THE GIRL WHO DARED TO THINK

BELLA FORREST

Before the Tower, humanity dreamed of flying.

We made great machines to lift us away from the earth, roaring on engines that growled with noxious fuels, then rockets that shot us into space. But once we were there, we realized it wasn't enough. We grew restless. We waged war. We won, and we lost, and we brought the earth to its flaming knees. The sun tore open our irradiated, weakened atmosphere, and life dwindled to ash.

And now, nearly three hundred years after the end, we survived. Hidden behind the thick outer walls of the Tower, we served the monstrous structure that was both our salvation and our prison.

Once, we had dreamed of flying. Now, we didn't seem to dream at all.

"Squire *Castell*." Gerome, my commanding officer, snapped me out of my musings, and I cringed. I'd been daydreaming again, and not about productive things. That was not in service to the Tower.

I turned away from the window I had been gazing through and, forcing an apologetic look onto my face, met my mentor's mildly disapproving gaze. Gerome's dark eyes reflected nothing, but his face reset to its normal stoic expression. After a moment he gave a barely perceptible nod and turned to the man next to him, the thick fabric of his crimson Knight's uniform creaking slightly, the sound magnified by the narrow concrete walls of the service hall we were standing in. "As I was saying, this is Squire Castell. She will be accompanying us, Mechanic Dalton."

Dalton, a 'seven' from the Mechanic Department (or Cog, as we referred to them), glanced pointedly at Gerome, and even out of the corner of my eye I could see the look of disgust he was shooting me. No doubt he had seen the number on my wrist and condemned me—which meant today was not going to be the brand-new day I had promised myself it would be.

No—it seemed both of us were destined for mutually assured sniping. Dammit.

It wasn't either of our faults; whenever any department needed to use a Knight's equipment, our protocol was to provide them with an escort— and these occasions were typically used as training for Squires like me, so we could learn our future duties when we became full Knights. This time —like most times—we needed to go outside to repair a few of the solar panels on one of the Tower's outside branches.

Dalton shot me another irate glance and I realized he'd said something and I had missed it. *Strike two,* I thought to myself. Gerome was turning and moving down the passage away from us both, heading toward the elevator just a few feet down the hall so I realized Dalton must have told him the level we had to get to. I moved to follow, but Dalton held out a disdainful arm, blocking my path.

"You'll come up after us," he said with a sniff. "I don't want to risk the psychological contamination."

A twinge of anger ran up my spine, but I looked away, biting my tongue.

As always, the narrow passageways in the shell were practically deserted. We were in its depths so there wasn't much to look at—just pipes and concrete and steel walls.

"I can't believe they sent a *four,*" Dalton muttered as he turned toward the elevator. I couldn't control myself this time. I opened my mouth to say something when Gerome shot me a look over his shoulder, his message clear. *Stay back—do not act.*

Yeah, okay. Fine.

The two men stepped forward onto the elevator's exposed steel-gray platform. Several beams of blue lights shot out from the platform and I heard the computer begin chirping out their names, identification codes and rankings as they began to rise. I watched as they were quickly lifted up toward the next floor, disappearing from view. I wondered if the system ever failed. Gerome was okay but I felt Dalton could benefit from a long fall to a cement floor.

You're part of his detail for today, I scolded myself. Gerome would have been disappointed; my thought had been dishonorable for a Squire —or anyone, really. Besides, Dalton's dislike of me was for a reason. A stupid reason, but one I was not helping with my negativity right now.

Level 173, Squire, Gerome's voice buzzed in my ear.

Sighing, I pressed the button, watching as a new platform slid out of the wall and covered up the exposed shaft the elevator ran through. Taking a deep breath to mentally prepare myself for the scan, I stepped inside and waited. Almost immediately the lights came on, and I felt a dull pain in the back of my head as the neural net surrounding my cerebral cortex buzzed with activity and the computer ran its scan of my credentials.

"*Identity verified: Squire Liana Castell, designation 25K-05; you are cleared for elevator use.*"

I fruitlessly prayed for that to be the end of it, eager to get moving. The computer, however, was not done with me.

"*Your number is currently four,*" its artificially rendered feminine voice chirped. I scowled, and once again felt a throb in the back of my head. It was bad enough that Dalton disliked me because of my number; for a stupid *computer* to remind me of it was just downright depressing. I leaned against the wall of the shaft and waited for it to finish the worst pep talk in history. "*For a Squire of the Citadel as well as a citizen of the Tower, it is recommended that you—*"

"Seek Medica treatment," I recited along with the machine, the speech ingrained. It lectured anyone ranked five or lower—but the lower you were, the more the computer had to say. "Yeah. Got it."

"Your well-being is for the well-being of the Tower," the computer said. *"Remember that, as a Squire, it is your duty to—"*

I knew the rest of its speech by heart. The damn thing regurgitated it every time I so much as breathed too close to a high-security area. *Your number is too low. Have you considered Medica treatment? Maybe it's time to find new friends!* I made a face and then uncrossed my arms, pushing up off of the wall as the platform began to move, my eyes watching the painted numbers on the walls glide by.

A four. I was a lousy four, and the end of my Knights training was drawing near. If I didn't raise my number before then, I'd fail to meet the ranking requirements to be a Knight. Consequently, I'd be dropped from my department, and essentially become homeless, doomed to try to find another department to take me in before my number fell to a one and I got arrested. All before I turned twenty-one. My parents would make a case for me and get me extensions, I was certain, but they could only buy me so much time. Not very much at all.

My eyes caught the number 150 as it slid past and I turned, a trill of excitement interrupting my bleak thoughts. I waited patiently until, like dawn breaking, I was greeted with a section of glass paneling. Here, the elevator shaft was now exposed to the inside of the Tower behind a glass tube that ran up and along the walls.

The walls of the Tower were actually a shell—one that was, by design, for defensive purposes. It contained two layers—the outermost layer holding the hatches into and out of the Tower, with a grand set of stairs inside, wrapping around the Tower, and seemingly endless. The innermost layer contained hundreds of floors that held a collection of things—service tunnels and quarters mostly—but the floors of its lowest section housed the machines that kept us alive. The lowest floors were also the densest floors, as they bore the weight of the entire structure.

As a result, not all of the elevators connected with the floors at the top; they typically stopped at the highest available level, meaning the citizen inside would have to walk to the next elevator if they needed to go any higher. The lift I was in, however, and a few just like it, ran all the way up the interior walls.

My eyes soaked up one of the more beautiful sights in our Tower (beautiful sights were few and far between, after all): the artificial light emitting from the walls was set to 'morning' and rays of bright light were beginning to cut into the shadows of the dim nighttime lighting, revealing three structures dangling from the ceiling. Their bases were massive at this height, and from this angle I had a full view of all three of them, gleaming in the artificial morning light. The glowing white walls of the Medica's smooth-sided cylindrical structure were closest on this side, the white almost too bright to look at directly. Circular walkways girdled the giant cylinder—one for each of its sixty floors. The walkways were thin and white, interrupted only by steps that ran up and down between floors, and the bridges that connected the structure to the rest of the Tower. Opposite the Medica was the Citadel, with its black-and-crimson-lit arches, dark steel edifices, and stylized walls, borrowing heavily from Gothic architecture to distinguish its cylindrical shape. Between them dangled the luminescent blue-and-black cone-shaped structure of the Core. Its circular levels were stacked, the widest level connected to the roof. Each level below was slightly smaller than the one above it, making the whole thing appear like coins of different values stacked together from largest to smallest. The Core was the heart of the Tower and the heart of Scipio... *Our benevolent computer overlord.*

The net in my head buzzed, warning me that it was detecting a strong spike of negativity, and I quickly broke the thought apart and shut it away. "Stupid," I muttered, catching a flash of my scornful amber eyes in the glass as I spun away from the view to face the wall. I glanced down at my wrist.

The band wrapped around my bronze skin was made of black microthread, a smooth material that was thin but practically unbreakable. Mounted atop it, the digital display that showed my number was glowing a soft, irritated orange—our overlord's little reminder that I wasn't good enough. Scipio, the great computer that monitored the nets in our heads and used the readings to determine our worth, had never liked me.

Supposedly he didn't have emotions, but I had long suspected that he took some perverse pleasure in my failings. He'd never had any faith in me. Then again, neither did my parents. Or my teachers. Or anyone really, except for my friends and my brother Alex.

Alex had explained that the number was a representation of the concentration of positive versus negative thoughts in your brain. The net couldn't exactly read direct thoughts but it read the feelings associated with them and, through some sort of complex algorithm, could perform an ongoing risk assessment on the citizen in question, to determine the likelihood of dissidents. The thing was, I didn't consider myself dissident. In fact, the most aggravating thing about my existence was the number itself, which seemed self-defeating.

The elevator slowed as it approached Level 173, where Gerome and Dalton were waiting. It halted at a cut-out section of wall, and I stepped out quickly. The elevator hovered for a moment behind me, awaiting new orders, and then sank back into a slot in the wall to await its next rider. I was halfway down the ramp connecting the elevator to the floor when the tip of my boot caught on something—my other foot, of course! —and I pitched forward, starting to fall. Gerome moved quickly to steady me. Being a confident man, he used his right hand, which meant I caught sight of the number there: a cool blue-colored 'ten' shimmered against his pale skin as he grabbed my upper arm. A perfect citizen. Gerome was a prime example of how being perfect could make a person boring.

I straightened and shot a glance at Dalton. He was standing a few feet behind Gerome; he tilted his chin away from me, refusing to meet my eyes.

I clenched my jaw. It was beyond unfair. Dalton's ranking of seven was so average that the typical citizen of the Tower wouldn't bat an eyelid. Since we had met, however, he had looked down on me. The way he was acting, you'd think we were here on a secret mission sent straight from Scipio, not to fix malfunctioning solar panels, and that I (the lowly four) was his lone obstacle, rather than his escort. The worst thing was, he could get away with it; he obviously knew from experience that the odd spike of righteous superiority on his decent track record wouldn't lower his number. It made my blood boil.

"Peace, Squire," Gerome said, clapping a massive hand on my shoulder. "Cogs have never been the most social of our departments."

I grunted in response.

Gerome looked at me. His face resembled the holographs we had of the ancient Greeks: chiseled, each feature designed as if by an artist. His thin, distinct eyebrows rose up under hair that had just begun to go silver at the temples, and his cleft chin jutted toward me like an accusation.

"We don't want you slipping any lower," he said, his voice devoid of empathy. "Your number is low as it is. Have you considered—"

"Medica treatment?" I muttered, looking at the metal flooring so Gerome wouldn't see me rolling my eyes. Dalton moved down the service hall ahead of us, and I moved quickly to follow, hoping that walking would keep Gerome's lecture brief. "Yes. My parents have been talking about it quite a bit."

Gerome caught up to me with one swift step. Up ahead, Dalton had begun climbing a steep set of narrow stairs toward a rectangular access hatch. As he pushed it open, I saw the black outer walls of the shell waiting beyond.

"Your parents are good citizens," Gerome said. "Strong. Capable. Champion Devon made them Knight Commanders for a reason."

I grimaced, looking away. "They're very perfect."

They had wanted me to be, too. They'd been disappointed.

Gerome stopped at the foot of the stairs, and the way he snapped his heel against the floor made it clear that I was meant to halt as well. I did so, wondering if I had gone too far. Gerome hated sarcasm like a cat hated water.

"Lord Scipio spared you," he needlessly reminded me in that soft patronizing tone I got from nearly everyone. "You were a second-born twin, illicit and undeserving. Your parents yielded your life to his judgment, and he deemed that you would live. Must you continue to throw these... tantrums?"

My face grew hot and I curled my hands into fists, feeling my nails biting into my palm. In a way, he was right. Each family was allowed two children by law, but my parents had given birth to my older sister Sybil before I was born, and even though it was by seconds, I was younger than my twin brother. My mother, overflowing with maternal instinct, had been willing to kill me right then and there. Excise the excess, so to speak. Scipio, however, ordained that I would live. For a time, my parents had thought that made me special. A chosen child, destined to lead the Knights into a glorious new era.

When Sybil died unexpectedly when I was five, grief only inflated their opinion of me. As I grew a little older, I began asking questions about Sybil's death, trying to make sense of it. It came to a head when, at the age of seven, I made the mistake of asking why Scipio hadn't prevented Sybil's death, and my mother had responded by slapping me across the face and hissing words I would never forget.

"He chose you over *her*," she had spat, her eyes glittering with tears. "You have a destiny—but when you ask questions like that, it makes me wonder if he made a *mistake*." Her number had dropped to a nine that day—the first and only time I ever saw it happen. Of course Scipio didn't choose me over Sybil; the computer couldn't prevent death and Sybil's demise had nothing to do with Scipio having allowed me to live. But that was the day I learned to never question Scipio's decisions out loud.

Eventually my parents' grief faded, and they turned their attention fully on me and Alex, trying to make us into carbon copies of them, essentially. They wanted so badly for us to carry on the family tradition. Which was why they were astounded when Alex, upon turning fifteen, defected from the family profession—he was recruited from school into the Eyes, Scipio's private order of engineers and residents of the Core. After that, all expectations fell firmly on me.

As for the destiny my parents had hoped for? Well, I found out a year after Alex defected that it wasn't even true. The only reason I was alive was because another child had been stillborn. I wasn't special. Scipio hadn't cared about me; he had been correcting a population imbalance.

"I can't help how I feel," I muttered.

Up at the access hatch, Dalton had turned and was shooting fiery looks in my direction. I found myself suppressing the urge to throttle the man.

"You *can*," Gerome said, his tone firm. "You just *won't*."

When we finally topped the stairs, Dalton was practically frothing at the mouth with impatience. He muttered a few words in the Mechanics' tongue, a language unique to his department, as we stepped out onto the landing. I stared at the massive staircase heading down, the ensconced lighting making the stairs appear to extend for eternity into the darkness, pressed between the scorching heat outside and the confines of the Tower.

"Are you quite ready?" Dalton asked in the common language.

I tried not to glare at him. Really, I did. I concentrated every ounce of effort I had on keeping my face still. But I could feel my lips twisting, my eyebrows shaking. Before my expression could grow any more gruesome, I turned away.

Gerome gave me a disapproving look as he gently set down a bag he had been toting on his shoulder. "Squire—can you please help Dalton into the lash harness and give the safety briefing?"

I nodded and squatted down to open the bag, pulling out the harness with its heavy black dome set on the back. Locating the top, I picked it up carefully and turned, holding it out to Dalton. The man screwed up his face in the now familiar look of disdain—but because Gerome had ordered me to do it, he had no choice but to obey. He held out his arms and allowed me to help him put the lash harness on.

"These are the lashes," I said as I helped him settle into it. I began pulling on straps, tightening the harness around his shoulders and chest. "When used correctly, they can prevent you from falling. Where would you like them fed through—your arms or your waist?"

"Arms," Dalton said bitingly, and I blinked but wisely kept my mouth closed. Arms were fine, but only if you needed to move fast. The waist was better if you had work to do, but it wasn't my place to question a seven, so I didn't.

Coming around behind him, I felt around the base of the case and grabbed one of the two metal ends at the bottom, pulling out a long line and threading it through the small loops in his uniform, underneath his arm, and finally through a small eyelet at the bottom. I repeated the process on the other side and then began double-checking each strap, to make sure the harness was secure.

"Okay," I said as I worked, not wanting to waste any time. "The tip of the lash is designed to absorb ambient static electricity as it flies through the air, building up a charge so that it will bond with anything it touches —metal, glass, you name it. To use it, simply—"

"I know how to use it, *Squire*," Dalton practically spat, his patience apparently coming to an end. "I'm a seven, and the Cogs designed and built them for the Knights, if you'll take a moment to remember."

"Of course," I said, trying to remain patient. "But I'm supposed to—"

"I'll be fine." End of discussion, apparently. I took a deep breath in, trying to calm some of the resentment that had boiled up in my gut.

"Ready when you are, Cog Dalton," I said, trying to make my tone as cheerful as possible.

Dalton sighed, then looked over at Gerome, who had rethreaded his own lash to come out from the small eyelets over his hip, just above his belt. Lashes were standard equipment for Knights, so our harnesses were worn under our suits, the lines running through internally designed channels. I had configured mine that morning, knowing we were going outside, in an attempt to prepare beforehand. Apparently that effort was going to go unnoticed.

"Does she have to come?" Dalton asked as he approached the exterior hatch—the only one that led onto the branch. "I would feel much better if it was just you, Knight Nobilis."

And I would feel better if you slipped off the branch, I thought, then flinched. Bad thoughts. I was having a really hard time controlling them today. Well... every day, really.

Gerome's voice was patient as he spoke. As if he'd had this conversation too many times before. "She's my Squire," he said. "She needs training to be a productive member of the Tower. She'll be no trouble. I stake my reputation as a Knight on it."

Honestly, if it had been up to me, I probably would have just stayed in for the day. Going outside the Tower was always something of an ordeal, and one look at Dalton's sneering face had told me how much more unpleasant the excursion was going to be. Still, it was my duty as a Squire to follow Gerome around and do what he said. And besides, if I *didn't* do it, my parents would probably have me executed or something.

Dalton bit his lip and then sighed in defeat. "Fine," he muttered.

He shoved the exterior hatch wide open and a blaze of bright morning light slashed in. We'd chosen this time of day so as to avoid the intensity of the sun; it would take some time before it started heating the night-cooled air. All the same, I could feel the warmth of it prickling against my skin as I looked out over the solar branch.

The branches were beautiful, in their own way. Massive slats of solar panels spread some three hundred feet out from the Tower, forming a full platform one could walk on. I hopped out after Dalton, watching as he fidgeted with the lash harness. The things weren't standard issue for mechanics, and, despite his claims to the contrary, he didn't seem to know how it worked. He pulled the cable from its wrist holster and stuck the glowing tip to the ground. It fizzed, and I winced.

"You'll want to be really forceful with those," I called. It was a novice mistake; lashes were designed to be flung with speed and force to absorb the friction in the air and form a static burst when they connected.

Dalton looked up.

"The lashes," I said, tugging one of my own out. The tip shone with blue light. "You have to really slap them on."

Dalton stared at me for a moment, then turned away without a word. He stepped away, using his cable to lower himself off the edge of the solar branch and down the side.

"He really should be more forceful with that," Gerome said, peering out beside me.

I felt a small stir of pride at that. Gerome, like most people aside from my weapons trainers, rarely told me that I'd gotten anything right. Even this wasn't praise per se but at this point in my life, hearing that I wasn't a *complete* colossal failure was worth *something*.

I peered out over the edge and watched as Dalton slowly descended, the feed in his suit lowering him down. The view was breathtaking; the vibrant green of the river below, coupled with the brighter yellow desert —a desolate wasteland. Coincidentally enough, it was called The Wastes. The sky was already a bright blue, even though it was early morning—but there was nothing to diffuse or block it with. There was rarely a cloud in the sky, and the mountains in the distance were barely visible on the best of days—the heat from the desert acting as a mirage to hinder the view. But on nights when the full moon was out, they could be seen, sitting very small, to the south. Everything else was vast, empty and devoid of life.

Gerome slapped down his lash with a forcible *tink*, the electricity pulsing in a small series of arcs around the impact point, and began to rappel down slowly, following Dalton. Without wasting another moment, I moved to one side and stepped off, not bothering to throw my own lash until I was plummeting. It hit the side of the branch with a click and the harness arrested my fall by feeding out more line to slowly catch me. I braced my feet on the side of the glass, taking care not to damage the solar panels, and threw my second lash down. It stuck firm, and I released the first line as I kicked off, dropping down a few more feet and coming to dangle from the very bottom of the branch, my heart pounding.

As cocky as the move had been, my stomach lurched. The Tower was over a mile tall and the sides were sheer. I could see the world splayed out below me, and the massive wall of the octagonal Tower. The thing was flawless and brown, the perfect form broken only by the great solar branches jutting out of and around the gargantuan block. Hanging in thin air from the side of the monstrous edifice was terrifying. And exhilarating.

Gerome dropped beside me, beating Dalton down. Gerome, of course, had attached his lashes the proper way, and his descent was a bit more controlled than mine.

I scrutinized Dalton's faltering progress above. The mechanic was *slow*. His every movement was so plodding that I wished I could do the job myself. It would have been one thing if he had been doing it safely, but he didn't even seem to know how to use the tools correctly. He was handling them like they were going to *break*. He placed his free lash so gently each time, letting it lower him down before he gingerly placed the next one to repeat the process. It would have been comical if it wasn't also deeply dangerous. All it'd take would be one failed connection and Dalton would get to do his best bird impression for over a mile-long drop.

Then again, it wasn't really his fault. Despite his proclamations, he was using Knights' equipment. The Knights were very protective of it—lashes included—which was why whenever anyone from another department requested their usage, they got a pair of Knight escorts with it, to make sure their equipment got returned in working order. I just happened to be one of the escorts today. It also wasn't his fault he was out here; it was common for sevens and sixes to get selected for the more dangerous work—they were of a high enough ranking to be reliable in their duties but a low enough ranking to be expendable.

I scanned the underside of the branch and quickly identified what we were there for. A clump of wiring had fallen loose, spilling out through a break in the metal plating. It happened sometimes—the air was still right now, but winds whipped by at high speeds and would cause shearing to some of the plates, until they broke off or the screws came out.

I threw out a hand, letting another lash fly, pulling me in closer to the damage. Dalton was just reaching it as I did, and began lashing himself over quickly—so quickly, in fact, that I paused and allowed him to go first, which earned me a sullen, angry look as he lashed by. I waited before I resumed my movement, careful to stay far enough away so that the man wouldn't feel inspired to actually start talking again.

Dalton drew himself in close to the exposed wiring. I winced as he used his fingers to connect his lash to the metal surface above, not even watching for the flash that confirmed its attachment. He then began fiddling, tugging a wire this way, then that, and I relaxed a little—his lash was holding. I let out a yawn, releasing the lashes with my hands, trusting my weight to the harness and settling into the lines. Some might have felt worried, hanging that high up. Me, though? In spite of any trepidation I felt at the height, I always felt more at home on lashes than I did on the ground. They were my wings.

"Watch him carefully," Gerome said, coming to my level.

I glanced at Dalton. He definitely didn't strike me as the criminal sort, but then again I was a four. According to Scipio, I was pretty rife with dissident urges of my own.

"If it was up to me," Gerome muttered, "a seven would have no place here. It is a respectable number, but the branches are too valuable to risk. There are nines among the mechanics. I would rather they do it."

I felt a spark of irritation.

"And a four?" I asked. "Where should *she* be?"

Gerome shook his head. "You're different, Squire. *And* you aren't touching any of the machines directly."

And there's the truth of it. So long as I wasn't actually doing anything, Gerome would overlook my number, for now.

I looked back at Dalton and paused. The man had given up on sorting through the wires and was now poking at the branch's wall with one of his lash cables with increasing desperation, the other one holding all of his weight—one had disconnected. I raised an eyebrow. It looked like he couldn't get the thing to reconnect.

"Gerome?" I said. The way Dalton was handling the lash wasn't just unsafe; he was going to—

There was a flash of blue light and Dalton's only connection broke. The lash tore free. He attempted to turn in our direction and had just enough time to reach out a hand to us before gravity began its deadly pull.

Gerome let out a shout of surprise and I saw his arm moving, a cable spinning from his hand to strike the metal surface beside where Dalton had been hanging, but Gerome had always been cautious, precise, professional with his lashes. Dalton was plummeting, desperately throwing lashes in all directions in a futile attempt to save himself.

I didn't like Dalton. He was a pompous ass, cruel to those he viewed as inferior, and smug in his assurance of his technical knowledge. But I couldn't let him die. I began retracting my lashes as I spun upside down on them, letting the slack pull in before I kicked off the bottom of the branch to send myself torpedoing earthward. In an instant, I was staring at the ground, over a mile down, the sheer brown expanse of the Tower rushing by my side.

He's a jerk, I thought as I fell. He'd been nothing but abusive. But, hey, here I was, falling through the air. And there he was, plummeting down just feet below. What choice did I have, really? My body moved on its own.

I pressed my arms and legs together to move faster than Dalton, and tore through the air toward where he was flailing about. I felt the pressure of the wind against my body, the air blazing against my suit. I gritted my teeth, pushing forward, and with a guttural yell I reached out and grabbed one of Dalton's flailing lashes by the cable, avoiding the tip—that would have hurt like hell and the shock through my suit could knock out my own lashes, which would be bad. I pulled the line to tug us closer together until I could get my arm around his waist. He clung to me, and I could feel him vibrating with terror as we dropped.

I whipped my head around to stare at the Tower as it streaked by. To Dalton's credit, the shot *was* tricky. Estimating the angle to throw at and the drag on the line, the shot needed to be precisely and forcibly executed. I sucked in a breath, paused for an instant, then fired the lash.

It struck the side of the Tower and rebounded, the tip sparking angrily. I cursed, glancing down. Another branch was hurtling toward us, solar plates glinting like teeth. In my arms Dalton was thrashing about like a panicking fish. I was sorely tempted to hit him upside the head, but instead I turned back to the Tower. One more throw.

I threw. The lash spun through the air, colliding with the side of the Tower. It buzzed and then, with a flash of blue, it stuck. I felt the jolt in my arm as our fall was slowed, and then we were swinging, our feet practically skimming the lower branch before we hit the side of the Tower. My legs were already braced for the impact, and I managed to catch our collective weight with a grunt.

"Hold on to me," I ordered, and I felt the terrified Cog wrap himself around me as the mechanisms in my harness helped pull us up. My arm now freed, I threw a second lash through the hole in my uniform at the wrist, arcing it so it landed fifteen feet above us, and I slowly began to pull us back up to the branch where Gerome was still hanging.

Dalton was still flailing about like he was going to die. I shot him a look. "Would you *hold still?*" I snapped. "I really don't want to drop you."

A lie—but hey.

Back inside the Tower, I reached up and ran a hand through my black hair, panting but flushed with triumph. The cool air washed over my skin, and in that moment I could have kissed the nearest air circulation unit. At my side, Gerome actually gave an approving nod.

And then I looked at Dalton.

The mechanic was staring at me. I expected gratitude, or at the very least some joy at being alive... but instead I found nothing but hatred.

"What makes you think," he said, voice soft, "that you can just... handle me like that?"

My stomach dropped and for a moment my mouth didn't seem to work at all.

"I... *What?*" I managed.

"I was fine," Dalton snapped insistently. "I was fine, and you felt the need to—"

"You were *not* fine!" I retorted, taking a step toward him and suddenly aware of the baton I wore at my side. I wondered if a sharp blow to the side of the head would improve Dalton's temperament.

"My lashes were fully operational," he replied. "I was entirely capable of saving myself, and certainly didn't need a *four* to come to my aid."

"Well, excuse *me*, Mister Seven," I said. "It looked to me like you were falling to your death. Maybe next time I'll just let you get on with it."

"Liana." Gerome's voice held a note of warning, but I didn't care. I was too frustrated to apply any sort of brake to my mouth.

"Maybe you should!" Dalton sneered. "The idea of a *four* thinking I needed saving, of laying hands on me! I have a family, you know. I can't even imagine what my wife would say if she knew."

"She'd probably rather have you saved by a four than have you come back in a bag, Cog," I hissed. "Or, you know, not in anything at all. It's hard to get bodies back when they've fallen off the damn Tower."

"*Liana.*"

I turned sharply, glaring at Gerome. "And what do *you* want? Are you going to scold me, too? I saved a life—and even if he won't admit it, you know I did. Was it *wrong*? Was it *bad*? *What*?"

Gerome's features were somber as he reached out, seizing my right arm and lifting it so that I could see the dial on my wrist. Tears pricked my eyes as I stared at it. It couldn't be right. It couldn't be. The number shone hot and red, though. *At risk.*

"Oh, dammit," I breathed.

2

I stared, stomach churning, at the dial on my wrist. A tremble rolled through me. Being a four had been bad enough as a Squire. But no matter what department you were from, once you hit three, Medica treatment was no longer just recommended; it was *required*. If you were a two you were placed in confinement on your floor and sent to mental restructuring, a rigorous process of intensive drug cocktails and heavy indoctrination designed to raise a person's number by completely rewriting their personality. If I dropped to a two, I would be automatically expelled from the Knights. Ones disappeared into the dungeons of the Citadel—I wasn't even sure what happened to them.

"A *three?*"

I looked up, my whole body numb. Dalton was gazing down his long nose at me like some kind of pompous vulture, thin tongue darting out to wet his lips. I tried to press down a surge of disgust at his presence. Such thoughts were not helpful right now. I could practically *feel* Scipio leafing through my emotions via the net in my head.

"Liana..." Gerome began, but I turned away.

"It's fine," I said, not sure where the lie came from. "I—I'll get it sorted out."

"The Medica will sort you out, you mean," drawled Dalton. "At least *I* won't have to deal with you again."

I glanced back as Gerome turned on the engineer, his eyes flat as stone. "She saved your life, Cog."

Dalton stood up a little straighter. "I still had my lashes. I was perfectly capable of—"

"I have been training with lashes my entire life," Gerome said matter-of-factly, "and Liana is already twice as talented as me. I respect your loyalty to the Tower. I respect your commitment to its values. What I *cannot* respect is your flippancy toward its Knights. Unless you're trying to mar your record and bring your number down, I suggest a change of temperament."

Dalton had gone pale, and now he nodded shakily.

I glanced at Gerome. The speech had been defensive, but it wasn't meant as complimentary. How very Gerome: the facts, flat and simple, with no emotions or loyalties beyond himself and the Tower to get in the way. I appreciated the support, but sometimes I wished the man would show me something that resembled actual kindness—not the damnable cool statement of facts.

"Liana," he said, and this time it was not a tone that allowed me to ignore him.

"Yes, sir," I said, shoulders slumping.

"You will be required to visit the Medica tomorrow," he said. "They will give you what you need in order to be a productive member of this Tower."

My gut clenched. "Yes, sir."

"For now," he said, "I think it would be best if you—"

A low buzzing cut him off, coming from the net in my head. The vibrations seemed to flow together, until my eardrums rattled with sound that wasn't there. I bit my lip; direct messages had always left me with a vague sense of vertigo.

Squire, a voice said in my head. I recognized Scipio, and shivered.

The programmers had chosen a soft, male voice for him, and for some reason whenever he spoke I imagined a young man, blond, sitting upon a throne, sword across his lap. He was regal, condescending, and completely at ease in his power. I wasn't sure if I hated, loved, or feared him. He merely was what he was.

There is an incident that requires your attention. A 'one' has appeared in the Water Treatment facilities. You are to assist in apprehending him. Immediately.

Scipio's words rang in my ears, and for a moment I stood, frozen in shock. I had expected a reprimand, not a call to duty. I watched as Gerome's iron façade twisted. He turned away.

"Something has come up," Gerome said. "I need to—"

"I got it too," I said hurriedly.

Dalton's stare darted between the two of us like we were mad.

Gerome stared at *me*.

"Confirm to me what you heard," he said.

I looked at Dalton, not particularly wanting to give the man the gossip that he wanted. The communication had been for Knights only. All the same, Gerome wanted an answer.

"A one has appeared in Water Treatment," I said. "I am to assist."

Dalton let out a gasp but Gerome just nodded.

"We're taking the plunge," he said.

Dalton, predictably, gasped again. I, on the other hand, offered the first genuine smile of the day.

The plunge was a sheer shaft that ran almost the entire length of the Tower, from the ceiling to the lower levels. Unlike the elevators, this tunnel was narrow and didn't always run in a perfectly straight line. For an experienced Knight, lashing your way down the plunge was simple, but, much like the drop outside, my stomach never failed to lurch when I leapt out into the empty air. The narrowness and random changes in the tunnel meant there was little room for error. It was one of the faster ways of getting to a lower floor, but at least one Knight a year died due to a mistake that sent them slamming off wall after wall in free fall, often getting no time to place new lashes before they hit the bottom of the passage. Seeing the deadly shaft of pipes and exposed beams, and leaping into it was as thrilling and terrifying now as it had been the first time I'd done it.

I'd be lying if I said I didn't love it.

Gerome leapt into the narrow shaft first, and I managed to last three whole seconds before I followed, a mad grin on my face. I placed my foot into nothingness and then allowed gravity to take me, throwing my lashes at the last possible second to arrest my descent down.

Gerome stared straight forward, his short hair barely moving as we hurtled toward the ground. His approach was methodical: a flick of the wrist here or there to keep himself perfectly centered as he shot downward. By contrast, I was a meteor. I spun and whirled, dancing about him as I let my feet clip the walls, grinning in spite of my mentor's disapproving glances. My teachers had always been very firm on the fact that the plunge was for emergency transportation only, but they had been forced to remind me several times over the years. Something this wonderful couldn't just be for when things were bad.

"When we arrive," Gerome shouted, his voice barely carrying over the wind roaring in my ears, "you are to stay with me. We'll search the perimeter indicated by Scipio while others search the interior."

I shot out a cable and yanked myself away from where a beam cut across the path, slipping my slim form through the narrow gap between the beam and the wall, leaving the wider space for Gerome's muscular form. Once I was past it, I took the time to answer. "Wouldn't it be more efficient if we split up?" I yelled back.

"We're not splitting up."

I winced, and for a moment I was all too aware of the low number on my wrist. Of course Gerome wouldn't want me to go off on my own now.

"Yes, sir."

Coming to a halt in the plunge was never easy, but Gerome managed it nicely, throwing a hand in either direction so that the lashes he shot out caught the walls simultaneously, at the same elevation. He came to a halt just above the exit we needed to take, which was little more than a door-shaped hole.

I speared one lash to the top of the exit and shot past Gerome through the narrow space, throwing another lash up and back to catch the door-frame as I passed through. I eased the latch and the cord gave a gentle pull at my wrist, slowing me until I landed, feet skidding along the ground.

Behind me, Gerome eased himself through the doorway. "Being flashy will get you killed," he grunted. "We have procedures for entering and exiting the plunge for a reason, Squire Castell."

I wanted to make a face but held the impulse in, opting for a curt nod instead. It never seemed to matter that I could do things nobody else could. My expertise, and what I could accomplish with it, meant nothing in the face of the immutability of the Tower. It was all I could do not to scream sometimes.

Gerome strode off and I fell into line behind him, my boots slapping moodily against the floor.

"So, what do we know about this guy?" I asked, trying not to think about the fact that my own dossier had just been flagged and passed on to the Medica. Gerome would have the information on the individual we were looking for—sent along with our orders.

Sure enough, he pulled a small, pen-like device from his pocket and held it up to one side. An image flared into view over it: a picture and several lines of text.

"Grey Farmless," he said, reading off the information. "Citizen designation 49xF-91. Looks like he was initially raised by the farmers but his parents petitioned the Department Head to drop him and they did."

I blinked, looking at the face with renewed interest. Getting dropped by your parents was a rare occurrence, but it did happen. When a parent simply couldn't take their own child's presence, or else thought them a bad influence on their floor, they could "drop" the child, essentially rendering them homeless to go find a new floor. It was extremely rare for any Hand to drop their own children, which made me curious.

In the picture, Grey's mouth was twisted into the smallest of frowns, his soft, dark brown eyes staring intently toward the camera. His hair was a light brown or dark blond—it was hard to really tell—and his square jaw framed lips set at a slight scowl. He wasn't classically handsome, but there was something sultry in the dry disdain of his features that made my heart skip a beat, and I quickly pushed the feeling back—it was woefully unprofessional. There was something else stamped into his features. It was subtle, but there: a *bitterness*—that I couldn't help but recognize in myself.

"What did he do?" I asked.

"Hm?"

"Why did they drop him?"

Gerome scrolled through the notes.

"Doesn't say," he replied eventually. "I do see that his number dropped before it happened, though. Might have just been natural prejudice against a dangerous element." I shoved my right hand behind my back, biting my retort clean in half. Picking a fight with Gerome about calling the lower numbers "dangerous elements" made about as much sense as saving Dalton had, and I was done doing stupid things today.

The search proved boring. Water Treatment was a fascinating process, or so I'd been told. Intricate, delicate, and deeply scientific, the mesh of vein-like pipes kept the Tower from dying of thirst, grew our crops, and provided energy. This floor, however, held nothing of the supposed majesty of the profession. Everywhere I looked it was pipes, pipes and more pipes. Some glass, some metal, they tangled together into complex and intricate knots with only sparse room left for walkways to wind between them.

"Why would someone even be *in* here?" I asked, using a lash to tug myself up and over a particularly large pipe that had been built directly across the footpath.

Gerome pulled himself up over the same pipe without so much as a grunt.

"It makes sense," he said. "Good place to hide. Not to mention, these pipes go into the Depths."

I cocked my head at that. The Depths, as the council had taken to

calling them, were a series of caverns and maintenance shafts at the base
of the Tower. Supposedly they had become too irradiated to inhabit, but
sometimes people would talk about *undocs*, the undocumented citizens
of the Tower, hiding down there. It didn't seem likely to me. If there were
people down there, surely the council would have done something about
them by now. Besides, there was nothing to live off of in the dark, under-
powered floors that made up the Depths.

As I was contemplating the idea of someone actually trying to live
down there, a figure emerged from behind a nearby pipe.

I froze, looking him up and down. He was taller than I'd imagined
from the picture, and better built. Also, his hair was a little lighter, and he
looked more rugged; a layer of stubble had grown along his jaw. All the
same, this was our guy. I raised a hand, but found myself momentarily
speechless as his intense brown eyes locked with mine.

As he shifted, his wrist came into view. His band glowed hot and red,
like an angry burn.

"Gerome," I finally blurted.

My mentor turned, and I could feel his eyes zoning in on the young
man. Gerome wasted no time.

"Citizen Farmless," he said, advancing, one hand unslinging the stun
baton from his waist. "You are hereby placed under arrest by the order of
the Knights. Should you fail to comply, you will be—"

Grey didn't even wait. He turned with alarming speed and darted
back the way he had come. Gerome cursed and broke into a run. I took
off after him into the maze of pipes.

The guy was *fast*. He swung under and over pipes, his feet never
missing a beat, never faltering for an instant as he sprinted ahead. Within
moments he had a sizable lead. Growling, I thrust a hand forward and
sent a lash spinning out. It collided with a pipe, and with a flex of my
wrist I let it surge me forward at a breakneck pace.

I was almost near the fleeing man when I saw a familiar grayish tube
just beyond him. An elevator.

That's fine, I thought. The scanner would read his number. The
elevator would hold him in place—like any other person with a ranking of

one attempting to use them—and we could just grab him when it refused to move.

That was what I was telling myself as Grey stepped onto the platform and the blue lights erupted from the bottom, moments before it began to lift him upward. I nearly slammed into a pipe as I gaped, dumbfounded, at the machinery. It hadn't even chirped out his ranking, and it *always* recited rankings if anyone lower than a nine was present on the platform.

Grey had the nerve to grin and actually waved at me as he disappeared behind the wall. I felt a burst of annoyance at the odd sense of pleasure his acknowledgement brought me.

Gerome entered the room just as I seized on that annoyance, racing up the ramp and onto the platform that slid out of the wall to support me. I didn't break my movement as I flung the lash up, attaching it to the underside of his elevator and letting it haul me up as I dangled in the shaft. Below me, the blue lights of the computer flashed red in warning— indicating that someone (me) had broken protocol.

"Liana!" Gerome bellowed, as I disappeared into the shaft. "Get to C-9 and head him off! I'll come around the other side."

His voice carried after me as I pulled myself up toward the panel above, reeling in so fast the line seemed to whistle. I couldn't stay under here for long—it was too dangerous.

The elevator began to slow and I waited until it had almost stopped before disconnecting my lash. I fell a few feet down, and flung out both lashes so they attached to either side of the shaft. The lashes fed out as I continued to fall, and at the last possible moment I reversed the feed and had them reel me back up—faster than was safe but I needed momentum. As I shot past the lash points, I disengaged them, angling my body up and through the now exposed doorway. I landed with a hard thud of my boots, a few feet behind Grey.

Grey froze and turned, his eyebrows jacking up into his hairline as he gazed at me in surprise. On impulse, I raised my hand and waved at him. He blinked, and then ran.

I felt a smile bloom on my lips as he sprinted, and flexed my shoulders, suddenly confident. *This* was what I had been made for. I felt my worries slipping away, my concerns staying far below with my supervisor as I lashed my way after him—through the pipes that crisscrossed the room, skimming surfaces as I shot lash after lash, in pursuit of Grey.

Because of his speed, and the pipes being so dense, I lost him behind a few, overshooting his location, too fast to stop. I swung back around, letting the swing of the last lash carry me back in a reverse trajectory and releasing it at just the right moment so I could land on an outcropping of pipes. I stared at the floor below, trying to find him.

The room was silent—only the occasional sound of water gurgling or steam escaping could be heard. My eyes scanned the piping he had disappeared behind. After a long moment, I lashed down to the catwalk below, looking for any sign of the man.

He hadn't disappeared after all—but had come to a stop by a junction of pipes and was now hunched over one, rooting around like a farmer planting seeds and not a man being pursued by the Knights. I coughed as I unsheathed my stun baton, releasing a menacing hum of electricity.

"So," I said, drawing out the syllable, "are you going to introduce yourself, or...?"

He spun around, his dark blond hair mussed and touching the sides of his face. His eyes found mine immediately, his muscles surging and tensing beneath his clothes. He didn't exactly look like a villain to me. Then again, I was a three, so maybe villains were just my type.

I tapped the tip of my baton against some of the piping, letting a thin tendril of power curl lazily up from it.

"Awkward silence works too, I suppose," I said, taking a step forward.

I failed to anticipate his speed, though, and he moved close, grabbing my wrist and attempting to break my hold on my baton. Alarmed, I reacted instinctually, striking a low blow with my foot in an attempt to get him to move back or upset his balance. His foot came up to block my blow, and I froze as he kicked it away.

I launched another kick, which he blocked as well, his hand still firmly wrapped around my wrist. We stared at each other, tension radiating from both of us.

"How do you know to do that?" I asked after a pause, looking at his feet.

He smiled, a flash of white straight teeth. "You're pretty, for a Shield," he said, referring to the Knights by their nickname.

I glared at him then thrust out my arm, my fist clenched, intent on knocking the smug look off of his face. He blocked the blow with his forearm, and then slid his arm around my waist, pulling me tight against him. I flushed and looked up at him, extremely uncomfortable at his proximity and the way his brown eyes lit up as he looked down at me, that cocky smile still clinging to his lips.

"Let go of me," I said, forcing air back into my lungs as I tried to fight my way out of his arms.

Grey smiled a slow, arrogant grin. "Let go of a pretty girl in the middle of a dance? My mother raised me better than that."

"Apparently not, *Farmless*," I spat, and was immediately mortified by my own words. They sounded harsh and cruel—spoken out of a nervousness that stemmed from the feeling of being trapped.

Grey's jaw twitched and he abruptly released me, keeping cool despite the simmering anger burning behind his brown eyes. He sucked in a deep breath as he took a slow step back, creating a little bit of room between us.

"Liana!" I heard Gerome's voice from the tunnels behind me, clearly looking for me, but I ignored it, keeping my eyes on the oddly untroubled fugitive in front of me.

"Citizen Grey Farmless, designation 49xF-91—to be precise," Grey informed me, his tone exasperated and curt. "May I ask why, exactly, you feel the need to brandish a weapon at me, Squire?"

I gave him a confused look and he gestured to the glowing display on his wrist. "I already know your number," I informed him, baffled by his odd behavior. "It's a one, Citizen Farmless. I've been given full authority to take you into custody."

I slapped my baton against the ground, forcing a shower of sparks, in an attempt to re-establish control of the situation. He seemed to be having a hard time getting it through his head. I wondered whether maybe that was because he was off the medicine handed out by the Medica for all twos and ones. *The medicine I would soon be taking*, my mind reminded me, and I pushed the thought away. Now wasn't the time.

Grey lifted his arm, turning it to display his number.

"Not a one, Knight. Sorry to disappoint."

I stared. The end of the one seemed to have gotten lazy, curled around, cooled to a soft blue.

"A six?" I said, dumbfounded.

"Nine, actually," he replied with a suffering sigh, "but who's counting?" He looked pointedly at the three on my wrist, one sandy-brown eyebrow slowly lifting.

"You were a one," I insisted, trying to force the flush from my cheeks.

"Well I'm not now," he replied. "Funny how the world works."

"I can't just let you go," I said. "There's no way that—"

"Squire Castell."

I turned and saw Gerome approaching, his own baton held loosely in one hand. He moved straight toward the young man, who took a step back and lifted his arm again.

"I'm a nine!" he announced. "There's been a misunderstanding."

Gerome paused, then turned toward me. His slate-gray eyes seemed to stab clean through me.

"This *is* the same man, isn't it?" he asked.

"Yes, sir," I answered, somewhat unsure of how that was possible.

I shuffled uncomfortably, glaring at the man's number. It couldn't be right, could it? But to think otherwise would be to assume that Scipio was wrong, and if I wanted to start claiming that, I might as well arrest myself and spend the night in a cell.

Gerome looked at me, then at the man, his hard eyes seeming uncertain. "Very well, then," he murmured after a pause. "We cannot arrest those in Scipio's grace. The Citadel apologizes for any inconvenience you have suffered, Citizen."

Grey gave him a shrug, donning an expression of mock sincerity. "That's no problem," he replied. "I just want to help the Tower run as *smoothly as possible.*"

I stared at him. His words were dripping with sarcasm, his eyes glinting with amusement. How the hell was he still a nine? It didn't make any sense.

"You were a one!" I erupted, gesturing at him. "You fled from Knights of Scipio's order!"

Gerome's baleful gaze fell on me this time, and I shrunk under it. "You know as well as anyone that Scipio marks criminals with a one, to make their capture easy and assured. If he is not a one, then he has committed no crime."

"But—"

"We're done here, Squire," Gerome said, his voice gaining a hint of steel as he turned and walked away.

I could only stare at his retreating form. It seemed that Gerome was as indifferent to crime as he was virtue. Actions didn't matter to him, or to the other Knights. It was all about Scipio and the number you happened to have flashing on your wrist. They were off the hook for everything else. Gerome was too indifferent to even admit there must have been some kind of mistake. But I couldn't exactly blame him, either; this was the only protocol he knew.

I, however, couldn't stop thinking about it. In all my years of having my accomplishments ignored, I hadn't really stopped to consider the things a high number could get away with. Now, my mind was abuzz. This *couldn't* be right, could it? And yet, it was happening.

I shot a lingering look back at Grey. He was lounging against a pipe, his eyes bright with quiet amusement. As I turned to follow Gerome, Grey gave a mocking salute, a smug smile tugging at the corners of his lips.

Oh, I'm going to figure out exactly *what you're doing.*

3

I followed Gerome along one of the many bridges that connected the shell to the entrance of the Citadel, the Knights' headquarters. The giant cylindrical structure was dark and foreboding, stylized with great arches and loops of metal tempered to look like stone. The level we approached had high, towering walls, and lining those walls were gargoyles set upon platforms. Blue-and-silver banners bearing Scipio's insignia (a tower wreathed in lightning) hung from the structure, and high above I could hear the whoosh and snap of Squires and Knights lashing between the arches of the Citadel, practicing their art.

Reaching the looming front doors, Gerome was waved through, while I was brought to a stop, a crackling baton barring my path. I looked up and met the eyes of Lewis, a Knight who had sparred with me once. I had even thought of him as friendly.

"Nobody below a ranking of four is admitted here," he said, his voice unyielding. "You may take the residents' entrance, as you still live with your parents."

I looked to Gerome, but the man just shook his head. I should have expected the reaction, to be honest. Gerome would have arrested his mother and spared the devil based on the number on their wrists. I bet the devil was good at cheating the system too... maybe I could find him and he could give me some tips.

"Go home, Liana," he said, rubbing at his brow. "You need to speak with your parents."

I bit my lip. "What about my report, sir?"

"I will handle your report," said Gerome. "I was there. At any rate, the testimony of a three is inadmissible in the records. Dismissed."

He never said "goodbye" like a normal person might have. So I shouldn't have been surprised when he turned and disappeared into the darkness of the building beyond without another word. In front of me, Lewis continued to hold his baton, eyes level with mine.

I swallowed hard as I stared at the man. It wasn't even that I liked giving the reports, but it was my job. To be disallowed from even doing paperwork somehow felt like a bigger slap in the face than anything else I had experienced.

What am I going to do—write a treasonous report? I thought bitterly. Then I tried to catch the sour thought, bundle it up and send it to some part of my brain where it wouldn't be noticed. I couldn't allow myself to fall to a two. Happy thoughts.

Hey, you okay? a soft voice in the back of my head asked.

I jumped and stared at Lewis. He just brandished his weapon again, apparently concerned I might try to force my way in. I took a step back and exhaled, looking around. It hadn't been him talking, and there wasn't anyone else around, which really only left me with one option: my dear brother, with his personal access to Scipio's communication networks.

"Alex?" I muttered softly, knowing the implant in my ear would pick up the sound and transmit it back to him.

Literally and metaphorically coming at you through your thoughts, buzzed the voice in my head. *I went to check in on you and saw your number had dropped. What's going on?*

I smiled and walked away from Lewis to settle down on a bench. Alexander had always been the first to ask what was wrong. I rarely heard from him these days, except in a crisis. My parents hadn't taken kindly to his decision to leave the Knights, even to directly serve Scipio, and as a result he never visited. I missed him, truth be told. There was something earnest and good in Alex that was hard to find elsewhere, and it often made me wonder just how he had come to work with Scipio.

"It's nothing," I said. "Stupid run-in with a moronic Cog."

A pause.

Your ranking has slipped to a three, Lily.

I scowled at both the patronizing voice he used, as well as the nickname. He was the only person who called me that and I wasn't fond of it.

"So?"

So, three is when compulsory Medica treatment kicks in. Not to mention, your apprenticeship is nearing an end. They could drop you.

I let my head fall into my hands, a wave of defeat rolling through me. Alex had never been one to mince words, and he knew me well enough to know exactly what I was afraid of. My number had fallen because I couldn't stay positive, keep my thoughts in a good place on a consistent basis. The Medica was going to fix those thoughts, whether I liked it or not. And I had to do it, or risk losing my department forever.

"Maybe it's just a bad day," I muttered. "Maybe it'll be better in the morning." Using the net to communicate was weird; it always looked like someone was talking to themselves, although everyone knew they weren't. Or at least hoped they weren't.

It won't be.

"Gee, thanks for the reassurance."

A soft chuckle. *Would you rather I coddle you with lies?*

I watched as a pair of stiff, straight-backed Knights in crisp, crimson uniforms strode by, heading toward the building. Everything about the place was so rigid. So stiff. Was this really all there was to life? Rules, and grappling with your own brain out of the terror of ever, even for a moment, thinking something bad?

"What's it like, working for the Eyes?" I asked, partially to distract myself.

Alex sighed. *Work, work, and more work,* he admitted. *But it's fasci-*

nating. The sheer amount of data we have access to, you wouldn't believe it.

Data, he'd said. People's emotions screened and compiled into a revolting blob of *data*.

Did I say something?

"No."

Your negativity concentration—

"You're reading me!?" I cried, jolting to my feet and causing a nearby Knight to shoot a disparaging look my way.

I'm just watching your screen while we talk, Alex said hurriedly. *I like to keep an eye on you.*

"Alex, that's..."

Would you rather I didn't?

I paused, considering. "No," I said eventually. As invasive as it was, as bizarre as it was to think that someone always knew my inner state of mind, it was comforting to know that someone cared enough to look. To look at that negativity and not just slap a number on it but ask *why* my thoughts looked that way. Alex had always been different like that, and I adored him for it. It gave me hope, knowing that someone like my brother worked with the Eyes.

The net in my brain continued to buzz, but Alex didn't speak for almost a minute.

Things are changing, he finally said.

I tilted my head up, looking at the Core. The great computer was located somewhere in there, but the Eyes never let anyone other than other Eyes inside. Even their trainees, called Bits, weren't allowed inside, until after they had passed copious screenings.

"How so?"

I can't say. Or maybe I'd simply rather not—I don't know, he replied. *Just... get your number back up, and stay away from any more moronic Cogs. Or just Cogs in general.*

I chuckled at the tone of his voice—it was dryer than the desert outside. Eyes and Cogs were notoriously bad at getting along, and it seemed Alex had picked up that characteristic as well.

So it is possible to get some positivity out of you after all, he drawled. *Anti-departmental humor works like a charm every time.*

"Seriously, though, it's creepy for you to just... read me like that."

He was right, though; I was smiling.

You sure? I thought it was endearing.

I laughed. "Pretty sure you don't have any idea what's endearing about you."

There was a silence, then a sigh. *I have to work.*

"I know."

You going to be okay?

I stared down at the number on my wrist. "I don't know," I replied honestly.

Another silence.

I'll do what I can, he said.

The buzzing in my head cut out, and just like that Alex was gone. With the noise, and my brother gone, I abruptly felt very alone. I thought about going home. About seeing my parents. But they didn't care about anything more than the number on my wrist, and now that I had finally dropped—as they expected me to—I suddenly didn't want to. The only thing that could possibly redeem me would be if I went off and managed to catch an entire gang of criminals—and even then it might not work. Both of them were Knight Commanders, the highest rank in our Order without becoming Champion, and that seat was held by Devon.

I realized that I didn't want to go home. In that moment, perhaps it was more that I couldn't. I turned, moving back across the bridge, intent on finding an elevator to take me back to Water Treatment.

The elevator decided that the three using it needed an insultingly long lecture on immorality in exchange for travel back down to Water Treatment. I waited, stewing in sullen silence, for it to finish and deposit me where I needed to go. I quickly went back to where I'd confronted Grey. He, of course, was long gone, but the pipes along the wall still bore the faint black mark where my baton had struck as I flew out of the sky to arrest him. Flew out of the sky and saw his wrist.

A nine.

I gritted my teeth as I walked forward, scanning the area for something, *anything* that might indicate what had happened. He had been a one. I had seen it, and even if I hadn't I would have known. The easy smiles, the spark of character in his eyes; those things died when someone's number got higher. Even aside from that, why would he have run if he wasn't a one?

I moved up to the place where he had been hovering, but there was nothing obviously different about it. Uncertain, I lowered my hand into a gap between the pipes and rooted around in the little pocket within.

"So, Grey Farmless," I muttered. "What were you rooting around for over here, huh?"

It was a stupid venture. Grey was cleared. Even if I had found a bloody knife and a confession to murder, the man would have been free to prance about the Tower while people looked at me like I was going to burn the place down. To the eyes of the world, a nine was all but infallible, and a three was just waiting to explode. Still, something drove me. I needed to know the truth.

Just then, my fingers brushed against something. It was small, smooth, and the contact sent it rolling away from me. I cursed, scrabbling for a moment, and just managed to close my hand around it before it got away. Yanking my hand out, I held it before me, then slowly opened it.

It was a pill. And while Medica pills were brightly colored and well labeled, this one was a nondescript white, the sides completely blank.

Hello... What might you be?

I rolled the pill in between my fingers, thinking. *I ought to take it to Gerome* was the first thought that came to my head. This was important. Significant. As I thought about it, though, I pictured Grey. Cocky, self-assured, and so... *himself.* So much more himself than anyone I had ever known—and so unafraid to be so. He didn't act like someone worried their number would fall. He didn't act like someone who was worried about their number *at all.*

I stared down at the three on my wrist. Medica treatment. Mood-altering pills. Liana—vanished.

I shoved the pill into my pocket.

4

"A three?"

My mother's expression could have wilted crops. My father's probably would have caused them to combust.

"It's nothing," I said. "Just—"

"It is most certainly *not* nothing, young lady," my mother replied, her voice soft. Lethal. I looked over at her and didn't see my mother, but the Knight she was—everything perfectly in order, from the smooth, ebony braid dangling down her back to her shiny black boots. Nothing was ever out of place, out of line.

They were both still wearing their Knight uniforms. In fact, that was all they ever wore, the commander's insignia shining on both of their chests, right over the heart. They had other, non-uniform clothing, but they never wore anything except their crimsons or the thin undergarments used for sleeping.

"We have been waiting your entire life for you to step up. Become the child this family needed. This, however..." My father pushed away from the dining room table at which we were all seated and began pacing the tight confines of the space. "A three. Scipio's grace, we'll have to send her to the Medica, Holly. I mean, do you *want* to get kicked out of the Citadel, young lady?"

I kept my face carefully neutral at the question, but even the expectation of pain wasn't enough to keep my heart from hurting at the sound of it. My father spoke the words as if they hadn't been on his mind every day for the last month. Like I didn't suspect that he was excited to finally have the opportunity to "correct" me. It made me feel heartsick and raw.

My mother's expression twisted. "We know people in the Medica," she said, turning to me, the Knight fading slightly back into my mother. "You'll be okay, Liana. We won't let you fall any farther, I promise. You're not going to lose your home."

It was interesting how they only ever made promises when they were promising to do something they wanted anyway, but the fear of losing my home was deeply rooted in my heart: I didn't have anywhere else to go, and I wasn't suited for anything else.

"I was hoping I wouldn't have to go to the Medica just yet," I said, already knowing their response. "Maybe give my rank a chance to bounce back?"

"It's too late for that," my father replied. "I'm not letting this get any worse than it has. We've tried to be reasonable, really we have, but it is clear that you are incapable of handling these... dissident thoughts."

The word "dissident" made me think about Grey, his one miraculously changing to a nine, and I nursed the smallest spark of an idea. Maybe if I could present it right, they would hold off on sending me to the Medica.

"Speaking of dissidents, Gerome and I were called in to arrest a one down in Water Treatment today."

That caught their attention. My mother's eyebrows lifted.

"A one?" she asked. "I heard the alert go out, but I wasn't aware he had been apprehended. What was his name again?"

"Grey Farmless," I said excitedly, leaning closer to her. "We happened upon him in one of the service ways. As soon as he saw us he began to run, and I chased after him, using my lashes. He got into an elevator, and—"

"What a stupid thing for a one to do," my mother said with a laugh.

My father answered with a knowing chuckle. "Well, there's a reason they're ones."

I took a deep breath, trying to ignore the sudden stab of insecurity their comments created, wondering if they would talk about me like that, if I fell even farther.

"Then what happened?" my mother asked.

"Oh. Well, I thought the same as you," I said, successfully picking up the thread of the story, trying to act like their comments hadn't bothered me. "That the elevator wouldn't work—but then, to my surprise, the platform began to *move*."

"What? How?"

"I don't know," I replied, answering my father's question. "All I know is that it started moving almost immediately. I knew if I didn't act fast, I'd lose him. So I used my lash and attached it to the bottom of the platform as it traveled upward. You should've seen it! As soon as it started to slow, I disconnected the lashes and used the cables to launch myself into the room. He thought he'd lost me, but—"

"Liana," my mother admonished. "That was dangerous! You could've died!"

"I know, Mom," I said, a pleasant wash of guilt flowing through me, the pleasantness a result of her showing concern for my well-being. "I was careful. Anyway, I caught up with him, and—"

"And you caught him?" my father interrupted. "How? Where?" He glanced at my wrist. "And your number didn't improve? Liana, you know that it's not just about what you do; it's about your *dedication* to what you are doing."

I bit my lip. "Well, yes, but that's not the point. You see, when I saw him the first time, I could've sworn his number was a one. But when he showed it to Gerome and me... it was a nine."

My parents stared at me blankly.

"He was a one," my mother said flatly. "Ones don't become nines just like that."

I made a non-committal gesture, suddenly nervous at the look in her eyes. A look that said she didn't believe me. "*He* did," I said. "You can ask Gerome."

"So in the end," my father huffed, "you didn't *actually* catch anyone, did you?"

I flushed, my head dropping. I shook my head. "Well, no, but I—"

My father's long, heavy silence caused me to fall silent. "Oh, child," he said, and he actually took a step closer. I could smell his breath, spearmint with a hint of metal. "Why would you even bring it up?"

"Because it doesn't make sense—I swear, his number was a one when we saw him, but it jumped up eight ranks. Is such a thing possible?"

"No," my father said flatly. "No one has increased their ranking so fast like that before. You must have been mistaken."

"But I wasn't," I insisted, meeting my father's gaze head on. "Gerome even saw it. He was a nine. I just don't understand why Scipio would raise him up to a nine, but drop me down to a three? I think there must be something wrong with Scipio—some sort of problem with his—"

My father slapped my cheek, hard—but he'd hit me harder before, when my questions became too dissident for his tastes. I blinked back the shock of tears at the pain that suddenly blossomed on the side of my face and began to throb, as if still radiating ripples from the impact site. I clutched at it and looked at him, at his angry gaze.

"Yours is not to question the will of Scipio," he snarled. "Yours is to do your work, and do it well. With your two hands you—"

"Mete out justice and bring order to the Tower," I said, forcing my words out through clenched teeth and aching jaw, knowing he expected me to speak the Knight's Oath with him, word for word. Always a sign that I had really screwed up. The words were practically ingrained into my brain; I could probably recite it in my sleep at this point. "We shield the Tower from those who would do it harm. We hold the line between order and chaos. We lay down our lives in service to the Tower."

My father nodded at me approvingly and took a step back. I looked at my mother, and found her eyes hard and gleaming. She agreed with what my father had done. And I'd done even more damage to my standing, in their eyes, with my story. Unfortunately for me, that was how things always seemed to go whenever I tried to talk to my parents. Only this time, it hurt all the more, because now they were willing to kill who I was in order to get a more capable daughter.

"Squire Liana, by my power as a Knight Commander of the Citadel, you are to seek Medica treatment tomorrow. There will be no arguments, no exceptions, and no complaints. You will serve the Tower." My mother's words held the ring of finality to them.

I scowled at the floor. I hated it when she did that. Took off the mask of mother and put on the mask of commander, like they were utterly interchangeable. I met her gaze and lowered my hand from my cheek, trying not to wince at the sting. Managing a curt nod, I turned and made for the front door, needing to be anywhere but there.

"I want to hear you say it, Liana."

I froze at the steel in her voice. "I will go to the Medica tomorrow," I managed, barely able to force enough air through my vocal cords to produce a sound. I squared my shoulders and continued toward the door.

And just like that, she was trying to be my mother again.

"Liana, where do you think you are going?" she asked, and I heard her step up behind me. I instinctively took a step away, closer to the door.

"Out," I said. "I need to think. Settle my mind before tomorrow."

I heard my father begin to speak, but my mother cut him off. "Let her go. Tomorrow these little tantrums will be over and done with once and for all."

I didn't wait to be excused. I shoved open the door and rushed out into the hallway beyond.

As soon as the door automatically locked, I leaned my back against it and turned my head toward the narrow ceiling, exhaling slowly and fighting back the urge to cry. I didn't know what I had been expecting; they rarely cared about anything I had to say. Why had I ever thought that story about Grey Farmless would give me an out? Neither of them could ever hear anything past what they wanted to hear. They had never really let me make my point. Or maybe I had—and I'd just screwed it up.

Feeling absolutely dejected, I made my way down the hall, needing to continue my journey and get as far away as possible. My parents lived in the lower levels of the Citadel, where the other high-ranking Knight Commanders lived. We had lived on this level for the past ten years, although Alex's room had been given to our neighbors after he had been accepted into the Core—the walls of his room were reprogrammed so that the door on our side was sealed to us, but open to them. I liked these quarters better than our old ones; it meant that I was closer to the wide lash openings that led directly to the outside of the Citadel—exactly where I wanted to be.

I turned right and then left again, following the wide halls and keeping my head down so as not to draw any attention to myself. The walls of the Citadel were all exposed dark steel, carved with intricate designs during the cooling process so that they looked like they had been stacked, like rudimentary brickwork. I came to a stop at the lashway—a cut-out section of wall leading to the outside walls of the Citadel. I could see the gleaming black-and-blue walls of the Core through the twisting arches and gargoyles that ran around the Citadel. There was a soft sound as I took a step to the edge, and the light around the door turned from white to red, pulsating in warning.

"You are approaching a lashway," the familiar, clipped voice announced. "Please make sure that your lashes are ready."

"Thank you," I said as I stepped over the edge, already pulling my lashes into my hand. The air caught my hair, pulling it up, and for a moment I didn't throw any lashings. I just fell, oddly peaceful, watching the view of the exposed lower level rush past me. A mother and child, walking hand in hand over one of the flat bridges from the Medica. A young pair of Squires sparring as they lashed by, their batons emitting sharp flashes of light. A statue of a man, eyes held high, hands open and accepting.

Why can't they just stop and listen? I wondered. *I know I'm onto something here with Grey and Scipio...*

I tossed out a lash, hitting a column and letting the cables slow my fall and pull me closer to the structure before detaching again, keeping close to the Citadel walls and arches, which collapsed inward the farther down it went. If I didn't, my lashes wouldn't be long enough to hit, and I'd continue falling until I reached the bottom. Then I probably wouldn't do much of anything, after that.

Why can't I just... please them? I should have been a perfect Knight. I loved the athleticism, the speed and exhilaration. The Knights were stiff, but at least I *knew* them. The Citadel was my home—I didn't want to go anywhere else. I didn't have anywhere else to go.

I just wasn't suited for anything else, not really. I wasn't smart enough to be considered for the Eyes, nor would I work for them. I still couldn't understand how Alex could, but it was his life. The Cogs were too insular, the Medics too coldly logical, and I couldn't swim well enough to go to work with the Divers in Water Treatment. All that left were the Hands, and I wasn't sure I could grow a potato, let alone be responsible for feeding the massive population of the Tower.

I threw another lash reflexively, the harness tightening as it caught, slowing me down and drawing me closer to the building. I disconnected it heartbeats later, just as reflexively, my mind still churning.

You do ask a lot of questions, a traitorous voice in my mind announced, adding to the frustration. So what if I did? What was wrong with a liberal dose of curiosity? Why did Scipio only want us to look down and not ask questions? What did he have to hide?

I threw yet another lash out, only this time I had it draw me up, and slowly began to climb, one lash at a time, up the edifice of the Citadel. I didn't make myself climb like the other Knights—hand over hand, mutinously devoid of any fun. I played. I didn't zig, I zagged. I used gravity and the winch in the harness to my advantage, sometimes going down so I could flip up to higher levels, casting my lashes up at the apex of the climb, barely latching on to a column or arch, or even the sheer walls of the Citadel itself.

But even with a smile cracking my face, my cheeks flushed from exertion, the dark seed of doubt remained. What if something really was wrong with me?

Something inside me eventually gave, and I spun myself onto a landing, hitting the ground hard and stumbling forward. A nearby Knight reached out to catch me as I toppled, and I caught his arm with my hand, managing to avoid making a total spectacle of myself.

I straightened, a grateful smile forming and dying on my lips in the speed of a glance. His eyes were on my wrist, the three illuminating the horror and revulsion on his face. He quickly snatched his hands back, as if afraid I would suddenly decide to keep them with or without his permission, and took a big step back. It could've been funny, if it weren't so visceral.

Am I a degenerate? I asked myself as I watched him scurry away.

For a moment I stood there, the people milling about and keeping their distance from where I had landed. My own little bubble, with nobody in it. I thought briefly of my friends, but they weren't Knights. They weren't my people. *These* were my people—and they hated me. When they didn't even *know* me.

"Squire Castell."

The voice was as soft as the man's footsteps had been. I hadn't even heard him approach. I looked over, and felt my face redden immediately.

The last time I had seen Theo he'd had a beard, a mop of dusty blond hair, and a sense of humor that could make even our surly training officer smile. We'd sparred often, and hard; he'd been the only person who could keep up with me. We'd been the lowest-ranked squires, both of us fives at the time. He'd been the only person I could remember ever joking with about my number, and I had wound up nursing a pretty big crush on him for the better part of the year. I had never been able to find the nerve to tell him about it. I wasn't even sure if he reciprocated it, or if I'd taken ordinary moments between us and somehow imagined them as something more. I was too nervous.

And now he was standing right in front of me. I hadn't seen him since he'd graduated. I'd cried for a week, that perfect image of us taking shelter from the world in each other's arms broken. I wasn't proud of that, but he was my first crush, after all.

He'd changed. His cheeks were clean-shaven now, his hair trimmed to a military cut. His eyes, which had once held so much life, now looked dull and flat.

"Theo," I said, stepping toward him, instantly concerned. I wanted him to be sick, but I knew that look all too well. "Are you all right?"

"I am well," he replied, his voice stiff. "It's disappointing to see that your number has fallen so low. I had high hopes for you."

I winced. The words felt harsh, like salt on an already festering wound. "That's pretty condescending coming from a guy who used to say Scipio made his number low because he was so much handsomer than everyone else," I snapped defensively, not needing him to point out the flaws I was already beginning to pick apart.

"Things change," he said. He raised his wrist, and I saw the number there. A crisp eight, purple and gleaming. "I was young, irresponsible, and foolish when I was at the academy. My thoughts were naïve, but insidious; I was everything a Knight should *not* be."

I took a deep breath, putting my burst of anger aside. "I thought you were fantastic as you were," I admitted after a moment. "I... Well, when we were at the academy, I had a huge crush on you."

"Perhaps that is why you are a three now."

I blinked at his response, a surprised laugh escaping me. I didn't know why I sometimes did that, only that it happened at the worst possible moments. Theo gave me a disapproving look, and suddenly the urge to get away was overwhelming. I was about to make an excuse to leave, when a chime sounded and Theo looked down at the indicator on his wrist.

"Excuse me," he said, reaching into his pocket.

He pulled out a bottle of pills, each one bright red, with "MSM-7" printed on the side, and I cringed as he shook two pills into his hand, knowing I would soon be taking something similar. I couldn't look at his face without seeing my own future burned there, and I hated it. It was like watching one of the Water Treatment people getting sucked into a pipe: it was terrifying, yet I couldn't look away, even as a queasy feeling began churning in my stomach.

"You're on Medica pills?" I said, the question more a statement.

"Yes," he said. "They saved me, Squire. I am... better, now, than I was." He looked me up and down. "As you will be, soon."

I don't want to be like you, I thought, my hands shaking. *I want the number... but not like that.*

He wasn't just changed. Theo, as I knew him, was *gone.* Soon, there would be another stranger walking around. A Liana who was pert and prim and obedient, doing everything right. She wouldn't be me, though.

"I have to go," I said, a numb fear settling deep into my bones.

Theo inclined his head, and I stepped away, the people parting quickly to let me pass, fear and disgust on their faces. I could hear a mother whispering to her child as I left, her fearful words catching my ears.

"Psychological contamination," she whispered, and inside, my conflict raged. How could I be better? How could I avoid the Medica? How could I get my number up without losing who I was?

It wasn't anything I did that was the problem, it seemed. It was my mind. My mind, which was so treacherous that it could infect the minds of others without so much as a glance. Because I asked questions. Because I just didn't understand.

I looked up at the spires of the Citadel. The Tower was massive, but it was nowhere near big enough for me to ever be able to hide from my problems. I kept combing through my mind, trying to tease out ideas on how I could fix this by tomorrow. The only thing I could settle on was to pray that Scipio found some shred of mercy for me tonight. Or developed a sense of humor. Possibly even grew a soul or two.

My thoughts invariably brought me back to Grey, his miraculous nine, and the pill in my pocket. I pulled it out and stared at it, thinking. What if this *was* a pill that could change your number?

After all, that was what the Medica gave out, wasn't it? But why was it different? *How* was it different? And how did Grey get his hands on it?

What if it was a new pill that the Medica was trying out? Ones had occasionally been used as test groups for new medications in the past; maybe this was a new pill they were developing. Something that corrected our emotional imbalances without taking away our personalities.

Still... the possibility existed that this had been created outside the

Medica. It just looked so different from any of their pills—plain and without any serial numbers. They wouldn't make something like that without marking it... which meant the pill was contraband.

Could this really be a way to cheat the system? It was preposterous— there was no way to escape a system that was literally seated inside your brain. I had never heard of such a thing. *It couldn't be possible, could it?*

I stared at it, weighing the options. If I was honest with myself, however, it wasn't much of a decision to make. After a couple of minutes, I tucked the pill back into my pocket.

It was simply too dangerous to take a pill I knew nothing about. It was too dangerous to assume that it did what I thought it did. I was desperate, and my mind was trying to fabricate a way out—the perfect mental state to do something really stupid that could even turn out to be life-threatening.

Once I'd thrown out the notion of trying the unidentified pill, it didn't take long to come to a conclusion about everything that was about to happen. All the pieces of my messed-up life were pointing to one very upsetting but not entirely unexpected conclusion: I was going to the Medica tomorrow, whether I wanted to or not.

5

Thankfully, I managed to buy myself more time by scheduling my appointment to the Medica for *after* my bi-weekly apprenticeship lessons. My parents had considered making me skip them, citing my shameful number as a reason, but it seemed I had been on the ball this morning, and had cleverly delayed my sentence by reminding them that the lessons *were* in service to the Tower. How would it look to Scipio if I put my needs before the Tower's?

Needless to say, it had worked, so here I was, in one of the communal annexes in the shell—the one closest to the Citadel, which made it the one to which I was assigned.

The apprenticeship program was supposed to be a way of giving each citizen of the Tower a baseline understanding of the other sections. A Knight could come to understand the importance of the greeneries (the farming floors), or an Eye could learn the inner workings of Water Treatment. Twice a week, a group of youths assembled to be taught something new by a member of one of the departments, and we all either pretended to be interested, or, like my friend Zoe, actually *were* interested.

I entered the small gray room full of chairs with uneven legs and others around my age with a certain amount of trepidation, and was, unsurprisingly, met with stares. My peers took one look at my ranking... and then walked away from me without so much as an excuse. One girl actually turned pale, like my number was a disease that she could contract. For an instant I was tempted to chase the timid thing and tackle her. That, however, was once again probably a good indicator as to why I was being sent out for Medica treatment.

I looked sullenly at my wrist—funny how something as insignificant as a number could make people believe the best or the worst about you. I sucked in a sharp breath and pushed the negative thought out of my head; if I wanted to avoid the Medica, then I had to get my number back up. I *had* to think happy thoughts.

"Whoa, look at you, you rebel."

My lips twitched into the closest thing to a smile I'd worn all day, and I turned to find my friend Zoe, her hand on her hip, her long brown hair braided down the center of her skull, the sides of her hair shaved close. It was the custom of the Divers—the workers of Water Treatment—to shave part, if not all, of their hair.

Zoe was twenty, like me, and a Roe, a trainee in Water Treatment. Unlike me, the only reason she hadn't been accepted into Water Treatment was because she was putting it off until the last possible moment, while she waited for her application to the Mechanics department to be accepted. She might have been a great Diver, but the girl lived and breathed machines.

"As you can clearly tell, yesterday was a stellar day for me," I said wryly.

"Ah, sarcasm," Zoe said dramatically, clutching her fist to her breast and gazing wistfully up at the ceiling. "Thy name is Liana, and we have met before."

I snorted out a laugh, but the levity of the moment faded quickly under the looming weight of my Medica appointment. Zoe gave a long sigh and sashayed over in the hip-based gait that all the Divers seemed to have, as if walking were just swimming vertically. She slid her arm over my shoulder, and I shivered. The arm was both cold and wet; Zoe, like most Divers, preferred to simply dive into the access hatches in the pipes and swim to wherever she needed to go. Even the suit she wore, designed to be water-repellent, never quite seemed to keep her dry.

"Tell Mama Zoe all about it," she said, her tone maternal. "Zoe is here for you now, you poor child."

"Oh, God, she's talking about herself in the third person again," another voice cut in loudly over my laugh, and I looked up to see Eric pinching the bridge of his nose under his spectacles, shaking his head in mock disapproval.

Eric was an old friend from the nearby greenery, and unlike Zoe and me, he wore simple clothes, his brown hair held off his brow by a sweatband, his strong arms, streaked with dirt, emerging from short sleeves. Eric never seemed to feel the chill of the Tower.

"Zoe knows how to drown people," Zoe said, giving Eric a salacious wink, and he smiled broadly at her.

"Does Zoe know how to give Eric a hug?" he teased back, and I rolled my eyes.

The two were so into each other, it was actually kind of painful to watch sometimes. They flirted constantly, but when it came to actually admitting their feelings or taking a chance on a relationship, they invariably chickened out, and in the most ridiculous of ways.

Zoe's arm slipped off my shoulder as she moved toward him, seemingly confident. Eric stood waiting, an inviting smile on his face. There was a moment—I felt like I could almost see it—in which they seemed so hopeful, so optimistic that this was it, this was when it was finally going to happen, and then... Zoe's hand trembled slightly, and she suddenly whipped around to face me so quickly that the end of her hair slapped wetly (and loudly) off of Eric's face.

"Wait, do Zoes ever actually hug Erics?" she asked cutely, acting both completely oblivious to the fact that she had just smacked Eric in the face, and like she hadn't just completely lost her nerve. I bit the inside of my cheek to keep from grinning at her; as friend to both of them, it was my duty to tease them about it mercilessly. But only in private—never with the other around.

Eric slowly wiped water off his face, shaking his head. "Smooth," he muttered as he shook his hand, water dripping on the gray floor. "Can't wait to return the favor. So, Liana, what's up with the three?"

"Yeah, what happened?" Zoe asked, taking a step closer to me, her mouth tugging down in a small, concerned frown.

I quickly told them about Dalton's ungrateful attitude after I saved his life, and the fight that led to my number dropping, before telling them about Grey. And about his one morphing magically into a nine. Luckily, we still had a few minutes before class began, so I was able to get through the tale before we were interrupted by the arrival of the instructor.

"I still don't understand how he did that," I finished, staring at the floor. "I tried to make my parents see that there was something more going on, but all they cared about was that *my* number had dropped."

"How did you say it?" Eric asked, giving me a knowing look, and I sighed.

"Not very well, but they barely even let me speak! They didn't care! Their trust in Scipio is unshakable. If there's a nine on his wrist, then Scipio put it there."

"They're not wrong," Eric said softly, and I gave him a sharp look. He held up his hands, his eyes widening. "No! God, I'm sorry. I didn't mean that how it sounded. Well, maybe a little, but—"

"It doesn't change the fact that no one has ever cheated the system," Zoe finished for him, meeting my gaze with her own vibrant blue one. "I mean, think about it, Liana. How could his number change like that? Did he hack his own net? Does he have the background for that?"

"No, he was a Hand originally, but they dropped him, so maybe—"

"I'm going to stop you right there," Eric said, with no small amount of disdain. "There has never been a Hand accepted into the IT department, not once, in the history of the Tower. They hate us. Notice how they only ever send their first-year Bits down here to teach us? It's because this is primarily a Hand school."

"But they do the same thing at other schools," Zoe pointed out.

"We're getting off topic, guys," I cut in. "Not to be needy, but I got a lot on my plate, and unfortunately not a lot of time to talk about it."

"Oh. Yeah. Sorry, Liana."

I smiled at Zoe. "No problem. Now, he might not have had the code, but..." I hesitated. Thought about the mystery pill I was carrying even now in my pocket. Suddenly, I didn't want to tell them—not yet. Mostly because it could be nothing, but partially because it could be *something*. Something illegal, which meant something dangerous, and I didn't want to recklessly jeopardize them before I understood the size and scope of what was going on. "What if something is wrong with Scipio?"

"Don't even think *that*," Eric hissed. "Asking questions like those in a public place is dangerous. People get scared easily, especially if they think something's wrong with Scipio. Don't you remember Requiem Day?"

I shuddered. Requiem Day had been one of the more horrific chapters in the history of our Tower—the day when Scipio had crashed. It was the first time in the history of the Tower that he had gone offline, and because his subroutines controlled so many aspects of Tower life, when he went down, we went down. Oh, yes, the greeneries continued to collect electricity, but there was no way for them to pass it down to Cogstown without Scipio's help.

On that day, the Tower's population had been close to forty-one thousand people when the lights cut off. People plummeted to their deaths in the elevator shafts and Knight after Knight died in the plunge. On the second day, people began to panic—with none of the services functioning, and no way to net each other, the lack of information regarding other sections of the Tower made people scared about what they were going to eat and drink. It wasn't until the evening that people really started to turn on each other.

When the lights came on during the third day, there were only thirty-two thousand people left alive.

"That is a really good point," I said, looking around. Luckily, we were far enough away from the few other students in the room that they probably hadn't heard us. Still, I lowered my voice. "Fine—so what if he found a way to cheat the system?"

"It's not possible." Eric's expression was adamant even as he shook his head back and forth, denying the very premise. "No one has been able to cheat the system."

Not that we know of. It was on the tip of my tongue to say, but Eric's somber expression stopped me. It took a lot for Eric to look serious, and I didn't want him dwelling on possibilities that could jeopardize the eight on his wrist.

It took a long moment before anyone was willing to speak again.

"Couldn't your parents ask for a deferral and give you a chance to raise your number on your own?" Zoe asked, and I glanced over at her to see the thoughtful expression on her face.

"They *could,* if my parents, y'know... actually cared about who I was. But no—my parents have wanted me to get Medica treatment since my number hit five, but I refused. Now that it's a three..." I trailed off with a sigh, finding it unnecessary to carry on with the sentence. They knew what the stakes were. They knew there was no way out.

"What if you got it to go back up before your appointment?" Eric asked.

We both looked at him.

"I've been trying," I said pointedly. "I think I'm broken."

"You're not broken," he replied. "Just think positive thoughts. Scipio just checks for concentrations of positive versus negative, right?"

As much as I loved Eric, he really could be dense sometimes. It wasn't his fault—he was just one of those naturally pleasant people. He enjoyed almost everything. In fact, I'd never heard him say a cross word about anything. As a result, his number was eight, and even though he hung out with morally questionable people (meaning *me*—Zoe's number was a six), that number had never once twitched as a result.

Zoe quirked an eyebrow, her head tilted all the way back to stare up at him.

"It's not *quite* that simple," she corrected him. "Scipio uses complex algorithms to..."

I watched Eric's eyes glaze over as Zoe warmed to one of her many areas of expertise. Her father had run a shop down in Old World Market—one of the common areas toward the bottom of the Tower—

trading this and that for that and this. He specialized in books, mostly tech manuals and the like (although I knew that more than a few of the outlawed works of fiction had found their way through there). His main profit came from recovered and restored tech manuals, and he sold them to a few interested parties with higher ranking in the appropriate department (as per the law), but not before Zoe got her chance to read them.

And I swear to God, she had a photographic memory.

Luckily, our instructor interrupted her rant partway through. He was a tall, fit man whose head was shaved bald, and a Diver's mark shone blue on his white scalp, the tattoo wrapping around the back of his skull in intricate little lines. He smiled kindly around at everyone as he came to a stop in the middle of the room, nodding his head once.

"I believe this is Room 937D, is it not?" he asked in a pleased voice, gazing around the room.

"Yes, sir," Eric said before anyone else had quite gathered themselves.

The man looked at Eric, then gave a kind smile of approval toward the eight shining on Eric's wrist.

"*Leristas*, young man. I am called Phineas Lute, and I will be teaching you the special language the Divers use to communicate under-water. Does anyone know what the language is called?"

My hand shot up immediately, and Zoe gave me a coy smile as she kept her hands folded across her chest. Diver Lute looked over at me, and nodded expectantly.

"Callivax," I said. "Named after Anthony Callivax, the first Praetor of the Divers."

"Very good, Squire..."

"Castell," I said, brimming with pleasure. Maybe I could use this class to get my number back up! *Diver Lute seems nice—maybe he's a little different.*

A small hope, but it never hurt to have them.

Until they were crushed moments later. His eyes flicked to my wrist, the approving smile on his face growing tight and forced.

"Squire Castell. I see you are a three?"

My cheeks burned as I realized that everyone was now staring at me, and I nodded.

"Yes, sir."

"Why are you here and not at the Medica?"

"I wanted to come here first. I didn't want to miss out on an opportunity to learn how to be of better service to the Tower."

"You wish to be of service?" he asked, sounding surprised by my statement.

"Of course I do," I said a bit hurriedly. I cringed, not wanting to seem argumentative, and cleared my throat. "I'm just not quite sure how to do that."

"Well... you have to follow the Water Ways, my child."

"Oh, great," Zoe muttered, her voice so low it was almost impossible to distinguish from the hushed whispering of my peers around me. "Typical."

The "Water Ways" was the spiritual belief system that all the Divers followed. Their ideology followed every other departmental philosophy—protect the Tower at all costs—but had spun a religion around it. A lot of it was based on the collective history of the Tower, but with moralistic rules about not being negligent or dissident, lest you get exposed to the toxic waste the machines in the Tower generated.

"The Water Ways can save you, child," Diver Lute said kindly, his eyes urging me to say something.

"Oh." It was all I could come up with, considering the uncomfortable level of attention I was currently receiving. "I'll have to think about that."

His face became disappointed rather than disapproving, but I didn't care; his assertion that I needed the Water Ways to fix myself was irritating. He didn't know me, but clearly the number on my wrist told him I was a lost soul in need of an intervention, and now that was how he would treat me. It was just so damned galling—I had gotten an answer right, and he should've left me alone. Not turned me into a spectacle for the whole class to watch, a warning to all of them to keep their numbers up.

"You do that, child. In the meantime, you'll need to come up here and stand with me for the class. Protocol says that I must keep you within reach at all times."

"Would protocol allow me to vouch for her, sir?" Eric asked, standing and angling his wrist to show Diver Lute his number. Irritation rolled over me as I looked up at him, silently condemning a system that would force a babysitter upon me. Of *course* I needed an escort; I was a dangerous element. I couldn't even learn in peace. "I can keep a careful eye on her, and that will allow you to teach us without worrying about what she is doing at all times."

"I don't think there is anything in the protocols that disallows it," the older man drawled, giving him a considering look. "You two are friends, are you?" he asked, obviously noting the fact that Eric and Zoe were the only two anywhere near me.

"Yes, sir," said Eric, so quickly that I let go of my annoyance. It cost him nothing, yet meant the world to me, and suddenly I was grateful for his friendship, and that he was willing to spare me any humiliation. "Liana is the daughter of two Knight Commanders, and a Squire herself. This is a temporary issue, and I'm willing to take full responsibility for her actions."

Phineas nodded, his smile growing wider. "See that you do," he said, then turned away. "Now, if you could all take one of these manuals, we'll begin."

"Thanks for that," I muttered as the class began to pass around a stack of small gray manuals. "I did not want to be standing up front as some sort of visual warning for what happens when your number gets too low."

Eric grinned at me, a big, lopsided thing. "What good is being an eight if I can't look out for my friends?" he asked, waving his wrist about.

Zoe laughed and punched him on the shoulder. "Look at you, acting all chivalrous," she said. "Are you using this hero thing to try and romance her?"

"And risk certain death? Pass. I mean, I love you, Liana, but not in the romantic sense. I just wanted to spend as much time with you as I could before you went into the Medica."

I knew he didn't mean it—Zoe reached over and smacked him with one of the gray booklets, and the look he gave us was immediately contrite—but it didn't matter; it hurt all the same, the knowledge that I would be in the Medica in a few short hours. I looked at my friends, and realized what I was about to lose. I felt the pill in my pocket, and thought of the mysteries I would never solve. Inwardly, my mind began to churn, trying once again to find some sort of way out.

Learning Callivax didn't seem all that important after yet another unsurprising defeat on my never-ending quest to get my rank back up.

6

The Medica was comprised entirely of sheer, curved white walls, brilliantly lit by thousands of lights so that the whole floor was almost glowing. It seemed so pure—a beacon of light in the darkness—but all I felt was dread as I crossed the wide, flat bridge that connected the Medica to the Tower. I'd taken the long way around along the Tower's inner shell, trying to delay the inevitable.

I lowered my head and looked at my wrist. The red three glared sullenly back at me, chiding me about my inability to make it change, and I suddenly had the urge to try to tear it off with my teeth and throw it over the side.

Exhaling in an attempt to soothe my nerves, I began walking toward the glowing white light. I didn't really have a choice in this, but there was no reason I couldn't try to make the most of it. Who knew? Maybe this wouldn't be as bad as I was making it out to be.

I tried to hold on to that thread of hope, but it evaporated and died even before it was born. I couldn't even bring myself to try to believe that I'd come out of this possessing the same traits that made me *me*. Theo was proof of that.

I have to do this, I thought to myself. *It's this or I lose my home.* I was already a three—if I fell to a two, the entire department would drop me, and when I turned twenty-one, I'd have to try to find a new department. If I wasn't accepted before I became a one, then I'd be locked away deep within the Citadel, and I had no desire to learn what exactly they'd subject me to there.

The queasy feeling in my stomach continued to grow as I fell in with a rush of people, their uniforms a mix of white, crimson, green, gray, blue, and orange—each color representing a part of the Tower. I should've blended in, but everyone around me kept a wide berth, the number on my wrist somehow managing to carve out my personal space in a wash of people.

My eyes immediately saw the sign hanging over the wide door on the bottommost level: *Ranking Intervention Services—3rd Level,* with an arrow pointing at the stairs some hundred feet away. I fingered the end of my lash and sighed; the Medics did not allow lash use on their structure, unless it was absolutely necessary. That meant I had to walk.

I climbed the glass staircase that wrapped around the side, the thing barely shifting despite the fact that it was suspended from the platform above, up to the third level. This level was quieter, the floors deserted. People moved much faster on this level, I noticed. As if they were afraid of being seen there.

The entrance was a wide-open space in the side, and through the glow of the walls I discerned a desk with a woman sitting behind it shimmering into view. Her blonde head was down, her eyes on the screen in front of her while her fingers flew over the glowing keyboard on the desk.

"Name and designation?" she asked when I arrived, not pausing or bothering to take a look at me.

I licked my lips, my mouth suddenly dry. "Liana Castell," I managed, wiping a sweaty palm against my thigh. "25K-05."

Her fingers flew over the board, and the next thing I knew, my face was being projected on the desk. "Liana Castell," she announced, finally looking up at me to reveal a set of tired blue eyes. "You have fallen to a three. Medica treatment is now mandatory. Do you understand?"

"I do," I lied, because no, I didn't understand why I needed to subject myself to this, and I didn't understand why people felt they needed to subject me to it either. Why did I have to be positive in order to serve the Tower? Why did we have to use ranks to decide who was worthy of our time and who wasn't? "My mother made an appointment for me with Dr. Bordeaux."

There was a flicker of recognition as the woman gave me a considering look. "Your parents must really care about you," she commented. "Dr. Bordeaux has a very impressive record with helping potential dissidents change their outlook. He's also notoriously difficult to get an appointment with."

This was all news to me—my parents had made the appointment with him. I wasn't surprised he was recognizable; only the best could help salvage their waste of a daughter.

"Oh. What makes his... technique so effective?"

The woman arched an eyebrow at me as her fingers tapped something out, the movement barely making a sound in the stillness of the room. "That information is the Medica's intellectual property, Squire Castell. My words were meant to offer you solace, not incite conversation. Please follow the lights, and, as always, have a good day."

Her fingers came to a sudden stop, and an excessively cheerful noise sounded, a series of green dots appearing on the ground and leading away from my current location, off into the depths of the pristine white building. Her tone had been curt, dismissive, and I found myself not wanting to stick around.

And her words had *not* offered me comfort; in fact they had the opposite effect. I was now worried that Dr. Bordeaux was an over-medicating kind of a guy, or performed questionable procedures on healthy people in the interest of science. It had happened before—a few Medics going off the deep end and cutting on people unnecessarily—but it generally happened when they were lower in rank. Of course. Just once I'd like to see a ten go off the deep end—maybe then people would stop putting so much faith in the stupid ranking system.

Still, the thought of a rogue Medic running around made me shudder, and I forced myself to remember that the Medica had stricter security protocols now. I followed the green dots through the curved halls, which were bisected by long, straight ones, and finally turned down a long hall and moved forward. These rooms appeared to be patient rooms; the glowing citizen designations by each door were my only evidence. The designations were followed by rankings—all of them twos. Twos were kept in isolation within Medica walls, so they could be monitored closely. These twos were supposed to be the least harmful—the more dangerous individuals among them were carted directly off to the Citadel for restructuring.

I swallowed hard and picked up the pace, my shoulders hunching as my mind imagined the people inside screaming and banging their fists on the walls, trying to get out. If there were ever a perfect reminder of why I was here and what I was trying to prevent, that would be it. It did nothing to settle my continuously fraying nerves, though.

Before long, I was greeted by the strange sight of a section of wall seemingly evaporating into a gradual brightening of the wall around it. I lowered my hand from my eyes as the bright glow receded, and saw an empty space in the shape of a doorway where the wall had been moments earlier. I looked inside and found a tidy office, the wall-screen depicting a painted landscape of green fir trees against a bright blue sky, a flock of birds frozen above them.

"Please enter, Squire Castell." A gentle old man's voice invited me in, his voice synthesized, telling me it was automated. Still, I liked the voice. It seemed kind.

I stepped inside, and there was a humming sound behind me. I turned, saw that the door was suddenly gone, and took a step back as my heart skipped a beat. I felt trapped.

"Sit down, girl," the elderly voice firmly commanded. "Your heartbeat has increased significantly, and I'm detecting a heightened amount of adrenaline. You have nothing to fear from me, Squire Castell."

I swallowed and backed farther into the room, trying to calm down. "No, you're right. I'm sorry. I'm nervous."

"That's all right, dear," he replied. "Everyone is, their first time here. It's completely normal."

"Oh," I said. Somehow, the synthesized voice had managed to comfort me. It was nice, if a little odd. Normally the machines in the Tower were coldly critical, but this one seemed... different. "Do you work with Dr. Bordeaux?"

It laughed, a delighted sound, and I blinked, taking a step back and looking at the walls around me.

"You should be asking if Dr. Bordeaux works with *me*."

"That's enough, Jasper," a firm voice announced, and I turned to see one of the walls open in a flash of light, a man's silhouette standing there. When the room dimmed to its regular glowing whiteness, I could see a man holding a white plastic pad in his hand and looking at me expectantly. "Squire Castell, I want to thank you for coming in. Can you please sit down so we can begin?"

I nodded and sat in the nearest seat available to me: a red bucket chair. Dr. Bordeaux—presumably—came around a short table to sit in an identical chair opposite me. He smiled and placed the plastic pad on his lap. He tapped it, and it immediately lit up.

"I see Jasper ran a cursory exam, but I'll need a bit of blood as well," he said, pulling something from a pocket in the white coat he was wearing. I leaned forward and held out my hand, and he quickly took a blood sample.

"What is Jasper?" I asked, watching him put the sample in a slot on the wall.

"He's different," Dr. Bordeaux said.

"He seems like Scipio. I mean... he seems more lifelike than the other automated voices in the Tower."

"Thank you," Jasper said, and I smiled.

Dr. Bordeaux turned and gave me a sharp look, his eyebrows drawing together over his nose. "That is a very astute observation, Squire Castell. However, it is also treading on council secrets, so I would suggest you not mention it to anyone."

I nodded automatically, but in my mind questions began to tumble about. Why would Jasper be a council secret? What made him special? The council had lots of secrets—it was a common gripe in every department—but to have actually stumbled upon one? It was definitely interesting, and worth noting. I had to bite my tongue to keep from saying anything while I calmed my mind.

"I'm sorry," I said, after a moment.

"No need. At the very least, it told me something very important about you."

"Oh?"

"Yes," he said as he sat back down, settling in. "You ask too many questions. Why do you think you do that?"

I frowned, shifted in my seat, and thought about the question. "I don't know... Just, sometimes things don't make sense."

"Like?"

I pressed my lips together, my jaw tightening. "I don't know," I said after a moment, the lie less heretical than the truth. "I can't think of an example."

Oh, I could think of several, but I doubted he wanted to entertain my thoughts and opinions regarding the ranking system, Scipio, or how everyone running around in service to Scipio and not each other seemed stupid to me. Why did my rank mean that I was seen as inferior, even though I'd never even done anything other than entertain an emotional thought? What was so wrong with emotions? As an AI, Scipio was supposed to be programmed with them. Did he ever have a bad day? Did he ever feel bad about himself when everyone treated him like crap for not working optimally? What gave him the right to judge us?

"I see." He tapped a few things on his screen and looked at me, the pair of spectacles perched on his nose turning white from the light of his screen. "All right, Squire Castell, we're going to do some word associations."

I bit my lip and shifted. "What is that, and why are we doing it? I thought I was here for medicine."

"Not everyone has the same problem," Dr. Bordeaux replied patiently. "Some low numbers are caused by depression, or grief, or hormonal imbalances. We can't treat every case in the same manner, which is why we do a psychological examination as well as a physical one. What will happen is this: I'll say a word, then you, without thinking, say the first word you can think of. Do you understand?"

I nodded, but inside I was suspicious. It seemed too easy a test. I had expected more torment, but hey—the appointment was still young.

"Trees."

My brain spun. For a moment, it was just blank.

"The first word that comes into your head, please."

"Green," I blurted out.

His face remained neutral as he tapped my response onto the pad. "Scipio."

"Computer."

The answer came easier this time. I could feel my brain leaning into the task, growing more accustomed to it with every word he said.

"Knight."

"Stern."

"Blood."

"Mistake."

The words started to come faster, my responses rolling off my tongue as he tapped away.

"Fire."

"Water."

"Friend."

"Zoe and Eric."

Dr. Bordeaux gave me a look. "Try to limit yourself to single words."

I flushed. "Sorry."

"Insurrection."

"One."

"Sadness."

"Home."

"Tower."

"Prison."

I felt that word slip out before I could catch it, and saw Dr. Bordeaux pause. He looked up at me, his brow thick, then slashed out the answer in a few quick flicks of his wrist. I watched them, instinctually knowing I had just completely destroyed any chance of getting out of here without medication. Comparing the Tower to prison was not an appropriate thought for anyone living here, end of story. It was all I could do not to bang my head against the wall.

"The test results have been collated into a report for you, Dr. Bordeaux," Jasper announced, his voice stiff and affronted.

Great—apparently I had offended him, too. I closed my eyes and tried not to give in to the despair of knowing that I couldn't even keep it together for this exam, this one exam. I heard Dr. Bordeaux get up, and when I opened my eyes, his back was to me as he examined the screen on the wall, reading the results there. He sighed heavily, and, with a swipe of his hand, dismissed the report.

"I was hoping it was a hormone imbalance or something easily treated, but it appears you've been exposed to some other psychological contamination at some point." My mind went to Grey, and then immediately dismissed the thought. My problems had started long before I met him. Besides, I had come to the conclusion that psychological contamination wasn't an actual thing: I'd never been in contact with a one before I started falling. Therefore, my so-called problems were just me. Little, inadequate me.

"I'm putting you on something we call 'Peace,'" he announced, and immediately a slot on the wall opened, a tray morphing into existence with a burst of light. Massive red pills began to pour from the wall into the dish, falling in what seemed to be a never-ending tide. I watched as the tray then poured the pills into a wide pill bottle, a lid placed on top of it by a slim robotic arm that extended from the wall. The bottle then dropped into the waiting hand of Dr. Bordeaux. "The chemical name is Parlexotalopram," he said, a forced smile coming to his lips as he held it out to me.

I took the bottle with numb fingers. "Will I have to be on these for life?" I asked, fearing his answer.

"I don't know," he replied honestly. "We've had more than a few people become stabilized enough that we could wean them off, but right now the majority of Peace users need it continuously."

I bit my lip and stared at the red tablets. They felt heavy in my hand, as if they were ready to drag me down into the depths of the Tower.

"Side effects?" I squeaked out, hoping somehow it wouldn't mean the end of everything that culminated in my personality, like it had with Theo.

"Nausea," Dr. Bordeaux announced gently, his face knowing. "Memory loss, suicidal impulses, and loss of sex drive. You may feel dizzy for a few days, but the sensation should fade."

"Oh." He didn't need to tell me more—these pills were exactly what I feared most. The slow death of my *self*, trapped behind glassy, dead eyes. At least it would be in service to the Tower. Finally, Scipio and my parents would get the version of Liana they'd always wanted, never mind what it did to me.

At least you'll still have a home, my mind whispered at me. I couldn't help but wonder if the price was worth it. Maybe that was why I was a three.

"Sir, Squire Castell's dopamine levels are falling, and I'm detecting increased signs of depression."

"To be expected, Jasper," Dr. Bordeaux said. I looked at him, and his smile was kinder now. "It's good that you feel so sad about this, Squire Castell. It means you recognize a problem, but are resolved to do something about it. These will help you, I give you my word. Now, take two in the morning and two at night, with food. The first week you'll be a little groggy, but give it time and be patient. Okay?"

I nodded, still too numb to do anything but sit there.

"Liana." I looked at him again and blinked. "This will fix you," he said.

And the bottle seemed to grow heavier still.

My parents were waiting for me when I exited the Medica, the pills still in my hand, my palm sweating around the bottle. At first I didn't see them. I was so wrapped up in my own apprehension and suffocating fear of the pills that I nearly walked right by them. My father, his Knight Commander coat slung over his shoulders, caught my arm with one meaty hand and brought me to a stop. I turned, saw the concerned look in his eyes, and almost broke down in tears, the urge to beg him not to make me do this sitting thick and acidic on the tip of my tongue.

I pushed it back, stamped it out, and looked up at him. "Dad?"

"Hey," he said softly, his eyes flicking to the pills. "We wanted to be here to show our support. You okay?"

I nodded and held out the bottle. "This is Peace," I said. "Dr. Bordeaux gave it to me. Two pills in the morning, two pills in the evening."

I licked my lips, and my dad pulled the bottle from my stiff fingers, giving the case a good shake and nodding at the heavy rattling sound. I suddenly wished I hadn't told him that, but it was all I could think to say. If I hadn't, maybe I could've taken less, started out more slowly. Now that I had blurted it out, they'd make sure I took the dose. No more, no less.

"I know you're nervous, but this really is a wonderful thing," my mother said, one slender hand coming down on my shoulder. I was sure she meant it to be a loving, reassuring gesture, but as soon as she touched me, all I could feel was revulsion. They were on board with drugging their child and killing off enormous parts of her personality until she became an empty shell like them.

"Dr. Bordeaux is supposedly very good," my father added. "His work with threes and twos is unparalleled." He fiddled his thumbs, seeming to wait for a response from me. When I offered none, he continued on his own. "Do you want to take your first dose now? It's close enough to the evening that I think it would be okay."

"I'm supposed to take it with food," I mumbled, trying to stave off the inevitable.

"Well... why don't we head over to the Lion's Den, and we'll use our ration cards to get some fry-bread for dinner. You love fry-bread."

"Sure," I replied numbly to my mother's suggestion.

The Lion's Den, an open market in front of Greenery 10, was perpetu-
ally busy, people moving through the tight alleys around produce stalls
and food carts with small tables and chairs parked around them. We
managed to find a table that was unoccupied, and my father collected our
ration cards so that he could order. My mother tried to engage me in
conversation, but all I could do was stare out at the crowd, too depressed
to even pretend to care. Eventually she gave up trying.

Later, after my fry-bread had been cooked, served, and largely
uneaten, my father placed the pill bottle in front of me, my mom setting a
cup of water beside it. My hand moved, but it felt like it belonged to
someone else. Someone else poured two of the pills into someone else's
palm. Someone else lifted them to my mouth. Someone else swallowed.

Someone else got up from the chair.

7

I rolled over in bed and stretched, slowly coming awake. A yawn cracked my face, and I peeled back my mutinous eyelids to peer around. It took a second for my brain to identify my surroundings as my room. It was just a clean version of it.

I sat up, confused by its tidy state. Gone were the clothes that normally formed a massive pile on the back of my old, beaten-up stuffed chair. The debris of pens, maps, doodles, and homework had vanished from my workspace, and only a pad and stylus remained, set just so on the surface.

Slipping gingerly out of bed, half expecting some sort of neat-freak monster to grab me, I pressed my feet to the cold metal floor, letting its chill assure me that this was real. The juxtaposition was too jarring. I couldn't seem to remember how I'd gotten here.

I looked up at the display over my door, staring at the date and time-stamp lit up in green numbers. Staring at it. Because I couldn't seem to make sense of the numbers. They were wrong.

Yet deep down, I knew they weren't. I combed through the broken bits of memories I could conjure in my mind, trying to explain what could've happened to me. I had been at the apprenticeship classes, then we had gone to Water Treatment, and then... The Medica. The pills. My parents. My eyes darted back up to the display, and I felt my stomach sink.

That was why the numbers looked wrong—a week had passed. A whole week since I had taken those first two pills, and I didn't remember a single moment of it. Something, someone, had hijacked my body and taken it over, and I had no memory of anything I'd done.

Nauseated, I looked over to the small nightstand next to my bed, and saw the bottle of pills, two already set out and waiting next to a tin cup containing water and a wrapped nutrient bar. I stared at the pills with revulsion, then quickly scooped them into my shaking hands, deposited them into the pill bottle, and threw the thing as hard as I could, desperately needing it *not* to be in my hands anymore. I heard the bottle hit something and then land on the floor, spinning across it and rolling toward the closet at the foot of my bed. I curled up in a ball and pulled the blanket over my head, trying to calm the rising tide of panic threatening to tear through my chest.

A week. An entire week, I thought, fighting back tears. I had no idea what I'd been like—*who* I'd been like—and that terrified me. I could've done anything and never known.

Why was I suddenly me again? Had I missed a dose last night?

Or was this what it was going to be like? Brief periods of lucidity during which I was in my body, but looking at the life of a stranger?

I shuddered, a burst of anger at the injustice of it all making me throw back my blankets and look around. If this girl was taking over my life, I might as well get to know the new Liana.

No, I thought to myself, perhaps a bit maliciously. *Her name is Prim.*

I got up and moved over to my desk, intent on checking the pad. It was password-protected, but my usual password worked—thank God. I couldn't imagine what it would be like waking up and knowing that a version of myself had changed my passcode.

I went to run a nervous hand through my hair, and paused when a flash of orange at my wrist caught my eye. I focused on it, and was momentarily shocked by the number emblazoned there.

Five.

It flickered to and fro between four and five, as if it could sense my conscious mind rebelling against the drugs that had clouded it, then settled on five again.

I took a deep breath, trying to gather some calm and force it into my body. I could stop taking the pills now. It had taken me years to fall from five to three, so this had to have bought me some time to figure things out for myself. Like a little boost to my morale or something. I looked down at the five… and saw it flicker again with the thought.

"I don't think I have years," I admitted out loud. I honestly wasn't even sure I had days.

I began searching through the pad, opening up recent files and studying them. It was strange to see things in my handwriting—things I didn't remember writing. I had notes on water treatment, suggestions about improvements to Tower security, and even (this made me gag slightly) a quote from Gerome scribbled in a margin. It seemed that Prim was an industrious and conscientious student.

Well, that's good for Prim, I thought. *But that isn't me! I don't like notes—I like action! Why is that such a bad thing?*

It dawned on me that this room was no longer even my room—it was hers. Sure, it was filled with my things, but she'd made them hers just by putting them away, creating a space that was just as familiar as it was foreign.

I needed to get out.

I pressed the button, and my door slid open with a pneumatic hiss. I stumbled out and into the hall, looking around, trying to find the other ways that Prim had taken over my life.

My mother looked up from where she was standing by a bookshelf in the small communal space we shared. "Good morning, sweetheart," she said as I stepped out of the hall.

I paused. *Sweetheart?*

"Hey. Mom." This was so incredibly awkward. She never called me sweetheart, but the way she said it told me that today was not the first time she had done so. Which meant that somewhere in the forgotten memories there were examples of her saying it to Prim. Not to *me*. That meant there was a version of me she loved.

She looked over at me, a warm smile touching her lips. "Gerome just came by, sleepyhead," she said.

If she didn't stop with the pet names, I might run screaming from the room.

"Oh? What did he have to say?" I asked, trying to focus on the question and not give away any of the emotional turmoil I was feeling.

"He said he was really impressed with how you've been adapting to your new medication and stepping up in your responsibilities." She shut the red Knight's manual she was holding and placed it neatly back onto the shelf. "I just want you to know, your father and I are so very proud of you. We see you finally becoming the woman Scipio always knew you could be."

I nodded, my mouth dry. "That's nice." Prim was succeeding where I had failed. God, I hated her so much.

My mother's smile flickered, and she took a step toward me. "Are you feeling well? You seem strange."

"No, no!" I said quickly, suddenly terrified she would figure out that something was wrong and make me take those pills. I forced a smile onto my face. "I'm fine, just a little groggy."

She prowled closer, though, her eyes sweeping me up and down. "Is your medication okay? Should I talk to Dr. Bordeaux for you?"

"Mom, that's one of the side effects," I reminded her, recalling Dr. Bordeaux's words. "I'm sure it will pass—maybe some air will help. I might go find Zoe and see if she's free for a walk."

"The six," she said, her voice flat, and I blinked, confusion radiating through me. My mom had never had a problem with Zoe before. What was her problem now?

"I'm a five," I quickly pointed out, my mind grasping for straws. "There must be *some* things she can teach me."

My mother grimaced, but then nodded. "I suppose you have a point there. But when your number levels out as higher than hers, I expect you to end the relationship."

My heart pounded against my ribcage as I stared at her, defiance already creeping into my spine. My relationship with Zoe would end over my dead body, and not a moment before. My mother looked at me expectantly, and I kept my tongue in line, trying to come up with a non-pithy reply that made her believe I was still Prim.

"Yes, ma'am," was the only thing I could stomach saying, and even then it came out strangled. My mother must not have noticed, because she turned back to the shelf to pull out another manual, and flipped it open.

I made my way back to my bedroom, shutting the door and taking a deep breath. I needed to get out of there—which meant I needed to get dressed. I looked around the room for my uniform, trying to figure out where Prim had put it, and it finally dawned on me. The closet.

I threw the doors open, and sure enough, a fresh suit was right there—hanging from a hanger, all nice and proper. I glared at it, mentally condemning it for being complicit with Prim. It now felt like it was hers and not mine. I grabbed it and quickly put it on, though, eager to get out. I tucked the Medica pills into my pocket, took a small bite of the nutrient bar and sipped from the water, then made sure to say goodbye to my mom before I left. That was probably something Prim would do.

I made my way to the lashway, and didn't hesitate, just flung my lash as I raced through it. It hit one of the arches with a *plink*, and I swung out, using the momentum to launch myself higher. As I flipped, I felt something of my old self returning. The sheer drop, the trill of my heart as I lashed through the air, made my problems fall away, if only for a moment.

One lash. Two. I felt my body respond to each cable I threw, as though it was waking from a deep sleep. I threw in an artistic flip at the end, and landed gently.

Bet Prim doesn't do this, I thought as I added a little flourish at the end, looking around and expecting, even hoping for, the level of dismay that had always appeared when I got too fancy with the lashes. It would make me feel like *me*.

"Nice landing," a passing Knight called, flashing a thumbs up.

The smile slid from my face. I had made landings like that over the years, and the lower my rank was, the more people looked at me like I was wrong for doing it. Now, they appreciated it, and the only difference was the stupid five on my wrist. That just made the compliment feel fake.

I shoved my hands in my pockets and headed for the nearest footbridge that connected to the shell, moving fast. The Tower was in dawn mode, the artificial light brightening. I looked over at the east wall as the lights changed, starting off low and rising as the sun did. I paused to watch it, closing my eyes when the light reached the footbridge, the rays pure and warm. I let them heat my face for a moment, taking pleasure in the feeling, as well as the knowledge that it was *mine* and not *hers*. Eventually I left, heading into the shell and moving through the service tunnels and access hatches, going nowhere in particular. Everywhere I went people waved, greeting me, asking how I was doing. While I had once been seen as diseased, I was now seen as normal.

Once again I felt Prim's presence, a stain on my mind, and moved deeper into the passages, taking less-used halls to avoid running into anyone. I ducked back as I stumbled into a group of six men wearing orange uniforms and wielding massive tools, prying up a bit of floor, and forced myself to stop and reconsider how I was going to get around the Cog work party.

"This is madness," I muttered under my breath as one of them gave a cheerful wave in my direction. How could one little pill affect me so much? More importantly, how was it able to make me work if it wasn't even *me* driving? Was this how everyone on Peace felt? The irony of it being called "Peace" was not lost on me, in my current war-torn state, but I let it pass as I headed deeper into the shell, finally finding access to the plunge to get some solitude.

I jumped through the doorway and let my first lash fly, using the plunge to shut my restless mind off and force it to focus on the task at hand. I spun in the air, losing myself to gravity and relying solely on my wit and reflexes to guide me in and around obstacles. When my fall came to a sudden halt, I swung into a doorway, throwing lash after lash at the beams across the ceiling to propel myself forward. The tunnel opened into a huge collection of beams and girders—a section of the shell designed purely to brace and hold the weight of the Tower.

I spotted the glowing green arrows painted on the sides of the beams, following their directions up and to the next access shaft. When I spotted it, I immediately swung myself over it, tumbling in the air and then righting myself so that I was falling feet first. I'd judged the distance correctly, and was now falling through row after row of beam walkways, perfectly positioned in the middle so that I wouldn't have to adjust my position. My eyes caught a splash of glowing blue paint, and I threw a lash, angling toward it and through the door right underneath, landing on my feet in the middle of a hidden Water Treatment hatch.

My breathing came in sharp pants for a few moments, and sweat was beading across my forehead and the back of my neck. That had been a stiff workout. I waved my hand across my hot cheeks, trying to cool them, and my eyes caught the number on my wrist, instantly grounding me.

Five. Just like that, my problems were back, pressing down heavily in my thoughts to remind me that there was no way to escape. The five flickered, battling with a four, and I shut my eyes and lowered my arm, trying to calm down.

I looked around the room for the designation number so I could figure out where I was, and how I could get to Zoe. I desperately needed to see her, talk to her, hear her thoughts. She was incredibly insightful when it came to things like this, and I could use her practicality right now. It also wouldn't hurt to have someone tell me exactly what I'd been doing for the last week. Maybe filling in the gaps would help ease some of this discomfort.

I found the room number and quickly began to push through the pipe room, heading for the elevator that was somewhere ahead. As I approached the tall opening, I could hear the sound of rushing water, and realized I was about to cross onto a catwalk suspended over the massive hydro-turbine that supplied massive amounts of energy for the Tower.

I stepped out onto the platform into a mist of water, my hair immediately going damp. The water churned white as the wheel spun at a moderate pace, crashing down to be gathered into the water storage tanks below. This was the first step in treating the water, and there were thousands of ways the water was utilized after it was processed. I didn't really understand how all of it worked, but, much like the view from the elevator, it was another beautiful sight the Tower had to offer.

I walked down the catwalk, thoughts and ideas running around in circles in my head. When I looked up, suddenly, there *he* was.

He had one foot braced on one of the lower rungs of the railing, his elbows resting on it as he looked out at the massive waterfall. The water roared all around us, kicking up mist and an occasional breeze, but he just watched it all. His hands were busy cutting an apple, and his mouth moved silently, as if going over a list, or reciting a poem. His nine shone bright blue on his wrist, but his face was wild with expression and unabashed emoting that was captivating to behold. He smiled as if something he'd mouthed was silly. He laughed as if he had some private joke—which I instantly wanted to be in on. It was unlike anything the Tower demanded, and I simultaneously envied him... and desired to know how he did it.

He finally saw me staring at him like a freak, but instead of walking away like any sane person would, he took a good look at me, then smiled.

My heart skipped a beat, and I instantly forgot about Zoe.

8

The smile flickered and was quickly replaced by wariness, and he frowned at me. "I'm still a nine, Squire."

I shifted, self-conscious. "I'm not here for that. I didn't even know you were here. I was just—"

He looked at me, his brown eyes reflecting his disinterest in what I was saying, and I broke off. His knife flashed, catching the light from overhead, and he crunched into the fruit, his gaze once again on the waterfall.

I waited for a second, to see if he would say anything, and was disappointed by his lack of interest in doing so. A part of me wanted to just keep walking past. Another part kept me rooted to the spot, reminding me that he had a way to keep me from meeting my current fate.

"I like it down here," I announced, and that earned me another side-long glance. He shifted, turning slightly toward me.

"Oh?" It was barely a syllable, let alone a question, but I went with it, just happy to get any sort of response.

"Yeah. Here and the elevators that run along the interior of the shell

—where you can see all three buildings from far away. Also outside. Whenever we have to do a repair mission, I like—"

"A view," Grey cut in. I met his gaze and was surprised to see a lopsided grin there. He slid another slice of apple into his mouth and then offered me a fresh one. "Got this from a Hand up near the Menagerie," he said, referencing the section where animals were reared.

"How?" I asked suspiciously, even as I accepted the slice.

His gaze was smug as he arched a solitary eyebrow. "Come now, even you couldn't accuse a nine of stealing," he said, his eyes sparkling. "A woman up there gave it to me. She was inspired by my ranking, or some such nonsense."

Nonsense. He'd said it almost as an afterthought, but there it was. My eyes flicked to the nine and back up to his face, which was once again angled toward the waterfall. I needed to know how he'd done it. I had to. Because more pills like the ones I'd been taking would slowly drive me insane, and I'd become a statistic in one of Dr. Bordeaux's studies.

It occurred to me that I was a statistic no matter what I did, and I set fire to the idea until it was ashes, and focused on Grey, my task clear: get him to confess how he changed his number, and use it. But I had to go slow; whatever it was, it could be illegal or possibly even embarrassing. He needed to feel confident before confiding in me.

"I see your number went up," he said. "Good for you."

I looked down at my wrist and then slapped my hand over the number, shifting my weight. "Thanks," I said. "But I'm not sure how much longer it'll be there."

He looked back at me, his brows furrowed, but he said nothing. After a moment he shoved away from the rail to stand before me. "You want something from me," he said flatly. "What would that be?"

I stood there, the question starting and stopping at least a dozen times in the space of a heartbeat. I was taking a dangerous risk, now that I thought about it. If I took a moment to believe in Scipio, then it would mean that somehow Grey had earned his forgiveness. And if I accused Grey, a nine, of cheating the system, my rank might tap-dance its merry way back down to four, and then three all over again. And then where would I be?

"Yes," I admitted after a pause, looking at him through my eyelashes. "I do. But... I'm having a hard time asking it." He started to roll his eyes, and I impulsively took a step forward, grabbing his arm and looking at him. "I'm sorry, I just... feel like I've woken up in this stranger's life, and I feel more out of place than I ever did before. I can't remember anything from the past week, my mother is finally praising me, everyone is acting like I'm some sort of hero instead of the villain—which is also uncomfortable in its own right—and now I'm standing on a catwalk, unloading on a complete stranger I tried to arrest over a week ago, because I'm not sure what to do."

I finished my rant right around the same time as my mind began to scream out an alert that maybe I shouldn't be saying what I was saying, and I looked down, heat rising to my cheeks and pooling there, until I was sure they would start to smoke. Grey didn't say anything, but a quick glance up told me he was watching me with an unmistakable look of sympathy. As soon as I tilted my chin up to confirm it, it disappeared behind a tight, neutral mask.

"Well, that was a lot to take in," he said after a moment. He folded the knife and slipped it into his pocket, while depositing the apple core into another one. I watched as he turned to leave, my heart sinking into my stomach, the urge to kick the railing increasing with his every step as he walked away, when he suddenly called, "You coming or what?" over his shoulder.

I followed, my heart pounding in my chest as we quickly crossed the long catwalk until we were at the doorway at the other end and stepping into a wide space filled with pipes. They rumbled all around us with hidden floods, mirroring my own hammering heart.

Everything about him was just different. His cocky smile, his arrogant attitude—it was mysterious and intriguing. It was also the thing that made the nine on his wrist all the more wrong: he was just too full of life to hold a nine.

"Which medication do they have you on?" he asked loudly over the rattle and gurgle of the pipes.

"Peace," I replied, tugging the edges of my uniform down self-consciously.

He shot me a glance over his shoulder, his brown eyes once again sympathetic. "They had me on that during my third treatment."

I recognized the opportunity and seized it, reaching out and putting a hand on his shoulder while my other hand withdrew the little mystery pill of his that was still, thankfully, in my uniform's pocket. It was odd, because it had been in a fresh suit, which meant Prim had been moving it, but she hadn't done anything with or about it. Still, I was glad to find it there—I hadn't intended to run into Grey, so hadn't thought about where the pill could be.

"Is this the new medication they've got you on?" I asked, holding it up for him to see. "Are you testing it for them? What's it like? You clearly still feel like you, don't you? Just a happier you?"

He frowned. "What are you talking about?"

"This pill?" I asked—practically shouted—as I held the pill in front of his face.

He looked at it, and his face paled slightly as his eyes took it in. "Where did you find that?" he asked sharply, reaching for it.

I held it back, clutching it in my fist. "Oh, no, you don't," I said, taking a step back. "Not until you tell me what it's called and what program in the Medica is using it. How long have they been testing it? And—"

"That is my personal property, and it's none of your business," he said, his hand reaching out again. "Now, if you will—"

"No," I said, evading his grasp. "I need you to tell me. I really don't mean to embarrass you, but I need to know. What is this?"

Grey watched me, his entire posture indecisive. "I can't tell you that," he said after a moment, and I met his gaze.

"Why not?"

He sighed and ran a hand through his hair, the dampness of the previous room causing a few blond locks to stand up crooked, giving him a wild look. "It's not my place to talk about it."

"Whose is it?" I demanded.

He looked away. "I can't tell you that, either."

I let out a frustrated breath and tried not to growl. "What *can* you tell me?"

"That you should give me that pill and walk away from this. It's dangerous."

"That means illegal," I said, and he winced painfully. "This isn't from the Medica. You're working with someone."

"I'm done talking," he said, turning to move away.

"Wait," I cried, racing around him and blocking his path. "I won't tell anyone, I swear. Just tell me about these pills! I can't go back on Peace. But if I don't, I know I'll drop to a one before too long. I need something else, please. I can't keep doing this."

Grey clenched his jaw, his eyes looking up over my head, a vein in his forehead ticking. "You don't understand; I *can't* trust you. You're a Squire. So please, leave me alone—before I'm forced to report you for harassing a nine."

I gaped at him, surprised by the cruelty of the threat, and then got angry. He moved to push past me, and I slammed a hand on his chest and forced him back, shoving him into a wall. His eyes widened in surprise as I held him there.

"I need your help!" I said. He pushed against me, trying to get leverage to break the hold, but I resisted him, using a nearby pipe to brace my foot and keep him from moving.

He stopped, giving me a probing glance. "Look, I'm an apprentice to a rather eccentric doctor. He works in solitude, creating new drugs for the Medica all the time, and I deliver them. What you found was one of the pills I was transporting."

"That's a lie," I said angrily. "You were a *one*. The Medica would never have trusted you with that job before you miraculously became a nine."

Grey sighed. "Fine," he said after a moment. "Ease up a little, and I'll tell you. For a price."

I took a step back, eyeing him warily. "What price?"

His answering grin was slow, giving him time to smooth out the wrinkles in his clothes. "A kiss."

I felt my face go instantly scarlet. I had only ever kissed one boy before, and believe me when I say that it wasn't on a whim. I had agonized for weeks, building up to it. Picked the right time and moment. Here, surrounded by pipes, did not seem like the right moment. Grey didn't even seem like the right *person*.

"Oh, wow," he said with a whistle. "That's an impressive shade of red. Don't tell me you've never been kissed before." The teasing note in his voice threw me off, and I took another step back, decidedly uncomfortable.

It had taken so much courage to build up to my first kiss, and in the end it hadn't mattered. He had not shared my attraction. And this felt even less comfortable—the location was all wrong, murky and loud, and Grey was... mysterious. Adventurous. It made me want to know what he was hiding, and why he would demand a kiss for it.

I was actually considering this, I realized with a nervous flutter in my stomach. As odd as it was, I really was—because I needed answers. Needed a way to avoid becoming Prim again.

I reached out and grabbed Grey by the front of his shirt.

"Hey, wait," he said, the smile vanishing from his face. "No, I didn't mean—"

"Shut up," I said as I took a step into him, my eyes on his lips. "I accept your terms."

"Right, but I think I should—"

I lifted up onto my tiptoes and pressed my lips against his in a chaste press, cutting off whatever he was saying.

He grew very still for a long moment, and then his arms came up and slid around my waist, dragging me close. The kiss changed, grew hungrier, and I broke away and took a step back, my hand going to my lips in shock. I'd never been kissed like *that* before.

I met his eyes, and noticed that his cheeks were flushed. "Now," I said, panting slightly as I brushed a lock of black hair from my face. "Tell me."

He spread his arms, looking embarrassed. "I told you," he said, his cheeks growing darker. "I didn't mean it. I meant what I said earlier: I *can't*—"

"Are you *joking*?" I exclaimed, taking an aggressive step forward. "You told me you—"

"You were holding me against my will," he pointed out, his embarrassment fading. "You weren't taking no for an answer. I just thought it'd get you to back off... I didn't know you'd take it *seriously*."

I flushed, embarrassed that he'd seen how far I was willing to go, and suddenly the urge to get out was upon me. I couldn't have felt more vulnerable, desperate, and exposed if I had walked into the Knight Commander's office and declared Scipio's programming to be filled with some pretty serious flaws.

"You're an ass—and you *deserve* to be a nine," I spat, turning and breaking into a run to get as far away from him as possible.

"Wait, Squire... I'm sorry!" he called behind me, but I ignored it, throwing my lashes up to move away from him even more quickly.

I made my way to Zoe's quarters, my bleak outlook turning downright dismal after my encounter with Grey. Zoe's quarters sat over the massive turbines below, in the bottommost level. In fact, the first time I had been there, I'd expected the entire floor to vibrate from the force of the machines below, but it was surprisingly silent, and still.

Diver sections all looked the same: brightly colored murals decorated the walls, depicting scenes significant to the Water Ways. From the eradication of the great cities to the history of the Tower, the murals all showed a river of flowing water—the Tower's lifeblood. I stepped gingerly through the offerings of specially crafted incense and bits of food left in front of them, and continued through the halls until I arrived at her quarters.

I pressed a button and waited. A moment later it slid aside to reveal Zoe, her blue eyes narrowed suspiciously at me.

"What do you want?" she demanded. "Here to tell me to try treatment again?"

I swallowed. "Uh, no," I replied. "I didn't actually tell you that, did I?"

She frowned. "Three times," she said. "You also told Eric that he was 'very sweet,' but that 'associating with low numbers would be harmful to possible futures in the Tower.'"

I buried my face in my hands. "Ah, hell."

Zoe examined me for a long moment. "That's really you, isn't it?" she finally asked. "Not the princess?"

"I've been calling her Prim," I said dryly. "Her hobbies include studying, cleaning, making my parents love her, and now, apparently, doling out unsolicited advice like an elevator computer."

"Now you see why I don't take the elevators," she said with a grin, stepping aside and ushering me in.

Zoe's house was different from mine, but then again, Divers were deeply religious people. Furniture was absent, replaced with colorful and intricately embroidered pillows and mats, to separate them as little as possible from the Tower. The sitting area surrounded a small fountain that shot a stream of water a foot off the floor, backlit by blue lights, which served as the family altar. The altar was adorned with small offerings, placed on the rim of the bowl the water spilled into— half a pear, some more incense, a wedding band. A glowing image of Zoe's father filled the wall behind the fountain, his eyes watching us both.

"So," Zoe said as she waited for me to kick my boots off before leading me to her room, "what happened, and how are you back? I can't see Princess Prim not keeping to her scheduled dosages."

I immediately flopped onto her bed and tilted my head up toward the ceiling, watching the clear, glowing pipe of bubbling water shooting by overhead.

"I honestly don't know," I admitted balefully. "I just woke up today feeling normal. No—not *normal*. Like I was waking up from a nightmare to realize I was living a stranger's life." I looked down at my feet, my legs in the perfectly pressed uniform. "And suddenly I just couldn't take it anymore. I got out of there as fast as I could."

Zoe sighed and tossed her hair over her shoulder, then crossed over to her desk. Several slim books stood in a line, their covers of various colors. She pulled out a red one and began flipping through it, slowly turning around. Then she paused and began to read.

"'Procedures performed by the Medica in order to prevent dissidence are more often than not met with failure. Medications that have been developed thus far have no lasting effect on the subject, and are—'"

"Summarize, girl," I interrupted, and she looked up at me, her nose wrinkling.

"You're no fun." She pouted as she put the book back in its rightful place, treating it gently. "Basically, we develop a tolerance to the medication eventually, and some people are just... naturally immune."

"Of course I am one of those people," I breathed, and she gave me a sympathetic look. I placed my face into my hands and exhaled. "Why can't I just catch a break?" I mumbled, my voice coming out muffled from behind my hands.

"I didn't catch that, but if you're whining about why life isn't being fair to you, I suggest you take a look outside this Tower and think about whether history has been fair to *humanity*."

I sat up, her words like hot lead being poured into a lethal mold. "That's great for humanity, Zoe, but I'm having a bit of a selfish moment over here, and would appreciate some sympathy. I mean, how can I be expected to succeed if my body or mind or whatever won't even get with the program? I really don't want to find out the hard way what restructuring is."

She blinked at me, her angry face withdrawing some, and sighed. I knew why she was angry—she didn't like pity parties or people feeling sorry for themselves. It was her biggest pet peeve.

"Do you think you can maintain your number for a while at least? Maybe I can do some research or something."

By way of response, I held up my wrist. The orange five held firm.

"Apparently not," Zoe said gravely. "That didn't take long."

"What do you mean?"

She frowned. "You were a six yesterday," she said.

"What am I going to do?" I asked, my eyes still on the pipe overhead.

Zoe lay down beside me and wrapped an arm around my waist, hugging me. "I don't know," she admitted. "But the drugs have got to go. That's first and foremost."

My mind flashed to the pill in my pocket and the kiss Grey and I had shared, and I flushed with embarrassment and shame, grabbing one of her pillows and shoving it over my face.

"Oh, God, Zoe, I made a complete idiot of myself today, on top of everything else."

"What? How is that possible? It's only ten in the morning!"

"I know," I groaned as I removed the pillow and rolled onto my side so I could face her. My fingers traced the outline of an elephant on the bedspread before me, gold in a sea of royal blue, and I sighed. "Do you remember that one I told you about? The one that suddenly became a nine?"

"Yeah. That happened on the day you became a three."

I smiled, pleased that she remembered. It might seem like a small thing, but it made me feel important, knowing that she actually listened and cared about what I told her.

"Well, anyway, I ran into him, and..." I flushed, the blush growing hotter as I forced out the words. "...I wound up kissing him."

Silence met my confession, and when I looked up into my best friend's face, I could see the incredulity there. "You kissed a potential criminal," she said flatly, her brows furrowing. "Now I know you're off the drugs for sure. Princess Prim would never do that."

"He's a nine," I said defensively. "So technically, Princess Prim wouldn't have a problem with kissing him."

The thought backfired as I realized the implications of what I had just said: as long as I took those pills, I would never really know who I was kissing—or why. Kissing Grey didn't seem so bad, under that light. Sure, it had happened under false pretenses, but at least I got to make the decision—even if it was the wrong one. It was *my* bad decision to make. Not hers.

Zoe stared at me, then gave me a small smile. "So how was it?" she asked.

"Zoe!" I chided, grabbing a pillow and whapping her in the face with it. But my mind flashed to that hungry kiss, and I felt another blush coming on. This time, however, I managed to push it back, needing to take this seriously so she would too. "Look, I think this guy has some information on a case I'm working on. He told me he'd give me the information *if* I kissed him, and I—"

"Say no more," she said with a smile, sitting up and pressing on a panel on the wall over her bed. "This is a classic romance story arc," she said, pulling a battered book from the now exposed compartment. I alone was privy to this little cache of illegal books, and it had never once occurred to me to turn her or them in. Besides, she let me borrow *Charlotte's Web* regularly; it made me see spiders in a whole new light, and now I let the little things run loose in my room. Unless they touched me, in which case the truce was ended. It was a shame fiction books were contraband—the stories held in their pages were nothing short of magic in our glum existence.

"Yup," she said after thumbing through a few pages of her romance novel, a smile on her lips. "Guys tricking girls and stealing kisses? Classic romance trope. I wonder if he had this book before I did."

I gaped at her. "Seriously? What, are you predicting our marriage?"

Zoe gave me an incredulous look. "What? No! Life isn't like a story, Liana. So, what information were you trying to get from him?"

"I can't really talk about it," I lied. It took me a moment to figure out why I was so determined to hold this back from Zoe. I had to remember Grey's behavior during our conversation, confirming my suspicion that there was something illegal about the pills. I didn't want her to have any knowledge about it, just as a precaution, until I knew more. "Not until I have something more concrete. I know he knows something. I just can't get him to tell me. I practically begged him, Zo. It was humiliating, and I'm so embarrassed. Especially after that stupid kiss."

"You went through all that and he still didn't tell you anything?" she asked, incredulous.

"Not a thing."

"What an ass."

I smiled. "My words exactly."

"So what do you want to do about him?" she asked, and I smiled. This was what I loved about Zoe the most: she was a woman of action. You came to her with a problem, and she immediately focused on the solution. It was what made us the best of friends.

"I've got to do something if I want to keep my number from dropping. I'm just not sure what I *can* do as long as he's a nine."

"Well, all you want to do is get him to answer some questions, right?"

"Right—but I have no idea how to figure out where his assigned quarters are. I could've when I was a six, but now that I'm a five..."

"Oh, leave that to me," Zoe said with a wide grin. "I'm interested in meeting this guy, and giving him a piece of my mind for bamboozling a kiss out of my best friend. And possibly giving him a boot to the rear, as well."

"Oh, Zo, I missed you," I said, wrapping my arms around her and giving her a hug. She squeezed me back, and I could feel her smile.

"I missed you, too," she said into my hair, and for a moment, I felt like everything was going to be all right.

9

Z oe's method of tracking Grey, it turned out, was to rely on the natural paranoia of the citizens of Water Treatment.

"They *hate* outsiders," she needlessly explained as we raced away from an older woman who had given an extremely detailed report of exactly where 'the suspicious-looking man with brown eyes' had gone. "We'll have his location inside of an hour—I'm sure of it."

She hopped onto a pipe, then grabbed onto the rung overhead to swing out and over a wide gap that ran several floors deep. Reaching out with her other hand, she grabbed another handhold. I watched her over-hand progress as she practically flew over the gap, and then used my lashes to follow, more confident in my abilities with *them*. I landed on one knee next to Zoe, who was stretching out her arms, and stood up. We shared an exuberant grin.

"Oy, Knight!" came a voice.

I turned to see an old man's head peeping up from a narrow gap between the floor and a large pipe, bushy eyebrows furrowed in concern. I trotted over and knelt down, instinctively hiding my number behind my back.

"I'm a Squire," I informed him. "Can I help you?"

"Bah," said the old man, craning his neck to try to get a look at my wrist, then giving up. "I heard you two were looking for someone."

I blinked in surprise and then furrowed my brow. "How'd you hear that?"

"The pipes, girl!"

"We tap out messages on the pipes," Zoe said, stepping on the tail end of the man's statement. "We have the fastest gossips in the Tower," she added.

"It's not gossip—information is critical down in the pipes, girl," the old man admonished, pulling himself out from the narrow gap with two skinny arms. "And you shouldn't peer down your nose at the ways of your people, especially when those ways save lives."

Zoe flushed, her cheeks bronzing over, and I recognized the frustrated look, having worn it myself a time or two.

"Sir, did you see someone?" I asked, trying to put the conversation back on track. The old man pulled a cloth out of his pocket and opened a sliding hatch over one of the pipes. He dipped the cloth in the water racing by and then began washing off some of the grime and soot that had collected on his face.

When he spoke, his voice was muffled by his ministrations, making it difficult to hear. "Saw a young man, dark blond. Had a suspicious look to him. Too expressive, if you know what I mean."

I did. That description matched Grey to a T. Still, I needed a bit more to go on—after all, how could I be sure it hadn't been some other dark blond man who looked super happy after getting kissed sometime earlier?

"Was he a one?" I asked, and the man turned and gave me a look, water dripping from his eyebrows.

"A nine. That's what was so odd about him. I told myself, that right there is a suspicious thing."

I grinned, glad I wasn't the only one who saw the oddness of Grey carrying a nine. After all, nines never exhibited much in the way of emotions. "Which way did he go?"

The old man jabbed a finger toward a beam of grayish light filtering upward. "I asked him, and he said he was going to Cogstown, which meant he took the elevator," he said, a note of disdain in his voice. "Can't say I'm surprised. Cogs always been trouble, since day one. And this one had damned beady eyes, you know?"

I didn't know, and I didn't agree, but I kept my opinion to myself. "Thank you, Diver," I said, and he waved a dismissive hand over his head.

"Give me a ride," Zoe ordered as soon as I turned around, and I groaned, but bent over while she climbed up on a pipe behind me. She gently settled onto my back, and I took a moment to adjust and shift her weight around until she felt balanced. I switched the settings on my suit so that the leads came out of my waist. I needed them lower to help center our collective balance. If I was going for speed or accuracy, I used the wrists. Her arms wrapped around my neck, and within moments I was lashing us both up and toward the beam of light the man had pointed out.

I landed on a platform about midway up, the yellow markings next to it telling me the elevator was ahead. Zoe slid off my back and looked down the narrow hall.

"This area always gives me the creeps," she said softly, flicking on her flashlight to provide more illumination than the dim red bulbs provided.

"Me too," I replied, eyeing the gloomy shadows that threatened to swallow the hall in the flash of one bulb blowing. It was a simple, primitive fear—the fear of the unknown that could be lurking there—but it was fear all the same. "So... do you have a way to get us into Cogstown proper, and not the reception hall the elevators dump all non-Cogs into? Because I don't have the ranking to override the elevator protocols."

"I'm going to hack the elevator," Zoe replied with a grin. Her hands dipped into her bag, and I gaped as she pulled out a small black pad, modified, like the ones the Eyes always carried. Upon closer inspection, I could see that it wasn't *exactly* the same; in fact, it looked like she had pieced it together out of odds and ends from around the Tower.

"How'd you get that?" I asked, warning bells going off.

"This thing was five months in the making," Zoe said excitedly. "I've actually hacked two elevators with it already—nothing too exciting; I just wanted to see if I could do it."

"Zoe!" I said, wide-eyed as I watched her drop to her knees in front of the shaft. She rummaged around in her bag, pulled out a screwdriver, and began unscrewing something from the back of the black metal control panel that sat just outside of the elevator, a long metal rod holding it up in the air.

"What?" she said. "I had a manual on how to fabricate your own pads —in case of emergency—and it was too fascinating to pass up. I had to learn how to code, and it took me ages to find something that taught me how to do that. The Eyes really don't like their manuals floating around."

"Zoe, if you get caught—"

"I'm not doing anything that could hurt the Tower," she insisted. "I'm not touching the security protocols, or any of the base functions. I'm just overriding the controls to make them think we're Cogs, okay?"

"Yes, but this is pretty serious. I just want to make sure *you're* sure you want to do this."

Zoe gave me a withering look as she lowered the now freed panel to the floor. "You *asked* me to be here. Besides, do you want to find this guy or not?"

I did. Still, I couldn't help but feel guilty. Zoe was tampering with the Tower, and that was a severe offense, and always came with a charge of terrorism. Altering anything in the Tower without permission was like that, as the smallest change could cause catastrophic failures (or so the department heads wanted us to believe). In Zoe's case, it would be made worse, as she was tampering with something that didn't fall under Diver jurisdiction—another big no-no in the Tower. I looked at my wrist and found myself wondering if I was actually carrying some sort of psycholog- ical contamination. If Zoe's number fell because of me, I would never forgive myself.

"Damned thing!" Zoe said as sparks shot out from where she was connecting a wire. She shook her hands and stared down at the pad, the screen turning her face a soft aqua blue. A screen popped up, and she sat down and began inputting commands into it. "So, I found a pretty exploitable flaw in the elevator's security protocols, and have written an algorithm of my own to make use of it. I trick the system into performing what it thinks is a test, and tell it what floor to go to." A platform slid out of the wall, covering the shaft, and she grinned victoriously as she began disconnecting the lines and screwing the plate back into place, making the entire thing look just as it did before.

I looked around while she did this, keeping an eye out for anyone approaching, but the halls were deserted. She stood up and nodded toward the elevator.

"Let's go," she said, gliding over the ramp and coming to a halt on the platform.

I followed her quickly, crossing my arms in preparation for the inevitable elevator lecture, and then smiled when the voice never came and the lift began to descend. Apparently, it couldn't chastise people during a test, and I wasn't going to complain.

I felt a trill of excitement as it moved—this would be my first time actually inside Cogstown proper. Cogs were very protective of their home, and didn't like uninvited guests visiting. Knights with a rank of eight or higher could overrule the protocols, but Gerome and I had never had cause to go down there even once during my apprenticeship. Suffice it to say, the two of us were going to draw some attention.

"I'm still surprised you didn't accept recruitment into the Eyes," I commented after a second, and she gave me a sharp look.

"The Eyes aren't the only ones who need to know how to code. The big machines that keep us alive are run by computers. Only the best Cogs can speak the language, and that's only because IT tried to revoke all of the copies that contained coding, citing that all computers and codes fall under their jurisdiction. They actually got a majority vote in the council initially, and got their hands on a lot of the copies before the Cogs managed to get the council to overrule their decision. Of course, it was too late—and the IT department had secured, and then conveniently misplaced the books taken in the first place. But some of them still exist, hidden by their owners before they got confiscated, and—"

"How do you know that?" I asked with a frown. "That's not taught in school."

"My grandmother was a Cog, remember? When I was young she used to tell me all sorts of things about the history of Cogstown, ranting about the IT department and the many ways they've tried to eliminate the entire Cog department."

"What?" I said with a laugh. "That's preposterous. All of the departments are necessary to keep the Tower functioning. None is more crucial than the other—it's part of the Oath."

The Oath was something we'd had to recite every morning, afternoon, and evening in our interdepartmental education centers, when we were young. It was basically a way of remembering that we were all in the struggle to survive together, and an acknowledgement of our dedication to serving the Tower, ensuring our continued survival.

Zoe shrugged and shook her head, her eyes watching the numbers as they dwindled down. "I guess if you did something to try to eliminate an entire department, you wouldn't really want anyone knowing about it, would you?"

It was an excellent point, but I still wasn't convinced. Interdepartmental spats had existed pretty much since the inception of the Tower. Jurisdictional disputes, departmental reorganizing, and more than a few hotheads had created rifts over the centuries of forced cooperation. Rumors always flew this way and that during those times; someone would get blamed for something or other, and then legends were born, with heroes and villains. The legends would become part of a department's history, and a lot of them were taken out of context and got a little out of hand.

Her grandmother had probably just told a story from her own mother. Likely, if I were to go back into the public history of the department, it would result in finding a memo about the coding books being collected by IT to ensure that all data was input into the computer, so that in case of a catastrophic event, like, say, the loss of a department, the other citizens could have the knowledge available to try to salvage the situation. It had been blown out of proportion—like most interdepartmental memos were. Centuries of living together and serving the Tower meant that sometimes departments would start fights with each other, at times erupting into full-blown group attacks and guerilla warfare. But the whole idea that a department had ever moved against another to wrest more control for themselves was unrealistic to say the least.

"Heard back from the Cogs about your transfer?" I asked after a moment, and she frowned, shoving her hands into her pockets.

"No," she said glumly. "I'm worried my mom intervened or something. She's close with the Praetor, and I'm one of their best workers."

"Can he intercede like that?" I asked, blinking at her. Praetor Strum was the head of Water Treatment, and had the final say on who could and could not transfer into or out of his department. He also served as the head pontifex of the Water Ways, giving sermons to his people once a week. Unlike IT, who never allowed people to transfer out and only a handful to transfer in, they were normally more relaxed about department members' changeover. In fact, I wasn't aware that they had ever stopped anyone before.

"He can, if he can make a strong enough case against inducting a Diver to the ranks of a Cog. It would be harder to do, since I'm first-generation and my mother came from the Cogs, but..." She trailed off with a sigh and ran the edge of her thumbnail over one brow, as if massaging a headache away. "I just like machines."

That was true. For as long as I had known Zoe, she had loved to tinker. Give that girl parts, and she'd show you a robot. Or an IT pad. I felt an empathetic pang for my friend, knowing that all she wanted was to work on the big machines, and that politics and interdepartmental disputes were getting in the way of her happiness.

I knew that if she were a Cog, she'd be a ten in no time flat.

Wrapping an arm around her shoulder, I rested my cheek against hers and hugged her close.

The concrete wall suddenly transitioned to glass, and I lifted a hand to block out some of the bright light from the beams on the ceiling, the lift continuing to drag us down. After a moment, the light grew far enough away for me to lower my hand, and I blinked as I took my very first look at Cogstown.

Steel girders jutted out everywhere, some of them making a frame, others ending abruptly in thin air. I could see the wide spaces in between —as if they were their own levels. In some ways they were, thanks to the metal plating that had been welded over the gaps. The makeshift levels were awash with activity. Men harnessed to safety lines climbed girders, while others crossed massive gaps, sliding down a single line. Parts of the open spaces were welded over, creating rickety-looking landings. The landings grew denser as we descended, and I could see more and more people.

There were improvised homes everywhere, but with no doors—open, much like the greeneries, only more chaotic and busy. Hammocks hung over empty spaces, while metal baskets lifting heavy tools rose and fell all around them. I saw one man sleeping while a heavy basket with a spanner half my size swung dangerously close, missing him by inches as it was hauled up.

I stepped out of the shadow of the platform, and made for the light. Girders were rooted to the floor all around us, and the makeshift floors above were blocking out the light, giving the wide space we were in a terribly exposed feeling as we moved forward. We walked for fifty feet before we stepped into the light, and I got my first direct look inside Cogstown.

Great, ponderous machines turned and growled, the gears slicing into shafts of light to create strange shadows as they moved up and down. Cogstown was seemingly built around and over them, catwalks and rope bridges running to and fro overhead, people climbing everywhere. The base of the village was here on the ground floor, with tent huts built around the machines, hammocks inside, and electric cooking elements everywhere, topped with pots or pans. I could see stalls of fruits and vegetables—this morning's shipment from the farms—and people shopping for supplies, their ration cards out and at the ready.

Zoe whistled as she looked around, spotting one of the vendors with corn cobs. She shot me a glance. "You ever had Cog-style corn before?" she asked, and I shook my head.

"C'mon, let's see if anyone has seen our man," she said, grabbing my hand and pulling me over to the cart. "*Akkani-kal*," she said in greeting, and I smiled—it seemed her grandmother had taught her some Cogspeech as well.

The vendor behind the cart, an elderly man with rheumy eyes and a slight tremor in his hand, looked up at us, and smiled kindly. "*Akkani-ko,*" he said, his voice, still strong, coming from deep in his wide chest. "What could bring initiates of two different departments into Cogstown? How did you even get here?"

Zoe smiled and held out her ration card. "One corn cob—and my grandmother is a Cog. She's given me permission to access this floor for visitation."

The older man nodded as he pulled one of the sizzling corn cobs from the fire element. I watched him roll it in something ground up on a plate before handing it to Zoe, and realized he had added some sort of spice mixture. Zoe didn't wait to bite into it, her white teeth flashing.

She made a happy sound and passed the rest of it to me. I quickly finished it, and was amazed by the spicy and aromatic flavors there. It was incredible.

"Just like my nana's corn," Zoe said with a smile. "Thank you."

The old man nodded and returned her ration card, having swiped it. "My pleasure." He scratched his beard and held her gaze. "Why are you here, Roe?"

"We're looking for someone," I said, wiping the grease off my lips and discarding the cob. "He's about six feet tall, dark blond hair, brown eyes, not wearing any uniform. His name is Grey—Grey Farmless. Do you happen to know him?"

He looked me up and down. "What's he done?"

I stepped forward, donning a smile. "Nothing that I know of, but I have some questions regarding his whereabouts a few days ago."

"He in trouble?"

I frowned. This man clearly knew him, but was acting very oddly about giving us the information. I studied him for a long moment, and then realized he was keeping his hand behind the stall, hiding it. I was all too familiar with the gesture—as I constantly felt the need to hide mine.

"May I see your wrist, Citizen?" I asked, hating myself for even pulling that card.

The man blanched, then stuck out his wrist. An orange four glittered there.

I studied it and studied him, then gestured for him to drop his hand. "It's all right," I said softly. "I'm honestly not that much higher than you. But you and I both know what it means *not* to be so low, and what it means if we are of service to the Tower. Grey isn't a Cog; he's a Hand. An ex-Hand. Where is he?"

The man looked at me, and nodded. He jerked his head down a path to the left that had multicolored ribbons dangling overhead, diffusing some of the light filtering in from above.

"He's in one of the private rooms—C19, I think," he said gruffly. "Living with an ex-doctor named Roark. Cogs-bred, that one, so I'm sure he's not involved with Grey. Just roommates is all. Grey runs errands for him. Follow the path till you get to the quarters. On the other side of Bellows." He pointed to the massive machine in the middle of the room, the centerpiece of the market.

"*Grandle,*" Zoe said to his retreating back.

"*Slep krin tuok,*" the man replied.

I looked over at Zoe, whose eyebrows rose into her exposed scalp as she looked at the man. "We should go," she said, grabbing my hand and dragging me down the path he had indicated.

"How could you do that to him?" she asked after she and I had moved a sufficient distance away. "That wasn't very nice, using his number like that."

I shifted guiltily. "I know," I replied. "I didn't like doing it either, but he was interrogating us, and I got the feeling that he wasn't going to tell us anything if he didn't like our answers. But I'm... I'm not very happy that I did it."

Zoe's mouth turned down, and she stopped. "I thought it was the return of Princess Prim," she admitted. "You handled it much more nicely than she would, I think, but still... it wasn't like you. What information does this Grey guy have that you want so badly?"

"I told you, I can't talk about it." *For your sake,* I added in my head, suddenly feeling guilty for even including her in all of this insanity. What was I even doing down here? I'd already confronted him once today. Now I was going to do it again, with Zoe. She'd know what he looked like —she could identify him if questioned. It put her at risk, especially if they found out that she had met with us. I was fine putting myself at risk, but her? I couldn't stomach the idea. "You know what? Maybe you should go. You got me down here, but I think—"

"Liana, what is up with you today?" Zoe asked, her eyes searching mine. "You're acting really weird."

I hesitated, and then shook my head. It was too late to send her back; she was intrigued, and she wanted to at least see Grey. Maybe having her there would keep him from throwing me out, but it would also mean he would have to watch what he said. I'd have to find a way to get him alone —but maybe Zoe could help me with that.

"All right, look... I need to talk to Grey in private," I said softly. "The information he has, if I'm right, could be very sensitive, and I don't want it getting out before I can do something about it."

"Oh." Zoe blinked, and I could practically hear the gears in her head moving as she considered that. "Well, he's living with someone, right? Maybe I can keep him distracted while you talk to this guy. Speaking of which... you sure you're going to talk, or are you going to *kiss* him again?"

"You're disgusting," I said with a laugh, shoving her in the arm. "And yeah, that seems like a reasonable plan. C19, right?"

"That's right," she said. "Let's get over there. Follow me."

I followed her as she began weaving through the people bustling around. She slid through them seamlessly, while everywhere I went I seemed to get jostled and bumped into, like it was some sort of sick game. Then again, it could've been my bright Knight uniform, which screamed that I didn't belong.

Suddenly the aisle narrowed considerably, dead-ending at a ladder, and Zoe began climbing it, following the signs. We had to climb up two levels, onto a grated floor that bore a resemblance to the other floors in the Tower, with the exception of the exposed girders and absence of walls, which opened the hall up on one side. Doors appeared in the wall every thirty feet or so, at first only on one side, but as the passageway continued it became boxed in by apartments on the other side too, creating a long hall. We followed the numbers into it, the lighting in this area once again dim and red. Eventually, we stopped in front of a door, "C19" emblazoned in orange paint on the front.

"Do we just knock?" Zoe asked.

I nodded. "It's all we *can* do," I said, reaching out to do just that.

"It's you," a voice said behind me, and I whirled, my hand going to my chest as my heart began to pound in alarm. I hadn't even heard anyone come up behind us.

I gaped at Grey, taking in his spiked, damp hair and the bag of food in his hand, surprised to see him. He stared back, his eyes wary and cautious. After a moment he stepped up to me, and my heartbeat began to thunder in my ears, drowning out everything as he drew inexplicably close.

For a second I imagined him kissing me, pulling me to him and doing it slowly, gently, tenderly... but then he pressed his palm to the door. It slid open, and I fell in, dragging Zoe with me.

"Might as well come in," Grey said as he stepped around us, not bothering to help us up. "You did come all this way."

10

I looked up from where I lay flat on my back and saw his legs retreating deeper into the dwelling, bypassing a door on the right and moving through an archway into a communal living space. The smell of sulfur and chemicals hung thick in the air, and I heard Zoe sneeze twice in rapid succession.

We helped each other up and dusted off our uniforms.

"What do you think?" she whispered furtively. "If he is a criminal... Well, he is cute. I can kind of see the appeal."

"Shut up," I said, my cheeks heating slightly. "Let's go." I tugged on the edges of my uniform to straighten it. A quick glance at my wrist showed me that the war between four and five had started again on the walk over, and I exhaled, stepping into the compartment.

The house was warm inside, the heat of a furnace sending ripples into the air, but I kept my uniform buttoned, unwilling to show vulnerability to whoever was inside.

Zoe followed at my heels and quickly closed the door, while I continued deeper into the dwelling. I stepped into the communal living space and paused to take a look around, expecting to see a dining room table or some kind of seating, but finding none of the usual objects one could expect. Instead, I was looking at a small, basic laboratory. A table supporting several machines I didn't understand and lined with tubes stood in the center of the room, surrounded by tall shelves filled with specimens. An old man was leaning over the table, one eye pressed firmly to a microscope, his mouth moving as he muttered to himself.

He looked up to grab a mug of steaming tea and take a sip before turning back to his microscope, seemingly oblivious to the two young women darkening his doorway. The old man wasn't even sweating; he looked as calm as a cat. I heard a rattle just past him and looked up to see Grey in a small kitchen nook connected to the side of the room. That was it—just the door in the hall, and this.

I stepped farther into the room, letting Zoe in behind me, and Grey glanced up at us as he set a head of cabbage down on a wooden block, knife in hand. "You guys want cabbage soup?" he asked as he neatly cut the cabbage in half.

"Cabbage soup?" the old man sputtered, looking up and around. "Guys?" His eyes found us, and he paused. Then he zeroed in on my crimson Knight's uniform, and a flash of anger consumed his face.

"Who is this?" he snapped at Grey. "Who have you brought into my home, boy?"

"*This*," Grey said, casually pointing at me with his knife, "is Squire Castell from the Citadel. She's the one who tried to arrest me last week. I'm sure you remember me telling you."

"That's nice," the man groused. "But that doesn't explain why she's here."

He looked around, not nearly as good at masking his emotions as Grey, and I could see the nervousness on his face plain as daylight as he examined some rows of samples. I followed his gaze, and saw nothing but liquids in a range of colors in their containers, tiny labels marking them. I took a step closer, trying to study the labels and make sense of the very small print, but he quickly grabbed the tray in front of me and clutched it to his chest.

"My work is delicate," he hissed. "I would like you to remove these two from my space. Immediately."

Grey sighed as he artfully sliced up a carrot. "She knows where we live, Roark—she could just come back."

"Then you need to do something about them!"

"What would you propose I do?"

Zoe finally found her tongue and stalked around me to look at them both, her finger pointed. "Excuse me," she said testily, "but would you explain what the hell you mean by *do something about us*?"

"We could kill them and throw them into the Depths," the old man continued, ignoring Zoe's statement, and I had to reach out and catch her arm before she could launch herself at him. My other hand went automatically to my baton.

"Calm down, Zo," I ordered, and I speared the old man with a look. "Are you threatening a member of the Knights?"

Grey lifted his hands, knife-free. "I certainly didn't mean *kill you*," he said. "But you're doing a lot of snooping, and it's beginning to feel like harassment. I was thinking I should report you."

The man stared blankly at Grey, then shook his head and turned to me.

"Your name," he said flatly.

"Squire Liana Castell, designation—"

"I don't need your designation," he said, cutting me off and waving his hand irritably. I noticed the crisp blue ten on his wrist, and a trill of excitement ran up my spine. "I can tell by your expression that you're not going to let this go, so I'll keep it brief. My name is Roark. I'm a chemist helping to develop Medica mood adjustment therapy."

I blanched, thinking of the pills waiting for me back home, and he must have guessed because he raised one eyebrow. "No, not those pills. I'm conducting research on alternative methods and their effects on a user's outlook, to see if there are other, healthier ways of helping a person's ranking."

I leaned forward, unable to keep the eagerness off my face. "Have you found one?"

He shrugged noncommittally. "I have found some interesting chemical interactions, but my work is private, sensitive, and secret."

Here he took the time to actually glare at Zoe, Grey, and me individually. I didn't pay any attention to it, instead looking at the tubes now in his hand. I thought about the pill in my pocket, and Grey's miraculous rank improvement. About how he was here in Cogstown.

"Does the Medica have you working from here?" I asked after a moment, and he glared at me.

"What part of 'secret' don't you understand?"

"The part where if this was Medica-sanctioned, you'd be doing it in the Medica, and not in Cogstown."

Roark glared at me for a long moment, and then looked pointedly at Grey, his expression thunderous.

"It's time for both of you to go," Grey said, turning his gaze to me. "Roark's tired."

A flare of panic rose in my chest, and I realized I might have gotten too aggressive in my questioning. I just wanted to know if there was a way for me to stop the insanity of Peace and Prim, while improving my number.

"Wait!" Everybody stopped, staring at me. I flushed, but spoke anyway. "You said your name is Roark, right?"

The old man nodded.

"Roark," I said, "I'm sorry for interrogating you, but I'm here because I need help. I want to be a Knight, you see, and the ranking requirement is—"

Roark raised an eyebrow. "I know what it is, and I don't care. Shields aren't welcome in my home. Get out."

"Please," I said, holding out my wrist. "They've got me on Peace, and it's killing me!"

Roark looked at my wrist for a second, seeming to notice the four/five fighting again, and then looked away. "Get this Shield out of my house, Grey."

I wanted to scream at him, yell at him, beg for some semblance of humanity, but Grey's hand unexpectedly landed on my shoulder and I looked over at him, at the carefully reserved features he was holding on his face. There was nothing I could say that was going to change his mind, I realized. Suddenly, I just felt tired; this was my one chance to get away from Prim, away from losing myself to the meds—possibly even stronger meds, if they found out Peace wasn't working—and he wasn't going to help me.

"Thank you for your time," I managed after a pause, before turning slowly toward the door. "Come on, Zoe... We should go."

Grey just watched me leave, and I moved back out into the cool tunnel. Zoe was quiet beside me as I headed back toward the ladder, pausing when the wall disappeared, revealing the open space of Cogstown some thirty feet below. The entire Tower was one complex machine, everything serving a purpose, everything sharing a goal: keep us all alive. It was something you knew, but rarely got to see in action. All the gears, all the steam, all the electricity feeding in and out of each and every little thing. It all fit together so well, but in that moment I felt like a cog that didn't quite fit, and I could feel the hammer coming down, trying to force me into place.

Zoe broke the silence, nudging me with her shoulder. "Hey," she said. "What's really going on? You think he's working on a cure for the Medica and slipped Grey some?"

"I don't know," I replied. "Honestly, Zoe, this wasn't even something I planned on reporting to the Citadel. I just was looking for a way out. I think I'm getting desperate."

"I hate to say this, but you have to go to the Medica and report today," she said with a tight nod. "If you don't, it won't be long before you get to two and your parents are forced to drop you."

As if I needed the reminder.

"But if I go to Medica, I turn into something that isn't me."

She reached out and took my hand, giving me a wry smile. "I'd rather have you alive than lose you forever to restructuring. You need to be in a department. No department means—"

"No work," I finished for her, looking up and watching some Cog children run fearlessly across a narrow pipe overhead, their bare feet slapping against it as they darted by with a laugh. "No food on the ration card, no service to the Tower, the fall to becoming a one taking a matter of days, depending on how optimistic you can be. I know."

"Sounds like a blast when you put it like that," she quipped, and it brought the shadow of a smile to my lips. "Come on. I'll walk you home."

"Hold up."

The voice was Grey's. He was trotting up the hall behind us, and came to stand before me just as I turned. He was ever so slightly taller than me, and met my eyes with that warm brown gaze of his. I watched him warily, wondering what he wanted, and secretly hoping that Roark had changed his mind.

"I'll walk you two out of Cogstown," he said. "They probably already know you're here, and they might try to scare you before you leave."

"What? Why?" I asked, baffled by his unexpected statement. I looked at Zoe, hoping for clarification. She knew almost everything, it seemed.

She opened her mouth to reply, but Grey beat her to it. "They don't like outsiders here, and tend to want to make them leave afraid."

I laughed darkly. "You're an outsider," I said. "You're a Farmer, aren't you?"

"Not anymore," he said simply. "But they know me here; if I'm with you, you won't be bothered. Besides, I doubt you'll want to hack the elevator right out in the open in front of everyone."

He gave me a pointed look, and I kept my face neutral, revealing nothing—though my heart was beginning to pound again. It was stupid, but I couldn't help but feel a bit pleased that he thought me so capable.

Zoe rolled her eyes and tapped him on the shoulder. "Hi," she said. "I'm the one who hacked the elevator. How did you know we had done that?"

"Lucky guess. Also, I saw the pad in your satchel. It's an IT design, right?"

Zoe raised an eyebrow, clearly impressed, and nodded. "It is. And you're right—I don't want anyone to see me doing it. So... thanks for escorting us, and we really should get going."

"No arguments here. Shall we?" They both looked at me expectantly.

I didn't want to leave, but I also couldn't argue that we had to get going before the residents of Cogstown started messing with us. Grey was apparently being kind and offering to walk us out, which I hoped was his way of making up for being a jerk earlier. I remembered the kiss from earlier and felt myself turning pink as I let him take the lead, climbing down after him, the air full of thick steam and the smell of shaved metal.

We reached the elevator without incident, which gave me time to think. Grey's appearance meant another chance, another opportunity to try to get the truth. I just had to find the appropriate moment, and an idea was already spinning in my head. Grey went to the security box and slipped a little metallic chip into the top. It turned blue, and a platform slid out expectantly.

Zoe stepped forward onto the platform and looked back at me.

"You coming?"

I looked between her and Grey, then shook my head. "I need to talk to him for a minute. Go on ahead."

She frowned, but didn't argue. Instead she looked over at Grey and speared him with a lethal look. "I'd better see her soon," she informed him, and he flashed her a charming smile.

"Hey, *she* wants to stay to talk to *me*," he announced, but she didn't back down.

"Yes, and you were the one who stole a kiss using underhanded trickery," she snapped back, and, to his credit, Grey paled slightly. "So I reiterate: I'd better see her soon. I know great places to deposit bodies so that they're never found. I'm just saying."

"Zo, it's okay," I said. "I'll be all right."

Her face softened as she looked at me. "All right, but I expect details. And I want to know more about whatever it is that's going on with Roark."

"If I find anything else out, I'll tell you," I promised, and she nodded before giving me a hug. She let go at the last possible moment, and I watched her begin to rise.

"You know that if you do find anything out, you can't tell her, right?" Grey asked casually, and I gave him a sharp look.

"Why not?"

He looked over at me and then shrugged. "Not important. You wanted to talk?"

There was no dismissing what Grey had said, and my mind had already pounced at the opening. He was here, he wanted to make sure I understood that I couldn't tell Zoe anything... he was going to tell me. I knew it.

He leaned a hip against the elevator console and crossed his arms, looking at me expectantly. I wished he weren't so handsome when he did that—so free and so casual, as if things in this Tower weren't messed up and everything was fine. I guessed having a nine on your wrist meant a certain peace of mind. I wanted that. Desperately.

"You have something that could help me," I said.

He looked away. "Roark said—"

"If I wanted to talk to Roark, I'd have stayed and done that," I said.

He looked back at me, and some of the haughtiness fell away. "I'm sorry," he said, "about earlier. You were just pushing me around, and I didn't like it, but I didn't want to hurt you. It was the first thing I thought of that might get you to back off. It worked... I just didn't expect you to take me seriously."

I sighed, lashed myself up to a beam overhead, and perched on it, needing to sit down. Grey shot me a curious expression, and I tapped the spot next to me, an open invitation. He sucked in a deep breath and began climbing up one of the vertical beams supporting the one I was on, using the tips of his fingers and boots, and doing it with some ease. He walked out to me, confident, even though the beam was only a foot wide, and then paused, giving me a questioning look.

"Don't make a girl feel awkward," I said. "Sit."

He did so, looking at me uncertainly, as if I were a poison he wasn't certain he had the antidote to, and we sat there together for a moment, watching the machines churn and hiss.

"I'm not stupid," I said after a long moment. "I know you took that medicine and it made you a nine. I also know that you aren't acting like a nine—you've got far too much personality for it to be believable. Which means that either the meds he's working on are a genuine cure for nega-tive thoughts, or he's created something to cheat the system."

Grey said nothing.

"And I get that you can't tell me why," I added. "I live in the Citadel, and am training to be a full Knight. My parents are both Knight Commanders, both ranked ten. I'm the last person you'd want to admit anything to, and I get it. But... I'm not joking when I say I need this. I don't want to be thrown out of my department, but I don't want to be a zombie anymore, either. I promise, if you tell me, I won't tell anyone."

He looked at me. "If I am a nine," he said carefully, "then you just asked an upstanding citizen for a way to undermine Scipio. Aren't you afraid of the consequences of that?"

I let my head fall into my hands. My fingers felt cold against my fore-head, every strand of hair like a nerve ending as I tried to hold my anxiety inside my body and stop it from bursting out. Saying it felt wrong—like I was committing sacrilege. It took every ounce of courage I had to answer his questions.

"Yes, but that doesn't change the fact that I still want to do it," I admitted. "Because I can't keep being the version of me that they want. I won't survive another day on this stuff, Grey. I can't. The last week is a blank slate for me—I remember nothing, but everyone treats me as if I was walking on water, instead of drowning in it." I sniffled and scrubbed my cheeks, trying to keep back the tears that were threatening to spill over. "If I have to cheat to get my number and keep my sanity, then it's worth the risk."

He looked at me for a long time while I sniffled and snuffled, still fighting back an overwhelming sense of despair. Finally, he sighed heavily and, from out of nowhere, produced a clean handkerchief.

"My parents were eights," he said. "I was a seven."

I dabbed my eyes with his handkerchief and looked at him, baffled by his sudden change of topic. "But what does that have to do with—"

"Shut up a minute," he growled, and I stiffened reflexively, but relaxed when I realized he wasn't angry or irritated. Whatever he had to say was painful. "My parents, they were eights, but they wanted to be more. They wanted *me* to be more, and when I wasn't... well. They started piling on responsibilities. Duties. They forced me to keep a 'positive thoughts' journal, and to list three things every day about the Tower that made my life better. You know what happened?"

"Your number went down," I replied. The story was almost too familiar. In fact, it was similar to mine: my parents had demanded more and more of me after Alex left, but my ranking only ever went down. It was exceptionally demotivating and incredibly depressing. I guessed Scipio never considered that some of us were far too sensitive for the ranking system. All I knew was that it was beginning to feel rigged.

Silence.

"Yeah," he said eventually. "It went down. Way down. So far down that they dropped me."

He grimaced and shook his head. I knew most of that from his dossier, but I still hurt for him. He had been abandoned because they'd demanded more—and then shamed him when he couldn't perform to their expectations. It was unjust, and it had ripped him away from the only home he had ever known, and thrown him into the Tower all alone, to fend for himself. He was lucky another department had picked him up. If they hadn't, he would've been rounded up with the other underage kids, who, when they turned eighteen, were shuffled down into the dungeons of the Citadel if they couldn't get into a department of their own, slated for restructuring.

My parents had been oppressive, controlling, downright mean at times, but they had never even mentioned dropping me. It had been unconscionable for them. Maybe Sybil's death had changed them in that regard. I couldn't really be sure. It was a marked improvement over wanting to have me killed at birth, so...

"I'm sorry," I said. It was all I could think to say in that moment.

"Roark took me in," he said with a shrug. "And things have been fine. Good, even. I feel like I have a purpose here, and my number is high enough now that nobody even bats an eye at me. It's funny—I don't do anything different, but nobody cares. All anyone ever cares about is the number."

That, too, rang true. I found myself leaning in a bit, drinking in his words. After hearing about positivity for so long, and moving forward with your chin held high, no matter how much you were hurting, it was refreshing to see someone so down to earth. So real.

He looked at me, and I felt my heart skip a beat. I snapped my eyes away.

Don't be stupid, I thought. *You don't even know him.*

"Roark and I," he said, seeming not to notice my embarrassment, "we want to help people, like he helped me. But he has a grudge against Knights, and honestly it's hard to argue the point with him."

I scowled. "Why? What did we do?"

Grey's voice was soft as sunlight, and cold as wind. "The Knights killed his wife," he said simply.

I sat there, my head already shaking in outright denial of his words. Knights didn't kill. We just didn't. We captured, guarded, and protected. To kill a person was to break one of Scipio's cardinal rules. It was to instantly reduce yourself to a one, and be tagged for arrest and exile.

"That's not possible," I said.

"Tell that to Roark."

"I will. Right after I call him a liar."

"Wait—are you mad?" he asked, leaning back onto the palms of his hands and eyeing me. "Why are you mad?"

"Because that was a lie," I said, still upset. "The Knights don't kill. If he says they killed his wife, then he is a liar."

"Whoa! Roark might be a bit touchy, but he's not a liar. Besides, if they were killing people, do you think they'd let a Squire know that?"

"My parents are Knight Commanders," I said. "They could never have killed anyone. They couldn't." Except for me, that was.

"You also said they were tens," he fired back. "You think they'd clue you in to something that's probably a secret?"

I glared at him, my jaw clenched so tight that it ached. "I want to go. I want to go *right now.*"

I began pulling my lash out, intent on swinging out of Cogstown if I had to, but he reached out and laid a hand on my wrist. "Wait."

Looking over at him, still seething that someone was going around accusing Knights of murder, I was surprised to see a contrite expression on his face.

"I'm sorry. This is clearly a sensitive topic for you, and I shouldn't have brought it up."

I pursed my lips at him, considering him for a long moment, and then sighed. "Why did you come after Zoe and me? Was it really just to walk us out?"

He sighed too and pulled something out of his pocket, cradling it between his hands. It rattled, and I realized he was holding a bottle. Our gazes met, and there was a stillness between us, so intense that I was afraid to breathe—or maybe the air was too thick.

"These are for you," he said hoarsely, offering them to me. I hesitantly held out my own hand, and he dropped a bottle into it. Pills: small, white, and unmarked.

"Take these," he said. "You might find them a more palatable alternative to the Medica drugs."

I looked between the bottle and him, something warm curling up in my throat.

"But Roark said he—"

"Roark's not here," he said, rising to his feet. "And one benefit of being dropped is you develop sticky fingers." He held his fingers up and wagged them back and forth, then stepped out into the air. I reached for him, but somehow he twisted and caught the edge of the beam with his fingertips before dropping the remaining three feet to the ground below. He moved over to the elevator and inserted his chip, and I used my lash to lower myself gently to the floor, the pills clenched between numb fingers.

"This is you," he said, guiding me onto the waiting platform. "See you later, Squire Castell." He gave me a sweet smile as the elevator began to rise. "Oh, and only one a day!"

"Goodbye," I said, still stunned by the change of events. I looked down at the bottle in my hands and felt the weight on my shoulders lighten significantly. "And thank you!" I shouted as an afterthought.

Belatedly, I wondered if he had, by filching these pills, gotten himself into trouble with Roark... but then decided that if he had, I would do something to help him out of it. Even if it meant going down and talking to Roark again—although I wasn't sure I could do that and let his insidious rumors about the Knights slide. But I was willing to give it a try.

Especially if it meant having access to more of this medication in the future.

I looked at my wrist, and was unsurprised to see a four gleaming there. Only this time, I smiled at it. But it was more like a baring of teeth, really.

11

I stayed away from home for as long as possible, taking time to net Zoe just to tell her that I was okay—I didn't want to say anything more yet. The walk back to my room was a silent affair. My number, which had since dropped even further to a three, drew stares, and people muttered as I passed. Strangely, I felt more at home this way. At least it was honest. At least it was *me* being judged.

I stopped outside the door leading to my quarters, knowing my mother was waiting inside, and took a deep breath. Under no circumstances could I let her see the new number—not before I got a chance to try Grey's medication. If she did, she'd haul me off to the Medica and Dr. Bordeaux, and they'd probably make me take the pills in front of them.

Pressing my ear to the door, I waited until I was certain she wasn't in a front room, and then slid the door open and closed. The only movement between the two actions was me stepping quickly through.

"Liana?" I heard my mom's voice call from her bedroom as I moved down the hall.

"Hey, Mom!" I shouted as I made it to my door. "I'm not feeling well, and I'm going to go to bed early. See you tomorrow!"

"Okay. Feel better, honey."

I slid my door closed and engaged the magnetic locks, exhaling slowly and closing my eyes, trying to press away the panic that had formed in the short distance between the door and my room. She'd bought it, and she didn't know. I was safe... for now.

I moved to my window and sat down on the sill to stare at the bottle of pills in my hand. I shook one out and pulled the other from my pocket, and compared the two. They looked identical, but without any markings it was hard to tell. It could be that they were some sort of poison or memory-loss pills, but I didn't feel like Grey would do that to me.

I pressed one to my tongue and swallowed it dry. Dropping the second one back into the bottle and screwing the top back on, I stared out the window, and idly wondered how long it would take.

My view from my window was one of the better ones, in my opinion. It held the normal loops and swirls and lines of the Citadel, but through it, I could see Hadrian's bridge—one of the bridges that ran from the Citadel to the shell. It was a calliope of colors, set in a mosaic. The artificial light was starting to go down, turning orange, and the white rails of the bridge glistened and gleamed, while bright blues, greens, and oranges blazed through the dark arches.

A pair of Squires lashed past, playing some sort of game that appeared to have no rules. I leaned forward, watching how they handled their lashes and twisted their bodies, and was moderately impressed. They were fast and accurate, but could improvise. Those were critical skills for lashing.

I shifted, following their progress, but eventually my eyes drifted down to my wrist, the urge too strong to resist.

The pills from the Medica had evidently hit me instantly—I certainly couldn't remember anything after taking the first set. I could barely remember getting fry-bread before swallowing them. I didn't know what to expect with this pill, or how long it would hold, but I expected it to work almost instantaneously.

But no—not these, apparently. Not according to the angry red three that still adorned my wrist.

I sighed and got up, moving over to my bed and lying down on it. I kicked off my boots, letting them fall to the floor at the foot of my bed, and undid the front fasteners of my uniform before shrugging the coat off and tossing it to one side. The pants quickly followed, and I climbed under the blankets. I shifted back and forth, trying to get comfortable, and then looked up at the display. The entire ordeal had taken two minutes.

I looked at my wrist. The three glared stubbornly back.

I sighed. Again.

Lowering my arm, I stared up at the dark ceiling and began to feel doubt. Maybe Grey had given me a placebo. Maybe I was immune to them. Maybe he'd tricked me. Maybe I needed to take another.

Over and over my thoughts tumbled while I lay in bed, keeping my mind active even when I closed my eyes. I tried to doze—to make my mind go quiet enough to sleep—but it didn't work. It couldn't be stopped.

Liana?

I started in surprise, my heart skipping a beat and kicking the air out of my lungs for good measure. I had been so engrossed in my thoughts that I hadn't even noticed the buzz starting at the back of my head. I looked down at the indicator on my wrist, and sure enough, Alex's name was displayed on it.

"Alex, do you have to override my indicator every time you call? How do you know I'm not in the middle of something?"

A moment of silence, then a hum.

Please, you're never in the middle of anything, he teased. *And I have to override your indicator so you won't ignore me! Congratulations on your new number. Impressive progress, for so short a time.*

I frowned. "It went back down again," I groused, rolling over to my side.

Dips aren't uncommon.

I sighed.

I'm sorry I didn't get in touch sooner, he continued. *Things have been strained up here.*

A burst of affection came over me, and I was suddenly glad he'd called. If this was going to be my last night as me, then I couldn't imagine a better way to spend it than chatting with my brother.

"What's going on?"

A quiet noise.

I can't really talk about it, he said.

"Alex," I chided, softly.

Another pause, and I could almost see him. I missed his mannerisms; as irritating as they had been, I could almost imagine him doing them all in the space of the silence. Gnawing his lower lip. Scrunching up his nose to hold his glasses tighter. Combing his fingers through the front of his hair.

You can't tell anyone.

"Of course."

I'm serious, Liana.

I looked at the pills on the table. I wasn't about to rat Grey out, and I barely knew him. Alex was my twin. Not to mention, if he was even willing to bring it up, it meant he needed to talk about it. Better me than someone who *would* turn him in.

"I swear I won't breathe a word of this to anyone."

I heard a noise and smiled when I realized that Alex was drumming his fingers on his desk.

It's Scipio, he said.

That got my attention. Alex had transferred to the Eyes specifically because he wanted to work with Scipio. The great machine had always fascinated my brother, drawn him in like sweets would any other child.

"What's wrong with Scipio?" I asked—cautiously, though my mind was ablaze. Of course something was wrong with Scipio—what else could explain people like Grey and I trying and trying and trying but never going anywhere but down? Of course, if Alex was just figuring this out now, we needed to have a long talk about his observational skills.

I don't know what's wrong. Not exactly, anyway, he said. *I think... I think Scipio's losing it a little.*

A chill ran down my spine at the edge of anxiety in his voice. "Losing it?"

He's getting more extreme, Alex said, and his words were quieter now, as if he was speaking in a jumbled whisper. *More violent. He's using the Knights more viciously, and punishing low numbers more aggressively.*

I swallowed, thinking about Roark and his claims. "Punishing them how?"

Alex began to talk, then cut off. I heard a set of footsteps moving by.

People have died, Lily, he said.

"What do you mean, people have died?" I asked. "Alex... have you heard something about the Knights?"

Silence met my question, and I waited, heart in my throat. I almost gave up waiting for an answer, but after a moment I heard a soft breath, followed by his voice.

I don't know. All I know is that it is a good thing you got your number up.

I frowned. "Alex, when was the last time you checked it? Because it isn't the best right now."

I'm looking at it now, he said, sounding confused.

"Well, then I'm glad you're impressed with my three, but—"

Have you checked it? Alex asked, bemused.

I looked down at my wrist, expecting to see red. Instead, I saw blue. A blue so cool and calm that I had a hard time reading the number there. My wrist hadn't *ever* looked like that.

Sitting primly at the base of my hand was a glowing nine.

I don't think you have anything to worry about with a nine, Alex was saying. *I'm genuinely unsure what they gave you to spike you that fast, but it does make me feel better. I gotta go, but I'll check in soon. Tell the folks I said hi, all right?"*

"Wait, Alex. I want to know more about Scipio," I said hurriedly, but he didn't respond, and I could tell by the now inactive net that the call was over. I exhaled and looked back at my wrist. Still a nine—certain, still, and confident.

I lowered my arm and considered my own feelings. Did I feel any different? Was I feeling the urge to do anything differently?

A quick assessment revealed two things. Number one, other than the shock of seeing a nine on *my* wrist, I felt relatively normal. A little excited, but ultimately, I still felt like me.

Number two, the only urge I had was to go down and use my ration cards to get some fry-bread and see if I couldn't scrounge up some berries. Which was pretty normal, for me. Not that I was going to follow through on that urge, either. Going outside now with a nine on my wrist was just as dangerous as the three; I worried people would notice incongruities with my behavior compared with that of other nines or tens. I had to be careful not to reveal anything to anyone, and keep my emotions hidden as much as possible.

Grey's pill had worked, and just in time too. With Scipio malfunctioning somehow, I could've sunk to a two and gotten booted from the Citadel before it got fixed.

But that didn't stop it from happening to other people.

That thought haunted me for several hours after that, and it took a long time to go to sleep, the nine suddenly feeling heavy on my wrist.

"I don't know how this is possible."

My father sat opposite me at our dining room table, his eyes flat with shock, his hands playing excitedly across the tabletop. My mother was next to him, a broad smile splitting her features.

I shrugged, trying to act nonchalant. "Neither do I," I blatantly lied. I looked down at my wrist, and the nine smiled back, bright and cheery. "It was just like this when I got back from my walk."

It was morning, and I had spent the better part of the night trying to decide how to explain the significant increase. Luckily, the last time they saw me I was a five, not a three—but rising four ranks overnight wasn't normal. I considered concocting a tale of heroism, but that seemed a little far-fetched, and was too easy to disprove. My next thought was that I could tell them I went on a spiritual quest and came out understanding my place in service to Scipio, but the thought was so nauseating, I immediately dismissed it. There was no way I could be convincing in the retelling, so it was better to pass.

In the end, I decided to opt for something as close to honesty as I could manage: I took my pills, met with Zoe, came home, and boom, nine status.

"Anyway, I really need to get going," I said, glancing toward the door. "I have my apprenticeship."

My mother shot to her feet, dragging my father up with her. I canted my head toward her, alarmed by the intensity on her face, the wide-eyed panic on it.

She gave me an incredulous look as she saw me staring up at her, and frowned. "Liana, you're going to be late!" she exclaimed. "We don't want your number dropping, so the best thing to do is to keep doing what you've been doing. Now get up and get to class, dear."

I barely had a chance to grab my things before she literally pushed me out the door. I stood there, blinking in the hallway, confused by the sheer enthusiasm still seeming to radiate out from our quarters. Was this what it felt like to be loved, like I'd always wanted to be? Was this what it felt like to be accepted?

Not at all a bad feeling, if I did say so myself.

I turned and began walking, my mind automatically drifting to Grey and the pills. He'd given me enough for a month—I'd counted—but who else were they making this for? It was illegal, that much was certain, yet it was giving me a second chance at life in the Tower.

It could be dangerous. By taking these pills, I was putting myself and possibly my friends and family at risk. And Grey was running around out there, someone who knew what I was doing. If he was compromised... I wasn't sure I could count on him not to turn on me. Or vice versa.

Grey's story about Roark and his wife flashed across my mind, and I felt the dull burn of anger, but a greater sense of disorientation, the thought leading me to my brother's words last night. *Something's wrong with Scipio.*

My feet paused in their stride, and I brought myself to a slow stop, trying to calm the sense of foreboding settling over my bones. I was being paranoid. I was stressed about what I was doing with Grey's pills, and Alex's comments were just adding to an overactive imagination that tended to focus on impending doom rather than looking on the bright side.

And there *was* a bright side—I was a nine.

I just wished I knew what that meant for the future.

The apprenticeship annex held its usual smattering of bored young adults when I arrived. Unlike before, however, they did not part when I approached. Instead, they waved or offered a smile as I slid by. It took me a minute to find Zoe and Eric standing in a corner, Zoe gesticulating wildly as she spoke.

The pair of them looked up as I drew near, Zoe's smile fading as she gave me an apprehensive look. I knew she was worried about my number, and wondering what had happened after she'd left. I gave her a nervous smile as I walked up.

"Hey, Liana," Eric said cautiously, his eyes flicking over to Zoe. "I heard you were feeling more... like yourself?"

His face screwed up at the end of his statement, a mixture of awkwardness and naiveté that brought an amused smile to my lips.

"I am," I said. "Very much so."

Zoe stepped forward, tilting her head to try to get a look at my number, and I caught myself moving to cover it. I had to be careful not to do that now; nines wouldn't try to hide. They had nothing to be ashamed of.

"A *nine!*" she exclaimed, her eyebrows rising, and Eric whistled, a low, impressed sound. Zoe's eyes met mine, quizzical, and I could hear her unspoken question: *Did Grey help you?*

I hesitated and gave an imperceptible shrug. I felt bad for lying, playing dumb, but with the nebulous nature of my relationship with Grey, and the origin of the pills, it wasn't worth the risk of telling her. She was a six, and I knew she'd never betray me, but she had been exposed to way too much already. It could be dangerous for her to learn more.

"A nine *and* the side effects wearing off? That's seriously impressive."

"Thanks," I said with a smile, but I felt the urge to fidget under their scrutiny.

"How'd it happen?" Eric asked, and I sucked in a deep breath, the lie I'd told my parents slipping out more easily this time.

"I'm not really sure," I replied. "It happened after I met with Zoe. I dropped down to a three, and then it was a nine."

"No miraculous realizations?" Zoe asked. "No heroic deeds?"

"Nope. Maybe Scipio's finally getting my sense of humor?"

Zoe frowned, but seemed willing to drop the subject for the time being, probably just as unwilling as I was to bring it up in front of Eric. I knew there'd be hell to pay later for withholding information, and I would have to tread very lightly, but for the time being I was safe from any other interrogations.

"Does that mean I won't get any lectures about why I shouldn't fraternize with dangerous lower numbers like Zoe again?"

"Scipio's grace, no," I said. "Please, fraternize with the low numbers until I'm forced to arrest you."

Eric grinned. "It's good to have you back properly. Those drugs did a number on you."

"They really did," Zoe agreed, as if she hadn't known already, and I realized she hadn't told Eric about our escapade yesterday. She held my gaze, her eyes sharp. "So who's up for Phineas, week two?"

I frowned, racking my brain for a memory of who Phineas was. It took me a few seconds to remember the class right before the Medica, and our lesson in Callivax, the hand language of the Divers.

"Is he still teaching us?" I asked, confused. "I thought he was only supposed to be here for a few days."

"He extended," Eric patiently replied.

"Great," I muttered, running a hand through my hair. "Now I'm behind in a class I've been attending for the past week."

"Don't worry—the class has really become a spectator sport. Now we all just watch the showdown between Zoe and Phineas. She has a nasty habit of correcting him."

The look Zoe gave us was one of pure smugness. "I'll stop when he stops giving out the wrong information."

I shared a conspiratorial smile with Eric. "Of course you will," I drawled sarcastically, and Eric chuckled as we began to move toward the classroom.

Phineas was already inside, a series of shiny tools and equipment strewn all over the long table at the front of the hall. He glanced at the three of us as we entered, and then looked back down at one of the pieces he was fiddling with.

"Ah, Eric, I see you are still associating with Zoe and Liana. I assume Liana's number is still holding steady at a six?"

"Actually, no," Eric replied, grinning at me approvingly. "Liana is now a nine."

Phineas looked up at me, brow and scalp wrinkling in surprise. His eyes darted down to my wrist, and then back up to my face. "Extraordinary!" he exclaimed. "To rise so far, so fast? Tell me, did you take some time to learn of the Water Ways?"

I hesitated, and then shook my head. "Not that I can recall, sir. I went to the Medica and they gave me some medication. I'm afraid it's affected my memory some; I can't seem to remember the past few classes we've had together."

Phineas looked disappointed, but then grinned broadly. "No matter. It is good to see your treatment is so effective. Your story could inspire other lost souls like you. You really should come to a service."

"I'll think about it," I said, very uncomfortable. He nodded, and I used that opportunity to excuse myself, hurrying over to some open seats toward the back of the room and dropping into one. Zoe arranged herself in the seat to my right, while Eric dropped down on the left.

"Well that was awkward," I said, pushing my hair behind my ear. "Zo?"

"Don't look at me—my mom's the religious one in the family. I always found the Water Ways too... mystical for my tastes."

I chuckled, and we fell into a companionable silence as a few more students straggled in. Soon, Phineas started the class. First we reviewed a few of the more important signals for Callivax—mostly directions and warning signals—and then went over a few of the symbols for identifying a water treatment pod's function within the Tower.

"Hot and cold running water is marked by color," Eric recited, as if from rote memory. "Blue for cold and red for hot."

"Very good," Phineas replied. "And who knows what the hot water is for?"

"Creating steam for condensation in the greeneries," one of the Medica students said tentatively.

"And helping heat the forges in fabrication down in Cogstown," Zoe added lazily.

"Correct. It's imperative you pay attention to these functions. Hot water will always be in glass pipes, as our glass-fabrication process can withstand the heat coming off the water. Now, can anyone tell me why they are hot?"

"It's part of the purification process for cleaning it," a Cog boy with wild orange hair said. "There's a lot of radiation still in the water, and heating it is just one of the many steps for cleaning it."

"Very good. Now, who can tell me—"

"Excuse me, Master Diver."

Gerome's deep voice was familiar, but when you weren't expecting it, it really sent a shiver down your spine. I felt myself go straight as a post, and turned to see Gerome standing there. How on earth had he just *appeared* like that?

"Knight Commander," Phineas said, offering a little bow. "I was just going over safety protocols. Is there a problem?"

"Liana has no need of more than basic Water Treatment training," Gerome announced firmly, and I frowned. "She intends to become a Knight. Don't you, Liana?"

"Uh, yes," I stammered. "But I'm not certain I should miss—"

"You're required in the Citadel, Liana," Gerome said, fixing me with a pointed look. "Immediately."

A chill ran down my spine as the room got quiet. I sat there for a moment, but then stood up. Zoe gave me an alarmed expression, and I knew what she was thinking. It was the same thing I was thinking: I'd gotten caught.

"You can get notes from one of your friends, Liana," Phineas said congenially. "And I will see you next class."

Somehow my legs propelled me forward toward Gerome, who was now opening the door to allow me access to the hall. I stepped past him and came to a halt on the large platform, looking up at the Citadel hanging over four hundred feet away. My heart began to pound.

How could they have found out so soon? Had my number been flagged for rising too quickly? What if they had found out about the pill? What was going to happen to me?

At that moment I felt very much like I was in freefall, with the added spike of fear and adrenaline that came from missing a lash connection. Only this time, I wasn't sure there was a lash hold within distance that could save me.

"Squire?"

I blinked up at Gerome, who was looking down at me, and realized he was waiting for me.

"Sir?" I said, coming around to face him at attention. It was more habit than anything, but it was ingrained, something familiar, and it helped keep the growing fear at bay. Not by much, but it helped.

Gerome studied my face, his expression thoughtful. "You look a little pale, Squire. Are you unwell?"

"No," I said, and then belatedly realized I could've lied. Clenching my teeth together to prevent a curse from slipping out, I quickly scrambled, looking for something to explain my paleness that didn't rhyme with "terrified beyond belief that you caught me doing something potentially (definitely) illegal," and managed to fabricate one from seemingly nowhere.

"I'm just surprised, sir. I didn't expect to see you today. I'm not on duty."

Gerome frowned, his eyebrows meeting over his nose as he drew them together. "We were supposed to meet today, remember? We discussed this on Tuesday."

I frowned, doing the math, and my frown morphed into a scowl. *No, you and Prim discussed it. Liana was not around.*

Then relief washed over me as I realized he wasn't there to arrest me. We just had something we needed to talk about, I guessed. I took a deep breath, trying not to let my relief show in front of Gerome. He'd notice.

"I'm sorry, Knight Commander," I said, shaking my head. "I must have forgotten. It's a side effect of the medication, you know. Can you refresh my memory?"

"Of course," Gerome said smoothly, nodding us toward the bridge. "But it's a lot better if I just show you."

13

Gerome and I walked in relative silence back toward the Citadel, and I used the time to collect myself... and speculate on what this appointment could be. I still had no access to memories from when Prim had been in control, so that didn't help me. Could it be an early assessment? Was he recommending that I be promoted to full Knight? A rush of excitement went through me at the thought. I looked down at the nine sparkling on my wrist and felt the corners of my mouth quirk up. But I quickly forced them down. Nines did not smile that often.

The guards loomed ahead, and I turned my wrist out as I approached, watching their recognition turn stupefied as they took in my new number. As if they had never expected me to reach that rank.

"Your number has risen so much, Liana," Gerome said as we entered the main terminal—the centermost levels in the Citadel, reserved as offices for receiving complaints and running missions. "I was satisfied when you had increased to a five, but when I heard from your parents that you had reached nine, I knew you were ready for this. Ready for the chance to serve Scipio properly."

I thought about the possibility of a promotion and found myself smiling again. "It's my honor to serve Scipio in whatever way I can," I informed him, and he gave a tight nod. He ushered me onto an elevator— we actually had to wait a minute for a group of Hands heading to another level—and then we were descending.

"So where are we going?" I asked, the breeze of displaced air from our descent causing my hair to blow around my face. I gathered it and twisted it into a ball, securing it with a band, and looked over at Gerome, who was watching the numbers descend.

"To the prisons," he replied, and I frowned. Why would we be going there?

Because this is a ruse, a scared voice inside me whispered. *He's leading you like a lamb to slaughter, and you're falling for it, hook, line, and sinker.*

I pushed through the fear and propelled myself forward off the lift as soon as it hit, trying not to gag at the stale scent of dried sweat already radiating from the dimly lit tunnel. This part of the Citadel was different from the rest; instead of dark, mottled metal, the walls were grated, with thin slits of red light coming through them and washing everything with the color. Exposed yellow bulbs in the ceiling glowed dimly, but it made the entire area seem grungy, and a foreboding feeling settled at the base of my spine. I suddenly did not want to be here.

Gerome continued forward, oblivious to my hesitancy. I watched his departing back, considering the elevator behind me, and managed to talk myself out of the urge to run away. Running would mean guilt. Running wouldn't be something a nine would do.

We were halfway down the hall when the first glass window appeared. I looked through it, curious, and paused when I saw a medical table inside, covered in straps, with long, mechanized arms that held gleaming needles ominously hovering over it. The table was, thankfully, empty, but I cringed to think about the views ahead. Were they going to be empty as well, or... were there going to be people in them?

"Gerome? What is this?" I asked, unable to help myself.

Gerome paused, some ten feet ahead of me now, and turned back, looking at me. "I know you've never been here before, Liana... but surely you know what we do down here."

Restructuring. The final process to try to salvage the best traits possible in a one or two. The process was a secret, known only to the highest-ranked members of the Citadel. My stomach roiled as I eyed the table in the room, the mechanical arms holding long needles poised and ready over the headrest, and I was suddenly grateful beyond words that Grey had given me that pill. A three had been too close to this fate. Far too close. I looked down the hall past Gerome, at the windows ahead, and he, for once, seemed to understand what I was feeling.

"It's okay to be nervous, Liana," he said. "I was too, when I first came down here. Be that as it may, I made sure to schedule this for a time when treatments weren't happening. All the rooms are empty right now."

I exhaled, and was suddenly grateful to Gerome. Grateful, and surprised—it didn't seem like him to protect me from anything. That also meant there was a reason he had done so. And that meant, whatever restructuring entailed, it was pretty awful. I shuddered and moved away from the window, eager to be out of this hall.

I kept my eyes down as we walked, only glancing ahead and not through any more windows as we moved. I couldn't bear to see those tables, imagining myself on them, let alone any of the people I cared about. If I stared, it would stop me cold. I would look just the way I felt, which could clue Gerome in that my nine might not be as genuine as he thought. The door at the end of the hall was wreathed in red lights, and Gerome came to a stop in front of it.

"Knight Commander Gerome Nobilis," he announced.

There were a series of beeps and chirps from an unseen machine, and then the lights turned green one by one as the doors slid apart.

"Welcome, Knight Commander Nobilis," said a voice. I frowned when I realized it was the same clipped, regal-sounding voice they used for Scipio. If this machine was using Scipio's voice, did that mean it was networked with Scipio? But that shouldn't be possible—there were inter-departmental rules against it, so that no department could gain influence over another. I must have been mistaken, but I filed it away to bring up with Alex later.

The door slid open and Gerome stepped in, me close behind him, eager to get away from the hall. This room had to be better than the hall, at least.

The hope died almost immediately as I turned and took in the room. It was divided into two areas—a viewing chamber on one side, our side, and a cell on the other, a thick layer of glass separating us. There was a door on the viewing side—off to the left—that presumably led into the cell. Inside the cell, a woman was propped up in a corner.

She looked small. She was thin, her arms and legs curled in upon each other like roots seeking nourishment and finding only air. The dirty skinsuit covering her form was shredded down to rags and stained with blood and grime, so much so that it was hard to make out the color. Her hands flopped weakly against the wall, and I realized she was using her own blood to draw something on the wall behind her. Her mouth moved as she smeared her blood around, but whether she was singing or talking, I couldn't tell—there was no sound.

I could see the *one* on her wrist, plain as day. And suddenly Grey's voice was back in my head.

The Knights killed Roark's wife.

"Gerome," I said softly, questioning. I needed to remain calm—I couldn't give myself away—but I needed to know. "What are you doing to her? Is this part of restructuring?"

Gerome didn't seem to be listening. He stared into the cell, his eyes hard and merciless.

"These people," he said, approaching the glass until his breath fogged it. "These... ones. They are a rot upon our Tower. Have you ever spoken to your farmer friend about what rot does to a tree, Squire Castell?"

I shook my head, walking up to the glass.

"It gets inside," Gerome said. "It gets in deep. There comes a point when cutting it out would cause the whole thing to collapse."

The woman was crying. Tears spilled down her cheeks, leaving trails in the dirt, her hand slapping against the ground now. Was she tapping out a beat? Humming a song? There was no sound coming from the other side of the glass—the devices that normally enabled communication had been shut off.

"Scipio invented the ranking system to help us find the darkness in our society," Gerome said, and as he looked at the woman, he was his usual self. No pity. No empathy. No emotions. Just Gerome's stark, unflinching face. "He invented it so we could be safe. Strong. Before, we were left to deliver justice based on crimes, evidence, and arbitrary things. Now we have the justice communicated to us by something greater."

But I could barely hear him. The woman's body had begun to shake with sobs. I could see now that the tattered rags upon her frame were gray beneath the muck. A mechanic, then. I looked at her long fingers and saw that at least one was broken.

"What are you going to do to her?" I asked.

Gerome ignored me. "Your remarkable climb has been going so well," he said, and there was real pride in his voice. "With your skills and improved mindset, you stand a chance of becoming the very best of us. That is why we decided to show you this early, Liana. That is why you are here. Why we are all here."

I gave him a look. "What are you going to show me, Gerome?" I asked, my mouth dry and my instincts pleading with me to just turn away, to run and hide. But I couldn't listen to them; I had to know what was going on.

The woman clutched her knees to her chest, and I could see long marks, burns, running up and down her pale skin. What had they done to her? How could they treat another person like this and not *feel* anything?

"Ones are a threat to the Tower, Liana," Gerome said, finally meeting my gaze. "We have to remove the threat."

There was a click.

I spun, and saw Gerome pressing a red button beside the viewing glass, his eyes fixed on the woman.

"They're rot," he said. "And unless rot is rooted out, it will topple the whole tree."

I turned back to the cell and watched in horror as white gas began to pour from the vents in the ceiling, curling down like tendrils of sentient smoke and reaching for the woman. Her mouth opened, but I couldn't hear her scream as she scuttled toward us, pressing herself against the glass. I pressed my hands against it too, trying to reach for her, but the pane of glass didn't evaporate.

"Gerome!" I cried. "What are you doing? Stop this."

What are we *doing?*

"Keeping the Tower safe," he said. There was no emotion there. No humanity. "At any cost."

The woman's eyes were inches from mine. Panicked. Desperate, as she clawed against the divide. I saw the gas swirling around her head, coiling down her arms and midriff in languorous tendrils. I had to stop this. I had to do *something*. I was a nine, now. Didn't that count for anything? Wasn't that supposed to mean that things were different?

I whirled, intent on stunning Gerome with my baton and getting her out, when she collapsed, her body jerking and shaking in seizure. It lasted for a moment, resulting in her going rigid, her back bowing as her limbs quivered. Lines of blood snaked from her nose, eyes, and ears, and when she opened her mouth, foaming red spittle burst out in a pop.

Then she fell silent. Still. Eyes wide open and staring at me with hollow accusations.

You let this happen to me, they said. And I couldn't disagree. I took a step back, and then another, horrified and unable to tear my gaze from her lifeless eyes.

Gerome pressed another button, and there was a humming sound as the gas was sucked from the room. The woman's hair fluttered as the vacuums did their work. Behind me, a pair of Knights entered, speaking in hushed tones as they opened the side door dividing the viewing room and the cell. Moments later they entered the cell and, with practiced efficiency, lifted the corpse and carried it from the room.

I hadn't moved an inch through the entire process, merely watched it, an odd numbness beginning to settle into my bones and muscles. I was pretty sure I was in a mild state of shock, but I needed the numbness right then. I needed Prim, because I wasn't certain how long I could maintain the façade.

"How are you doing?"

I looked up to see Gerome gazing down at me, and was surprised to see one big hand settled in a strangely paternal gesture upon my shoulder. "I was shaken the first time I saw one of those," he added, when I didn't immediately respond. "But you must understand. This is for the best, Liana. That woman didn't have a hope of rising back up for longer than a few days, and everyone near her would lower as well—Scipio gave us all the data, told us what needed to be done." He sighed. "It is the only way to save the Tower we all love."

Prim felt like nodding, so I nodded. I could still see the pink streaks on the glass where the woman had been scrambling in her efforts to escape. I wanted to protest, to scream and kick and cry, but Prim overruled it. Gerome's hand on my shoulder was heavy, and suddenly I couldn't bear it touching me, feeling revulsion radiating from the site. Prim had me step away, toward the glass, and I hated her for it, even though the action continued to keep me safe.

"You'll handle the next one," he said when I continued my silence.

The words speared through me, and I felt my knees weaken. Even Prim couldn't stop the bile rising into my throat, but she managed to swallow it down, forcing me to breathe through my mouth in long, slow breaths. They weren't steady, but they were slow.

Gerome didn't miss any of it.

"The first time you see one is never as difficult as doing it yourself for the first time," he warned as he pressed another button, which produced an eerily pleasant chime sound. "It's never easy doing the right thing, but it does get easier. I promise."

The door on the far side of the cell slid open, revealing a dark holding area beyond. A figure was being pushed forward, shoved into the cell, a one glowing bright on his arm. As he came to a slow stop and lowered his eyes, I felt my heart lurch and the world around me deteriorate and fall apart before my eyes.

"It's just the press of a button," Gerome said. "And they feel no pain."

In the cell, the prisoner stood, gazing around with brown eyes. His clothes were just as I remembered them; it had only been a day since we had talked. His hands were balled into fists, and he had a long, bloody cut across his chest.

"Just one button, and the Tower is safe."

In the cell, Grey turned, and even though I knew he couldn't see me, it felt like he was looking straight at me.

The Knights killed Roark's wife, his voice taunted in my mind. And this time, a Knight had to kill Grey.

14

"Liana, the button?"

Prim's and my eyes flicked over to Gerome, and the big, red, glowing button on the wall just over his shoulder. I felt her consider it, her practicality cold and unyielding. I jerked her back and took over, unwilling to let any aspect of me—drugged or not—commit that atrocity.

"Liana?"

I had to stall for time, figure out a way to get him out of there, get him to safety. It wouldn't matter if it was Grey or someone else; I couldn't allow this to happen. I couldn't kill him. My heart pounded in my chest, but I kept coming up with nothing, my mind flashing to the woman's eyes and imagining what it would be like to see Grey's eyes in their place. Or Zoe's. Eric's. Alex's. My parents'. Mine.

I imagined the helplessness of being in there, no control, in pain from whatever brutal treatment I had endured, only to have my life stolen from me. The only crime committed: the failure to conform.

"Liana."

"I can't," I blurted out honestly, unable to think of anything else.

Gerome stared down at me with his cold, flat eyes. "You can't?" he repeated.

I made my head bob, and suppressed a look at Grey. I was fairly certain the glass was one-way, but I didn't want to risk the chance I was wrong. If the glass wasn't one-way, I just hoped he didn't give away that we knew each other—if he did, I would never get him out of there.

Gerome took a deep breath, then actually smiled. "That's all right," he said. "I was reluctant my first time, too, and for good reason. It is hard taking a life, as it should be. If it were easy, it wouldn't be right. I'm sure you'll come to realize that soon, and understand that these are sacrifices we make for the good of the Tower."

No, I won't, I replied in my head, feeling the heat of my conviction rushing through me.

"For now," Gerome said, "we'll let the matter be."

I felt a moment of relief, then realized what he was saying. If I didn't kill Grey, would *he?*

"Sir? What will happen to him? Will he be returned to restructuring?"

I wasn't sure what prompted me to ask the question about restructuring, but as it left my lips, I realized that I desperately wanted to know. After all, it was supposedly what these cells were all about: rehabilitation of the most depraved ones, if possible. Not to mention, I'd seen Grey only yesterday. That meant they'd caught him between then and now, and it didn't seem like they had done anything to him like they had to the woman. Yet.

"Restructuring rarely works," he informed me. "The success rate has only been six percent, and even then... well, let's just say this way is more humane. We perform it for a week to give them one final chance, but more often than not, it's easier to bring them here and be done with it. Sometimes Scipio agrees. This one, for example, skipped restructuring per Scipio's orders. This one is for you to kill, Liana. Now, I suppose I can give you some time to come to terms with what you have to do, but I can only keep him aside for you for a week. After that, he's overstayed his welcome."

He smiled at his own quip, and I felt a surge of revulsion at how casually he could joke about such things. It was all I could do to hold it together.

Looking at Grey, believe it or not, helped steady me. I had bought time, and no small amount. Now I just needed to come up with a way to get him out of there.

I watched as he settled onto the floor and began staring up at the ceiling with a frustrated look on his face. He never gave any indication that he had seen me, confirming my suspicion that the glass was one-way. I felt a brief flash of anger as I realized the Knights not only murdered, but they did it like cowards. Then I put the feeling aside. Anger wouldn't help me or Grey now. The glass was one-way, and that was a good thing, I hoped. I wasn't sure how yet, but there was an advantage, I was sure about it.

I thought of Grey and wondered if he knew that just beyond the vents, a mass of poison was waiting for him. Then I thought of myself and hoped I'd be enough to stop it.

He's yours to kill.

Those words echoed around in my head until they were all I could hear.

I couldn't remember walking back to the elevator. Nor getting off at my level and entering my home. I didn't remember taking off my uniform, crumpling it into a ball, and tossing it away. All I could remember was feeling cold, like an icy needle had been plunged into my heart and frostbite was radiating down into the rest of me, threatening to petrify me to a block of ice.

I came to in my bed, the blankets hauled up over my head and my knees drawn to my chest. The reality was there, unforgotten, but somehow I managed to channel the ice that had been threatening to freeze me earlier into some semblance of control.

"Contact Alex Castell, IT47-4B," I said aloud, tapping the indicator with my finger, and I felt the net buzz under my command. It was dangerous to reach out this way, but I had to trust that Alex would immediately delete the conversation between us as soon as it was finished. He would've done it last time, after mentioning the problem with Scipio. And he would do it again.

The net buzzed, and then a soft computer voice informed me that he was unavailable. I felt a burn of annoyance—he could always remotely activate my indicator to connect his call, but, I didn't have that ability, which meant, to be fair, he needed to take the damn net whenever it was me. I almost tried again, but stopped when I realized that if I pushed too hard it would draw too much attention. I canceled the order and ran a hand down my face, trying to think of a way to get in touch with him without drawing attention to myself.

A soft knock on the door sounded, and I looked up, my heartbeat increasing. *Gerome changed his mind and is making me do it tonight,* I thought, and I trembled and scooted away from the door.

"Liana?" My mother's voice was muffled through the door, but I was instantly relieved to hear it. *She'll know what to do.*

I got up and crossed over to the door. I almost threw it open immediately, but caution held me back. I couldn't explain it, but something told me to wait to see what my mother wanted before blurting out the problems I had with what I had seen today.

I pushed the button, and the door slid open, revealing both my parents standing there, their faces expectant. I was immediately on guard.

"Aren't you both supposed to be on duty?" I asked, realizing the time.

They looked at one another, then smiled at me.

"Gerome told us you were performing your first expulsion today," my mother said, and I blanched.

"We wanted to be here for you when you got home, but it seems you beat us here," my father said, his voice soft. He stepped forward, his eyes careful but undeniably excited. "How did it go?"

I stared at them, too horrified to speak. They *knew*. They *did* it.

"With Gerome," my father added, tilting his head. "Did I get the day wrong?"

"No, dear," my mother said. "It was today. Gerome netted me a confirmation." She angled her head toward me. "Did something come up?"

"No." It was easy enough to get the word out, because I was screaming it on the inside. There was a bitterness to it, if I thought about it. Of *course* they knew about it. Of *course* they had done it. They were Knight Commanders, and Gerome's equals (although Father had trained him). They had always known. Why else would they be so eager to put me in the Medica? They had known the fate that would have been in store for me if I hadn't improved my ranking. If I hadn't met Grey and gotten those pills. And now he was going to die, and they expected *me* to kill him.

"I didn't do it," I finally told them, my gaze meeting theirs headlong in open challenge.

My mother's eyes flashed in alarm at the defiance I'm sure she saw there, but my father nodded sympathetically. "Gerome had a hard time at first, as well," he said. "He's a compassionate man, as you are a compassionate young girl. Believe me, dear, after this time you don't ever have to do it again, if you don't want to."

"I don't?" I asked. "Then what if I don't want to hurt anyone the first time? Dad, this is *wrong*."

"No, this is as Scipio has ordered."

"It's *murder*," I spat, and once again I was rewarded with the fiery brand of a hand across my cheek. And she didn't hold back.

"I am *ashamed* of you," my mother declared. "You don't even know all the tragedies this Tower has suffered because of a one's plot to destroy it. Black lung, a virus created in the first fifty years of the Tower, cost us half the population, most of them children. A one created it. You think when Scipio finally made the decision to start doing this we weren't all shocked by it? That I wasn't appalled? But this is the bottom line. This is who we are. We serve this Tower, and we keep it safe, by any means necessary."

I stared at her for a long moment, and then looked away. She must've interpreted it as a sign of me backing down, but in reality, I just couldn't look at her anymore without feeling like I was looking at a monster.

"I'm sorry I hit you, Liana," my mother said after a pause, her breath coming out as a tired sigh. "I know this isn't easy for you, but this is what you must do to join the Knights and fulfill your duty to Scipio. He clearly has faith you can do it, so take the time you need, and then do your job. If you cannot, then there will be no home for you in the Citadel, and we will be powerless to help you once you leave for another department. Do you understand?"

I met her gaze long enough to nod once, and then my hand reached out and slapped the button, shutting the door between us. I heard a muffled exchange of their voices, followed by the sound of them walking away, and flicked on the magnetic lock.

I walked back over to my bed. Sat on it. Crossed my legs and started to think about what I could do. With Alex unavailable, I had to figure out a way to break Grey out by myself.

The only way to get them to spare him was to get his number up. I looked over at the bottle of pills he had given me. If I could get one inside, then maybe...

I dismissed the thought immediately. His ranking would never naturally go up that high under those conditions. It wouldn't be believable, and they could kill him anyway.

That meant another trip to Cogstown to talk to Roark. I doubted the old man wanted to see me again, but I was fairly certain I was going to need his help. Which meant I needed to involve Zoe.

Which meant I needed to tell her everything.

I sighed and turned toward the window, looking at the view outside, but only seeing the woman's eyes waiting for me. I put my hand against the window, and as I did so the nine there flickered, blurring... and then cracked. A one appeared on my wrist, bright and red and angry. It took me a moment to realize what was about to happen, and then I was fumbling for the bottle, opening it and spilling several pills into my hands. I got one in my mouth and dry swallowed, then held up my wrist and stared at it.

"Come on," I muttered. "Before the alert shows up—come on, come on!"

The one flickered back to a nine. Good—apparently once it was in your system, it worked faster.

I heaved a sigh of relief. For the time being, I was safe. But Grey had these pills too, and he had been caught. If I was going to get him out of that place, I needed Roark's help in more ways than one.

I stood, well aware that it was late, and got dressed. Tonight was not a night for feeling sorry for myself; it was a night for doing something about it.

15

I decided halfway down to Zoe's that I wasn't going to involve her after all. The closer I got to her, the more difficult it became to breathe, and I suddenly imagined her on the other side of that glass, painting pictures in blood and humming a song that no one could hear. And I couldn't risk it. I couldn't risk her.

So I turned away from her quarters and did something a little more dangerous—I took the plunge. As a general rule, no area of the plunge was ever safe. Yet the parts leading into Cogstown were especially perilous. Most Knights never bothered to try, opting to take the elevators to the main halls outside of Cogstown.

Taking the plunge here required quick thinking, ingenuity, and near-perfect timing. One wrong move and they'd find my body torn apart by industrial cables, or worse. The reason it was so dangerous was that it changed as repairs were made, the internal structure modified, restored, modified again. It was constantly changing, and had been for hundreds of years. As a result, the place was littered with obstacles. Knights over the years had updated the painted signs inside the plunge, adding new ones or removing obsolete ones as they were discovered, but every time a

Knight stepped into the Cogstown plunge, they knew there was a chance something had changed since the last time a Knight was in there. And that meant I had to proceed with utmost caution.

I stepped up to the edge and looked down, already noting the places where light shone, marking the safer path.

Playing it safe, I lashed over to the adjacent wall and slowly began to lower myself, letting my eyes grow used to the dark. I adjusted my position slightly as I descended, keeping a careful eye out for unknown obstacles as I navigated the metallic jungle that seemed to have grown in all sorts of directions.

It took a while before I began to grow more confident, allowing myself to pick up speed as I learned to trust the marks. I kept a careful eye on the marks for the landings that led back into the Tower, and eventually spotted a small orange gear mark, and made my way over to the doorway it stood vigil over.

Boots firmly on the ground, I followed the hall until it abruptly ended at the now-quiet market in the center of town. The lights were dim, replicating nighttime, and the only lighting came from lamps on tall posts deposited haphazardly along the streets of the market. It took me a moment to orient myself, but once I figured out where I was in relation to Roark's place, I began to move, winding my way through the quiet, still streets.

I kept my head down and my hands in my pockets, trying not to draw too much attention to myself. Adrenaline was coursing fiercely through my blood now, every shadow or movement setting my heart racing in a wash of fear and terror. I knew Scipio couldn't read my exact thoughts, but how had he not noticed the high concentration of negativity I was experiencing when compared with my ranking? And what would happen when he did?

My heart practically stopped when I realized that the Eyes must have figured out something was off. They had noticed the discrepancy of the massive jump from one to nine, and that was how Grey had gotten caught. It wouldn't take them long before they caught on to me as well. Maybe that's why Alex hadn't taken my call—he had realized my ranking had jumped in the same way and was furious with me. Or was covering for me. Or had gotten caught. The thought brought me up short, and I had to fight off the impulse to call him again.

It took a moment to talk myself down from that ledge, but I managed. The logic I used was harsh, but honest as well: none of that was under my control. If the Eyes came for me, they came for me. Until I had more information, I was being paranoid, and that was counterproductive. I needed to get to Roark to get his help with Grey.

That did something to lessen the fear, and I began moving forward again. I was determined to see this through, even if it meant going against myself. I managed to get back to the ladder leading up, and chose to lash up the girders onto the third floor. I moved quickly down the hall, the memory of yesterday still fresh in my mind, the ghost of Grey everywhere.

I knocked, pushing the morbid thought out of my head. Grey wasn't dead. Yet. And he wouldn't be, if I had my way about it.

Silence met my knock for several long moments—until I was certain that he wasn't in—and then a voice called, "Who is it?"

"Squ—Liana Castell," I called. I couldn't force the honorific out. It just jammed in my throat, heavy and disgusting. I wanted nothing to do with the Knights now that I knew what they were doing to people. "I need to talk to you."

I heard a low curse from the other side of the door.

"I thought I made it pretty clear I'm not interested in what you have to say," Roark snapped, his voice closer to the door.

"Grey's in trouble," I said flatly.

There was another pause, followed by a sharp click, and the door sprang open.

"Where is he?" Roark demanded as he came into view, and I blinked. His hair was unkempt and wild, and it looked like he hadn't shaved today. Dark bags lay under his eyes, and he seemed nervous and agitated.

"He fell to a one and got arrested," I said, unable to meet the man's gaze.

His eyes narrowed. "What? How? Grey's a nine."

"We both know that isn't exactly true," I said softly, and I pulled the bottle out of my pocket, letting him see it. His eyes widened, and then he grabbed me and hauled me inside. He shoved me hard against a wall and threw his arm over my chest in a surprisingly strong move.

"How did you get those, and are you alone?" he snarled, glancing quickly out the door. "And what have you done with Grey?"

I sucked in a ragged breath—the pressure of his arm adding weight to my diaphragm and making the move difficult and strange—and met his gaze. "I'm... alone... Grey's alive... for now."

Roark blinked and then took a hasty step back, his eyebrows drawing together. "So, there aren't any other Knights ready to burst into this place?"

"No," I said, rubbing my sternum with the flat of my hand. "And for the record, they'd be after me as well as you." I held up my wrist and showed him the nine there, and he gave it a hard look before closing the door.

"Why are you here?" he demanded.

"I need your help—I want to save Grey."

The old man scrutinized me, before finally nodding. "Might as well come in," he said gruffly, "and tell me what you know about Grey."

"I'm here to see if you can help me help him," I announced. "But I have some questions of my own."

Roark ignored my comment as he moved deeper into the dwelling, and I took a moment to straighten my clothes and run a hand through my hair. Then I followed. Roark was already pulling a set of test tubes out of a small refrigerator with ultraviolet lights shining inside of it. The whites of his eyes glowed under the light as he pulled out another set of tubes, giving him a sinister look.

He straightened and gently kicked the refrigerator closed, setting the two trays down on the table. Then he looked at me. "How did you get the bottle?"

"If I tell you about that, and Grey, will you answer my questions?"

Roark stared at me, and then nodded. "Yes."

"Grey gave it to me," I said, setting it on the table. "Yesterday."

His eyes lingered on the bottle and then came up to me, waiting. I realized he was waiting for me to tell him everything I knew.

"I watched a woman die today," I said, the words suddenly spilling out of me, and Roark blinked in surprise, and then leaned closer. My eyes darted up to him, and then away. "My mentor killed her. Like she was nothing. Like she was worth nothing." I paused, and then drew in a breath.

"Grey was dragged in after her body was taken out. My mentor told me I had to kill him. I refused. Now they are giving me a week to change my mind and conform."

Roark's expression changed. A seething, unbridled hatred formed in his eyes, making me terrified he would somehow make me combust right then and there. I leaned away from the intensity of it. As I did, he moved, so quickly it startled me, and it took me a moment to realize he was moving over to a pair of chairs against the wall, stacked high with boxes, rolled-up charts, papers, and a general assortment of junk. He started clearing the chairs, and then glanced up to give me a pointed look. It was, I thought, the least courteous offer to sit I had ever received—but considering the circumstances, I stepped in to help. Within a few minutes, we were both sitting down.

"Give me the details," he said between clenched teeth, and I recounted each and every detail I could, especially regarding the woman's symptoms. He asked the most questions about those, but I was unable to answer most of them, because I hadn't noticed her fingertips or toes or black veins or anything like that.

We both fell silent for a long time after that—long enough for him to make me a cup of tea and for me to pull myself back together—and then he sat down again, clearing his throat.

"You had some questions for me," he reminded me, and I nodded.

"How could Grey have gotten caught?" I asked. "Is it something I need to be worried about?"

Roark gave a huff of approval, and leaned forward. "You ask a lot of smart questions, girl. The only problem with smart questions is that they lead to dangerous answers."

"I'm here for your help to break someone out of the Citadel," I replied. "My life is not currently without danger."

"Fair point. And to answer your question, yes, I think it is something you need to be worried about. Grey's close call with you over a week ago proved to me something I had long suspected: the body builds up a resistance to the drug over time. It won't last as long if you're taking it every day. The same day you came by, I gave him a fresh bottle just to make sure he would be safe. And that was the only bottle I gave him that day."

He gave me another pointed look, and I felt my stomach drop even lower as I realized the implications of what he was saying. I recalled Grey saying that he had sticky fingers, and had assumed that was how he'd get his own pills. Had he failed? Had he run out of time, or thought he had more time than he did? The bottle in my hand felt as though it were filled with rocks, uncomfortably heavy.

"I didn't ask him to give me his," I said, a bit defensively. "But he knew I was desperate and took pity on me. If you had helped me in the first place, then we wouldn't be here right now!"

"That's not useful," he chided, and I fell silent. I was right, but he was right as well: none of that mattered now. "Do you have any more questions?"

"Maybe later," I said, still dwelling on the fact that it was my fault Grey had gotten caught.

"Then allow me to indulge in a few more. What is Grey, to you?"

I looked away, confused by the question, and not afraid to admit it. "What do you mean?"

"I mean... why are you doing this?"

I shook my head at him, my brows furrowing. "You're joking, right? They're killing people up there! I would want to do something no matter who they were."

Roark blinked and cocked his head, his eyes appraising me, as if he had discovered some new and interesting facet to me that he hadn't been expecting. I didn't care. I was practically vibrating from my impatience. I had expected Roark to be a little more animated in his desire to rescue Grey. Now we were playing twenty questions regarding my motivations? He needed to take a hard look at his own before he started judging me.

"So, do you intend to try and rescue the others?" he asked.

I hesitated. I had considered that during my time in the plunge, and had come up with the sad truth that I couldn't. I doubted I could even access the level without another Knight accompanying me, and I didn't know the layout.

"No," I admitted. "Grey is the only one I have access to, which means he is the only one I can save. But just because I know him doesn't mean I'd give him preferential treatment. This is the opportunity I have."

"He told me he kissed you," Roark said softly. "You sure this isn't some emotional romance thing?"

I flushed in anger and stood up. "Why the hell are you asking me this? I'm here because I'm not a killer!"

"Peace, girl. I was testing your resolve on this. I can't have someone who will balk at the first drop of a hat."

I pressed my lips together but let it pass. He didn't know me, nor I him, so it was fair on his part to make sure I was made of strong enough stuff.

"You have a plan?" he asked.

"I was hoping you might have something you could give him," I said. "There's a way into the cell, and if I can figure out a reason or excuse to be inside, I can maybe slip it to him."

Roark stood up out of his chair and moved back over to the workstation. "I do have something that can help him," he said. "It's a weakened version of the pills he gave you, actually, but it should be strong enough to get him to a four."

"Really?" I said as I followed him, my eyes on the test tubes. "How does it work?"

Roark let out a huff. "As if I'm just going to tell you that," he said.

I rolled my eyes at him. "Let me rephrase. How long does it take to kick in?"

"Ah." He wore the ghost of a smile as he picked up a pestle and began grinding something in a tiny mortar. "Well, he already has some in his system, but I have to assume it'll be gone before you can enact whatever plan you've got cooked up. I can use something to activate the metabolism to boost it."

"Good," I replied, "because I'm not sure how much time they're going to give him. I have a little bit of time, but I got the impression from my mo—" I paused, unable to even mention her "—mentor that this should be done sooner, rather than later. A sort of... 'hurry up and bite the bullet' mentality."

The last part came out bitter, but I couldn't help it. I was doing everything I could to keep it together.

"Who are you?" Roark asked, breaking my bleak thoughts, and I looked up to see him staring at me. "You're unlike any Knight I've ever met."

"Thanks," I replied, willing to take that as a compliment after what I'd seen tonight.

I continued to watch him make the pill while I began generating ideas about how I could give it to Grey. Whatever I came up with had to be convincing, believable, and reasonable, and I couldn't risk letting Grey know who I was while I was in there.

Most of all, I couldn't get caught.

16

"Absolutely not."

Gerome looked at me sharply and blew out a pent-up breath of frustration, as if he were dealing with a petulant child. I watched him from the corner of my eye as I pretended to look up at some piping overhead. We were on patrol—which meant a lot of hours spent walking, trying to keep children from making too much mischief, or searching for thieves who were trying to steal food to save their ration cards (or who had lost their rations in illegal gambling). We'd been at it for six hours, and were heading back to the Citadel to put in our reports and meet with our Knight Commander to learn what our duties would be tomorrow. I was using the walk back to ask the one question I needed confirmation on: could I go talk with my prisoner, one on one?

I'd spent the better part of the night, after leaving Roark's with the pill for Grey, trying to think about how to get inside. Sneaking in was not a possibility, and I was only a young woman; I doubted I could force my way in. Which meant I had to be clever.

"Why do you want to talk to him, Liana?" Gerome finally asked, and

I looked over at him, giving him the carefully neutral face I'd been practicing in the mirror.

"Because I feel it's important that I do," I replied, and then I looked away, trying to act nonchalant. "What you're asking me to do is not something I'm taking lightly, Gerome. The surprise still hasn't faded, and I find myself wondering more about him. How his brain works, what his disease is really like."

I came to a stop before him and performed a perfect snap turn, coming around to face him, and stopping him short. "I have to see it and hear it, so I know what dangerous behavior to look for."

It was disgusting talking in that way—keeping my voice flat and disinterested while spouting the propaganda of bigots. But I knew approaching this emotionally would make everyone even more suspicious about my number... and how it was still at a nine. If I wanted this to work, I was going to have to finally play the role of perfect soldier.

At least now I have a good reason to, I thought, my mind already picturing Grey.

"I'm quite surprised to hear this coming from you," Gerome said carefully. "Your mother netted me this morning and told me about your little outburst last night."

I kept my face neutral and eyes blank—glossy and devoid of life. "My behavior last night was unacceptable. It must have been a fluke in my medication, no doubt brought on by the shock of what I witnessed."

He stared at me, and then nodded. "I can understand that. Now, back to your request. Even with your explanation, I still have to deny you."

"May I ask why?" I asked, the "may I" surprising even me. Who knew I could speak so formally when I wanted to?

"It has been proven," he said with the tone of one delivering a familiar lecture, "that being near a one is psychologically dangerous, even with our rankings being so high. Thoughts from their kind can be insidious; I've seen good Knights fall before, when exposed to them. In a matter of days."

His voice was soft, whisper thin, like brittle paper, and I watched as an old sorrow began to shine through his dark eyes. I knew he felt bad—

and I understood why he would—and all I could feel was sorry for the "fallen Knights" he was referring to. At the end of the day, they were murderers, and I was guessing that the reality of what they were doing had, in the end, overwhelmed their loyalty to Scipio. It was sickening that anyone would be willing to just put aside all basic human decency in service of a machine.

I waited what I felt was a respectful amount of time before resuming the argument, unwilling to let it go. "Be that as it may—"

He held up a hand. "Enough." His expression softened, and he put a large, club-like hand on his hip. "I think I see where you are going, Liana, and I need to be the first to tell you that it has been tried. And it has failed —multiple times."

I managed to keep my confusion off my face, but it was hard not to. I had no idea what he was getting at. "Sir?"

"You want to study him, right? See if you can crack the riddle of the ones? Many have tried, Liana, and at the end of the day, the reports are always the same: unknown causes. Some people are just dead weight. We live in hard times, and if we want to ensure our continued survival, the worthless must go."

"You mean the ones who won't *conform*," I practically spat at him. I was exceptionally lucky he didn't notice my flash of rage. I drew in a deep breath, trying to calm the churning anger that had blossomed under his callous words.

"Exactly. This society has no need for an individual who can't contribute."

I took a moment, as if to think about what he was saying, but was actually focused on getting back to the matter at hand, trying to reconfigure my argument in a way that would get me what I wanted. Determination and desperation were keeping me locked in on this trajectory. I just had to hope that neither feeling got me into trouble.

"Sir? I still very much want to meet the prisoner," I stated flatly. "Even with these definitive studies, I still have to meet him. I have to make sure I am doing the right thing, once and for all."

"Your faith should be in Scipio, Squire," he said sharply.

"My faith *is* with Scipio," I replied calmly. "But that doesn't change the fact that he will be the first person I am going to kill. That is a lot to ask of anyone, and I intend to do it, but there is only so far faith is going to take me. So please. Give me peace of mind that what I am doing is the right thing. For all of us."

Gerome paused, tilting his head from side to side in uncertainty.

"I cannot let you speak to him," he said eventually, and—to my surprise—with a touch of regret. "But I can let you see him again. Maybe that will answer any questions you might have?"

I followed Gerome back to the cell, still unwilling to give up on the plan of getting the pill to Grey. I held my eyes fixed on the end of the gruesome hallway, ignoring the windows with the trays and equipment inside. He opened the door into the cell, and I almost pushed ahead of him through the door to see Grey.

Grey was huddled in the corner, as far away from the door as possible, and had grown even filthier than before in the short time that had passed. Bloody scraps of fabric were wadded up in one corner of the room—from where he had tried to bandage the cut on his chest, I was sure—and I turned to Gerome, unable to even look at the sight.

My words, however, continued to come out flat and disinterested. "Do you ever clean the cells?" I asked. "Or them?"

"That would be a waste of resources on a dead man. Besides, once they are in, they don't leave until after the button has been pushed."

My mouth pinched in disdain, but I hid it with a turn of my head. "That seems cruel."

Gerome gave me a sad look. "Then push the button before it gets worse. Had you done it right away, it wouldn't have gotten this bad."

My eyes moved over to the button in question, then slid away in disgust. If I couldn't figure out how to get Grey the pill, then someone else would kill him—and I'd be dropped from the Knights and quickly be on my way to joining him in death.

"I'm not ready," I informed him coolly. "I might have been if I could have talked to him, but now I must find another way to come to terms with what I must do."

The lies were coming easier now, and while I knew that should concern me, I was grateful for it. I just had to be careful.

"Then things will only get worse," he said with a shrug.

I locked my jaw up tight to keep from replying, and looked back into the cell, studying it. I avoided looking at Grey as much as possible, knowing that seeing him in this condition could break me, and it was hard. My desperate and ill-conceived backup plan of slipping the pill into Grey's food had died when Gerome talked about not wanting to waste resources. And even if Gerome hadn't told me, it was painfully obvious that Grey wasn't being fed. I watched as one hand went to his stomach, a grimace sliding over his face, and felt sick to my own stomach.

"I've seen enough," I announced, turning around quickly.

Gerome didn't move toward the door.

"Liana, you are making this much harder than it needs to be," he said.

"Am I?" I asked, giving him a look while ignoring the burn of outrage at his words. "Killing isn't something that should come naturally, sir, and while I understand that Scipio has decreed this, that doesn't mean I can immediately perform the task. This is not easy, sir, and I don't think it should be. Please respect that."

Gerome just looked at me, his eyes stunned. "This is a shame. I had thought that if I brought you down here you would find the courage to get it over with, but I can see that you're not ready. We've shown you this too soon. Don't worry. Maybe in a few more months you'll be ready."

I started to nod, but then, out of the corner of my eye, I saw his arm move. It caught my attention, and I followed it, realizing quickly and with considerable alarm that he was reaching for the button. My heart stalled while a cold wash of ice shot down my spine, and suddenly I was moving. I didn't remember crossing the room, or putting myself between him and the button. What I did remember was his wrist in my hand, and the look of utter shock on his face.

"This needs to be done, Liana," he said, clearly baffled by my intervention. "You're not ready."

"You gave me a week," I informed him. "You promised me a week."

"I did," he said, pulling his wrist from my grasp and straightening. "But it's clear that you—"

"You gave me a week," I repeated roughly, not offering much in the way of leniency. "To think it over. You need to honor that promise."

He gave me a long, considering look, and it took me a moment to realize that he was impressed. The realization left me feeling a little hollow. Two weeks ago, I would've given my right arm for Gerome's approval. But now he was a murderer, trying to pressure me into becoming a murderer as well. I hated that he looked impressed because of the behavior I was exhibiting—almost as much as I hated carrying on this façade of being a good soldier.

And I hated seeing Grey in that cell even more, which was what made all of the negativity I was experiencing worth it.

"Very well, Squire," Gerome said with a nod. "You have six more days to execute him. I hope, for his sake, that you do so sooner rather than later."

I let any retort I had turn to ash in my mouth as I left, barely managing to make it to the lift and away from Gerome before I started running, putting as much distance between me and the Citadel as possible.

I navigated the halls, bridges, and lifts instinctively. My destination was largely unplanned—I just needed to get away—and somehow, I found myself perched on a portion of the shell that didn't quite line up with the levels above, creating a narrow, flat ledge that was about three feet deep, and had no railings to prevent the very sharp drop of 156 stories. Zoe, Eric, and I had discovered it after a run-in with a group of Kits—trainees from the Cog department. It was one of the only places you could find complete and utter privacy.

I anchored myself to the wall using my lashes and then massaged my burning thighs, staring out at the three buildings with my eyes on the

Citadel, and focusing on the lowermost level, where Grey was sitting in a tiny cell, waiting to die.

I pulled out the small silver pill case and opened it up to stare at the small, circular pill inside, then closed it with a snap and slipped it back into my pocket. I was disappointed I hadn't been able to get in to see him, but I wasn't ready to give up. There had to be a way to get the pill to him. Maybe there was an access hatch or something.

It was frustrating knowing that someone was going to die, and having time to do something about it but seeing the only plan I could come up with fail miserably. The irony that bureaucracy and protocols were costing him his life twice over was not lost on me. But that didn't help me see a way out of this mess.

The sound of grating caught my ears and a familiar voice spoke from behind me. "So are you mad, or are you just having a bad day?"

I turned to confirm Zoe's presence, and then nodded for her to sit down, still not ready to speak—but grateful that I wasn't alone.

I heard the slight squeak of her wetsuit as she moved and dropped down onto the ledge next to me, letting her legs swing free. "What's wrong?"

"I can't tell you," I replied automatically, and then flinched. Zoe didn't take well to being told what she could and couldn't know.

It was no surprise, therefore, when she chose to pry anyway. "*Yes*, you can," she said, emphasizing the "yes". "There's something going on with you, Liana. I've noticed it ever since that morning you showed up looking and feeling like your old self. Something is getting you down, girl, and that's not good for that shiny new nine of yours."

"Someone is in trouble," I blurted out, and then clapped a hand over my mouth in an attempt to pull the words back in. But it was impossible.

Zoe sat up straight, her pouty lips pulled downward into a frown. "What do you mean?"

I swallowed and looked at my feet, torn. I desperately needed her help and her advice, but I couldn't bear involving her in it. She could get hurt—or worse, wind up in a cell much like Grey's.

"Zoe, I'm sorry, but I—"

"You know what? Save it," she said, climbing back up to her feet next to me. "I'm your best friend, and I know when something is wrong with you. First your drama about that boy and your number, and then you show up a nine. You left class and never came back, and you never netted me to tell me what *happened* and why Gerome wanted to see you—and you've *never* done that. Is it the Medica medication? Is this Prim 2.0? I was so worried about you after Gerome hauled you out! And you didn't even let me know you were okay!"

I let her rant, watching as she spoke passionately, with the snappish temper that ran in the Cog-bred part of her, and all I could feel was tired and depressed. The problems between us were insignificant compared to what I had seen, and I felt as if I couldn't even pay much attention to them.

"Zo, you don't understand," I tried again, and I could already see the dark storm clouds of her retort beginning to build. I paused and then looked away, letting whatever sketch of an idea I had about what to say evaporate.

"Explain it to me," she demanded, dropping back down next to me and craning her neck and head out into open air to get a fuller view of my face. I slid a long lock of hair over my ear and sighed, meeting her gaze.

"It's dangerous."

"More dangerous than hacking an elevator?"

I nodded.

"How dangerous?"

"Very."

"Is it those pills?" she asked, her brows furrowing. "Did you get involved in something illegal?"

I kept my mouth shut and my jaw tight, but the words were there, threatening to spill out of my mouth. I wanted so badly to tell her everything I'd seen since last night. She was my best friend—and I needed to talk to *someone*.

"They're killing people," I whispered, and all the emotions that I had been holding inside spilled out in hot tears. My anger at my parents, my fear for Grey, my frustrations with Roark, and the feeling of being completely untethered and out of control. I sobbed into Zoe's shoulder, and she clutched me close, patting my back as I explained the whole situation. It took a while, and by the end my eyes felt red and raw, and I was hiccupping.

Zoe was quiet for a long time. "The Knights are killing the ones?" she finally asked, her eyes glancing over to me.

And I could see the hope there, begging me to tell her it was all a sick practical joke. "Yes."

There was another span of silence, and a glance at Zoe told me she was struggling to process this. Eventually, she said, "And they want you to do it as well, and it just so happens that the man they picked out for you is Grey."

"Yes."

Another long, halting silence. Then, "And you have a pill that could get his number up, but you don't know how to get it to him?"

"Yes," I grated out, trying not to grow impatient with her and her need to fact-check every point I'd told her. I dried some more tears while she stared off, deep in thought. "Look, I need a way to get this pill to him, but they won't let me into his cell before I've killed him."

"Which would be counterproductive," Zoe said hollowly. "What about his food?"

I met her inquisitive gaze with an angry one of my own. "They're not feeding him."

Zoe paled. "That's unconscionable," she declared.

"That's an understatement," I replied. "And a big one. It's *awful*. That woman... she looked so thin it hurts me to think about it. There's no way of knowing how long they kept her alive before they killed her—but it seemed like a long time."

Zoe turned even whiter, her lips losing color, and I reached out and took her hand. "This is why I didn't want to tell you," I said.

She shook her head. "You shouldn't have to go through this alone. I mean... No one in the Tower would ever believe... Do you think your parents have—"

"They have," I said harshly, my hand cupping my cheek, feeling the phantom sting of my mother's slap.

"Oh." She fell silent, and I did as well, still scrambling around for an idea.

"You said there was a white mist?" Zoe suddenly asked.

I blinked. "Yeah. Why?"

"How long did it remain in the room?"

"Gerome had it sucked out a moment or two after she... stopped moving," I replied, my voice coming out strangled at the end.

She rolled her lips between her teeth, her expression thoughtful. "What did they do with her, after they... after she... after—"

"They came in and dragged her out," I said, trying to understand why she was asking all these questions. "But what does that have to do with—"

"How fast?" she asked, interrupting me, and I frowned, trying to remember. Most of the details stood out with perfect gut-wrenching clarity, but my perception of time was odd—I had only been down there for a little over six minutes, but it had felt like eternity.

"Fast," I said, finally able to remember, and she smiled. "What?"

"I think I know a way to help you," she said. "But it's tricky."

"What is it?" I asked, allowing the thin thread of hope to rise up inside me.

"It's really simple when you think about it," she said with a small, sad smile. "You'll have to give him the pill *after* you press the button."

17

I blinked at Zoe's words and then gave her an incredulous look. "That kind of defeats the purpose, Zo. If we let them gas him first, then the pill won't exactly be effective."

She grinned at me, revealing white teeth, and shook her head. "It will be," she announced as she pulled herself back up. "C'mon, we gotta stop by my house. I need a pipe chart."

I retracted my lashes and let them pull me up before disconnecting them, still mystified by her statement. "Zoe, stop planning and start telling me what your plan is before you go running off the deep end."

"I always run off the deep end," she replied as she hit the button to the access hatch. It grated as it slid open, and she cast an eye at it as she passed through. "This door needs to be oiled," she chided.

I stepped in behind her and placed my hands on her shoulders. "Zoe. What are we doing?"

"We're going back to my house to get the pipe chart," she said, shrugging out of my gentle hold. "We're close to an elevator that runs all the way to Water Treatment. C'mon."

She darted away down the left tunnel, moving quickly. I sighed and followed her as she moved down the tight, narrow passages that seemed to run on endlessly throughout the shell. My legs, still aching from the mad dash up here, were already protesting the fast, jerking speed as I tried to keep up with my best friend, following the flashes of her blue uniform as she navigated them effortlessly.

We came to a stop at an elevator, and I stepped on, immediately wincing at the buzz in my head as the computer scanned us. It instantly checked my wrist, confirming the blue nine was still there.

I let out a breath I didn't know I had been holding and then crossed my arms, expecting it to start moving after it said Zoe's name.

To my surprise it didn't, and I began paying attention to the computerized voice.

"Verified—Roe Zoe Elphesian, designation 12WT-531. Your ranking is currently five. As a Diver of Water Treatment, it is your responsibility to—"

I tuned the rest out and immediately looked at Zoe, my eyes searching for her wrist. She was already holding it up, and as she stared at it, I could see the orange light from the number shining on her wrist.

"Zoe, I'm..."

She looked over at me and folded her arms over her chest, hiding the indicator. "It's to be expected," she said, her gaze on the numbers gliding by.

"I shouldn't have said anything. Your mom is going to—"

"Have to deal with it," Zoe replied, giving me a pointed look before turning her attention back to the shaft. I stared at her, feeling hopelessly guilty for opening my big fat mouth, and finally looked away. Soon Roark was going to have to start making enough pills for Zoe, too. It was the only way to keep her safe from what I'd already exposed her to, and to keep her from the fate we were trying to save Grey from.

The ride felt abnormally long, and the silence between us quickly became too difficult to bear. I needed to talk, to fill the air, but I knew mentioning her new ranking would not end well, so I focused on something else.

"Aren't pipe charts maps?" I asked.

"No," she said. "They're charts." She stopped talking, and I thought that was the end of it, but suddenly she had a change of heart, her body softening its stiff posture and turning toward me. "Actually, a pipe chart is *kind of* like a map, but it's designed to show each and every pipe that water flows through in the Tower. They're standard issue for all Water Treatment personnel, so we can locate and fix leaks quickly. Don't you remember this from class?"

I was shaking my head when the elevator slowed to a gentle halt, and I got off quickly, thinking. "Why do we need one?" I asked after a moment, following her down the fluorescently painted halls, which glowed brightly in greens, pinks, and blues.

We climbed up a series of stairs that led to a bridge over a massive glass pipe. I heard a wet splash and looked over to see two bald men diving into the water that was rushing through the pipe, arms first, with black, flute-shaped objects clenched between their teeth—artificial gills to help them breathe as they navigated the aquatic spaces. They were likely a work detail running repairs in the system, but their presence reminded me that we weren't alone, and not everything in the Tower was as private as it seemed.

We were heading down the stairs on the other side of the bridge when Zoe answered me. "Because I have an idea, but before it can become a reality, I have to check to see if it is actually possible."

I was unamused by her indirect answer, but went with it. Zoe was smart, and I had known her my entire life. I trusted her implicitly, because she had never steered me wrong, and she cared more about *me* than some stupid number on my wrist. I followed her through the open market that had been set up around the fishponds—a more peaceful and tranquil place than Cogstown's market—and through the wide hall that eventually narrowed and led to her quarters.

She pressed the button to open the door, and I stepped inside, directly into the living room. I was surprised to find Zoe's mother sitting on the couch, her suit dripping liberally onto the cushions even though she was fastidiously towel-drying it.

"Hello, Liana," she greeted formally, and I inclined my head to her.

Helena was a Cog-bred Diver, and had changed departments when she was just eighteen to marry Zoe's father. He'd died a few years ago of a heart attack, which was rare, but still happened from time to time. "Hello, Zoe, darling. How was your day?" she asked.

"Good," Zoe said, flipping her long hair over her shoulder. "Liana and I are going to do some studying. Is that okay?"

Zoe lied effortlessly, and I was impressed by how easily the fib slid off her tongue. Her mother gave her an appraising look and then turned to me, her smile pleasant. She was always pleasant; she was also deeply religious, having completely embraced the Water Ways. And she loved to tell everyone all about it.

"I hear you're a nine now," she said as Zoe clattered down the ladder.

I held up my wrist. "Yes, ma'am," I said. "Been pretty steady for the last few days."

She chuckled. Her own eight glittered on her wrist, the purple color making it seem more like a bruise than an eight. "Never thought you'd have a higher number than me," she said, smiling. "Scipio works in strange ways."

I thought of Grey in the cell. "It would seem so."

"Mom?" Zoe interjected, and her mother looked over at her.

"Yes?"

"May we go to my room?"

"Well, of course! Just..." She trailed off as her gaze lowered to Zoe's wrist, her eyes growing concerned. "Zoe, your ranking dropped."

Zoe's mouth formed a thin line. "I know." It was all she said.

"What do you mean, you *know*? What happened?"

Zoe kept her eyes on her mother, not betraying me with a glance, and the guilt that had started to settle within me churned back up. "It just dropped," Zoe announced.

"Rankings don't just drop, Zoe," her mother declared angrily, and I sensed she was just getting warmed up. "And five is dangerously low. We should get you checked into the Medica immediately. Or I can call the Praetor, and maybe he can find some time to light a prayer with you."

"I'm not a child, Mom," Zoe said. "I'm twenty, which means two things. The first is that I don't have to go to Medica, even if you order me to. It's not mandatory until I'm a three. The second is that next year, I'll be twenty-one, and Scipio will assign me my own domicile."

"Next year," her mother echoed. "But while you're under my roof, you will—"

Zoe looked at me. "Go ahead to my room," she said, her voice dangerously soft as she interrupted her mother.

"Are you sure? I can—"

"Go."

Her tone brooked no argument, and I kept my head down as I moved through the kitchen and into the hall beyond, finding Zoe's room just as the voices began to rise in the living room. They cut off with a pneumatic hiss as the door closed behind me, and then I was in Zoe's room, all alone.

I considered sitting down, but I was too nervous about the fight that was happening just past the door, and wound up walking around her room, pacing in uncertainty. What if Zoe's mother punished her and made me go home? I still had no idea what she needed the pipe chart for, nor any idea where the pipe chart was so I could look at it.

Checking her desk anyhow, I found a few pieces of paper covered with scribbles and little diagrams, and studied the pages. Zoe had written in very clean, block print all around them, and there were more than a few mathematic equations, notes on how each machine would function, and statistics on how pieces of machinery could improve Tower life. I stared at the pages for a long moment, trying to make heads or tails of the information, and then put them down, frustrated.

Before today, the only reason Zoe had to be unhappy was that she was still in Water Treatment, and couldn't transfer to Mechanics. If I hadn't told her about the Knights, I was certain she would have eventually found her way in, and would have been a ten in a matter of days. Now that she knew, however...

I began wondering how many lives I was going to destroy just by association. First Grey, who had sacrificed his safety for mine by giving me his pills and then gotten caught, and now Zoe, whose ranking had dropped because I couldn't keep my mouth shut. Were Eric and Alex next? Could I destroy their rankings with this knowledge?

Maybe they're already infected with my psychological contamination. I looked at my wrist, queasy, and then lowered my arm, unwilling to look at it any longer.

The door slid open, and I whirled as Zoe stormed into the room, all but punching the door's button behind her. Her face was red, her hands working angrily at her sides. She rested her back against the door, exhaling slowly and clearly trying to calm herself down. I wasn't sure what to say, and I felt like it was better not to say anything, rather than pry.

Finally, she looked up at me and frowned. "You haven't found the pipe chart yet?"

I looked around, baffled, and watched as she approached one of the exposed shelves with books on it and pulled out a thick blue book that was almost as wide as her chest. "This is one of the few complete manuals," she commented as she sat it down on the desk. "From before we started training people for specific areas around the Tower. It's been in my father's family for generations."

Which meant the heavy volume now on the table was at least two hundred years old. It was impressive, but did nothing to assuage my concern for Zoe. "Zoe, what did your mother say?" I couldn't help but ask.

"It's not important and not unexpected," she said, putting on a pair of white gloves. "And don't go feeling guilty, Liana. I made you tell me, just like I made the choice to help you." She carefully flipped open the book and began thumbing through the pages. "You shouldn't have to face all of this alone," she added, voice soft.

I couldn't resist the impulse, and reached out to hug her, feeling incredibly relieved to hear her say that. She leaned against me, but was careful not to touch me with her gloved hands, for fear any dirt from me would get on her father's book. After a moment, I let her go.

"Thank you," I said, reaching up to pat the area under my eyes to stop the waterworks that were beginning to start up. I sniffled anyway, and she rested her head on my shoulder in an attempt to comfort me.

"We're going to get this Grey guy out. Now, have you thought about the others and what we're going to do for *them*?"

My moment of happiness evaporated under her gaze. I fidgeted and shook my head. "I don't have access to them," I said hoarsely. "I couldn't get access if I tried, I'm guessing. The only one I have access to is Grey, so—"

"So Grey is the only one you can save." Her face was a sad mask, but she nodded, turning back to the book. "Then we'll save him and figure out what we can do next."

She opened the book, and it turned out to be even larger than it had appeared, with pages that unfolded into massive maps, and small, detailed notes and charts on each individual pipe. She flipped through it, page by page, while I hovered over her shoulder, trying to get a peek at what she was looking for. Eventually she got annoyed and ordered me to sit down—which I did, on her bed.

I was too nervous to stay still, though, and wound up spending my time fiddling with things or flipping through books. *She said she didn't want to tell me in case it wasn't possible,* I thought to myself, watching as she studied each map intensely, her gloved hands handling each page as if it were a piece of glass on the verge of shattering.

When she finally said, "Ah, here it is," I was by her side before she got to the "it."

"Here what is?" I asked, and then froze when I heard paper ripping. "Zoe!" I cried, appalled to see her destroying something she loved so much. Something her father had given her.

My best friend looked at me, the torn page dangling from her finger-tips, and gave me a defiant look. "The book is too heavy," she said calmly, folding the wide sheet. "And my father always told me that human lives were more valuable than books."

"He did not," I shot back, and the corner of her mouth quirked up.

"Fine, he never said that per se, but he did say *something* along those lines." She slipped the piece of paper into a plastic bag that sealed shut, making it watertight, and then slipped the bag inside her uniform. She handed me the book, which I obediently put back on the shelf.

"Let's go," she said over the hiss of the door, and I turned to see her already heading out. I quickly followed.

"Zoe?" Her mother's voice called from her room as we passed, and I hesitated, but Zoe didn't, continuing back through the kitchen. I followed her, realizing that her mother had managed to whip together a stew while Zoe was looking for the pipe chart. It was bubbling on the stove, making my stomach growl, but I ignored it as I followed Zoe to the door.

"Zoe."

Zoe pushed the button to the door, ignoring her mother's insistent calls, and stepped out, almost plowing right into Eric. He reached out to steady her, and she froze, tipping her head up toward him. I slid through the space around them and closed the door before her mother could call her again, worried that Eric might wonder what was going on.

The two of them stared at each other for a long moment, and I suppressed a sigh, looking around for a clock. I wanted my friends to finally admit their feelings to each other, but now wasn't exactly the best time. Grey was waiting, without food and trapped against his will, probably scared and very much alone. Maybe it was insensitive of me, but we needed to speed this along—without getting Eric involved.

"Hey, Eric," I said, managing to put a teasing note in my voice. "What are you doing at Zoe's house?"

Eric blinked, the dreamy look on his face evaporating as he realized he and Zoe had a witness, and removed his hands from her shoulders so fast you'd have thought she was toxic. Running a sheepish hand through his hair, he looked over at me and forced a nervous smile on his face.

"Hey, Liana," he said. "Were you invited to dinner too?"

This time Zoe blinked, and her face filtered through a series of expressions, from confusion to consideration to recollection, and in spite of the gravity of the situation, I found myself smiling. The awkwardness between Zoe and Eric was something I didn't have time for, but I wasn't really sure how to put a stop to it.

"Dinner," she groaned, placing a hand on her forehead. "I forgot."

There was a flash of hurt on Eric's face, and I recognized the beginnings of an episode from one of their dramatic lovers-but-not-actually-lovers fights beginning to form. This was the best moment I was ever going to get.

"She forgot to net you that her mother had to cancel," I slid in smoothly, taking a step closer to them. "And that's my fault. I showed up unexpectedly."

"Oh." Eric ran his hand down his neck. "Do you want to come over to *my* place for dinner?"

Zoe looked at me and then snapped her gaze back to Eric. "I can't," she said. "I want to, but Liana came by to ask me for some help."

"Oh? With what? Can I tag along?"

My heart pounded, but Zoe didn't panic. "No," she said, an apologetic smile on her face, "because I already gave it to her."

"Oh." He looked around awkwardly, shuffling his feet. "Then why can't you come for dinner?"

My heart stopped. It flat-out stopped as Eric picked apart Zoe's statements, trying to find a way to squeeze in some time with her. It would've been sweet, but his timing was just so bad.

"Because helping Liana set me back on my own work," Zoe explained effortlessly, once again surprising me with the smoothness of her invented alibi. "I've got some parts that I need to take apart, clean, and repair before the next shift."

"Oh, well, I can help you with that!" Eric exclaimed, a broad smile on his face. I couldn't stop myself; I grabbed hold of the first plausible idea I could to get rid of him as quickly as possible.

"She's lying," I said, and Zoe gave me a wide-eyed look of warning that told me she'd be giving me a piece of her mind shortly, depending on what I said. I ignored her, focusing on Eric's surprised face. "Sort of. I came over to talk to her about a boy."

I let the statement lie flat, and waited for Eric's reaction.

"A boy?" he asked, clearly confused.

"Liana isn't sure if he likes her, or *likes* her likes her, y'know?" Zoe said, and I nodded, thinking of Grey and borrowing some of the emotions that were there to bring a blush to my cheeks.

"I came over to ask Zoe to, um... watch us interact and give me her opinion."

This time the blush was genuine. I couldn't help it. The idea that I would ever ask anyone to watch me interact with Grey, or any boy I liked, was mortifying. The last thing I needed was my faux pas recited back to me.

"Oh, now this I've got to see." My head snapped up to look into Eric's amused face. Anticipation was already gleaming in his eyes, and I froze, my mind fumbling for some sort of explanation.

"Are you *kidding* me?" Zoe asked loudly, placing a hand on her hip. "How obtuse are you?"

Eric blinked, his wide smile faltering and then disappearing as he looked at both of us. "I... What do you mean?"

"Whatever Liana has with this guy is fragile! The last thing she needs is to show up with another guy around! It would send the wrong message."

"Oh. Yeah. I hadn't thought of that."

We fell silent, and out of nowhere I thought of the perfect way of getting rid of him. "Yeah, imagine how you'd feel if you liked Zoe and then saw her standing around with some other handsome guy."

Zoe shot me a look that promised me a fiery death was in my near future, but I kept my focus on Eric's horrified face. His eyes darted to Zoe, who managed to screw her features into a mildly neutral expression, and then back to me, his gaze filled with questioning reproach. I felt bad; I'd never insinuated anything about their feelings for each other in front of them both, but right now it was the only way.

"I mean, if I liked Zoe... I guess I could see... Yeah... I never really thought... I mean, it's not really my business who Zoe hangs out with, even if I did like her, so..."

I smiled at Eric's stammering, and then nodded. "I'm sorry if this disrupts your evening, but I'm sure Zoe will reschedule. Won't you, Zo?"

"Sure," Zoe mumbled, looking at the toes of her shoes. "I'll net you later?"

"Sounds good," Eric said, managing to collect himself. "Good luck, Liana. See you later."

I raised my hand in farewell, but I doubted Eric noticed it; he left so fast I would've thought his pants were on fire. I watched him go, then turned back to Zoe, surprised to find her standing right by my side, barely an inch separating us.

"How could you *do* that?" she exclaimed, her voice loud. "How could you call me out like that?"

Call *her* out? I blinked, trying to remember what exactly I had said to get rid of Eric.

"How did I—"

"You told him I was *lying*. Now anytime he looks at me, he's just going to think, *Oh, there is Zoe the Liar, with a capital L!*"

"I'm sorry," I said, somewhat defensively. "I panicked. He was being pushy about trying to hang out, and in case you don't remember, a man's life is on the line. I'm really sorry if I embarrassed you, but if your dad said something along the lines of *lives come first*, then I think this falls under that."

Zoe gave me an affronted look and then sighed, her shoulders rounding out. "You're right," she said. "And you were right to get rid of him. I don't want him getting hurt because of me."

"Neither do I," I said, thinking of her five. We both fell into silence. I couldn't tell you what Zoe thought about, but for me, it was a moment in which I prayed that we could pull this off without getting caught. "Where are we headed?"

"To the Citadel," she replied, patting the pocket with the pipe chart, and I nodded. The fastest route back was automatic for me after years of coming down to visit Zoe. I began to move down the adjacent hall, but Zoe caught my arm and gave me a look. "We need to be *outside* the Citadel," she added pointedly.

I sighed and began rethreading my lashes to come out through my belt. I was going to need my hands, it seemed. From the excited look on Zoe's face, we were going to do some climbing.

Just before the Anwar's Bridge—a gleaming black bridge that lay flat and wide to accommodate traffic from the nearby greeneries—we came to a stop. I examined the bridge and the people already lashing across it while Zoe pulled out the plastic bag containing the torn page of her book.

"We'll have to go down here," she said. "You'll lash us across under the bridge and down the side of the Citadel. We're looking for hatch 3B."

I nodded absentmindedly as I pulled my lashes out, immediately attaching one to the black railing. There was so much traffic around the Tower that we likely wouldn't be noticed, so now was a good time to get moving. Bending my knees, I waited for Zoe to climb on, and then took two steps forward and pitched us over the edge. Zoe sucked in a deep breath as we fell, but I was already moving, throwing my next lash out at the apex of our descent and disconnecting the first line. We moved at a steady rate, my arms flying to attach new lashes almost as soon as I disconnected the last, and within moments, I had taken us through the arches and columns and attached us to the smooth, slightly reflective surface of the Citadel. I looked around, studying the small marks along the side—designed for navigation and repairs—and began moving left and down, following the designations toward the hatch Zoe had named.

"There it is," Zoe said suddenly, adjusting her weight on my back so she could thrust out her arm and point to a spot a few feet below and farther left. I threw my lash to just past where the door would be and swung us over it, spreading my legs wide to brace our weight. I was studying the smooth surface, searching for a button or switch to open it, when Zoe reached over and inserted a long wire into a small, almost invisible hole between the 3 and the C. I felt something hard press up against my back but stayed still, not wanting to distract her from what she was doing. There was an electronic beep behind me, and then a door about three feet wide slid open.

I realized it was a crawl space that ran between floors, and sighed as I lowered myself to let Zoe climb in first. She did so as gently as possible, but I still got her boot on my shoulder and neck for a moment as she pushed farther in.

"Now that we're here," I grunted as I pulled myself in before retracting the lines, "you mind telling me what's up?"

Zoe had already pulled out the paper and unfolded it on the floor, a small light in her hand as she studied it and looked at the pipes running overhead. I looked as well, but still couldn't make heads or tails of the chart.

"You said they used a gas, right?" she asked, her eyes still darting around.

I thought of the woman with blood streaming from her eyes and nodded, stomach knotted. "Yeah," I said. "Why?"

She seemed to find what she was looking for, then, because just after I asked the question, she started folding up the chart. "I'm not sure yet, but I think that if it's coming out as a mist, they might have hijacked a water pipe to make the system do that. It's not designed to, so they had to modify something somewhere. They're probably using the pipes that put a small amount of humidity in the air."

"Oh. Wait, so they are using the humidity controls to distribute the poison?" I frowned, considering that approach and puzzling out the rest of what she was telling me. "What good is that going to do?"

"I'm not really sure, yet," she said with a tired sigh. "I have to see how they modified the system before I can figure out a plan of attack. But... I have a theory, and if I'm right, then I can make it so the poison is never introduced into the water in the first place."

God, I loved Zoe, but she clearly thought more highly of my cognitive abilities than was realistic. "Girl, can you please dumb it down for me?"

"Literally no appreciation for what I do," Zoe muttered as she began folding up the chart. "I think I can make it seem like the poison gas is coming out, but without any of the poison."

I blinked, considering her words. "So I press the button, but he doesn't die?"

"That's the idea," Zoe said, her eyes now glued to the pipes overhead as she began to crawl forward on her hands and knees. "There's only one place they could do it from, and it's in the junction up ahead. Did his cell have a designation number?"

It did, now that I thought about it, but I had glossed over it both times I went in. I forced myself to remember the walk down the hall, and the door, and after a moment, it came to me.

"5D," I informed her, following her through the crawl space.

The space went on for some twenty feet before it opened into a wide circular room, awash with pipes—both glass and lead—electrical boxes, wires, and cables. Zoe clicked off her light and looked around. The room was well lit with a bright white light... and she was already frowning.

"Some of these pipes are lead," she commented, consulting her chart. "But they shouldn't be."

She was right, although it took me a minute to recall why. It was from one of our classes with another Diver, named Lester, several months ago, when he was explaining how to identify which pipes did what. The only reason to use lead was when the water was toxic, or lethal. Those pipes were only used below, in Water Treatment. No toxic water was allowed past floor forty, as a safety protocol.

"Do you think that's where the poison gas is?" I asked, eyeing the pipes.

"No," she said, lowering the chart and studying the pipes. "If it were already in gas form, they'd need a way to vent it in. I don't see any sign of a machine to help them do that."

"They could be piping it in with the air?" I asked. "The mist is already coming through the vent."

She immediately shook her head. "Can't be done without some serious overhauls to the ventilation system, as they are all connected. Besides, it wouldn't be coming out as a mist if they were—the system is specifically designed to eliminate moisture inside of it to prevent it from deteriorating. The humidifiers are the only way they could pump it in and keep it contained."

"So then..."

"Give me a second," she said, taking a step forward and running her fingers against one of the pipes, following it. I fell silent, trying to be patient enough to let her work. I was grateful she was here, because it was unlikely I was going to make any sense of these pipes. And I needed to know what was going on. Grey's life depended on it.

"Ah, so that's what they're doing." I looked over to see her kneeling by some wires, her homemade pad connected to them.

"*What* are they doing?" I asked as she disconnected.

"Well, the good thing is that there *is* water in those lead pipes."

"What's the bad?"

"I'll get back to that," she said. "In the meantime, we have to get up *there*." She pointed to a wide lead pipe, and I could see now that most of the other lead pipes connected directly to it. The pipe in question didn't even look right; it looked more like a collection or drainage tank than anything else, the way it dangled from the ceiling.

We clambered up to the pipe in question, Zoe climbing up other pipes while I used my lashes. She squeezed into the space overhead, lying across the pipe, and began examining it, cocking her head this way and that as she read the mechanical notes on the side.

I couldn't help but feel useless as she worked. It wasn't my area of expertise, of course, but I wanted to be involved somehow. I tried to recall more of my education in Water Treatment practices, but those had been basic, and this seemed far more complicated. Presumably, this was the sort of thing they would only teach to someone who had been fully accepted into Water Treatment.

Zoe smiled. "I think I figured it out," she muttered. "This isn't a collection tank, although it's meant to look like one. The pipe leads to a heating element, where the water inside is turned into steam. This other pipe is where the water comes from."

She pulled a wrench from her satchel and began turning a bolt on the pipe, and I held up my hand to stop her. "Wait!" I cried. "What if the water is toxic?"

"It's not—not yet, anyway. The poison is coming from somewhere up in here." She patted the ceiling tile that the pipe she was working on came through.

"Right. But explain to me how opening it up won't expose us to the toxin?"

Zoe stopped, clearly thinking about it, then shook her head. "Excellent point, but I misspoke. It comes *through* here. Hold on."

She turned the wrench, and the pipe popped free of the joint holding it in place, disconnecting it from the ceiling. I expected water or something, but it was bone dry. Zoe went to work on the ceiling grate overhead next, and I took it from her and balanced it on one of the electrical boxes. If it fell I could get it quickly, but for now, I needed my hands free to help Zoe.

I turned back and saw that she was now standing on the pipe, bent at the waist and fiddling around in the space between the floor above and the grated ceiling in here. I heard tools clattering and banging, culminating in a loud "Aha!"

She withdrew from the space, her hands and face smudged black with dirt, holding a silver valve the size of my fist. "This is something we can work with," she said, dropping back down onto the tank and pulling out a screwdriver.

"What is it?" I asked, trying to study the design.

"It's a directional valve," she said as she set the screwdriver against it. "It is automatically controlled, and supposed to change between hot and cold, like in a shower. *However*, it isn't where it's supposed to be. I followed the two lines connected to it and identified one that funnels the water, and, presumably, one that funnels the toxin."

I frowned. "Okay, so let me get this straight—there's a line for water and a line for the poison. This valve controls which one does what?"

"Kind of. It's like how you can adjust the ratio of cold and hot water in your shower. Same thing here, but it's been modified to only have two positions—open and closed. I'm guessing it was designed to look like this to be overlooked by anyone making repairs. It's a common enough valve to be overlooked. Hiding in plain sight." There was a click, and Zoe smiled.

"And just like that, Zoe saves the day. I've adjusted it so that the opening sits farther back, so that when the button hits, it will still block whatever it is they are dumping in there from getting in."

"Really?" That sounded too easy.

Zoe nodded and stood up again, presumably to put the part back in. She fiddled around for a few more minutes and then lowered herself back down, her hands filled with tools and more smudges than before. She wiped some sweat forming on her forehead, leaving behind a black streak, and held out her hand for the grate. I handed it to her, and she slipped it over the pipe and began reattaching it to the ceiling.

"So, there is one problem," she said as she worked, and I nodded. Of course it couldn't be that simple. Nothing ever was.

"What?"

"I had to break it to fix it. So anyone they try to gas in that room after this is also going to survive."

"Good," I said, and she nodded.

"I agree, but it's only a matter of time before they call someone in to take a look at it. Once they do, they'll find the valve and see that it is damaged."

"Can't we just come back here and fix it afterward?" I asked, but Zoe shook her head.

"The entire part needs to be replaced, and as a Roe, I can't requisition parts." She looked at me, her eyes wide. "Look, they'll examine it, and they'll either think it's a manufacturing problem, or..." She trailed off, but I didn't need her to finish. When they found the part, they might figure out it had been tampered with.

"Is there any chance we can—"

I was cut off by a lash spinning up past my ear and connecting to a pipe above me with a flash of blue. A heavyset form twisted up through the air and jerked to a halt next to me, bobbing on the line. I looked over and stared into Gerome's hard, flat eyes.

"Gerome," I said, feeling sweat break out on the back of my neck. How had he known we were down here? Was this room monitored? Oh, God, could he have been listening in?

"Squire," he said with a nod. Then he looked to Zoe. His expression twisted slightly when he saw her number, but he held his derision at bay. "Roe."

Zoe had grown pale, but she managed a little wave before turning back to the ceiling.

"What are you doing here?" I asked.

He gave me a sharp look, his eyes flicking over to Zoe and then back to me in silent warning, and I got the message: she wasn't supposed to know about the prisoners above, and what was being done to them. I held on to that, comforted by it, as it meant he had no idea what we were up to. But that didn't mean he couldn't figure it out. With my outburst earlier... and now we were down here... it was too soon. He was going to figure out we were doing something to the cell, unless I was the very essence of calm and collected, and gave him nothing to doubt.

"I was... concerned about you after the vein of our last conversation," he stated flatly. "And I felt like I owed you a bit of an apology. You were right to stop me when you did."

An apology? From Gerome? I looked over at him and saw kindness there, but it was hard to reconcile the kindness with the man who killed people, and I looked away. "Thank you," I said, summoning up the neutral face and voice needed to deal with him.

"Imagine my surprise when I found out from the Eyes that you were in here. What are you doing?"

"She's here with me," Zoe announced, fitting the pipe back to the hole. "And I'm just here doing some checks on the piping, checking for corrosion or leaks."

"Is this an assigned task or...?"

"Not assigned," I said, knowing that if he checked, we'd be found out. "Roe Elphesian is one of the more overzealous members of Water Treatment. She tends to take on extra responsibilities, while I accompany her to learn."

"I see." Gerome looked around the room and nodded. "It's good that you want to learn more. We would all benefit from it. I just have to wonder, are you considering a transfer?"

His words were delivered casually, but I could feel the potential bite of anger building. He didn't approve of transfers. Luckily, I had no intention of transferring.

"Not at all. I am just doing everything I can to make my skills more versatile. You can never tell when something will break down."

"That's true. Very well. I'm glad I caught up with you, but you appear to be busy. We'll talk more on patrol tomorrow?"

"Of course, sir," I said as I activated the gears in my lash harness to lower myself to the ground I had spent the last forty minutes dangling over. "I'd be happy to."

Gerome landed heavily beside me, choosing to drop straight down instead of lowering himself like I had, while Zoe climbed down using the pipes. "Good. Well, you two keep busy. I'll see you tomorrow."

He left as quickly as he had arrived, but I still waited for several long seconds before I let out a pent-up breath. Beside me, Zoe was doing just about as well—although her hands were shaking violently, as if she were experiencing extreme cold.

"You okay?" I asked, and she nodded.

"Yeah, but... I would very much like to get home."

"Me too," I replied automatically, then realized that no... I didn't. She looked over at me and grabbed my hand, squeezing it reassuringly.

"Hard part's done," she said. "Now it's up to you to get him the pill after you 'gas' him."

"Yeah," I said, a touch bitterly. "Let's just hope he realizes what's going on, and fakes it."

"Think he knows any Callivax?" she asked hopefully, and I shrugged.

"Don't think it matters," I replied, motioning for the tunnel that led to the exterior of the Citadel—back the way we had come. I wanted us out of the room sooner rather than later. "The window in the room is one-way glass."

"Turn on the lights in the main room," Zoe said as she slipped into the crawl space. "One-way glass only works when the room is dark. Sign him the message using the basic alphabet—everyone had to learn that in primary school. If you make it look like the lights got turned on by accident, and keep the hand movements small, I doubt Gerome will even notice. We've come this far. Only two more steps."

Sure, I thought to myself as I dropped to my hands and knees to follow. *And then I hope Zoe's fix works—because if it doesn't, then I'll end up killing someone.*

18

The next morning I woke up early. Too early, really, but I couldn't sleep any longer. I was too apprehensive about what I was about to do, and I had spent most of the night tossing and turning. After a while, I realized sleep just wasn't going to happen. So I worked out—push-ups, sit-ups, and squats, followed by a hot shower. I wasted an hour playing with my hair. Remembered to use the lotion that my mother had gotten at the market. Got dressed. Ate breakfast. Sat on the couch and waited. Practiced my message in Callivax. Ran through everything in my head two million and three times. Prayed.

At six a.m., just as the morning lights were beginning to glow, I tapped my indicator and netted Gerome with a simple message: I'm ready.

Two hours later, Gerome came to collect me from my house. My parents watched me go with more pride than concern in their eyes, standing in the hall as Gerome and I walked away.

Each step I took was fraught with worry. I agonized over every aspect of the plan, ending each thought with a prayer: *Please don't let me kill this man. Please let him understand Callivax. Please let them let me go in there to move his body. Please don't let us get caught.*

We took the elevator down. I stood in silence, watching the numbers track down as we drew closer and closer to the floor, the vice-like grip of fear slowly tightening around my heart. Halfway down, Gerome broke the silence, reminding me that he was still there.

"I'm happy you finally came to terms with what you must do," he said. "You're going to make a model Knight, Liana."

"Thank you, sir," I replied, keeping my eyes forward. Inwardly, I seethed at his words. Murder shouldn't make anyone a model *anything*. If this was what our society had come to—murdering those who didn't quite conform or fit in—then maybe the destruction of our world had been well deserved. Nothing could justify what they were doing down below—I didn't care how much rhetoric they spat at me.

"Yes, well... I can see you rising to Knight Elite within a month. I'll be surprised if they don't automatically award you the rank when you become a full Knight."

"It's my honor to serve."

Gerome smiled, his teeth flashing white, and all I could think about was that poor woman he'd poisoned in the chamber. I looked away and kept my head down, the words I wanted to scream at him locked tight behind a cage of teeth, jaw, and determination to rescue Grey.

The elevator came to a halt, and we stepped out and began moving down the familiar hall. This time the rooms were *not* empty. They were also, as I came to realize, not soundproof. The screams, cries, and whimpers were their own form of agony. Hearing the desperation and the pleading made me feel complicit in their capture—and subsequent torture.

I couldn't look into the rooms, though, for fear of getting lost in the fact that I couldn't save the people suffering there. I didn't have the manpower, the resources, or the opportunity. Which meant they were all going to die.

If I managed to pull this off, the first thing I was going to do was find a way of showing this to the council, and hopefully put a stop to it. The laws were clear about execution—so the fact that it was happening was deplorable. But the idea that the Knights were responsible? It was... catastrophic. They'd *have* to get to the bottom of it.

Unless they knew. Everyone put their faith in Scipio, and these orders came from him. What if everyone already knew—and wasn't doing anything about it? Was on board with it?

Something's wrong with Scipio, my brother's whispered message shouted in the back of my mind. Maybe this was what my brother had been talking about—that Scipio had convinced the council that killing ones was the only way to keep the Tower safe. They would've gone along with it, if he presented enough evidence to support it. But Scipio wasn't supposed to do that; human life was supposed to be protected. That was his function.

I put the worrisome thoughts aside and focused on the task at hand. I could dwell on the problem with Scipio and the council later. Grey was the priority right now.

Gerome led the way to the door and finally came to a stop. "There's something I need to warn you about."

I looked up sharply. The last thing I needed today was a surprise.

He must have misinterpreted my discomfort, because he said, "Nothing to do with the one, I promise you. However, you will have a special guest."

"A guest?" I echoed, puzzled. My parents weren't coming, and the Knights wouldn't want Zoe or anyone else to know what they were doing down here... There was no one else it could be, except for Alex.

That thought would've brought me to a complete and utter stop if we'd been moving. As it was, I was having a difficult time staying upright. The thought of my brother being there, watching... That would mean he knew about it, and—

I forced myself to stop. I was being paranoid. Alex didn't know anything about this. I was sure of it.

"Yes," Gerome said, a small frown gracing his features. "When his schedule allows, he likes to be present for a Squire's first execution. He—"

"Likes to make sure that the right people end up where they belong," a second voice finished smoothly from behind us.

I spun, and for a moment it was all I could do to stop my jaw from slamming to the floor. The figure before me was a man unbent by age. His silvering hair was tied back in a tight knot, his goatee clipped to a careful point. A hooked nose speared out from between bright, glittering, dual-colored eyes—one blue and one brown—which looked down on me with a hint of judgment. He wore a broach in the shape of a silver hand closing around an eye.

Champion Devon Alexander, head of our department. The Champion of Six Bells, and the Defender of the Gate, so named for the feats he had completed during the Tourney the Tower held to select new Champions.

"This is Squire Castell, Knight Commander Nobilis?"

Gerome nodded, seemingly unfazed by the man's arrival. "Squire Liana Castell, Champion Devon. Daughter of Silas and Holly Castell, two of your highest-ranked Knight Commanders."

I was doing everything I could not to start shaking. This was the guest? A council member and one of the most powerful men in the Tower? His bravery knew no ends, if the stories were to be believed.

The man reached out a gloved hand, and before I knew what was happening he had cupped my chin, turning my face this way and that like an apple he was inspecting for bruises. I let it happen without protest. Now, more than ever, I needed to be nine material. One misstep, and Devon would be onto me.

"I can see the resemblance," he said, abruptly releasing my head. "She has Silas's stoicism. She was a twin, was she not?"

"Yes, but third-born."

"*Really?*" Devon's voice was high, almost incredulous. "What happened there?"

"Scipio spared her."

Devon's eyes darted toward me, and for a moment I thought I saw a flash of apprehension, and wondered what it could possibly be. Scipio's will was normally treated as a blessing, not something to fear. For him to react that way... It was really weird and off-putting.

"You must feel very blessed," he said after a moment, and I nodded, keeping my features as expressionless as possible.

"Scipio granted me my life. It's only proper that I use that life to serve him as well as I can."

Devon smiled, a tight-lipped thing, and Gerome coughed softly into his fist. "Shall we?" he asked, activating the door.

It slid open, and I held back to allow both of them through. I moved in behind them and closed the door, sealing us in. My eyes darted to the walls, looking for the light switch and finding it on the other side of the room. All I had to do was go over to it, "accidentally" turn it on, and pray that Grey remembered the Callivax lessons we had been given when we were young.

I looked over to see Gerome and Devon going over a file together—likely Grey's, which would probably need Devon's seal of approval—and took the opportunity, striding quickly to the light switch and turning to lean my back against the wall. My eyes darted around the room to Gerome and Devon. Devon was placing his thumb on Gerome's pad when I applied pressure to the switch and the room lit up.

Grey immediately rose to his feet, and I watched as his eyes slid over Gerome and Devon, finally landing on me.

"What the—"

I hurriedly began signing to Grey as the two other men looked up at the bulbs, still unaware of what had caused them to activate.

P-l-a-y a-l-o-n-g. I signed this using the Callivaxian alphabet, rather than any of the more complicated signs that the Divers were fluent in. All citizens of the Tower received rudimentary training in each department's language, but it was when we were young, and many people forgot them from lack of use. I signed it once, then again, and kept signing it, meeting his gaze and then looking pointedly at my hand down by my thigh. Praying he would understand what I was trying to tell him. Praying that he'd get it before it was too late.

"Liana, you're on the switch!" Gerome suddenly exclaimed.

I jerked with faux surprise and turned around, immediately flipping the switch and killing the lighting.

"I apologize," I said, trying to work just a smidge of mortification into my voice. "I didn't realize. Do you think... Do you think he saw me?"

I turned, keeping my face neutral, but with just a taste of apprehension.

Devon and Gerome both stared at me, and then Gerome gave me a friendly smile. "It won't matter—he'll be dead soon."

"Yeah, about that." I sucked down a deep breath and grounded myself, preparing to spin my fair share of lies. "Sir, I want to collect his body afterward."

Gerome and Devon exchanged baffled looks, and I barreled on. "My father and I were talking about this last night, and he told me that one of his Squires asked him the same thing once. My father, understandably, was confused at the time, of course, because he wasn't sure why. So he asked the Squire, and he said, 'If I kill this man, then it is my responsibility to see that his remains are treated with the utmost respect, for this is the last service he will perform for the Tower, and that is important.'"

"Who was this?" Devon asked, blinking over at Gerome, and Gerome shrugged.

"Not entirely sure, but the story sounds familiar."

I blinked and managed not to smile, but Gerome's acknowledgement had unwittingly given me validation. Too bad the story was a complete lie.

"When my father told me about it, I realized that was how I could cope with what I had to do here today. I want to remember these people for the sacrifice they made."

Gerome looked expectantly at Devon, and the older man stared at me, his eyes hard. "It seems like a reasonable request, but I fear you humanize them too much."

I fear you don't humanize them at all. While Gerome's participation in this was, in the loosest way possible, understandable, Devon's was not. He was a man who could actually change things in the Tower, but decided not to. And that made him worse in my eyes than anyone else involved in this monstrosity.

There was an abrupt movement in the cell, and I looked over to see Grey sitting back down, staring at the glass. I hoped he'd received the message I had risked so much to send. And understood it.

"Disgusting," Devon muttered. "Like an animal, really. Imagine what depravity it must require to become a one."

Gerome nodded, obedient as ever.

"We tried rehabilitating them," Devon said, his lip curling. "We really did. But no matter what we did, they fell, and they fell, and they fell, and they dragged others with them. Good people. Honest people." He shook his head.

Rehabilitating. Yeah, right—from what I had seen and heard coming from those rooms, rehabilitation was anything but. You couldn't get compliance from people by driving needles into their heads and scrambling their brains. They'd be lucky to function at all after something like that, but I doubted they could do more than perform the simplest of tasks. No creativity. No innovation. No thoughts.

Which definitely meant they weren't dragging anyone down with them, as Devon had stated.

I watched as Grey folded his knees to his chest, using him as a visual reminder to hold my tongue and keep from saying anything rude to Devon. Keep from giving us away. I hated being in that room with Devon, and found myself hating him more than I'd ever hated anyone or anything in my life.

"Do it, Squire," Devon said. "Earn your place. Show us why Scipio graced you with that nine."

I swallowed, and Grey looked up. I knew he couldn't see me, but in that moment I met his gaze. Held it. Here sat the man who had saved me. Who had taken a risk on me—and had been repaid with capture, with torture. The wound on his chest was turning yellow with infection, and I could see the tired pain he was in, the hollow hunger in his eyes. I felt my heart swelling. This confirmed all over again that my purpose was not to kill.

"Do it," Devon said again, his voice sharper this time.

My purpose was to save.

I slapped my hand onto the button, feeling a wave of terror flowing through me, seated deep in my bones, convincing me that I had just condemned a man to die. This wasn't supposed to kill him anymore—this would just be steam. *Please let it just be steam.* There was a click, a whirr, and then the gas began pouring into the room.

Grey's eyes grew theatrically wide when he saw the white mist pouring in, and he immediately flattened himself to the ground. He'd gotten my message, I told myself. He was acting.

Devon let out a little chuckle of amusement at that. "Does he think that will help?" he asked into the silence. My hand clenched into a fist as his words crashed into me, and I fought off the urge to hit him.

Noise from the other room was completely cut off, and I watched, clenching my hands behind my back until my nails bit into my skin. Anger shifted to apprehension and fear as I saw the first tendrils of mist slip into Grey's nose, and waited, apprehensive and nervous and certain that Zoe had made a mistake.

Please, I begged. *Please let this work.*

Nothing happened for a second, and then Grey gasped, his breath becoming ragged like he was struggling to inhale. His hand darted to his throat, scrabbling there until he scratched long, pink lines down his skin. I stared in horror as blood began to trickle onto his collarbone and he started to slam himself against the glass. Once, twice, three times he battered himself, eyes wide, before he tipped over and started convulsing on the floor, a slip of saliva spilling from his mouth. He kicked once. Again. Then he was still. There was no way to tell whether Grey was acting or not, which made it all the more terrifying to watch. I kept looking for a sign, but coming up short.

I hit the button to vent the gas two seconds later. I wanted to believe this plan had worked, but if he was acting, it was so realistic, and all I could hear were the voices in my head screaming at me that I had just murdered him. Something had gone wrong. I had just *killed* him. Devon was smiling in grim satisfaction, while Gerome wore the same steely expression as always.

I waited a moment, but that was all I could manage. In my pocket, I wrapped a sweaty hand around the pill case and opened it, letting the pill roll free.

"Sir," I said, my voice finding a strong note and holding it. "May I go inside now?"

"You may," Devon said, lifting a hand and waving it dismissively.

I moved over to the door and opened it. I followed a long, narrow hall down about fifty feet, until it opened up slightly. There was another door at the end of the hall, and I noted it, making an educated guess that it led to where the prisoners were kept when they weren't in the cells or rehabilitation rooms. I turned right to enter the holding area. An exposed tile shower stood outside the cell, as well as a heavy metal table. I walked past it, too, trying not to think about all the degrading things that might have happened in this room.

The first thing I noticed when I opened the door was the smell. The cell was obviously filthy, but the stench just reared up to punch me right in the nostrils. Excrement. Blood. And in the middle of it all was Grey, streaks of pink leading to his hands. He was so still. His eyes were closed. If he was breathing, I couldn't see it.

I knelt, putting a hand on his chest and hoping for a heartbeat.

His chest was still beneath my hand.

No. No! No! No! No!

Keep it together, I ordered myself, palming the pill. *Stick to the plan. He's alive.*

I reached for his chin, pretending to shut his mouth, and as I did so I let the little pill slip past my fingers and between his teeth. It was a small motion, shielded from the audience by my body. Hopefully nobody would suspect a thing.

Swallow, I thought at him, willing him to do so. *Don't let them find your Scipio-damned body with a pill in its mouth.*

As if in answer, I saw his mouth move. It was only a little, but the movement was definitely there. I felt my heart leap into my throat, then forced myself back into the moment. There was no time for emotions. I had to get him out of there. I lifted him, a full dead weight in my arms, and began dragging him from the cell. Luckily, I had been trained in how to move unconscious people without causing too much harm to myself.

"SQUIRE."

Devon's voice was cold as steel as he snapped out the command. I leapt, Grey slipping from my arms to collapse against the floor as I jerked around to stare at the Champion standing in the doorway.

"Sir?"

"Step away," he said, his voice sharp as he yanked his baton out, its tip igniting with blue light. "He's not dead. The gas didn't do its job."

I looked at him, then at Grey. How did he know?

And then I saw the way the Champion's head was tilting. The way he seemed to angle one ear skyward. He hadn't known. Scipio, however, had.

My heart pounded. I hadn't thought of that, but of course Scipio could tell he was alive—his brain activity had never stopped! I couldn't believe I hadn't considered that before. I felt like an idiot—a soon to be imprisoned, tortured, and gassed idiot.

On the floor, Grey sucked in a massive breath, his eyes flying open. He looked around, first at me, then at the advancing councilman. His face, if possible, went even paler. He tried to force a smile, but it came out shaking and lopsided, hardly a smile at all.

"Champion," he said, his voice as cracked as a shattered plate.

"Grey Farmless," Devon answered, rolling his baton between his fingers and stepping into the room, filling it with his presence. "You have been tried by Scipio, and found undeserving. Your punishment is to be expelled from the Tower, immediately, and in a way that offers no return."

Grey scrambled back against the far wall, holding up a hand. "I think there's a mistake," he said. "I—"

"Champion!" I called, my voice loud and strong, and I pointed at Grey's wrist. "His number."

The number, now orange, had risen to a four.

"Scipio's grace," Gerome gasped from the doorway, his eyes wide and filled with awe. "The experience changed him, Champion. He has seen the error in his ways."

Devon's eyes narrowed as he looked at the number. Then, from between clenched teeth, a single word slipped out.

"What."

It wasn't even a question. It was a cold, stark thing, like poison that he was trying to spit from his body.

I stared between the two of them, my heart thudding wildly in my chest. Devon did not lower his weapon, and continued to look at Grey with what could only be described as hunger. Gerome, in contrast, seemed awed, though, his brows drawn up in confusion.

"A malfunction in the system," Devon snarled. "Scipio marked this one for death. His will *must* be carried out. Squire!"

Turning to me, he jabbed a finger toward Grey. "Finish him!"

I hesitated, and then lifted my chin up a notch. "Sir, are you asking me to undermine the will of Scipio?"

"It's a trick."

"How?" I asked, feeling a little reckless. "Sir, Knight Commander Nobilis informed me that six percent of ones can make a recovery— perhaps Citizen Farmless is just a part of that percentile? What other possibility could there be? How could Scipio even be tricked in the first place?"

"I said," Devon hissed, "it's a malfunction. Now do what you came here to do!"

I saw the opportunity, and took a step back, forcing an appalled look on my face. "Scipio malfunctions?" I said, eyes growing theatrically large. Devon froze, and inside, I felt a grim moment of satisfaction.

Talk your way out of that one, Champion Alexander.

Gerome looked concerned now, and stared at Devon with worry bright in his eyes. "Champion, forgive me for saying so, but Scipio does not malfunction when it comes to rankings," he said softly. "To question this is to question the system. To question this is to cause doubt, uncertainty, and panic."

He said the words almost as a child would—full of hesitation, and afraid of having the world as he knew it torn apart.

Devon became very still for a moment, his back to Gerome, his face to me, and all I could see was the flash of intelligence in his eyes, cold, hard, deadly. He straightened himself up and tucked away his baton, smoothing out his uniform.

"Of course, you are right, my dear Knight Commander. I seem to have gotten a bit carried away today. Citizen Farmless, I am glad you have seen the error of your ways. I hope this will help you excel even more in the years to come."

Grey, seemingly running out of energy, slumped down the wall, his eyelids fluttering, and I moved over in a way that I hoped did not seem rushed.

"Sir," I said to Gerome. "He needs medical attention."

Gerome nodded slowly. "Liana, escort the young man out. I will net the Medica to come meet you in the entrance hall. See that he is taken to a proper place of treatment. I want his number stabilized and improved. Scipio spared this one for a reason, and we cannot let him fall again."

I nodded, saluting by tapping my heels together and placing my fist over my heart. "Sir," I said.

Gerome helped me carry Grey to the lift, Devon following a few languid steps behind the entire way. The two men rode the elevator up with me, and I kept my head down and supported Grey's full weight, keeping my mouth shut. Luckily, they were also quiet, for which I was eternally grateful—I didn't want them to start speculating about Grey's miraculous recovery in front of me. My nerves were so frayed that I wasn't sure how much longer I could keep any act or acceptable version of myself in the forefront of my mind.

At the top, we were all greeted by the Medics Gerome had summoned. They took him from me, and I nearly sank to the ground with relief. He was a heavy man—surprisingly so, given his lean form. I smelled now, but I didn't care. I was so close to getting him out of there. Half of me wanted to cheer, but the darker, less optimistic half reminded me not to stumble at the finish line. I was beginning to follow Grey, Gerome by my side, when Devon finally spoke.

"Not you, Nobilis." We all paused. "I need to speak with you. The girl may go."

I didn't need telling twice. I followed the Medica team as they began to hook Grey up to machines, wheeling him along all the while. I had to walk in double time just to keep up, but the farther away from the Citadel I got, the more relieved I felt. I knew we weren't out of danger—in fact, things were going to get even more dangerous. They would discover the valve. It was only a matter of time. But for now, I let myself feel the relief, and even permitted myself to smile as we moved. I had succeeded.

19

Grey was still sleeping after the medicine the Medics gave him, and I had been waiting for him to wake up, my patience dwindling. I felt certain that if we were going to get caught for taking medication that illegally altered our numbers, this was the place it was going to happen. I also felt certain that Devon was tearing apart the cell right now trying to find out what had gone wrong with Grey's execution, and it was only a matter of time before he discovered the valve had been tampered with. We needed to get out of here. Soon.

I rose from the chair I had been sitting in and moved over to him, putting my hand on his shoulder. "Grey?" I whispered, giving him a little shake. He made a noise, but didn't stir, his chest rising and falling in slow, even breaths. "C'mon... we really should get out of here."

"Why?"

The sudden voice in the room caused me to turn, the hair on my arms and neck standing up in alarm.

"You really are quite jumpy for a human, Squire Castell."

It took me a moment, but it suddenly clicked. "Jasper?"

"In the flesh, so to speak."

I looked around at the walls. Of course there was nothing to see, but it was a bit disconcerting just addressing the room. "Are you supposed to be here? I thought you only worked with Dr. Bordeaux."

"The computers in the Medica are networked together, so I go where I please. I like observing the other doctors."

"Don't you already know how to treat the patients?" I asked. "I mean, why would you need to observe?"

"I'm aware of hundreds of thousands of ways to heal a human's body," Jasper informed me gruffly. "But not the mind or heart."

"Do you... care?"

"Of *course* I care," he replied, sounding affronted. "Being a doctor is more than just handing out cures or delivering bad news. We should be making people feel better as well. Giving them comfort. I'm embarrassed to say my algorithms don't really cover that."

Embarrassed? That was... fascinating. I wondered how he had even come to the determination that his skills were lacking. Was it programmed in, or was it *him*? What *was* he?

I considered asking the question, then decided that, even directed at a computer, it felt a little rude. Besides, he was something I wasn't really supposed to know about, and I doubted Dr. Bordeaux would be pleased to know that his experimental program was revealing itself to me.

"Why are you here?" I asked.

"You're worried. I could sense it in your body language, heart rate, eye dilation, and the way you almost jumped out of your skin when I started speaking. What's wrong?"

I frowned. Hesitated, reluctant to ask for help with Grey and put my trust in a computer. "My friend is injured, but we have to go, and I can't seem to wake him up."

"He'll be up soon," Jasper replied. "Two or three minutes more, depending on how good his stamina is."

"Will he be all right to move as soon as he gets up?"

"Yes, but protocol states he has to be checked out by a doctor."

"It's an emergency," I lied. "He needs to go now... His father is sick."

There was a pause. "You're lying to me. You really shouldn't do that—my sensors are very sophisticated."

I shook my head. "Of course, you *would* also be a lie detector."

"In your defense, you are quite good at lying. The only reason I detected it was through a pupillary response in your eyes. I doubt most humans would pick up on that."

"Ah. Great to know that I can at least fool the humans." I paused, and tried to rein in my sarcasm. "Are you going to report me for wanting to take him out of here?"

"I should, but I won't, primarily because you're not acting like someone who wants to hurt him, but someone who wants to keep him safe. Why?"

I twisted around to look at Grey. He shifted slightly, as if he knew we were talking about him, but grew still again, his breathing slow and deep. He looked so peaceful like this, the natural suspicion on his face gone, leaving him looking innocent and young.

"He saved my life," I told Jasper after a moment. "In more ways than one. I owe him."

"I see. What would you call this feeling?"

I looked around the room, giving the walls and ceiling a touch of my incredulity. "I don't know—honor, duty, responsibility, guilt... compassion?"

There was a pause, and I got the impression (don't ask me how) that Jasper was considering what I was saying, weighing each word and trying to understand what it meant, how it felt.

"Thank you," he said, his voice softening some. "It's helpful to me for my own growth."

"You're welcome," I replied, surprised. Then, after a pregnant pause, I asked, "Can I help you with anything else?"

"No, but I can help you, in exchange for your lesson."

"Really?" I took a step forward, instantly excited. "How?"

"I'll mark him as released, and you can walk him right out the front door."

I felt a burst of happiness, but pushed it back, stubbornly refusing to feel it until I had examined all aspects of this with all the suspicion I could muster.

"Doesn't that violate protocol?"

"Not at all! I am a doctor, after all."

"But you're not supposed to be here."

"I'm a prototype computer system, Liana," he said, his elderly voice dripping with good humor. "We have glitches from time to time. I'll delete the memory of doing it, and they'll assume it was just an error."

"Really? So you screw up, and they basically forgive you for screwing up? Must be so nice to be a computer." I was unable to keep the bitterness out of my voice, even though it wasn't fair to Jasper that I was so frustrated. I was just so disgusted with the fact that they would spend more time trying to fix a glitched computer than a one or a two. Or their stupid broken system.

"I don't have anything to compare the experience to," Jasper replied. "But yes, I do enjoy being a computer, if that's what you're asking me. Humans are so... messy. It's fun to watch, but I would never want to be a part of it."

I blinked, and then shook my head. "I'm not sure how I feel about you calling us messy, but since you're not exactly wrong, I'll leave it alone. Just don't start getting too condescending on me yet."

"I will endeavor to remain uncondescending. Your friend is close to waking, so I will leave you now. I hope to see you at your next appointment with Dr. Bordeaux."

I opened my mouth to lie, and then decided against it, and nodded. "Goodbye, Jasper."

"Goodbye, Squire Castell."

Silence filled the room, but it was impossible to tell if he was gone or not. Then again, if he was networked to the computer in this room, was he ever really gone? What was Jasper, really? Was he a new version of Scipio, but on a smaller scale? Was each department getting its own AI? If so, were they linked? Had Scipio heard my conversation as well?

I pushed the thoughts aside, as they were not productive. There was nothing I could do about Jasper right then, except hope he carried through on his promise to help us, and that he wasn't networked to Scipio directly. I turned back to Grey, and noticed him moving more, on the cusp of waking up.

"How are you feeling?" I asked as Grey's eyelids fluttered open. He looked around the small private room in the Medica's clinical treatment ward, and groaned.

"Medica's... too... bright," he managed, and I smiled, looking around the white room and agreeing with him. His fingers reached for the dermal patch on his chest, and I hurried to grab his hand, stopping it just short.

"No touching," I said gently, pulling it back.

"Oh, God... leech patch?"

I gave him a sympathetic look and nodded. His wound had become inflamed and needed to be cleansed, and the leech patch did just that, pulling blood through it and separating out the contaminants of the infection, before returning the clean blood back into his body. The patch itself looked innocuous—like a cotton pad for stemming blood—but it was treated with special medicine designed to draw out infections on one side, and a chemical to neutralize it from causing further infections on the other. The result was a gnarly-looking crystallized formation coming out the other side, stained a dark yellow color, resembling sugar-glass candy, only it was dried. It wasn't pleasant, and was extremely fragile.

"Sad to say, but yes, and it hasn't been too fun to watch."

He relaxed back onto the thin bed and tilted his head toward me, his eyes softening. Searching.

"You saved my life."

My heart skipped a beat, and I looked away. "I just did what any decent person would do," I mumbled.

"No, Liana," he said, grabbing my hand, and I jerked my gaze up to meet his warm brown eyes, wary and afraid. I felt vulnerable, like he could see into the heart of me, and I wasn't sure how comfortable I was with that prospect. "You did something that no one's ever done for me before. Thank you."

I nodded wordlessly, uncertain of what to say. After a moment, I squeezed his strong fingers with mine. "I'm just glad I could," I admitted honestly. Then... "How could you give me your pills like that?"

Grey blinked, his brows furrowing. "How do you know I did?"

"I went to see Roark."

"And he let you in?" I nodded, and Grey whistled. "I'm surprised."

"Well, once I told him that you had been caught and they wanted me to kill you..."

Grey nodded, his face sobering. He raised his hand to look at his indicator and lowered it again. "How long do I have?" he asked, and I shrugged.

"I'm not sure. But we should get out of here as soon as possible. If they figure out our ranks, or how we modified the system to protect you, they will come for us, and I can't protect either of us here. We should get you to Roark."

"You're right," he said, sitting up so fast that I winced, my eyes going to the leech patch over his chest, the crystallized pus barely clinging to the other side. I could barely look at it, not wanting to see it crack open, but luckily it held.

"Lie down," I ordered, once I realized it was still intact. "If we're going to move, I have to take this off you."

I went over to the wall and pressed on the interactive screen, ordering up a set of gloves. I heard the rasp of Grey lying back down in a rustle of sheets as I began slipping them on. Turning, I saw him watching me, his head cocked.

"What?"

"How do you know to do that?" he asked.

"I take a lot of interdepartmental classes. They're a great way of escaping my parents' disappointment in me, of trying to make them see that I was trying..." I trailed off and sighed. "I'm not the biggest fan, but it's better than the alternative."

His face was sympathetic as I crossed back over to him and immediately got to work on the patch. The trick was to lift from the sides and not the corners, and hold it firmly, but not too tightly. I lifted the thing up, tossed it into the waste receptacle, and turned back to the wound, which was still oozing a little but looked much better than before.

"You'll need a dermal bond," I said, pressing gently on the skin just around the wound. The pink goop helped regenerate damaged skin and tissue in a matter of hours, instead of days or weeks. "And no climbing for a few days. Elevators only."

Grey's smile grew, and I looked up to see him watching me intently. "You have really gentle hands," he commented, and a flutter of nervousness shot through me.

I gave him an incredulous look and leaned back, pulling the gloves off and tossing them into the receptacle. *Ignore it*, I told myself, and I did. "I can't get a dermal bond, so hopefully Roark has some."

"Then there is no time to waste."

I looked up at him, and was surprised to see him already getting out of bed, a sheet wrapped low around his hips.

"Don't worry," he said when he saw me staring at the draped fabric. "I'm wearing underwear."

He winked, and I flushed bright red and turned away. "The screen—patients' belongings," I managed, in a weak attempt to tell him where his clothes were. "There."

I pointed to the far corner of the room, but didn't turn to look.

Luckily he got it, and I heard the sound of fabric sliding on skin. He was getting dressed behind me, and it was uncomfortable. Too much, too soon, too fast. I lacked the courage to even respond to his flirtations, because I was too worried about what I said or did. Then again, maybe I had already used up my courage quotient for the day, what with pulling all of that off in front of the Champion.

Thinking about the gaunt man with hungry eyes, so eager to kill Grey that he'd been willing to overlook Grey's raised number, still gave me pause. I was certain that he wasn't done, and that Grey had caught his attention, which meant both of us needed to be very careful now.

Using the elevator to get him back to Cogstown was fine, but if I was going to see him and Roark again, I was going to have to utilize the plunge and lashes more often to keep any future meetings between us as private as possible. Especially when they were supplying me with the medication.

"I'm ready," he said, and I turned to see him waiting, his chest still exposed under his torn shirt.

I wrinkled my nose playfully at him and smiled. "You'll burn those clothes as soon as you're out of them later, right?"

"Look at you," he said dryly. "Already trying to get me out of my clothes."

He winked at me, and I rolled my eyes before offering him some help. "Put your arm over my shoulder and follow my lead," I told him.

"Wait—the Medics have released me already? Nobody came in to give me the after-care speech or a condescending lecture about my rank."

"I'll be more than happy to give you a lecture about your rank, if you want one so badly. I'm pretty sure I've got the important bits memorized."

I had no intention of telling Grey about Jasper, because I still wasn't sure what to make of the computer. It seemed like Jasper had wanted to keep himself a secret, so I opted to respect that. He had offered us his help, after all.

"Hard pass. Not because I think you couldn't do them justice, but because I've pretty much memorized them as well." His arm settled onto my shoulders while my own arms went around his waist.

Together, we moved out the door and into the mostly deserted hallway, and I began guiding him toward the exit. We had been out of the room for barely ten seconds when a woman with bright red curls gathered in a massive explosion of color around her face walked up to us.

"And where do you think you two are going?" she asked.

I put on my best guard face. "I was told he had been released," I said, scrunching up my face in confusion. "I was ordered to help him back home."

"This is the first I'm hearing about it," she said, slipping a pad from her pocket and presumably pulling up the patient list. I watched her face closely, noticing the little line forming between her eyes.

"Apparently... I signed these orders," she said after a moment, her eyes flicking up at us in accusation.

"Oh. Did you forget?"

Grey made a sound in his throat, and I realized he was fighting back a laugh. I ignored him and met the woman's bright green eyes head on, daring her to challenge me on it.

She arched an eyebrow, her eyes narrowing. "No, I didn't. Because I didn't sign these."

"Are you sure?" I pressed. I took a step forward, leaving Grey to stand on his own. "I know it can get quite busy here at times."

"I'm sure," she insisted, slipping the pad back into her pocket. "There's something going on here, and I'm going to find out what."

I held up my wrist and yanked down my sleeve, revealing my nine to her. "Are you doubting my word?" I asked, trying to spear her with my gaze. "Are you doubting the rank and honor bestowed upon me by Scipio?" Beside me, Grey made another noise that sounded suspiciously like laughter, and I resisted the urge to turn back and smack him. If he gave us away...

"I... No!" she exclaimed, suddenly flustered. Her eyes darted around the hall for a second, and she licked her lips.

"And are you denying signing the orders to release this man? Even though you did it right in front of me?"

"I... I did?" Now she looked downright confused, and nervous. I decided to ease up then, and rested a gentle and concerned hand on her shoulder.

"Maybe you need to get looked at," I said softly. "Or get some rest."

"I... well... I have been tired lately," she said hurriedly. "I guess maybe I... I'm sorry, honored Knight. Please carry on."

I inclined my head toward her and began moving Grey to the elevator. The woman followed us for a few steps, but then fell back. A glance behind showed her still watching, though, and I raised my hand and gave her a concerned smile.

She smiled back and turned to leave, and I exhaled slowly.

"You're a good liar," Grey commented softly, and I pressed my lips together, uncertain whether that was how I wanted to be seen by him.

Grey must have noticed my discomfort, because he immediately began to backtrack. "Not that I think you're a bad person—your lies got me out of that horrible place, after all. I mean, not all lies are bad, if you really think about it. There's lying to make someone you care about feel better, lying to save a life, lying to protect someone, lying to..." He fell silent as we got to the elevator platform. "Does it bother you?" he asked, after a pause.

"Lying?" I asked, and he nodded. I considered it while the elevator's voice chided Grey about his number. Then I shook my head. "I've lied all the time, Grey—about who I am, what I am, how I want to be, my feelings toward the Tower and Scipio... My entire life is based on that lie, and I've hated it. But this time... I did the right thing, and if lying was the only way to do it, then I have no regrets."

"None whatsoever?" he asked teasingly.

I frowned, my mind instantly going to the woman Gerome had gassed. At how I had been too late to react and save her, even though I had desperately wanted to. In retrospect, if I had done that, then it might've been me in Grey's place, with no one able to get me out.

"How can you joke at a time like this?" I asked it without derision—I was legitimately curious—and he looked at me, surprise radiating from him. I glanced down at my feet as the elevator began to move. "I mean... you were almost dead. I *thought* you were dead. The Champion was there, and it was so... scary. I mean, how can you even laugh about *anything* right now?"

Grey's face sobered for a second, and he ran a hand down the back of his neck, massaging it. "I mean, I'm *alive*, Liana. When they dragged me into that cell, all I could think about was that my life was over. That was where and how I was going to die—and then suddenly you were there. Your hand flashing some sloppy Callivax, asking me to play along... And the next thing I know, I'm free. I can't be upset or sad or worried. Not right now. I'm too happy that I'm still here, y'know?"

"I'm just glad you're a good actor," I muttered. "I was worried you didn't know Callivax and wouldn't get it. Or that I'd get caught doing it."

Grey shrugged. "I probably would've done the same thing anyway, once I realized it wasn't working. Tried to get away when they transported the dead to the Medica for disposal."

"It wouldn't have worked—Scipio was monitoring your biometrics."

"Yeah, I picked up on that."

We fell into silence after that, navigating through the tunnels and heading for the most direct route to Cogstown. The silence wasn't exactly uncomfortable; it was more due to the state of exhaustion Grey was in. He leaned pretty heavily on me, and his feet were dragging.

"I should've made you eat something," I murmured, trying to keep us both from pitching over.

"You asking me out to dinner, Squire?" he quipped, and in spite of the ache in my shoulders and legs, I smiled.

"Do you ever stop flirting?"

"Not when a pretty girl is escorting me home. Or when she's just saved my life."

"I'm beginning to regret that decision," I replied, my eyes scanning the area above the archways, studying the symbols there and finding the one for the elevator pointing right. That meant it was close.

"Ouch," Grey said dramatically. "What? It's okay for girls to go out with the guy who rescued them, but for guys it's not okay?"

"What?" I asked, coming to a halt in the middle of the hall and giving him an incredulous look. "You cannot, seriously, be asking me out."

He grinned. "Suave, huh?"

"No, more like idiotic. We barely got out of that place, and we were damned lucky we didn't get caught. I'm glad you're happy to be alive, but I'll feel much better when we get to Roark's, get you some food, and hash out a plan for how to proceed, moving forward."

I began to advance again, the elevator within sight now.

"So... you think I'm stupid?" he asked. "That's rough. Most girls don't want to date stupid guys."

I made a very loud and annoyed sound, but couldn't help the smile that crossed my face again. If he were anyone else, it would seem obnoxious, but on him it was charming. Self-deprecating, with a twist of dry humor, but that confident smile. It was admirable, especially considering what he'd had to face.

And a part of me wished I didn't like it as much as I did. Because things were only going to get more dangerous from here on out, and attachments and attractions could become a liability.

Roark looked up from where he was pacing, his eyes wary and alarmed. The shadows under his eyes had darkened, and the creases on his brow seemed to have grown deeper, spreading from cracks into canyons. When he saw Grey, however, his eyes widened and relief shone brightly through.

"Grey," he breathed.

"Hey, old man," Grey said, stepping forward and away from my support.

Roark wrapped him in a fierce hug, tears springing to his eyes. "You damnable fool," the old man groused into Grey's shoulder. "If you ever give away your pills and don't tell me again, I swear I'll...!"

Grey pulled away, grinning. "You can't scare me today, old man. I'm alive."

Roark scowled. "Yeah, well, you're extremely lucky you are—and you owe a debt to Liana."

Grey looked over at me, his eyes steady and calm as they met mine. "I do," he affirmed. The look caused me to feel uncertain, the heavy, confident weight behind his words making me feel exposed somehow. And for some reason, I didn't hate it. It caused my heart to skip a whole sequence of heartbeats before breaking into a step-dance rhythm.

"You're injured," Roark grumbled, taking a step away and studying Grey. "And you're weak. I'm guessing they didn't feed you, did they?"

"They said it was a waste of resources," I replied, and I felt an accompanying burst of anger at the whole thing. "Listen, we need to talk about all this."

"In a minute," Roark replied as he inspected Grey's wound. "Did you stop by the Medica first?"

"We had to," I explained. "Gerome sent us."

"What did they do, and did they give him any medication?"

"Roark, relax," Grey said, his eyes opening and closing sluggishly. "Just a leech patch."

"And Zoponal," I added. Roark nodded, giving me a grateful look, and I knew he was asking in case he had to give Grey any additional medication, so he wouldn't give him something that didn't react well with what was already in his system. "I'm not sure what it is, just heard the Medics say it when they gave it to him. Is he okay?"

"He's going to be fine," Roark replied. "Zoponal is a sedative, a part of it lies dormant in the system until the heart starts beating too quickly, and then it goes to work."

"Zoponal is nice," Grey said, his eyes now mostly shut. Roark looked at him for a second, and then moved over to the table to pick up an injection gun and a vial. He popped the vial in and pressed it against Grey's neck, injecting the medication.

Grey murmured sleepily and then jerked upright, his eyes widening. "Oh, my

God," he said, slumping back. "I wish you hadn't done that."

"Pain is good, boy," Roark chided. "Reminds you you're alive. And I'll give you something for it later, but I wanted you awake enough to talk. They got you good, though."

They? Got him good? I frowned and looked at the wound on Grey's chest, now cleansed of the infection, trying to understand what could've left such a jagged cut. I remembered wondering about it earlier, but assumed he had just scraped it on something when he was caught. Now I was beginning to wonder.

"It was a baton," Roark said, noticing my curiosity. I arched an eyebrow, my hand automatically going to my own baton, when he added, "The tip of one."

I felt a shiver run up my spine at the words. While the batons were intended to deliver a harsh electric shock, the device that generated the electric pulse on the tip was actually quite sharp. Getting scraped by one while it wasn't charged was bad enough, and the scar it could leave was downright awful. But if it were charged? It was the focus point for the entire charge, which was strong enough to stop an organ, depending on where it was pointed. I stared at the red mark, wondering how many similar wounds my parents or Gerome had caused over the years.

"I'm sorry," I said. It was silly to apologize—it wasn't even my fault—but I still felt responsible. I should've known something was going on. I'd lived in the Citadel my entire life, and it felt wrong to have missed the Knights' cruelty this entire time. And now it had hurt a friend of mine—almost killed him. And I had been a part of the system that was allowing it to happen.

Then Roark began rolling up the sleeve on his own right arm, revealing a long white mark. "That's from when they came for my Selka," he said. "I wasn't inclined to let them take her."

He picked up a jar full of pink cream that I recognized as a dermal bond, and began applying it to the skin with a long, thin spatula. "Normally, the dermal bond would heal the flesh and leave no scar, but the electrical charge cauterizes the edges."

"Just like with burns," I said, thinking about my time with the Medica, and a few of the burn victims who had been healed but still had wavy scars where the fire had scorched them.

"Exactly," he said, smearing more pink goop into the wound. "You spent some time on Medica detail."

"I did," I replied. "Interdepartmental classes."

Roark smiled and took a step back, revealing Grey, his face still pale and his jaw clenched. "That stuff always stings," Grey grunted, slowly climbing to his feet. "I'm going to bed."

"No, you're not," Roark said, crinkling his nose. "You're filthy and hungry. Go take a shower and change, and we'll have something to eat waiting for you."

Grey shot an annoyed look at Roark. "And then bed?"

"And then *talk* and then bed."

"Fine," Grey grumbled. "I *guess* a shower and something clean would be wonderful."

He left through a door at the back, and a moment later, I heard the hiss of a shower starting up. Roark moved about the room, pulling down various foodstuffs and arranging them on a plate. Some slices of brown bread, a few grapes, and a leaf of lettuce.

"Bah," he said as he stared down at the motley assortment. "I was never any good as a homemaker."

I moved deeper into the room to take a look, and shrugged. "I'm pretty sure he's not going to care," I commented, and Roark's frown deepened.

"I should go get him something else," he said. "This isn't a meal that really screams *I just cheated death*, you know?"

I snorted. "I'm pretty sure whatever you eat just after that is going to taste amazing. So don't worry about it."

Roark placed the plate on the table with a clunk, and then looked at me. "I haven't told you thank you yet, have I?"

I shifted, uncomfortable, but made the decision not to answer. I really hadn't done this for thanks, and it made me uncomfortable. I shouldn't be thanked for doing the right thing—we should all just... do it. Drawing attention to it meant that I had done something extraordinary, but I hadn't.

"Well, thank you," he said, his eyes studying me. "It means a lot that you'd risk yourself like this."

"The risk isn't over," I pointed out. "And we're all at risk. I mean, what's your plan here? What are we going to do *now*? Sure, you've agreed to give me the pills, but that's just a stopgap, and people are *dying*. The Knights are probably tearing apart that cell to find out if anything went wrong, and guess what—something did go wrong! It's only a matter of time before they figure it out. Hopefully later, but with the number of prisoners I... heard down there... it won't be long. If they catch us, we're going right back into the cell."

Roark went silent, and then dragged a chair out from the table. "Sit," he ordered gently, moving away from it and taking the one on the opposite side. I sat down after a fraction of a second, and then looked at him expectantly.

"It's good that you're thinking of us as a 'we,'" he said, "because at this point we are, and we're all in it together."

"Yes, but to what end? What purpose? What is your ultimate goal here?"

I knew I came off as a bit angry, but the truth was I was frustrated. My patience was almost gone, and I was scared and tired—a dangerous combination that always led to emotional outbursts.

For his part, Roark didn't seem to mind my anger. In fact, his face looked almost vacant, lost in thought, and a bit sad. I leaned forward, concerned, but then his eyes flicked over to me and he began to speak.

"Her name was Selka," he said, and then paused.

I bit back a sigh and leaned back. Why did everyone want to do this kind of storytelling with me, during which I had to participate and ask questions to coax the story forward? Why couldn't anyone just be direct?

"She was my wife," he continued, just as I was about to ask the question, and I quickly closed my mouth, my frustration fading somewhat as I remembered Grey's words. "She wasn't the most beautiful woman, but I didn't marry her for that reason. She was fiery, passionate, ambitious... She started training at fifteen, was accepted into the department as a full Medic by the age of seventeen. I thought she was good enough to be the next Chief Surgeon after Marcus Sage—you know, if the old man ever bothered to die—and everyone else thought so, too. I loved her mind and her heart so very much.

"We'd been married for five years when it happened. She discovered something that changed... everything."

He was silent, and I didn't dare interrupt. Still, the quiet lingered as the elderly man struggled to get through the rest of the story.

"She was working in one of the Water Treatment health stations when some Knights brought in outsiders," he said.

I froze. "Do you mean undocs?" I asked. Undocumented citizens did turn up from time to time, but I hadn't heard of any being found in years. They were almost always the result of a family conceiving, bearing, and hiding a third child to keep it from being killed. Now the net also functioned to transmit biometric data to the Medica, making that impossible. But before, it had been a lot easier to get away with.

Roark shook his head. "No. People living *outside* the Tower. Beyond our walls."

I drew in a sharp breath. "That's not possible. The radiation..." The desert surrounding the Tower was the result of a nuclear detonation some three hundred years ago, during the End. The radiation was toxic, deadly, and kept us confined behind the shielded walls of the Tower. Over the years, the radiation levels had dipped low enough that we could go outside onto the wings for brief periods of time, but the ground was still too radioactive to even attempt to cross without an exposure suit, and even then, it was only a matter of time. The practice wasn't even allowed anymore, now that Scipio was fully operational.

Then again... Scipio relied on the Tower's continued function to keep him alive. He was powered by the hydro-turbines and solar panels. If humans left him, the Tower would fall into disrepair, and he would essentially die.

I looked up at Roark in alarm, and he gave me a withering smile. "How would we even know?" he asked, echoing my thoughts. "Anyway, the girl Selka treated was like nothing she had ever seen. The Knights told her the young woman was an undoc, but there had been procedures performed on her that no doctor of the Tower would ever consider, healing methods that were antiquated and barbaric. Her broken arm left to heal over the course of weeks, causing her pain, holes drilled into her skull for no good reason... and she had a genetic profile completely divergent from that of any of our citizens. She was alien, but just like us also—which means life *does* exist beyond these walls. No matter how many questions my dear Selka asked about the alien, she was met with lies."

I already knew where this story was going: Selka had made a mistake by asking questions, and I identified with her intimately. I didn't say anything, though, knowing the emotional turmoil the story was creating in Roark, and understanding that he needed to be the one to tell it.

"Questions," he said, "are bad for a person's number. Hers, once so high, dipped, then plummeted. She became obsessed with learning more about the outsiders, about how we might survive beyond the Tower. That was when I began developing Paragon, the pill you, Grey, and I are taking. A drug that could bring my wife's number up. Save her from scrutiny. Allow her to find her answers."

I let out a low sigh. "You were too late, weren't you?" I asked.

He nodded, a small movement that filled me with sadness for him. He had to be hurting so much right now. "I was," he said. "Her questions were too dangerous, drew too much attention. They came for her in the night, beating me half to death with their batons when I tried to protect her, and Selka... I never saw her again. I received notice from the Medica that she had died sometime in the night, while I was unconscious on the floor of our bedroom."

I swallowed. "*Who* came for her?"

Roark's eyes glowed with the slow burn of hatred. "Knights. Champion Devon was there, and a few others. I don't remember their names, but I'll never forget their faces."

Devon had been there. That was odd—why would the Champion show up for the collection of a one? It wasn't exactly a job requirement for him anymore, and I'd never heard of him doing fieldwork like chasing down criminals. Not since he'd won the Tourney.

"When Selka first met the girl... who brought the girl in?" I asked, curious.

"Some Knights at first. But she passed Champion Devon and Head Farmer Hart in the hall on her way out."

I frowned. "Head Farmer Hart?" I asked. "Did he come before Plancett?"

"She," he corrected. "And yes. Died... around the same time as Selka, now that I think about it. Damn shame, too, as she ran her department compassionately—accepting anyone, no matter their ranking. I think she would've let ones in there, if the laws had allowed it."

"How'd she die?"

"Hmm. I'm not sure, to be honest. I was pretty torn up over Selka, so I wasn't paying much attention to the world, y'know? Why do you ask?"

I opened my mouth to point out that both she and Selka had died after meeting this girl, so if anyone else who had been in contact with the alien girl had also died, then that would mean conspiracy. The door at the back of the room opened, and Grey walked in wearing clean clothes, his hair damp. I watched him for a second, and then turned back to Roark.

"I'm not sure yet," I said, suddenly changing my mind about bringing it up. No doubt Roark suspected the same thing, but since he didn't volunteer any new information, that meant he was either sitting on it, or he just didn't know. Either way, it didn't change the fact that I was curious enough to look into it on my own later. "I'd need more information, before I said anything."

"Well, let me know if you need anything," Roark said, sliding the plate over to Grey as he sat down. "Either way, it doesn't really matter. What does matter is whether you want in."

"In?" I looked at Grey, who was watching me intently while scratching absently at the now-fresh skin on his chest, which was smooth and whole except for the pink scar cutting across his torso in jagged angles.

"You want to bring her in on this?" Grey asked, arching an eyebrow. "Color me surprised. I never thought I'd see you work with a Knight."

"She's not a Knight anymore," Roark said. "At least, not really. She's with us, which means we tell her everything."

I smiled, pleased that Roark wasn't going to cut me out now that I'd rescued Grey.

"So you guys *do* have a plan?"

"Wait for it," Grey said, and flashed me a wink and that slow, burning smile that made my knees suddenly fill with pudding.

"Grey and I," Roark said, turning a fond smile on the young man, "have been continuing Selka's work, so to speak."

"As in..."

"Wait," Grey said. "It's better to tell her the stages. Stage one is—"

"Recruitment," Roark barked over Grey. "We need *people* in order to make this work, but it can't be too many, or we'll attract attention."

"Luckily, we are in the presence of Roark," Grey said, making a flashy gesture and topping it off with a bow that sent a ripple of pain over his face. "Master doctor and premier drug supplier of the great Tower of Scipio. Offering Paragon to those of low rank who are dissatisfied with life in the Tower, and offering them a way out in exchange for their expertise."

I blinked at him, my eyebrows rising, and then turned back to Roark. "Okay, but why are you doing this? Are you starting a... movement or rebellion or something?" If they were, I wasn't sure I wanted in. I didn't want to start a war in the Tower. Historically, they had never been successful, not to mention the amount of death they caused.

Grey laughed while Roark waved an annoyed hand. "No, nothing so preposterous and foolhardy. And don't listen to Grey; we only have some twenty-nine individuals at this point," he said. "Hardly the *premier* drug supplier."

I tilted my head. "But you can't possibly keep up with the demand of all the people who will need the drug," I said cautiously, thinking about all the levels of the Medica meant for housing the twos, and the prisoners in the Citadel. They all needed help, but there were too many of them. I'd know he was feeding me a lie about his intentions if he said that he could. There was no way.

To my relief, Roark nodded in assent. "I've spent the last decade making as much of the stuff as I can," he admitted. "I was waiting for the day when I could finally enact this plan. We'll find as many as we can, and keep them topped off. Until we can enact phase two."

"Which is?"

Roark smiled, and it was the first peaceful expression I had seen on him. He looked wistfully at his wrinkled hands, his eyes soft. "We leave," he said. "And we don't come back."

Everything stood still. *Leave?* The idea was ludicrous. Just because people had survived somewhere didn't mean we could find that place—or them. It didn't mean there was a surplus of livable land we could claim. We had no means of transportation through the Wastes. No supply of water once we left the proximity of the river, and we'd have to head east, because the river running west was tainted with toxins the Tower dumped into it. No food, because nothing grew in the irradiated desert. Oh yeah... and the desert was irradiated!

But there are people out there, my mind screamed at me, daring me to dream of the possibility of life outside the Tower. There were other people who *had* survived. Could we really just... leave the Tower and live somewhere else? No bloodshed, just those of us who couldn't survive life here, trying to survive and live our own lives?

I drew in a deep breath and looked at both of them. "So your plan is to deal drugs to recruit people, and then leave?" I asked, and they nodded. "I feel like I'm missing a few significant details between the two steps. Not to criticize... but yeah... I'm going to need a little bit more."

Roark let out a rough chuckle and nodded. "That's a fair point, girl. And we're more than happy to fill you in. After you decide whether you want to join us."

Life beyond the Tower. If it was a real possibility, it was incredible. It meant there might be something more than the eight massive walls keeping us inside. It meant there was hope for a new and different life— one in which we could live however we chose, free of being monitored and used as slaves to the great machine. It meant a life in which I wasn't expected to kill anyone.

"I want to join you," I said, making my decision. "I'm not sure if I believe your story entirely, but life outside the Tower is worth the risk."

"Okay, Squire," Roark said, and this time the term didn't seem to have any derision attached to it. It felt more like a nickname than a title. "Welcome to the revolution."

20

Unfortunately for me, being part of a revolution wasn't as exciting as I had thought it would be. Two weeks had gone by since I'd gotten Grey out of the Citadel, and I hadn't seen him *or* Roark since that evening when we had talked.

I understood the reasoning: we needed to keep a low profile, after everything was said and done. I'd just taken Grey out of the Citadel in somewhat suspicious circumstances—and being seen with him again could draw unwanted attention. It was safer to let some time pass, until we were certain that they weren't going to figure out I was the one who had saved him, and not Scipio.

After the Citadel, I grew better at hiding my emotional state from my parents and Gerome—but that didn't change the fact that I was certain we were going to get caught. That *I* was going to get caught. Whether it would be because of the stupid valve Zoe and I had tampered with, or someone in the Medica figuring out that Grey had Paragon in his system, was yet to be known.

As a result of my paranoia, and in an attempt to keep the people I cared about safe, I stopped going to the bi-weekly apprenticeship classes so that I could avoid meeting with Zoe and Eric. I felt bad—Zoe netted me fourteen times on the fourth day—but I needed to keep them away from all this.

After leaving Roark's that night, burning with a need to tell my best friend what had happened, a sinister thought occurred to me: when they discovered the valve and figured out it had been tampered with, Gerome would confront me about what we had really been doing when he'd caught us near the valve. If I carried out the lie, that Zoe was training me, then we would both go down.

This meant two things. First, in order to keep Zoe safe, I would have to confess, and tell everyone I had used Zoe in order to learn about the system so I could break the valve. Second, I had to stay as far away from her as possible, so that if I was caught, they would believe my version of events. After all, if we were still spending time together, then my confession would be less believable, as they would assume I was just trying to cover for my friend.

At least, I hoped those two things would keep her safe—who even knew if there was such a thing as justice anymore. But, with limited options and a smidge of hope, the decision had been made.

My days were still ablaze with routine, though, which helped keep the paranoia at bay. I made sure to keep my room clean —not because I desired tidiness, but because I felt like my parents were watching me constantly, waiting for me to slip up, doubting the nine on my wrist. I worked out, the need to keep in shape more important than ever before, in case they came for me and I needed to fight. And I worked side by side with Gerome, patrolling the halls and floors of the Tower.

Gerome still hadn't brought up what had happened with Grey. And he hadn't even attempted to schedule a time for me to murder some other person. I didn't ask, although part of me wondered if I should. I tried to believe that it hadn't been brought up because of my argument that Grey was just a part of the population who could improve. After all, it would seem like the only reasonable explanation to them, right? Then again, if they didn't agree, it might explain why he was being so cold with me.

I was being paranoid—Gerome was habitually stoic and stone-faced, and there was no reason to question his behavior now, save for what I had done. He probably wasn't acting oddly; he just had a neutral, somewhat bland demeanor. Like always.

If there had been a problem, it would've been mentioned by now. Surely, they'd have found the valve, and learned that most—if not all—of the poison hadn't reached the room. Surely, they'd have figured out that someone had tampered with it, and there was only one reason for anyone to have done so. Gerome had seen Zoe and me down there. Why hadn't he said anything about it?

Because they don't associate it with you, I reminded myself patiently. *They can't. Parts break down all the time, and a nine on the wrist is a massive deterrent for those who follow Scipio loyally, as a nine would never do anything to hurt the Tower or go against Scipio. I'm protected by the very system they created to keep people like me down.*

Basically, it seemed I was enjoying the benefits of being Prim, but without actually being her.

Except when I had to, of course.

———

I stared out the window of my room at a group of first-year Squires practicing baton fighting on their lashes, and turned away from it. I spent as little time at home as possible, but I still needed to come here to change clothes and eat. In a few short months, I would be in my own quarters, provided by Scipio, and I wouldn't have to look at my parents any longer... and see little more than murderers. I also wouldn't be putting them in danger by associating with them—because as angry and horrified as I was, I didn't want them to be at risk of execution, their tens thrown into question by my use of Paragon. They'd probably go in willingly, with how dedicated they were to Scipio.

I looked up at the digital time display over my door, and sighed. It was time to go, before Mom and Dad got up.

Slipping out of the house at five in the morning had become a part of my routine. My parents didn't start getting ready until six, so it was better this way—to be gone before they could check in and see how I was doing. It galled me that all they cared about was my ranking and how it affected them. I could imagine a pair of tens raising a one wouldn't reflect well on their parenting skills.

Then again, I was certain they would rationalize my one status however they wanted to in order to live with themselves, so what did it matter? I didn't care; I just wanted to get out of here.

And by *out*, I meant out of the Tower. Because, as insane as Roark's idea seemed, it was the only hope I had to cling to. It would mean freedom from Scipio and the insanity of the system. A system in which a ten's word was worth its weight in gold, while a four was seen as a disgrace already, propelling them farther and farther down with their negativity and fear. Psychological contamination threats kept the lower-ranked members of the population isolated, when they needed to be together, and loved. Efforts made to help them improve. Made to feel like they were worth something more than just an arbitrary number on their wrist. I couldn't be here anymore, living inside a broken system while I slowly died inside, watching everyone spend the rest of their lives as slaves to Scipio's needs. I spent every waking moment thinking about what could be out there. *Who* could be out there. How they had survived, and what life was like for them now.

Could they see the stars? Were there clouds that formed in the sky like they formed in the greeneries, when the heat from outside caused the water to evaporate, the water in the air growing thicker and thicker until it burst into a gentle rain? Did they have grass? What did it feel like? What did it smell like? What did it *taste* like?

I wanted to believe because I wanted to know. Before Roark and Grey, I would never have believed such hope existed. And now that I had it, I found I was impatient to do something about it. I hoped the next two weeks would go by quicker than the first two had. Because otherwise I was going to break down and make my own way back to Roark's.

I picked a path that would take me through the Lion's Den—the biggest outdoor market, which stood just in front of Greenery 10, the farming floor that jutted out the sides of the Tower like dark wings. They always grew the best food. It was the de facto capital of all the greeneries, as the Head Farmer had always resided here.

I was picking my way through the stalls, when suddenly the hairs on my neck stood on end. The sensation that I was being watched loomed over me. I slowed to a stop, my heart pounding up into my throat. I realized I needed to look busy, and turned toward the stall closest to me, becoming very interested in apples, while furtively searching the crowds for the source of this horrible sensation.

The feeling started to fade as I looked around, finding no sign of anyone watching me. It lessened considerably as I scanned the market, and suddenly, I felt very silly.

You're being paranoid, I told myself, turning away from the stall and heading back down the aisle. If Devon or Gerome knew, they would've come to question me already. Besides, even if they were watching, I hadn't given them anything to be suspicious of. I mean, I had, but I hadn't done anything bad recently, so...

I stopped in the middle of one of the narrow aisles between stalls and breathed deeply, trying to calm my fraying nerves. Truthfully, I was more concerned about the paranoia itself. I kept jumping at shadows, my heart hammering every time I saw a Knight heading toward me, and I barely slept anymore, thanks to the nightmares that seemed to find me. It was not a recipe for emotional stability.

"You okay?" a familiar voice asked, and I looked over to see Grey standing there in his battered green coveralls, his eyes glittering with humor.

I immediately looked around, my instincts screaming at me that something was wrong, and he took a step closer, concern radiating from him.

"Liana?"

"What are you doing here?" I asked, jerking my head around and meeting his eyes. "This greenery is right next to the Citadel! Do you think you should get this close, considering your recent brush with death?"

"Hey, whoa." He raised his hands, as if to soothe a startled animal, and I bit back the urge to growl at him. He wasn't sticking to the plan! Roark had promised me he'd be lying low for a month as well. "I swear, I didn't know you were here. I was just grabbing some breakfast before I ran a few errands."

"Yes, but around the Citadel?" I pointed out, still clinging to the same line of questioning. "I can't get you out of that room again if you get caught. I can't. They haven't even taken me back down there since that day. I—"

"Liana, calm down," he cut in, taking another step closer so that only inches separated us, and placing his hands on my shoulders. "It's okay. I promise. This is accidental, and I'm fine." He tilted his wrist toward me, revealing his blue, glowing nine, and I nodded, but I wasn't any less tense. We were so close to the Citadel, and Knights came through here all the time. What if Gerome or Devon came through here—and, being bachelors, they *would* be through here—and saw us together? I shuddered to think of it.

Grey studied me, and then looked around. "You need a day off," he said after a pause. "When's your shift?"

"This afternoon," I replied. "But we really shouldn't be—"

"You need to talk," he said firmly. "Maybe we shouldn't have just left things like we did. I've been pretty paranoid as well, but at least I've had Roark as my sounding board. You've been all alone with it. What about your friend, the one who helped me?"

I lowered my gaze, a pang jabbing into my heart. "I've been avoiding her... and everyone else. I didn't want to drag them down with me."

Grey frowned, his brows furrowing, and then nodded as if he'd just made a decision that I wasn't yet privy to. "Wait here for a minute," he said, his warm eyes earnest. "I'll be right back."

I opened my mouth to reply, but he disappeared before I could even say anything, leaving me standing there sputtering. I looked around, wondering if anyone had seen us. It was only five thirty in the morning, but the aisles were already packed with people in an array of colors, using their ration cards to secure their breakfast for the day. Again, there was no reason for it, but it felt like I was being watched, and the longer I stood stock still, waiting for Grey, the worse it got.

When he finally arrived, I was a mess of nerves, and he noticed. He shifted the bag he was now carrying to his other hand, grabbed mine with his free one, and began guiding me down one of the aisles. I let him, thinking he would let go of my hand as soon as I started to follow. But to my surprise, he didn't.

We quickly threaded our way out of the Lion's Den and down one of the wide platforms that jutted out from the shell and over open space. As soon as we were free, he slowed. We looked at each other, smiled, and looked away, and I felt a blush forming on my cheeks.

I pushed it back, not letting the nervousness that seemed to form every time Grey was in proximity flood in, and focused on the matter at hand. "We really shouldn't be seen together so soon," I said. "We talked about this. We agreed. You were going to keep a low profile in Cogstown and play the good reformed boy."

"Relax," he replied, releasing my hand. "If anyone asks, they'll probably attribute it to my life-altering near-death experience, and the need I might have to talk about it with someone who was there."

"I'm pretty sure they won't want to ask," I said under my breath, but he smiled, and I realized he had heard me.

"Yeah, probably not. I'm surprised they even let me leave. Why aren't they afraid I'll say something?"

"They probably want you to," I replied bitterly. "It's Scipio's will that you survived, and the Knights' will that you go forth and spread your message of enlightenment, so that others may learn what it is to truly serve."

Grey gave me a crooked smile and reached into his bag to pull out a white blob that I immediately recognized as bao: a steamed bun stuffed with a rich filling.

"It's curry," he warned as I took it from his hand, and I gave him a bored look before taking a big bite. Immediately the taste of spicy potatoes and peas caressed my taste buds in an exquisite combination of flavors.

I chewed and swallowed, barely registering the spice, and looked over at him. "So, you never answered my question. Why are you out of Cogstown?"

"Roark is crap about getting us food," he replied. "He barely knows what time it is. Anyway, we ran out last night. I had half a head of lettuce left for dinner tonight, and it won't last. Believe me, I'm not much of a morning person, but lately..."

He trailed off and looked away, and I recognized the look—it was one that had settled upon my own features lately—slightly glazed and weary. The look of a person not getting enough sleep.

"Same here," I told him, picking at the edges of the bao. "Keep having nightmares... Waking up thinking the Champion is just outside my room, about to press the button and kill me."

Grey's lips quirked up, but his eyes were sad. "This is my fault. If I hadn't—"

"Given me your pills?"

"I was going to say gotten caught. I have no regrets about giving you the pills."

We turned down one of the halls, and he stopped, forcing me to as well. "Liana, are you sure about putting distance between you and your friends? I mean, they must be worried about you."

I thought of Zoe and all the times she'd tried to reach out to me over the net, and shook my head. "Zoe helped me save you, and I know she wants to know what happened, but... if I tell her any more, I'm just dragging her further in. I can protect her better if I put some distance between us. In case I get caught, I can lie. Tell everyone I acted alone."

Grey was silent for a long time. "That is... very noble."

"No, it's not," I blurted out. I didn't think of it that way, and I felt unworthy of the word. I was hurting my best friend in the wake of my decision, and I knew it. It was killing me inside, and every day I had to fight with the selfish part of me that just wanted to go to her and break down. But fear held me in place, the fear of losing her forever, and that was not nobility. "She's my best friend," I finally said, unable to come up with anything better to explain. "I love her."

Grey nodded and looked ahead. "Okay," he said after a few seconds had passed, with the tone of someone changing the subject. "So, in the event that we aren't discovered or caught, your plan is what? Wait until we're ready to go and then grab her and make her come along?"

I bristled at his tone. "Yeah, actually." I gave him a challenging look, daring him to contradict me. "Is it that bad an idea?"

Of course, it wasn't the best idea—it was barely a concept, but without further information on the how and the when of this mysterious exodus, I was working with what I had. But he didn't have to point it out to me in such a condescending tone.

His eyes grew wide and he raised his hand, a sheepish smile on his face. "Not that I can think of; I was just curious. Would it just be her, or would there be anyone else?"

"Well, my brother, obviously. Although..." I sighed, my irritation at Grey fading as it was replaced with another, darker emotion, and I met his curious eyes. "He hasn't netted me in the last few weeks, and I'm nervous for him."

I had thought about him a lot the past few weeks, even tried to net him a few times, but he kept ignoring incoming transmissions. I was worried about him, worried about what he had told me, and hoping that he wasn't digging into information that was going to get him killed.

"He's not a Knight?"

I shook my head, a sad smile slipping over my lips. "No, he transferred to the first department he could." I changed the truth some, because I wanted to keep Alex's position as an Eye a secret. I didn't like doing it, but there was no telling how Grey would react to that bit of information.

Luckily, he didn't push for details, and I relaxed a little, allowing the exchange to flow more naturally. It was nice... and needed. I hadn't been able to let my guard down with anyone for fear of getting caught, but he *knew* all of my crimes already, and he was complicit. I could speak a bit more freely in front of him, without having to worry about someone chiding me for not being a better slave to the Tower. Or worse.

"Okay, so your brother, my personal hero, Zoe, and... your parents?"

My smile dropped almost immediately, and I let out a dry chuckle. "No, my parents were born to serve Scipio. If I didn't know any better, I'd say they were artificially constructed in his image."

Grey grunted, and I looked over at him to see him running a hand through his hair. "Sounds just like my parents. Oh, God, please don't tell me you're my sister or something."

I laughed. I couldn't help it, but the joke was so sudden, his face so theatrically horrified. We laughed together, but all too soon it dwindled down, until we were looking at each other and smiling. I looked away first, my heart starting to flop around wildly, and we moved a few more steps down the hall before he spoke again.

"So, anyone else?"

"What?" I asked, confused. It took me a moment to recall the thread of our conversation. "Oh. Well, we couldn't leave without Eric."

"Eric?" A pause. "Is he... your boyfriend?"

I fought back a laugh at the forced casualness in his voice. But I couldn't help it; I had to tease him. "Relax, Prince Charming. He's a friend, and a good one. He didn't abandon me when my rank started going down."

"Oh? Is he high?"

"An eight," I replied. "But don't hold it against him. He's just... one of those genuinely happy people. I don't think he could think negatively about anything."

"He sounds like a gem," he said flatly.

"He's a good guy," I agreed.

"I'm sure he is. What department is he in?"

"Farms."

"Of *course* he is."

I laughed, as Hand males were generally known for their rugged build and handsomeness, working in the fields all day, which was an attractive quality to a lot of women in the Tower. There were rather distasteful idioms based around the phenomenon as well, whispered from mother to daughter. If Grey had remained a Hand, he'd likely have another thirty pounds of muscle sculpted on his frame. I, for one, was glad he didn't have the extra bulk: muscular guys were not my type at all. I was a mind kind of girl.

We kept walking, eventually ending up in an elevator, the conversation changing to other things: how his recovery was coming along, how Roark was doing, and how the supply of drugs was holding up.

"I think we have enough to last forty people for a month," he said speculatively.

"Okay, but what's the end goal? I mean... are there forty people who are willing to come with us? Will they help us get parts and things to build some sort of..." I paused, trying to think of an appropriate word or phrase to describe what I wanted. "Transportation device?"

"Actually..." Grey smiled and stepped off the elevator. I looked up and realized we had gone up twenty floors to level 105. How we had gotten there was a mystery to me; I'd been focused on him and the way my heart had skipped a beat when I saw his flash of jealousy, and on feeling special—for the first time in a very long time. "Kind of, yeah. We aren't sure how, yet, but that's kind of the idea."

"What are we doing up here?" I asked, abruptly changing the conversation. It was a little rude, but we were clearly not heading for Cogstown, given that we were a hundred floors above it. I had assumed we were walking back there together, and I was reminded again that we shouldn't be seen together like this. It had been too long, and we were being too intimate. If we were being watched or had been spotted...

"We're going to see someone who can help us, and definitely needs our help. She lives in Smallsville."

Smallsville was the nickname for Greenery 11, while their opposite greenery, number 12, was called Biggins. Don't ask me why. Both greeneries specialized in most of the corn and wheat production in the Tower. Eric's family had lived in Smallsville since the beginning of the Tower, although his father was a former Knight.

It was also one of the most beautiful places in the Tower. It was a sprawling mess of green, and the air was humid and soft and smelled of wet grass. Water and dirt stretched out for what seemed like an eternity. Light from the sun shone brightly through the solar windows that encased the greeneries, just like it did outside. It provided the crops with precious energy without making them wither away and die from the extreme heat. Artificial wind generators—designed for pollination—blew periodically, making the long stalks of wheat sway and lean this way and that.

As we stepped inside, I immediately smiled, closing my eyes and absorbing the feel of the sun and the smell of the earth. I felt comforted and infinitely serene in that one moment. I couldn't help it—I *loved* it.

"Let's get this done quickly," Grey muttered, breaking my tranquility. I looked over to see him stalking forward with his hands shoved into his pockets.

I hurried after him along a dirt path, suddenly remembering that this had been his floor, growing up. Before he had been dropped.

"Is it hard for you?" I asked. "Being back here."

He let out a humorless laugh. "Let's just say I'd rather get out of here before anyone recognizes me," he replied.

He led me through a field of corn, which swayed to and fro in the artificial winds that danced across the floor. We followed a narrow path that twisted through it in slow-moving curves and bends; I knew from Eric that these paths were established randomly, so the corn could be tested to make sure it fit standards. As we pushed through, I stared at Grey's back. His dark blond hair fluttered in the breeze, his head tilting back and forth as he surveyed his surroundings. His hands, however, had clenched into tight fists at his sides.

"So," I said, thinking to distract him, "tell me more about this woman we're here to reach out to."

He blinked, looking back at me as if he'd forgotten I was there. "Her name is Sarah Thrace," he said. "She's just fallen to the rank of three. Her parents aren't speaking to her, although she's old enough to be independent, so they can't drop her."

He spoke the last few words with such vehemence in his voice that I felt myself pale slightly. Then I reached out and grabbed his wrist, pulling him to a stop. He turned, his face dark with anger, and met my gaze.

"Hey," I said, slipping my hands around his. "I'm sorry that your parents did that to you. It wasn't right, and it's sad that they never took the chance to know and love the real you. I know how awful that feels, and I'm sorry."

Grey's anger faded as I spoke, and after a moment his features had relaxed some. "Thanks," he said, and the word, though softly spoken, carried the weight of a significant amount of gratitude.

My chest began to feel warm, like something from within was glowing, as he stared into my eyes. A lock of his hair had fallen across his brown eyes, and I had the urge to reach up and push it aside, but I refrained, content just to stare at him. The kiss we'd shared reared up in my mind, and all I could think was that I wanted him to kiss me again.

This time he broke away, craning his neck to look over my head. I followed his gaze and saw a woman in a green uniform making her way down the path behind us, and within seconds he was pulling me behind him via our still-conjoined hands.

We walked at a fast pace for a minute, and then he slowed a bit, allowing me to come out of the half-jog I'd had to break into to keep up with his longer legs.

"So... how do we find her?" I asked, panting slightly from the sudden exertion.

He shrugged. "I have an address and a picture. We'll pay her a visit, and see if we can't... help each other out."

I frowned. Roark had told me that they offered Paragon to those who had fallen, and since then, I had found myself wondering *how* he did it. I wasn't sure if I was comfortable with the idea of using Paragon as a bargaining chip, and now it seemed I was going to be able to see and judge firsthand the method the two men were using to gain support. I wanted to get out of here, but there were lines I would never cross, and one of them would be using Paragon to extort labor.

We made our way through the fields and eventually came to a ladder that led down into the residential floors, through a hole cut in the floor itself, tucked against the shell. Normally, all residential areas had open access so that members of the Tower could come and go easily. Hands, however, had different concerns, and had sealed off the common entrances to their residential areas years ago, so that all visitors had to come into their homes via the greeneries. It was something about wanting everyone to appreciate the beauty and importance of the floors, and it was why people thought Hands were arrogant and self-serving (not Tower-serving).

The ladder dropped us onto a catwalk that ran down the length of a long pipe that fed water into the fields. We followed it as it turned abruptly at a wall, and led down thirty feet in a series of steep ramps that rattled and squeaked as we descended them.

We stopped to stand to one side as a group of Farmers moved past us heading the opposite way. A few cast curious eyes in our direction, and I managed a neutral face coupled with an occasional nod. Once they were gone, we started moving again, following the catwalk until it dead-ended against a wall, a hole cut into the steel. Markings etched on the side gave us the basic layout, and I was surprised when Grey studied it for a second, then looked sad.

"Her quarters are just down a few levels."

Eric had told me about this: when Hands started to drop in rank, they were assigned worse and worse quarters, pushing them closer to the greenery (and exit, to be dropped from the department). I understood Grey's sadness now; he knew she was close to losing her home, and he understood exactly what that felt like.

"Let's go," I said, swinging onto the ladder and moving down.

The hall we wound up in was brightly lit, with built-in shelves housing UV lights and plants, diagrams of root systems on screens below each one. The screens were interactive, so that Hands could brush up on plant care whenever they needed to. I stared—I had been to this floor several times, but I still loved seeing the simple dedication to life that existed here.

Everything about the residential floors and the greenery above made me feel safe. In a place where suspicion and fear ruled, it was so odd that Hands lived in perfect trust with each other, and as a result, their doors were always open. Neighbors often went in and out of each other's homes to chat or share dinner. Outside of a greenery, Hands were just as suspicious as the rest of us, but in here, they believed in each other. I loved that they had that sense of community. The Knights tried, with practice Tourneys and sparring competitions, but no one ever just came over to spend time with each other. No one actively visited their neighbors. Just a few words in the hall, and then it was over: bonding—done.

Grey, it seemed, felt differently. He stalked over to an elevator terminal and practically punched the call button, glaring at it until the platform slid out of the wall. We stepped onto it, and began to drop.

We heard the noises the moment we stepped out a few seconds later, two floors down.

"I don't care who you are," a male voice spat from down the hall. "The second your number fell to a three, you should have been removed from crop-rotation management. I've filed a complaint with Boss Lynx, and he says that he is personally looking into the matter."

A soft voice began to protest, but a meaty thud cut it off. I heard coughing, then retching. I surged forward, intimately familiar with that sequence of noises after combat training with the Knights.

"Liana!" Grey whispered as I moved forward, but I ignored it.

Turning the corner, I saw two young men cornering a young woman against the wall. She was doubled over and clutching at her stomach. Looking up at them with pleading eyes.

"Daniel," she said. "Stewart. I know you. Have known you for years. Why are you doing this?"

One of the men, a tall brute with a shock of dark hair, grimaced.

"We can't withstand a three in our midst," he said in a soft voice. "You put us all at risk. You have to go."

Anger began to burn, and I clenched my hand into a fist, drawing even closer. I was still unnoticed by either of them, and glad of it. In the mood I suddenly found myself in, I wasn't exactly going to give them a fair fight.

And I didn't feel bad about that, considering they weren't playing fair either.

The woman straightened, although it clearly cost her, and winced, looking directly at the men.

"This is my home," she said. "My place. My calling. You can't just take that from me because my number—"

The man drew his hand back and slapped her right across the face. Her words cut off instantly as her head was flung to one side, her hands clenching at her sides.

"I won't leave," she stated, and I caught the sight of tears welling in her eyes. "Not even Boss Lynx can make me."

I wanted to applaud the woman's bravery, but there wasn't enough time. The men's expressions were dark as they leaned closer, and I broke into a run.

I had the satisfaction of seeing one of them look up at me, his eyes widening in surprise, and then I slammed my shoulder into his chest, throwing him back into his companion. They stumbled back, the force of my impact too much for their balance, and I stood over them, baton out.

"That's damned well enough," I informed them coldly, making eye contact with both of them.

The two men looked up at me, their eyes wide with alarm and surprise... and almost immediately became contrite. I watched it happen, but didn't react, especially when that contrition morphed into alarm at the glittering nine on my wrist. A quick glance at theirs revealed a purple six and an orange five, respectively, and my anger tightened. If anyone should understand the plight of having a low number, it should be them.

"Knight," the one I had initially hit said, as he slowly picked himself off the ground. "We were simply attempting to—"

"Beat a woman in front of her own home?" I asked, my voice dripping with cool anger. It wasn't even an act. I was about three seconds from showing them both just how much a stun baton could hurt. "Yes, I can see that."

"She's a three," one of them muttered.

"Yes," I said. "And you're a five. He's a six. Neither of you is that much more devoted to Scipio than she is, are you? I wonder how long it'll be before I'm down here to escort *you* to the Medica. I think a trip to the

Citadel might be more appropriate, considering you're doing work that is not for your department. Clearly you hit your heads and can't recall that dealing with lower-ranking citizens is for Knights or Medics only."

The two paled and looked nervously at their numbers.

"Hurt a defenseless unarmed person again," I snapped, my anger a terrible thing, "and I will come down here personally to make your lives a living hell."

The two scurried away down the hall in the opposite direction, and I turned back to see Grey standing right behind me. He was grinning openly.

"That," he said as he came up beside me, "was very well done."

I flushed. "They made me angry," I said. "They had no right to beat on her just because her rank was lower."

"I agree. Personally, I think you could have roughed them up more."

I probably should have, but it was too late now. I made my way to where the woman had collapsed upon her knees, trying to catch her breath. I looked at Grey, my eyes seeking confirmation that this was the three we were looking for, and he nodded.

"Sarah?" I said. "Sarah Thrace?"

Wet eyes brimming with frustrated tears met mine, and she pulled in a shuddering breath.

"I don't want to go," she said. "Not to another floor. Not to the Medica. I can't."

I put a hand on her shoulder, and found her shaking. Disgust roiled up inside of me at a system that would reduce anyone to this when they had tried, but weren't quite good enough. I felt even worse when I thought about the fact that their torture ended with a trip to the first few floors of the Citadel. The entire system was rigged, just by its existence. It was impossible for a human (except for Eric) to be positive and dedicated to a system that just treated them like a statistic. And even his good nature only got him so far! To be a nine or a ten, you had to lose that bit of happiness, and fade away. Like giving over all free will to Scipio. What sort of choice was that? Death or blind obedience? I wasn't sure there was a difference.

"I'm not going to take you to the Medica," I said.

Her eyes widened as she looked between Grey and myself. "But you said..."

I shrugged. "I know what I said. Is there somewhere we can talk? Somewhere private?"

She nodded slowly, gesturing over one shoulder at the door a few feet away. "We can use my home," she said, rising to her feet. "Come in."

21

Sarah's apartment was a wash of green. Every corner, shelf, table, and flat surface available contained a potted plant, and every plant had a precise label containing the scientific name, the date the specimen had been planted, and how much water and light it needed. There were so many plants that they had begun to spread out into her living space, and she scurried about, lifting a few off the couch and dusting away any lingering dirt before motioning for us to sit.

"Sorry it's a bit of a mess, Knight," she said, her face flushed. She glanced at Grey with a puzzled expression, then set about dusting off a nearby chair and settling down in it, looking at us with cautious eyes.

I smiled, and then frowned as she closed the door to the hall using a button on her seat, almost as an afterthought. She was closing herself off from her own people—the ones who should be helping her, not hurting her—and I could see why. It was wrong of them to come down on her for her rank. The woman seemed amiable and pleasant, if a bit disorganized. I wondered what had made Scipio turn on her.

"Thank you, Citizen Thrace," I said.

"Please, call me Sarah." She looked down and away, a sad smile on her lips. "Thank you so much for earlier."

Grey sat down on the couch beside me and regarded the woman with a clinical eye. Sarah's own eyes darted between him and myself, and I let out a little cough. Then Grey started talking, a broad smile blossoming on his face and reaching all the way to his eyes.

"Sarah," he said, "it's a pleasure to meet you. My name is Grey Farmless."

"Yes," she said, exhaling slightly and shifting nervously. "I've heard about you. It was quite extreme what your parents did. Most of the floor felt that way."

Grey's eyes widened in surprise, but he hid it quickly, leaning back on the couch and placing an arm across the armrest. "I appreciate the sentiment. Thank you." I could he tell he didn't quite believe it, but we were here to convince her to do something big, and he wasn't letting his emotional issues get in the way. Which impressed me. "Anyway, we aren't here to talk about me. We're here to talk about you and your ranking. You were an eight last month. What happened?"

I blinked, new questions that I felt stupid for not having already asked him forming in my mind: How did he know that? How had he known how to find her, and how did he know about her rank history? Supposedly, the only people who had access to our rank histories were the Eyes. How did he know who she was, what her rank was, and what skills she brought to the table? Could Grey or Roark hack into Scipio? I made a mental note to ask Grey about this as soon as possible.

Sarah's expression had grown distant. She looked toward the rows of plants lining the entryway.

"My husband died," she said quietly. "An accident. Mechanical failure, they said."

Grey's expression softened, and he leaned forward. "I'm so sorry," he said. "It can be overwhelming to lose someone you care about. It's entirely understandable that you would feel pressured afterward."

She let out a little laugh, dragging a hand through her hair. "I just can't stop thinking," she said, the words bursting from her mouth in a sudden rush, "that if Scipio can see into all our hearts, and controls all the machines of the Tower, he should have seen this coming. And if he did... why couldn't he save Darren?"

I touched my cheek, remembering what had happened when I had asked the same question of my mother, and looked at Sarah. Grief was radiating from her, overwhelming and thick, and I felt her sadness—and empathized with it, despite the fact that it was putting her in danger. You couldn't ask questions like that about Scipio, not without being labeled a dissident. And I couldn't quite agree with her that Scipio was to blame for this. Oh, he was to blame for a lot that was wrong with the Tower, but not that. Scipio wasn't infallible—he couldn't predict *everything* that would happen, which meant he couldn't keep people from dying.

But he could use their deaths as an excuse to kick those left behind while they were down.

Grey nodded but stayed silent, allowing the woman to continue. I watched him, trying to understand what he was looking for.

"My number dropped," she explained. "After those thoughts started, it tipped down to a seven. It felt like Scipio was judging me for doubting him. Like my faith wasn't enough. And I just kept slipping and slipping. Soon my friends would no longer come over and visit me. Now my parents won't speak to me. The two men in the hall? They were my friends. I thought they'd stick by me no matter what. But once I hit three..."

Her voice broke, and she covered her mouth with her hand, tears leaking from her eyes while her shoulders shook. I couldn't bear seeing it without doing anything to comfort her and immediately moved to her side, placing my hand on her back and rubbing her shoulders.

"It's okay," I soothed. "It's going to be okay." I looked over at Grey, who gave me a small nod in confirmation, and I exhaled.

"No, it won't," the woman keened softly. She reached down, caught the hem of her shirt between two hands, and pulled it up. I gasped, a hand going to my mouth as she revealed a landscape of bruises. A mottled, angry series of marks. No wonder she'd still been able to talk in the hall—her composure in the face of violence had developed after being on the tail end of several beatings. I took in the sight of her bruises, and then gently moved her hand away, pulling her shirt back down for her. She continued her silent sobbing, and I comforted her. Grey stood up and went into her kitchen, returning with a cup of tea in his hands, having used the hot-water spigot and a tea bag he must have found in there.

She accepted it, the cup and liquid sloshing as her hand shook, and she took a moment to collect herself by taking a deep sip.

"Sarah," Grey started after she'd calmed down some, "it's not your fault that things have gotten this way, and it's not your fault that the people in this department are treating you so poorly."

Sarah's eyes filled with tears again, but she nodded, staring down at her hands clasped around the teacup in her lap.

Grey took a deep breath and glanced at me. "Sarah, what would you say if I told you there was a solution?" he asked.

She froze, then turned slowly, gazing up at Grey with apprehensive eyes. I also looked at him, and saw him draw out a small blue pill from his pocket. He wasn't showing it to her, though; he was just holding it. I stared. Paragon was white. What was that drug? What was he planning to do with it? I was more curious than alarmed—I felt strongly that Grey would never hurt someone in anything other than self-defense.

"I would say," Sarah said, carefully, "that I have an appointment to receive Medica treatment in two weeks, assuming I can keep my number up. And if I can't... well... then I'll be in the Medica a lot sooner, I suppose."

"Do you want that?" I blurted out. Grey shot me a warning look, but I plowed forward. "Medica treatment changes you," I said. "It makes you into someone you aren't. It improves your number, yes, but at a steep cost. Is that truly what you want?"

I wanted to know her answer—it was important to me. Grey and Roark shared my opinion on Medica treatment, but not everyone did. I suspected it was critical to know her opinion in order to determine who would be best suited to us and what we planned to do. After all, she didn't know the truth of Scipio, but if she was willing to let the Medica dope her so that she could continue being of service to the Tower, then she wasn't ready to come with us. It was ultimately her decision to make —just like it was mine, Roark's, and Grey's.

Sarah gave me a weary look. "Is this a test?" she asked.

I kept my face serious, but kind. "No."

She looked at Grey, her expression suspicious. "I lost my husband," she said. "I have been beaten by my neighbors, cast away by my friends and family. It's been hell to endure, and the person I've become now... I don't know... I miss my husband, but if I want to avoid the Citadel, I suppose I have to do what Medica says."

I felt my stomach sink, but was unsurprised by her answer. I looked around at the plants, the disorderly display of life and love that surrounded me, and imagined this place in three weeks. Swept clean, everything tidy and neat, and Sarah with those blank, drugged eyes. A version of her that didn't feel anything. A version that *didn't* miss her husband. Just like I had been a version of myself who alienated my friends and couldn't even remember what I had done with my family.

I sat back, wondering how I could reach her. After a moment, I exhaled. "My sister died when I was young," I said, and she looked up at me. "I... I didn't react well, but I wasn't in the ranking system then. If I had been, I'm pretty sure my parents would have had to arrest me as well, because I didn't think Scipio was good. I thought he was responsible."

"You were a child," she said, her hand reaching out to squeeze mine before pulling away. "You were in pain. I'm a three—a monster. I wouldn't expect you to understand."

I looked down at the nine on my wrist and smiled ruefully. I forgot, sometimes, what I appeared to be now. But I could almost see the one beneath the nine, red and struggling to get free. But one or nine, it didn't matter. I was still me: funny, sarcastic, tough, and smart. It might not be enough for Scipio, but it was good enough for Grey, Roark, Zoe, Eric, and my brother. And really, they were the only people whose opinions I cared about.

"Your name is Sarah Thrace," I said. "You love plants and life, and your passion for your husband drove you to desolation when you lost him. You take beatings without threatening retribution, instead seeking only to make peace. You are kind, and filled with grace and perseverance." I paused and met her eyes, and even though she had dried them not too long ago, they were now wet again. She balled her hands into shaking fists, staring at me with something between ire and hunger. I didn't stop talking.

"You are sad," I said, voice heavy with compassion. "True. But you deserve to be sad. You should be allowed to feel how you feel, without having it ruin your life as well. But we don't live in a place that accounts for all of that, unfortunately, and they want to take you and make you into something... diminished. If you go to the Medica, that wonderful human will be lost to us forever. But we can help stop that from happening, if you want us to."

Sarah let out a sharp laugh. "What can you possibly do?" she asked, voice throbbing with bitterness. "A dropped Farmer and a Knight? What power can you have?"

It was Grey who answered her. He looked into her eyes and reached into his pocket. This time, it was a white pill that he drew out, along with an accompanying bottle. Paragon. My brows bunched together as I watched him, and I carefully noted that the blue pill had disappeared. This just added to my mental list of questions for him after we were done here.

"This medicine," he said, "can help you avoid Medica treatment, if that's what you want."

The room fell deadly silent while Sarah stared at the pill and bottle.

"What is it?" she asked carefully.

"It's a pill that will change your number," Grey said. "For the better."

She didn't reach for the bottle, but stared at it with hot eyes.

"This isn't legal, is it?" she asked, her eyes darting over to mine, and I shook my head. Lying to her would just insult her intelligence, and she deserved to know what she would be getting into. She licked her lips nervously and looked back at the pills. "What would you want for them?"

I looked at Grey, curious to hear his answer. He leaned in slightly, offering up the bottle and pill. "Nothing now," he said. "And we would never ask you to hurt anyone or do anything to hurt the Tower." He hesitated, and leaned forward. "But we might need your expertise eventually, and when that happens, I hope that you'll be willing to help us. Though we won't force you to."

I paused a heartbeat, and then relaxed, relieved at how he was handling this. He wasn't strong-arming her into helping us, and I was eternally grateful. If he had, I might've had something to say about it, but for now, I was just happy that Grey and Roark were more interested in giving people a choice. Yet it was risky. What would they do if someone refused? I made another mental note to ask Grey, and then re-focused on Sarah, feeling the need to add something to what Grey was trying to say.

"You are so much more than a rank," I added on impulse, and her gaze snapped to me. "You are a person. Let yourself be who you are, Sarah."

She continued to stare at me, and then her hand darted out and snatched the bottle and pill, pulling them close to her breast. She clutched them there, breathing hard, like someone standing at the edge of a precipice.

"How do I know I can trust you?" she asked.

I smiled at her. This question, at least, was easy.

"Because we'd be in just as much trouble as you for giving them to you. Just like we have to trust that you won't tell *anyone* about these pills. Not a soul."

She bit her lip. Her feet twisted and fidgeted, tapping against the dusty floor. She unclenched her right hand, revealing the single pill.

"Guess I'll trust you then," she finally murmured, and then popped it into her mouth.

I watched her as she swallowed, then looked at us with a blank expression.

"Is it, uh..." she said, sweat breaking out across her face. "Is it a fast change? When will I feel it?"

Grey laughed. "You won't feel it," he said. "And yes, it's a fast change. Look at your wrist, Sarah."

She did so, and her jaw dropped. Where a three had sat moments before, the display now read five. I was also impressed—apparently Roark was improving upon them.

"That's not possible," she gasped. "I can't just... It can't..."

"It can," Grey reassured her. "And it did."

"A five?" she breathed, prodding at her number like it was some kind of illusion. "But I don't feel any different."

I grinned at her. "That's the point," I said. "The Medica's way is to strip away those traits that make you special and unique. Ours is to keep you who you are, but give you the freedom to be that person without worrying about what it means to your rank."

"The first pill I gave you is a diluted version of the pill," Grey added. "As are the pills in the bottle. We can get your number higher, but we want to stabilize you somewhere believable first, and then bring you up. In a month, I'll return here with more."

Grey went on to explain exactly how to take the pills, and once he was done, for the first time since we had met her, a smile had spread across her lips. It was still fighting with sadness, but the gratitude was there, shining behind her glistening eyes. "Thank you," she whispered, reaching out to take my hand. "Thank you for letting me grieve, and thank you for helping me. This is... incredible."

"I know," I replied, squeezing her hand. "And I want you to know that you're not alone. If you need anything, net me—just a short message. Say something like..." I looked over at Grey, who was looking at me with confusion and no small amount of alarm, but I ignored it. She'd need someone to talk to, and it was better to keep her close than not. This was no small favor to ask on our part, no small task for her. She'd need reassurance. She'd need a friend.

"I'll say the bread you ordered is ready?" she asked, and I nodded.

"It'll work. It might take me a while to get to you, so don't panic. If it's an emergency, say that my cakes are ready, all right?"

She nodded, her gaze returning to the pills in her hand. "If anyone asks?"

"Say nothing. Net me. Okay?"

Sarah met my gaze and nodded, the tremulous smile returning.

The joy on her face continued to be bittersweet, but I understood. She'd just lost her husband. At least she'd be safe now, and that was all that mattered. The thought made me feel good. Really good. Amazingly good, like I could climb the shell of the Tower with my bare hands. This was what being a Knight should be. It was about helping, not hurting, the people inside the Tower. This was what I wanted more than anything: to bring people hope.

She rose up out of her chair, and Grey and I followed suit, expecting her to ask us to leave. To my surprise, she wrapped me in her arms, drawing me into a tight hug. She smelled of dirt and tears and euphoria, and I hugged her tightly back, uncaring that we were practically strangers.

"Thank you," she murmured in my ear.

It was the best hug I'd ever had, I was sad to admit. But it was better late than never.

She moved on to Grey, and I saw his eyes widen as she pinned him to her, his arms wrapping around her all the same. Over Sarah's shoulder, our eyes met. Something moved between us, then. A gentleness. It was impossible to describe, but I thought I felt my heart moving a little faster.

There was hope, now, and my life burned a little bit more brightly than before. I was grateful that he'd invited me along.

Grey was quiet as we left the residential area and headed back into the Greenery, and after a while, I couldn't help but ask, "So how badly did I do in there?"

He looked over at me, the corner of his mouth quirking up, and he shook his head. "No more than I did."

I cocked my head. "Isn't this... what you do?"

"Sarah's the first I've recruited. Roark recruited the ones we currently have, and he was the person who convinced me."

"How many recruits are there?"

Grey shrugged. "I know a few of them from deliveries, but there are a few that Roark doesn't even want me to know about. People in high-level positions who need to be protected."

I blinked, sensing the answer to one of the questions that had formed during our exchange with Sarah. "Like an Eye who feeds you information on potential recruits?"

He looked sharply over at me, and after a moment of intense scrutiny, he smiled. "I knew you were smart, but that was some pretty good intuition. I'm impressed."

"And also not answering the question," I teased with a smile, though inside I was pleased that he had noticed that about me, and that he seemed to like it. I wanted him to like it.

"You're like a dog with a bone," he said with a laugh. "And yes—but I don't know who it is. For everyone's safety."

"For everyone's safety?"

"He's an Eye, Liana. If he feels he's threatened, he can find ways to hurt us. You know the Eyes are the second greatest force in the Tower, not for their physical prowess, but for their intellectual ability. He could gas us in our sleep or create fake arrests for us—whatever he wants. That's why Roark doesn't tell me. It's just safer."

"So... he's a man?" Grey gave me a sharp look, and I smirked at him for a second, before resetting my face to serious and asking, "And Roark trusts him?"

Grey continued to walk, but he grew silent, his face pensive. "He does—as much as anyone can trust an Eye. He showed Roark the flaw in the nets that Paragon takes advantage of, to help Roark strengthen it, so... he is trustworthy. To a point."

"Wait—if he showed Roark the flaw, then..."

"Exactly. He's been in on this from the beginning. But beyond that, I don't know who he is."

I took a deep breath, and accepted his answer. I, however, was thinking about it, and there was only one question on my mind: *What if it's Alex?* I could let it go for now, but as soon as I got a chance, I was going to try to pry the name out of Roark.

"So what about that blue pill you had earlier?" I asked.

Grey smiled, a short huff of air escaping him in a semblance of a laugh. "You really do *not* miss a beat, do you?"

"Let's just say you won't catch me resting on my laurels," I replied archly, and this time he did laugh. I liked watching him laugh; he looked lighter, free of the burdens that seemed to collect when we were together.

"The pill... is in case the interview does not go well." At my sharp glance, he added, "It's not poison, if that's what you're thinking. It's more of a contingency plan."

I raised an eyebrow. "Yeah, that answer isn't going to fly," I announced, picking up my speed and pivoting so that I could turn and block his path. "You've already told me this much. Why not tell me the rest?"

He stopped, our bodies inches apart, and grinned. "I'll tell you if you kiss me," he teased, and if possible, my eyebrow rose even higher.

"You really expect me to fall for that again?"

Grey's eyes were warm and filling with something I didn't quite recognize or understand... something that made it feel like all of the oxygen had suddenly deserted the area, and caused my heart to pound heavily inside my chest.

"*Expect*, no. Hope?"

My heart continued to palpitate as he seemed to sway closer, his eyes dropping to my lips. Nervous, I licked them, and his gaze grew even heavier, causing my skin to tingle and my face to blaze with heat.

"I..." I faltered, unable to find any words. I wasn't sure what to do or say... I could barely remember what we had been talking about before, and it had just occurred five seconds ago.

"Screw it," Grey said, and his arm shot out, his hand settling on the small of my back and drawing me in. I let him pull me tightly to his chest, his gaze never leaving my face, and felt my heart start skipping beats, the rhythm erratic and frantic.

He lowered his head, and I felt my chin tip up, eager for the feel of his mouth on mine. Our lips pressed together, and mine parted slightly, unwittingly giving him access to my mouth, which he immediately took advantage of. His other hand cupped the back of my head, holding it in place while he kissed me with a sizzling intensity that made my toes curl, made me want to melt into him.

I was lost in the kiss, drowning in it, until I heard a rustle of something coming from the stalks of wheat, and jerked away. From the corner of my eye, I saw something dark move, and I turned toward it, the paranoia from earlier flooding back in.

"Who was that?" I asked, my hand automatically going for my baton.

Grey, looking a bit alarmed himself, shook his head. "Who was what?" he asked, confused.

I looked over at him to see that he was genuinely baffled as to why I had broken the kiss, and frowned. I could've sworn I'd seen something, but... just like the market earlier, there was nothing there. The wheat swayed in the wind, but there were no sounds of anyone running away. There was nothing.

"I'm sorry," I said after a second, removing my hand from my baton. "I thought I..." I trailed off and met his gaze, suddenly nervous.

"It's okay," he said after a moment, his disappointment deteriorating. "This isn't the best place to be caught making out."

I chuckled, and then slipped my hand into his when he offered it, unable to keep a goofy smile from splitting my face wide open. I'd have to hide it later, but for now... for now I wanted to be Liana and not a nine. I wanted to be a girl, walking with a boy who had just kissed her.

And that's what I allowed myself to be.

22

Once Grey and I parted ways, I didn't expect to hear from him until the rest of the month we had originally agreed upon had passed, but to my surprise, he netted me only a few days later. My head buzzed as the neural net activated to notify me of the communication attempt, and when a quick check of my wrist showed me Grey's name, I immediately accepted it.

"Hey," I said, stepping off to the side to let the busier traffic on the platform running around the inside of the shell move past me unimpeded. "What's up?"

I was worried; his contacting me this way could mean a myriad of things, and my imagination was already starting to spin out of control, the foremost theme being Devon Alexander kicking down the door to Roark's little home, and Grey trying to warn me.

Hey. You got some free time?

Some of the alarm faded, because his voice came out calm and self-assured. "Yeah, why?"

I found another potential new friend. I was wondering if you wanted to come with me.

I smiled, instantly pleased. "You want me to come with you?"

Yeah. You were really good before. I figured I could use some of your finesse.

My smile grew even wider as my heart skipped a beat. Finesse. I liked that.

I considered his question, and found that I did want to join him. I'd enjoyed helping Sarah. It had filled me with a sense of happiness that had stuck with me the last few days. "I'd love to come with you. Where do you want me to meet you?"

An hour later, I found Grey waiting outside of one of the Water Treatment closets buried deep on Level 17. It was several floors away from Zoe's house, but I kept a careful eye out for her, not wanting to make contact unless I absolutely had to. Grey smiled when he spotted me and moved to meet me halfway.

"Hey," I said, stopping just short of him.

"Hey." He ran a hand through his hair and rocked back on his heels. "You ready?"

I grinned. "Obviously. Who's the target?"

"Silvan Wash," Grey replied. "Our friend in the Eyes notified us that he hit a three."

"Did he tell you why?"

Grey shook his head. "No, the process isn't very detailed, actually. With Sarah and Silvan both, we just got their names, housing designations, and ranks before they fell. Roark says that's all the Eye will give."

"How does he pick them? I mean... you are recruiting people who can help the cause, so to speak."

It was a question I had meant to ask a few days ago, but after that sizzling kiss, and the subsequent awkwardness afterward... well, it slipped my mind, to say the least.

"I asked Roark the same thing after Sarah. He's looking for those who have achieved high enough rankings in their fields to be useful to us, but then dropped rapidly. It usually indicates emotional distress, apparently, which is a window of opportunity in which we can offer them another way."

"Won't they climb back up once whatever it is has passed?"

He chuckled and glanced over at me, meeting my gaze almost immediately, because I was staring. Like an idiot. I looked away.

"Roark says his IT friend told him that once you drop to a four, it's almost impossible to get back up again without receiving Medica services."

Somehow, the news did not surprise me at all. If anything, it made me feel sad. It was just another layer to a system I had already known was rigged.

We made our way to the house of the man in question. Like with every home in Water Treatment, the doorway was flush with the wall, with a white call button in the middle of it.

As soon as Grey pressed it to alert Silvan that he had guests, a slat on the upper side of the door peeled aside to reveal two large blue eyes, topped by thinning eyebrows and covered with wire-framed glasses. He peered at us for a second, and then shut the slat.

Grey and I exchanged looks, before the door slid open with a hiss and Silvan stepped out. He was older than I'd expected, fine wrinkles lining his mouth and forehead. His eyes were wary, the dark circles underneath giving him a vaguely rodent-like look. He grew rigid when he took in my uniform.

"Knight," he said, offering a polite bow, shaved scalp gleaming in the bright light of the hall. He looked over, spotted Grey, and made a similar gesture. "Honored nine," he said reverently.

That didn't bode well, but then again, it could be an act. Maybe he was trying to ingratiate himself to us to start making a case against taking him to the Medica. It happened from time to time, but the Knights almost never chose to defer treatment to a later date. Besides, I wasn't a Knight yet.

"I'm still a Squire, sir," I said carefully, offering him a brief smile. "May we come in for a few minutes? There is something we want to discuss with you."

Silvan nodded without even a moment of hesitation and stepped out of our way to allow us inside. I entered, and found that the interior was covered with papers and sketches of mechanical equipment. He closed the door behind us before pushing past and starting to sweep his papers away into a pile. I grabbed one that he missed, taking a look, and saw what appeared to be a valve.

I turned it back and forth, trying to make heads or tails of it, hoping to identify its purpose, or even what it was.

"Please," he said, voice shaking as he shoved the disheveled stack of paper into a drawer on the other side of the room. "Make yourselves at home. What is mine is yours."

I hesitated, his anxious manner making me feel a bout of anxiety as well. I smiled at him in a way I hoped would make the man relax some. I had to wonder whether he was anxious about us being here because he thought like Sarah had thought: that we were from the Medica, coming to take him away for treatment. I couldn't help but feel sorry for the man. His clothes were rumpled, and he tugged nervously at his sleeves as I assessed him. He looked like he hadn't slept in days.

"Relax, Citizen Wash," I told him. "We're just here to talk. May I call you Silvan?"

His head bobbed, and he brought both hands to his temples and craned his neck. "I am honored to speak with ones such as yourselves," he said, voice soft. "I am not worthy. My tainted name should not come from the lips of someone like you."

He muttered something about a beverage and then moved off to the kitchen, leaving the two of us standing in his living room, looking around.

"I don't like this," Grey muttered.

"Me neither, but it could be that he's just terrified we're going to take him away to the Medica. Or, he's trying to act like a 'model' citizen of the Tower, but is petrified of being discovered to be something other than that. Let's give him the benefit of the doubt, okay?"

"Okay... Just... be careful with this one," he said.

"I will," I replied, just as Silvan returned with a tray of teacups, before moving back into the kitchen area, his hands flying to and fro. A kettle appeared, and was put on.

"Would you like some tea?" he asked, looking back at us with hopeful eyes. "I have chamomile and... oh... more chamomile."

His expression fell in disappointment at not having a variety of teas to offer, and I quickly spoke up. "Chamomile is my favorite," I told him. "I would love to have some."

Silvan's face brightened, and he nodded eagerly, drawing out a bag of tea before looking at Grey. "And you?"

"Chamomile is fine," Grey said apprehensively. I gave him another look, mouthing the word *relax* to him. His nerves were going to make Silvan jumpier, which was literally the opposite of what I had asked him.

Silvan busied himself for a moment, then froze, staring at his hands. I heard him mutter a curse as he spun back to face us.

"Please, have a seat," he said, gesturing almost frantically to the pile of cushions on the floor. "I'm so sorry, I should have offered that first. Your comfort is paramount while you are in my unworthy home."

"Silvan, there is nothing about your home that is unworthy," I said as Grey and I both sat, finding a position around a small floor table that sat in the middle. It might have been messy with papers when we had first walked in, but with them gone, the room was surprisingly tidy and neat. I doubted that the Praetor's own home was half as clean as this place.

Silvan's face darkened as he regarded his home, but then he shook his head, hurried forward, and seated himself on the cushions on the other side of the small table.

"So," he said. "How can I help you? Are you here to take me to the Medica?"

I looked at Grey, noting the tremor in Silvan's voice, and the look Grey gave me as he replied to Silvan's question was tentative. Cautious.

"Not exactly, but we do want to talk to you about your number."

Silvan looked up, a flash of anger flickering through his eyes. "I figured," he said. "It fell to a three just recently. I already have my Medica appointment for tomorrow, so don't worry."

There was a bitterness there, and that helped me relax some. What we were seeing was an act, I was sure of it. It was all a matter of making him comfortable, and he'd reveal himself.

"You don't seem... very eager to engage in treatment," I said, and Silvan looked at me, swallowing hard.

"I am," he replied, his eyes darting between Grey and me before he lowered them again. "I obviously want to be of service to the Tower, and to Scipio."

He looked at his number, as if expecting the three to have changed during his five-second speech, and when it didn't, he sighed. "I would do anything to get my number back up," he said.

"Anything?" I asked softly. "Surely your ranking isn't so bad. What caused the fall?"

"You mean how did I lose Scipio's favor? I was an eight, on my way to nine, before all of this happened, and it was jealousy that brought me down, I'm afraid. The head of my work group brought in a new Diver, and he's just... better than me. Faster and smarter and..." He trailed off, looking blankly ahead with unseeing eyes. "I'd been working for thirty years to get to where I was, and just like that, someone else walked in and could do it all as easy as breathing. It's not fair."

"You're not wrong," I said. Grey's knee nudged against mine in warning, but Silvan just thrust out his number. The three glowed upon his wrist, and he stared down at it with loathing in his eyes.

"I've given my entire life to the Tower," he muttered. "And it has deemed me unworthy. I have to fix it."

I hated seeing people like this, because it was all too familiar. Sarah's sadness, Silvan's anger—all reactions to a system willing to toss them aside for not serving in the way the Tower demanded. Even worse, the only way out was one that involved losing all sense of self in order to be met with approval.

"Does your anger make you want to do harm to the Tower?" Grey asked, leaning forward, and I looked at him, curious. What made him ask *that* question?

Silvan's eyes widened, and he made a frantic gesture. "Of course not," he said indignantly. "I may not be desirable to Scipio any longer, but this is my home. Besides, where else could I go, really? No, my only chance at redemption is Medica treatment."

"How does the thought of receiving treatment make you feel?" I asked.

Silvan looked around the room, considering the question, and then shrugged. "I don't honestly know. On the one hand, of course you don't want to have to take the Medica's fix. The people who take it are... distant and cold. But on the other hand... if there is a deficiency within me, I have to do something to fix it. I don't want to be a burden. I want to serve."

The poor, brainwashed man. Of course he blamed himself—I had too, more often than not, during my descent. He didn't want Medica treatment, not really. But he didn't think there were other options.

I opened my mouth to tell him about the pill, but was forestalled by Grey. "I understand your drive," he said. "And it seems your loyalty to the Tower is still strong, despite all of your troubles. Is that a correct assessment?"

Silvan's head whipped up and down so aggressively that I thought it might come flying off. I frowned at Grey. That question was loaded, especially to someone with the rank of three. They wouldn't deny that assessment, because if they did they'd be admitting their own dissidence against the system. And I was a Knight; no way he was going to admit that he didn't agree in front of me. Unless we explained who we were and what we had to offer.

"The Tower has rarely had a more loyal servant," Silvan reassured us amicably, his hands shaking. Behind him in the open kitchen, the kettle began to whistle softly, steam burbling up through the top and fogging the glass side of a pipe that ran across the ceiling.

"I can see that," Grey said. "So you are completely resigned to Medica treatment?"

A pause, followed by a nod. "I will keep my appointment," he said. "I will be better. I promise."

The direction the conversation had taken left me with a bad taste in my mouth. Grey wasn't telling this man he had another option. Instead, he was treating him like a sycophant. That was wrong, though—he needed to tell him what was going on.

"What if there were another way?" I asked.

"Liana," Grey said in a hushed voice, placing a hand on my shoulder in warning. But I shrugged it off, angry that he wouldn't even discuss the option. I understood that the man was saying all the wrong things, but I was certain he was saying them for all the right reasons. He was trying to protect himself.

I looked at Silvan, taking in the shadows under his eyes and the fear within them. He didn't want this. Who could ever *want* Medica treatment?

"You don't need to go to the Medica," I told him.

Silvan stiffened. His mouth locked shut, his eyes flashing. I moved forward to place my hand over his, the words flowing freely from my mouth now.

"*Liana!*" Grey said again, trying to stop me. "I'm sorry, sir; she's speaking out of turn. She doesn't—"

"There is a pill," I cut in, ignoring Grey and getting Silvan's eyes back on me. "It is called Paragon. It can change your number without touching your mind. It allows you to continue being yourself."

He stared up at me, his eyes confused and uncomprehending. "Are you trying to trick me?" he asked.

I wasn't surprised by his questions. If it were me in his shoes, I would ask the same thing, or something along those lines. Then again, I had to dig to find out. Here we were, offering him an option that seemed highly suspicious. I didn't blame him for not immediately jumping at it.

"I understand why you would think so, but no. We're not trying to trick you; we're trying to help you."

"I'm confused," Silvan said after a few seconds of contemplation. "Who are you, and why are you here? Are you with the Medica? Is this a new line of medication that they are testing out?"

"It is," Grey said smoothly, moving to stand up. "But I'm sorry; you don't qualify for it."

I gave him a sharp look, and his answering one was thunderous—

enough to give me pause. Biting my lower lip, I started to get up as well, but Silvan's question brought me up short.

"Why not?"

I looked at Grey and saw him frozen, alarm radiating from his features. "I..."

Silvan craned his head up so he could look at Grey from his seated position. "As I said, I'm loyal to the Tower. Shouldn't the Medica wish to give a devoted Diver the chance to improve?" His eyes shifted over to me, burning with intelligence. "Or is it illegal? Is that how you got your nines?"

A moment's hesitation held me in place, but once I realized it was too late to backpedal, I nodded. Grey, looking uncomfortable, glanced at me.

On the stove, the kettle had begun to boil in earnest, the soft whistle from earlier now a howling shriek that reverberated around the little room. Silvan stood automatically, brushing past me on his way to the kitchen, and grabbed the kettle to move it. The screaming died to a burbling hiccup.

"I know this is a lot to take in," I said. "I was just like you. I fell to a three and sought Medica treatment... but it was awful. I couldn't remember anything from when I was on the drugs. Any sense of myself was gone. But with Paragon, I can be me. I don't have to change in order to please the Tower. And we'd like for you to—"

With a feral howl, Silvan spun, the kettle coming around in a crushing blow toward my head. The motion came so fast that for a second I sat frozen, watching the container filled with boiling water arcing toward me. I was just starting to move, already knowing it was too late, when Grey darted over me, his hand pushing me even farther to the side as he flowed past me to take my place as target.

There was a loud noise as the kettle connected with the flesh of his forearm, a soft, sizzling sound, then a gasp of pain. I could smell something burning as Grey brought a fist around and jabbed Silvan in the side, under the ribs. Silvan wheezed as the air was forced from his lungs by the force of the blow, and Grey used his other arm to sweep the kettle out of his hand, sending it flying into the cushions. Silvan staggered back and then lunged at Grey, his hands coming up and together, fingers outstretched as if to throttle him, and I finally got my feet under me.

I threw myself at him, using my legs to push off, and caught him around the waist in a full tackle. We both went down, my shoulder radiating pain as I bounced off him and onto the floor. I rolled onto my side, gasping at the pain, and suddenly fingers were grabbing my hair, gripping me painfully. I reached up with my hands, trying to pry Silvan's fingers out of my hair, but he jerked my head up and slammed it down on the ground, so hard that my vision grayed out as pain exploded from the back of my skull.

"You're dissidents!" he screamed. "You threaten the safety and well-being of the Tower!"

He slammed my head down again, and the pain grew even worse. My thoughts were sluggish and disjointed, and I couldn't remember how my hands worked so I could stop him. My head was jerked up again, but then I felt some of my hair tear free as the hold on me was viciously jerked away.

I blacked out for a second, and came to with my hands on my head, trying to contain the agonizing pain radiating from the impact site. I looked up to see Grey's fist flashing up and back down, connecting with Silvan's face. Once, twice, a third... It was too much, but Grey didn't show any sign of stopping.

"Grey," I managed, my voice coming out a hoarse croak. His fist fell again, and I cleared my throat and started to pick myself up. "*Grey.*"

His fist froze in midair, and he turned back to me, the fury on his face morphing into complete concern. He let go of Silvan's uniform, dropping the dazed man to the ground, and crossed over to me, his hands going around my waist to help me right myself. I leaned heavily on him, more heavily than I cared to think about, and looked at where Silvan lay groaning on the floor.

"What happened?" I asked, still groggy. "Why did he—"

"Later," Grey said, his hand going into his pocket, and I looked down to see violent-looking red and brown flesh on his forearm where the kettle had caught him.

"Your arm," I managed, and he looked down at it, his face an angry mask.

"Later," he repeated, withdrawing a blue pill that looked identical to the one he had been playing with in Sarah's quarters. I remembered asking him about it, and realized I'd never gotten an answer. He helped me over to lean against a wall, then moved to where Silvan was slowly getting onto his hands and knees.

"What are you going to do?" I asked as he approached the man, and then watched as he put his arm around his neck—in a move I recognized instantly. "Oh." I looked away while Grey cut off the blood flow to Silvan's head—not because I couldn't watch, but because the room was spinning. I closed my eyes and focused on my breathing and not losing the contents of my stomach, and heard Silvan's brief moment of struggle before he blacked out.

When I peeled my eyelids back, fighting through the sudden tightness in my skull from the bright light of the room, I saw Grey rolling the man over and checking his pulse. After a moment, he pushed the pill past Silvan's slightly opened lips and forced him to swallow by massaging his neck. Finished, he straightened and immediately moved to gather me up, before guiding us both out of the quarters.

Back in the main hall, we both hobbled down the long tunnel, moving as inconspicuously as possible. Luckily, we were in the middle of a shift, so everyone else was either working or resting, which meant there weren't too many people to mark our passing. Silvan would be up shortly, screaming his head off about the two nines who had offered him an illegal pill that would make him a nine as well.

It made me wonder how Roark had dealt with these situations, and the blue pill flashed through my mind. It did something to them; I was now very sure of it, but I wasn't sure what.

"What was that you gave him?" I asked, once we had put a little distance behind us. Grey's arm around my waist tightened, and he looked at me sharply. I realized he was still angry. "What?"

"You should've followed my lead," he said, turning me down a side hall.

I looked away from him, my brows coming together as I thought about his statement. "Wait... Are you saying this is *my* fault? Because if so, then to hell with you. Your questions weren't exactly designed for him to give an honest answer without fear of incrimination."

"Liana, he was ready for Medica treatment, and—"

"He's been brainwashed," I interjected angrily, not liking the patronizing quality of his voice.

To his credit, he bit back what he was going to say, a muscle in his jaw ticking. Then he sighed, reaching up with his free hand and raking it through his hair, wincing when the burned flesh on his forearm pulled.

"I know he has," he said. "But he was also cutting his own flesh. Didn't you notice the scars on his arms?"

I thought back, fighting through the pain in my head. "No. I didn't. I mean... how do you even know he was cutting himself?"

Grey's face tightened, and he looked down. "I learned how to recognize it through Roark. It's a bigger problem in the Tower than many would think. He had multiple scars, some old and white, others pink and fresh, too regular and patterned to be accidental."

"Oh. But shouldn't that mean we should be helping him?"

"We are, by leaving him. The best place for him to go is the Medica. They have doctors to help with situations like this. Unlike you and I, Silvan can and will recover. But not if we recruit him." He held his arm up to look at the burn. "We couldn't take care of his emotional and mental well-being."

I felt a surge of guilt and looked away. "I'm sorry," I said as we rounded another corner. "I didn't realize."

We walked in silence for a minute, and then he said, "You shouldn't apologize. You were worried about him. That's not a terrible thing. It just didn't work out this time."

"Well, the next time, I'll just follow your lead."

"Next time?" I heard the surprise in his voice and turned to see a small smile playing on his lips. "You really want to do this again?"

"Well, yeah." Stopping, I looked up at him. "I mean, we're about fifty-fifty right now in our success rate, but... I really like doing it. I like trying.

It's the first time that I've ever felt like I made a positive change in some-one's life."

"And you didn't when you rescued me? Because that was a pretty positive thing for me."

I smiled at his teasing tone and began moving again. "Fine, that too," I replied dryly, rolling my eyes theatrically. "So you still never answered my questions, and I've had to ask them twice. Last time you offered me the answer for a kiss, and never delivered. It's turning into a pattern with you."

He laughed loudly, his eyes brightening, and just like that, some of my bumps and bruises faded away into inexplicable happiness. I waited for him to stop laughing, my own smile riding my lips, and he looked over at me, his eyes warm and appreciative.

"You're right, of course. Quite rude of me."

"Quite," I agreed primly. "So, are you going to make me ask a third time?"

"Not at all," he said, pressing the button to open a door that separated Cogstown from Water Treatment. The door beeped, and Grey withdrew his silver chip, holding it up to the scanner. The door hummed then, and then a digitally rendered woman's voice spoke.

"This isn't a regular entrance," it chimed brightly. "I suggest you bugger off, before I get mad."

I smiled in response and watched Grey roll his eyes and kick the base of the thick metal door three times. "Your mother is bad with tools," he announced, and there was a little beep.

"Password accepted. All right, I'm opening the door, but I don't want to see your face ever again," it said, just as cheerfully as before. The door slid open, and I stepped through.

"Man, when did the automatic voices get personalities?" I joked, and Grey shrugged.

"Well, each department has its own voices programmed for their talking equipment," he said, referring to any system that could communi-cate verbally with the citizens of the Tower. "The elevators are all networked together, so they use the same voice. But, yeah, they do have a little bit more personality lately. Maybe someone is experimenting, trying to give the voices more flavor. Anyway, in answer to your question, the pill I gave him was something Roark calls Spero. It's supposed to make him forget the last hour or so."

"So he won't remember us at all?"

"He shouldn't," he replied, and I exhaled. I had trusted that the pill was designed for a specific purpose to keep us safe, and I was glad that I had been right. Even still... he would probably wake up knowing he had been attacked, but with no memory of why. That was going to draw attention. I was suddenly glad we had gotten out of there as quickly as we had.

"Good. Now tell me we're going to Roark to get looked at."

"We are. We're going to have to—"

Whatever else he was going to say was lost when I caught a flash of movement from the corner of my eye.

I jerked back, my baton coming out in a flash of blue as I stepped around Grey, pushing him behind me. He made a surprised sound, but I ignored it, my eyes darting around the dark hall and tangle of pipes, searching. The hall appeared calm and empty, but I could've sworn I'd seen something. Just like in the cornfields, and just like in the Lion's Den.

"Liana? Should I ask if this is going to become a pattern with you?"

I heard the teasing quality in his voice, but immediately felt defensive. "I could've sworn I saw someone," I announced, spinning around.

Grey's eyes darted over my shoulder, looking behind me, but of course there was nothing to see. After a pause, he nodded. "I believe you," he said, meeting my gaze. "But whoever it is isn't here anymore. Let's just get to Roark's as fast as we can. He can check us out, maybe tell us what to do—okay?"

I eyed him, uncertain whether he was being completely honest about believing me. After a moment, though, I realized I didn't care if he believed me; if he wanted to get out of here, that was fine by me. Because my instincts were screaming at me to run as fast as possible.

"You have a minor concussion."

Roark spoke the words in a matter-of-fact tone as he looked at me from across the table in his little home. Behind him, Grey stood stone-faced, not quite meeting my gaze, but definitely waiting to gauge my reaction.

"I know what I saw," I said, perhaps a bit stubbornly. "It's happened to me more than once, Roark. Maybe twice is a coincidence, but three times is not."

"There's no evidence to support your claim, girl. You're the only one who saw anything, and this latest time, you had just suffered a fairly violent altercation. Safe to say it can account for what you thought you saw."

"Okay, but after we met Sarah I could've sworn I saw something in the cornfields."

"That particular crop is famous for freaking out non-Hands," Grey said quietly. "The artificial wind confuses them, given the lack of real wind inside the Tower. A few get sick from time to time."

I glanced over the white tufts of Roark's head at Grey, and gave him a withering glance. His comment hurt, and just confirmed my suspicions that he was saying what he thought he had to, to get me to follow him.

"But at the Lion's Den," I said, unwilling to let it go, "I could've sworn I felt like someone was watching me, and it wasn't a good feeling." I was right about this—we needed to be on our guard. I just had to convince them. "Guys, I am not the type of girl who freaks out over nothing or imagines things. I thought maybe I was stressed at first, but now... I think I'm being followed."

Grey and Roark exchanged looks, and then looked back at me. I met their gazes head on, and it wasn't easy. My skull still ached from Silvan's attack a little over an hour ago, my center of gravity slightly off sync with my eyes, making them tend to wander. Which made looking at them so hard, yet so necessary. I curled my fingers into the pain, partially to fight through it, but also to keep my hands from seeking out and gingerly probing the area where my hair had been ripped out. Roark had given me a band to help reduce the swelling and ease the pain, and, while it did help, I sort of wished he was more liberal with the pain medication.

"All right," Roark said, and I jolted back into reality. I had gotten a little lost in my aches and pains, and it took me a few seconds to remember what we had been talking about. I needed to get it together. "Tell you what I'll do—I have a contact who might be able to find out if someone has been following you. I'll reach out to him, and see if he can help us. Will that make you feel better?"

I nodded, some of my frayed nerves settling somewhat.

"Good," Roark continued, turning his attention back to the salve he was making for Grey's arm. "But if it comes back that you aren't being followed, I expect you to drop all of this. Agreed?"

"Yes," I said tartly. "Agreed." But even as I spoke the words, I realized I didn't care what he found out—I knew what I knew. And if I wanted to do something about it, then I was just going to have to figure it out myself.

A couple hours later, with Roark's tentative approval, I left and made my way back up to Smallsville, intent on seeing if I could find anything in the corn that would help prove my theory. I had an evening shift with Gerome starting at five tonight, but until then, I had nothing but time.

Even as I made my way up there, I recognized how flawed the idea was. Hands moved in, out, and all over the fields dozens of times throughout the day, and distinguishing one Tower-made boot from another was impossible, save for size and possibly weight. And even then, finding the exact spot where Grey and I had been standing would be almost impossible, as there was no way of distinguishing where on the trail we had been. But I had to do something. It was better than waiting or going home, so here I was.

The light, crisp wind that washed over me as I stepped out onto the floor was refreshing, but I couldn't let myself relax, not with the knowledge that, even now, someone could be watching me. That paranoia only grew worse as I was greeted by workers on the path, all of them eager or excited to see a nine. It was all I could do not to shove my hands in my pockets, put my head down, and stalk forward, but I had to be careful. A nine wouldn't act that way.

So I forced a blank expression onto my face and perfected my "yes, I see you" nod as I strolled down the path cut through the corn. I moved at a sedate pace, picking my way down the long path and eyeing each bend speculatively, trying to decide which spot was the one where Grey had kissed me.

That kiss. We hadn't talked about it—or at least not seriously—since we'd met up earlier today. Maybe we would've, had Silvan not attacked us, but after Grey's reaction to my assertion that I was being followed, as well as the lack of serious conversation about said kiss, I was left feeling confused and slightly hurt. I had no idea how he felt about me—I just knew that he had kissed me twice.

I hadn't stopped thinking about it, though, and maybe I was being too much of a 'girl' about it, but I really wanted to know what he wanted. Was he just being a guy and seeing what I would let him get away with, or did he genuinely like me? Did I like him?

I was angry with him right now, that much was certain, but did I like him? That was a bit harder to classify. Because on the one hand, yes, I thought I did. On the other, more realistic hand, I had tried to arrest him, then saved his life, then been saved by him, and... I felt pretty justified in saying that the mixture of emotions I was feeling about the whole situation just left me feeling... unsettled.

I paused as I crossed one of the footbridges running over an irrigation canal and looked out over the fields, trying to think. The issue with being followed and the issue with Grey were separate—yet mildly connected by his lack of belief in me.

If I really thought about it, I couldn't be angry with him for doubting me. Not once, but twice I had claimed to see something, only for there to be nothing there. If I were him, I wouldn't believe me either. He didn't know me well enough to trust my assessment of things, not like Eric and Zoe did.

As I thought of my two friends, and how I hadn't seen them in seventeen days and counting, my stomach twisted into even more knots. I frowned and leaned over the railing, allowing my elbows to hold me up as I watched the irrigation canal snake out through the massive fields. I wondered what they were up to... and how furious they both were with me. It wasn't like me to disappear. But then again, maybe they'd think it was just my medication.

I knew I was worrying Zoe. And it would only be a matter of time before she risked running into my parents just so she could barge into my room and demand answers. And I still wasn't sure what I would tell her if that happened.

"She is taking the Medica treatment," a familiar voice from some distance behind me said, and I turned, expecting to see Eric, bewildered at how I could be thinking about him one second, only for him to manifest the next.

"I don't think she is," Zoe replied, and I realized I had seconds before they rounded the corner and saw me, and quickly launched myself over the railing. I landed, just barely able to catch my balance before splashing into the water, and ducked under the bridge, crawling on my hands and knees into the tight space underneath. "I think she's avoiding me."

Hidden though I was, it took everything I had not to climb out from under the bridge to go to my best friend and give her a hug. Her voice had broken as she said it, and Eric sighed and said something softly, under his breath.

Then silence. I watched the water rushing by, trying to keep my heartbeat down, and wondered what they were doing up there. After a moment, Zoe sniffled.

"Eric... do you think Liana doesn't like me anymore?" she asked. "Like... maybe I did something to make her upset?"

Eric's reply was soft and soothing. "Zoe, there is nothing in the world you could do to make her upset. She loves you."

"Then why won't she net me?" Zoe snapped.

Eric sighed, and I heard the thump of his foot on the bridge and tried to curl up even more underneath it. The space was tight, however, and the bridge barely wide enough to accommodate two people walking side by side. If they came around the other side, they'd see me plain as day.

"Fine," Eric began patiently. "Why would she be mad at you? The last time you two hung out was when *both* of you were being weird. What happened after you left?"

My breath caught in my lungs, and I looked up, my heart pounding. The last day he'd seen us together was when we'd fed him that really awful story about why Zoe had to cancel their dinner plans. The day she had helped me save Grey's life. Zoe had said she wouldn't tell him, but she was positively smitten with Eric. She trusted him. So did I, to an extent—but there was a limit.

"I already *told* you. I helped her out and then left."

"Yes, but, I mean..." I heard the awkwardness in Eric's voice and bit my lip, praying he wouldn't dig too far. "I feel like you're not telling me everything. And I kind of thought... well... that we were better friends than that."

Zoe was silent. "Are we?" she asked quietly, and I could just imagine the insecurity on her face. "How long before your family convinces you to stop hanging out with me? My ranking has never been lower, and I'm definitely not the biggest fan of the Tower right now."

"Yes, but *why?*" Eric's voice was awash with frustration—the most negative I'd ever heard him in my life—and another pang of guilt shot through me. He was an eight because he was so upbeat, but if he was feeling the way he sounded—harsh and tense—then his rank was in jeopardy, and it was my fault.

Zoe sighed overhead, and I clenched my hands together, trying not to say anything. Going out there would only make things worse, because they'd demand to know where I'd been and what I'd been doing. And I couldn't tell them the truth, which meant I would have to lie. I might even have to be cruel.

Zoe sighed, and I heard footsteps. I closed my eyes as they thundered loudly overhead, and then opened them when they stopped halfway across. "Don't worry about me," Zoe said. "I'm sure I'll get over it. I just…"

She trailed off, and I wrapped my arms around my knees, trying to compress myself into an even tighter ball.

"Hey," Eric said. "You know you can tell me anything. I'm not like the others… I can take it."

"Oh, Eric," Zoe breathed, her voice so soft that I had to strain to hear it over the wind and the water. "I really want to, but Liana said…"

"She's not here! She's not even talking to us. Please, just tell me. Maybe I can help."

Alarm began to course through me as Eric tried to worm his way toward the truth, and I realized that I'd done Zoe a great disservice—I'd had someone to talk to about what I'd seen, but I'd denied *her* anyone to talk to about what I told her.

I heard her sigh, and in that sigh, I imagined her crumbling. Breaking down and telling Eric everything about what we had done. Putting him at risk. Panic gave speed to my limbs, and I tore out from under the bridge like a woman possessed, scrambling on my hands and knees.

I climbed to my feet immediately, taking a moment to find my footing on the steep embankment, and looked to where Zoe was now staring down at me, her mouth opened in a wide "O" of surprise, her eyes bulging. Beside her, Erik looked just as dumbfounded by my abrupt appearance, and I suddenly recalled that I had been eavesdropping on a very personal conversation. And now they knew that, too.

Well. Best way out was always forward. I hoped.

"Hey?" I asked, raising one dirt-stained arm and forcing a bright smile on my lips. Inside, my heart was quivering in terror, and I had to fight to keep it from punching out of my back and making a run for it. "How's it going?"

Zoe was *not* amused, and as her eyes narrowed to slits, I realized that, at the very least, I had prevented her from spilling her guts to Eric. For now.

"Where the hell have you been?" Zoe began, her voice snapping. Before I even had a chance to draw breath, she held up her finger, silencing me. "Oh no, scratch that. What the hell were you doing *down there?*"

I blinked several times, trying to think of an excuse. "I... was... inspecting the underside of the bridge."

Zoe's eyes narrowed even more, until they were just slits ablaze with fire, raging in fury. I wondered if she thought that squinting her eyes together tight enough would enable her to channel that anger into a laser beam.

"You were inspecting the underside of the bridge." Her voice was flat and emotionless, but those eyes told me to think carefully.

"Yes?"

"Just... the *underside of the bridge?*"

"Yes?"

"Really."

"Yes."

Her face scrunched into a tight knot, and then she tried to lunge for me, over the railing, her arms outstretched. I took a step back in alarm, and almost fell as my foot slipped on the steep slope. Luckily, Eric caught my best friend around the waist with his large arms, and held her pinned against his side. She kicked and screamed as she continued to try to get to me, but Eric didn't let go.

I used the time to climb out of the ditch and start to dust myself off.

Zoe's yells and hollers were dying down some, enough for Eric to look over at me and say, "She thinks that lie is insulting our intelligence. And I happen to agree."

My lips curled up in a smile, and I offered him a mock salute as I beat the mud off my boots. After a moment, Zoe went completely quiet, and I looked up to see Eric setting her gently on the ground. Her eyes met mine, and I saw a hardening in them before she whipped around and began marching away. My eyes caught her wrist, and I felt my heart stop short as I took in the four, winking mockingly and reminding me that *that* was my fault. I thought of what Grey had said—that after four it was almost impossible to get up without Medica assistance—and cringed.

Eric watched her go, turned back to me, shrugged, and then moved to follow her. I watched them *both* go, torn between following and running away.

Then I thought of the anger in Zoe's eyes, and how it was unable to mask the pain there.

I turned away from her, intent on telling Roark why he was going to recruit Zoe. Then, I was coming back up here and leveling with my friend.

I buzzed the door and waited, teetering on the precipice of banging on the door or *really* getting mad, when it slid open to reveal Grey, his eyes sluggish, as if I had woken him up. He stared dumbly at me, and I seized the advantage and pushed by him, heading deeper into Roark's home.

"Liana?" he said from behind me, but I ignored him and moved into the common space. Roark was sitting behind his workbench and looked up in surprise from his work screen, his fingers still on the controls.

"What are you doing back here, girl? You just left a few hours ago." His bushy eyebrows fairly bristled as he glowered at me, his blue eyes suddenly suspicious. "Don't tell me you saw someone following you again."

I ignored the question completely. "Zoe is a four, but she'll be a three soon. She's twenty, almost twenty-one, and with Water Treatment, but the girl is a Cog in her heart. She's untrained and built her own data pad, and not like the ones we use—like the ones IT uses. There isn't anyone more qualified to get us out of here or put together a transportation device. You don't just *want* her, Roark; you *need* her."

Roark stared at me during my entire speech. I'd spent the trip back deciding what to say and stripping it down to its most important and briefest points. Now I stood here, meeting his gaze unwaveringly—until I heard glass clinking so violently it set my teeth on edge.

I immediately turned to see Grey leaning heavily on one of the small UV fridges, his eyelashes fluttering. My feet moved of their own accord, and I crossed over to him to thread his arm over my shoulder and stand him upright. A few more steps with his sluggish and heavy body next to me, and I sat him in an overstuffed chair nearby. A book hit the floor with a *thunk* as he dislodged it from the seat, and I picked it up and set it to one side.

"What's wrong with him?" I asked, watching his head loll to one side as he immediately drifted off.

"Oh, him? He was scratching at the salve on his burn, so I sedated him."

I swiveled around to see Roark bent back over his work, his eyes focused on the glowing screen.

"Is he going to be all right?"

"He'll be fine. Just a little in and out for a while."

I made sure Grey was settled, and then marched back over to Roark. "Can you help me?" I asked, meeting his startled gaze.

"You mean, will I help your friend?" Roark said, turning back to his screen. "And the answer is no, I will not."

I had to bite the inside of my cheek to keep from screaming at him. "Look, she's the reason I was able to get Grey out. I cut her off after that day, completely abandoned her after giving her a glimpse of what was really going on. She is my best friend in the world, and there is no way I am ever leaving this Tower without her—okay? If not just because of what I asked, then because of what she did for Grey."

Roark leaned back in his chair and said nothing for what felt like an eternity. Then he sat up, rubbing at his forehead. He stroked the hair back from his brow, letting out a long breath before speaking.

"I knew a man, once," he said. "Name of Caduceus. We were as close as any two people in this damned Tower can be. We collaborated on research, lifted each other up when things were hard. I loved him as a brother, and was godfather to his child."

I grew silent and let Roark speak. I hadn't known him long, but I didn't have to know him long to know this was a hard story for him to tell. I was certain that whatever he was going to say, it was relevant, even if it wasn't clear in the moment. I hoped that it meant whatever I was about to hear would help me solve my Zoe problem.

"Caduceus was twice the scientist I am. If Chief Surgeon Sage ever managed to die, I think Caduceus would have made a fine candidate for the council, after Selka, of course. Not that Scipio would ever elect a seven like him. No, but Caduceus was methodical. Smart, but considerate, which is an unusual mix for the Medica."

He stroked his wispy beard, his expression full of distaste. "When Selka found out about the outside world, she swore me to secrecy on the subject. It would be between us, she said. We couldn't risk people dropping in rank, running off, causing a panic. We had to keep calm, and, more importantly, keep it to ourselves.

"Thinking back, it's easy to see why she wanted us to do so. She died, of course, and look at how I live now. Caduceus had heard about Selka dying, and showed up to beg me to let him help me with my grief, help me process, but I turned him away. And he quickly forgot about the old, dishonored man working in Cogstown."

I continued to stare at him, and he met my gaze, his eyes sparkling brightly with unshed tears, a crooked smile on his lips.

"The man's family is doing well. I check in from time to time. My godson has a son now, with a pretty girl he met when he was a student. The little boy shows as much promise in the medical field as his grandfather. Had I not done what I did, he would be dead, or disgraced. Do I miss him? Every day. Do I regret cutting him out of my life?"

There was a pause, and for an instant it looked like Roark was trying to convince himself of the next word.

"No," he said.

Silence grew in the room as I considered his words. After a long time in deep thought, I shook my head and looked at him. "There are parallels, sure, but there are some drastic differences. Zoe knows I was trying to save Grey, trying to break the law. She helped me do it. Caduceus was just your friend; he didn't know what was going on with you and Selka. Your behavior can be written off as grief—but mine? I just ran into her, Roark. She wouldn't even talk to me, *and* her number is dropping. You can't tell me that if you found out Caduceus was about to hit one tomorrow, you wouldn't help him out. I dare you to tell me that."

Roark folded his arms over his chest as I ranted at him, his gaze turning angry and then distant as I talked. I finished my speech and waited for him to respond.

He nodded and returned my gaze, his expression speculative. "I have to say that you do impress me, Liana. Your argument was fairly flawless. Let's hope this girl is as good as you claim with machines. We could really use a Cog, but, surprisingly, they are the one department with the highest job satisfaction. Go figure."

I smiled and allowed myself a moment of relief. He was going to let Zoe join us—which meant I was going to get my friend back. "Zoe is even better with machines than I said. When can I bring her here?"

"I imagine you'll want to do it as soon as possible, so let's say tomorrow."

"She normally has a shift in the morning, so I'll bring her by early in the afternoon," I said, quivering with excitement and starting a plan in my head about what I'd say to get her down here. I knew I still had to figure out what to do with Eric—no way Zoe was going to let us leave him behind when we finally left—but for now, she was my main concern. I'd figure out how to bring Eric in later. If he started to drop, then I'd bring it up, but hopefully we'd all be long gone before that ever happened.

"Good." Roark turned back to his work, this time lifting two test tubes filled with colored liquid—one blue and one a bright green—and pouring them into a beaker. "So I assume after this, you'll be ending your recruitment runs with Grey."

I looked up at him sharply, my eyebrows pulling tight together as I frowned. "No. Why would you think that?"

He shrugged. "Well, you got what you wanted: medication for your friend. You don't have any obligation to us, and if anything, we are in your debt. So I just assumed you would—"

"You really do not get me, Roark," I said, too tired to be incensed. "I *like* helping Grey. It's the first useful thing I've done in my life. We might be at a fifty percent success rate right now, but I don't care. I want to help, and I have no intention of going anywhere. Also, don't be surprised if Zoe wants to help as well."

A warmth washed over his features that made my stomach do a flip, and I realized that he was both relieved and pleased to hear me say that. I suddenly realized that he didn't like feeling isolated any more than I did, and that I had more in common with Roark and Grey than I did with my own family. Here, I felt wanted, needed, and appreciated. I belonged with these misfits, just like they belonged with me. Somehow, we'd found each other, and that made us all feel a little bit safer, and a little less alone. I needed it just as much as Grey and Roark did.

I opened my mouth to say something, then suddenly heard a rustling behind me. I saw Roark's eyes go hard and flat, directed just over my shoulder, and he stood even as I began to turn.

"Liana," said an all-too-familiar voice.

In the doorway, Gerome was brushing a bit of dust from the shoulder of his crimson uniform, his eyes sweeping over the little lab, lingering briefly on Roark, and then longer on Grey. He shook his head, expression cold and distant.

"Gerome," I managed, my eyes on my mentor, taking in his cold eyes and rigid stance. "What a pleasant surprise. What are you doing here? Am I late for our shift?" I wasn't—it was only four.

"To hell with that," Roark snarled. "You're in my home, Knight."

"The Knights go where there is a threat to the Tower, and no door can stop them," Gerome responded smoothly, his eyes returning to me. "What are you doing here?"

I hesitated, and then hoisted my chin up. "Citizen Farmless was assaulted by a three today, and suffered burns. I came here to help him file a report."

"Would this be Silvan Wash?"

Blinking in confusion, I looked away for a second, and then looked back up at him as a piece of the puzzle fell into place.

He'd been the one following me.

Gerome's face might as well have been carved from stone as he stared at me. "Why are you here?" he repeated.

I stuck to the lie. "If you know his name, that means they found him and got him to the Medica. Citizen Farmless was telling me he acted in self-defense."

"You're taking the word of a four?"

I placed a hand on my hip. "Citizen Farmless is a nine, Gerome. His experience changed him, for the better."

To emphasize my point, Grey weakly held up his wrist, and I realized that at some point he had woken up and figured out what was going on. Gerome hardly seemed to notice. He was still staring at the bottles of pills on the walls. "Changed for the better," he repeated softly. "Blessed by Scipio. Is that really what is happening here?"

I frowned. Gerome had never doubted a person's rank, not once, but the way he was talking was making my gut scream that he knew. It was impossible—he couldn't hear through walls or doors, and I doubted he'd been able to hear us clearly while following at a discreet distance. Unless...

My eyes darted around, pausing when I saw the black plastic box at his side. A tensor: a high-tech listening device that read vibrations through the walls and translated them into noise. The equipment was dear to the department, and only the Knight Commanders were permitted use. As a Knight Commander, he was trusted enough to have one in his possession, and he had used it to listen in on us. Had been using it for a while, if I had to guess.

Gerome shifted his weight to one side, uniform creaking, and placed his hand firmly on the handle of his stun baton—more a promise than a threat. His gaze slid around the room, and I frowned as his head swiveled. His cheeks were gaunt and hollow, and there were bags under his eyes that I hadn't noticed before. He looked like he'd been run ragged by something.

"Gerome?" I asked. "Are you okay?"

"I'm better than okay," he announced. "I am clearer in my duties to the Tower. Scipio explained it to me: he told me we had all been tricked, even him. He wants me to correct the mistake."

A chill ran down my spine at the words, and I took an instinctive step in front of Grey.

"Scipio spared him," I reminded him. "You were there."

"Scipio is great, Liana, but still just a computer," Gerome said. "A computer that can be tricked."

I blinked, my mouth going dry. This was getting more and more dangerous by the second. Gerome was either unhinged, or Scipio himself had sent him on this mad crusade. Either way, we weren't getting out of it easily. I needed to be careful about how I proceeded. I needed to keep him talking while one of the three of us scrambled to act.

"If Scipio was tricked," I said, "how was it done?"

With a languid motion, he gestured toward the rows of bottles. "What are those?" he asked.

Roark stepped in, his voice trembling with barely suppressed anger. "Antibiotics, mostly," he said. "I was forced out of the Medica, but I've never been able to stop tinkering."

Gerome's lips twitched. "Tinkering," he said, then turned back to me. "Tell me, Liana, what did you do to Silvan Wash?"

My hand was halfway to my baton before I could stop myself, but I quickly bypassed it to run the hand through my hair. "I don't under-stand," I said. "As I explained, I came here to file a report *against* Silvan Wash."

Gerome rolled his eyes, an exaggerated motion that looked cartoonish on his normally stoic features.

"You know I've been following you," he said calmly. "I'm sure you've already put the pieces together. If you haven't, I'll be very disappointed."

I went still, a chilling calm coming over me. He really did know everything, and there was no creating doubt in him. Now was the time to stand up. "I did," I told him. "But if you were following, and using the tensor, then you'll know—"

"That you and your demented boyfriend tried to force a loyal citizen of the Tower to take your little drug and plan an assault on Scipio? Yes, I figured that out. What I couldn't figure out was why you mutilated Citizen Wash's wrists, and why he couldn't remember anything. But before we finish here tonight, I'm going to find out."

His baton came out in a crackle of electricity, searing a blue streak into my eyes with its brilliance. He took a step toward Grey, who was still very much drugged, and I quickly moved in between them. "Gerome, please. If you saw his wrists, then you know that he has been doing it himself, for some time! We can talk about this," I begged. "You don't have to do this."

"Get out of my way, Liana," Gerome grated out, and a heartbeat later, he was drawing back his arm, the baton crackling menacingly over my head.

My baton was out and in my hand before I could even remember reaching for it, and I caught his baton with mine, my arm ringing in shock from the heavy weight of his blow. Sparks shot madly from where the electric ring made contact, but I ignored them and planted a boot in Gerome's knee, bringing the man down to my side.

A flick of the wrist disarmed him, his baton bouncing to one side with a loud clatter. His hand snaked up and grabbed my wrist in a vice-like grip, though, and I gritted my teeth as he twisted it. The baton dropped from my nerveless fingers onto the floor, and he released me. I staggered back a few feet, my hand around my wrist, and then spun and brought my heel to his face. He swayed heavily to one side, threatening to tip over, but his kneeling position on the floor helped him keep his balance.

He glared up at me, his hand on his jaw, and I didn't hesitate. I lashed out with a fist. He dodged it, rolling forward, and I whirled, lash already in my hand. I flicked out my wrist, hoping to hit him in the chest, but he swung out of the way. I let the harness reel me in and jumped into it as it snapped me toward the wall. I flipped, planted my feet on it, then snapped the next lash line out on the opposite end of the room. In a move I'd practiced a lot, I disconnected, kicked off, and retracted the new line all at the same time, building momentum.

Hurtling toward Gerome was a bit of an experience, but it was nothing compared to the moment of surprise I felt as he seemingly plucked me out of the air. I had a moment in which I was looking up at him, cradled in his massive arm, and then his mouth morphed into an angry shout as he slammed me to the ground.

The air left me in a giant whoosh, and my entire diaphragm locked up as I gasped for air. Then all I felt was pain radiating from my back, neck, ribs, and hips as my body struggled to remember how to breathe.

I came to a minute later to see Grey and Roark both grappling with Gerome, just a few feet away. The two men were holding onto one of the Knight's arms, which I now saw contained a stun baton, and Roark was struggling to inject something into Gerome's arm, fighting against Gerome's massive strength as he tried to drive it point blank into Grey's chest.

I watched in horror as Grey let out a hoarse cry of pain when Gerome's stun baton finally caught him in the side. He went down, his clothes smoking faintly. Roark followed with a cry of pain, and then Gerome was standing over us, his face grim, eyes narrowed.

Gerome had always been better than me. Better than anyone, really. I had been above and beyond him in lashing, but his combat skill was legendary. Never in my wildest dreams had I thought I would need to fight the man in earnest, but now he stood here, in my sanctuary, looming over my friends with his weapon drawn. And now that it was happening, I couldn't let him win.

I lashed the ceiling and used the momentum from the mechanisms in the harness to haul me up, one leg thrusting out to kick the baton out of his hand, the other catching him across the cheek so hard that he doubled over and stumbled back a few steps. I dropped to the ground and scooped up the baton, then exploded forward in a burst of motion, intent on stunning him into submission.

His hand whipped out and caught me on the jaw, and I spun, crashed into a bookshelf, and fell, books raining down on me as pain radiated up and down the side of my face.

I groaned, but would have made it to my feet if it weren't for the baton that smashed into my side. Lights danced before my eyes, and I felt every nerve in my body come alive with pain. I jerked for a moment, feeling my own sweat vaporizing off my skin and rising in a hot steam from my body. When my vision cleared, Gerome was standing over me.

There were tears in his eyes.

All I could do was stare as he looked down at me, the tears falling liberally down his cheeks. I was lost as to how to process the sight of him crying. It was alarming—this wasn't like him at all.

Then the baton in his hand let out a roar of power as he loomed over me, sending a shot of fear straight down my spine.

"You were the daughter I never had," he said. His eyes flicked up, and he leveled his baton toward where the two men lay. "Don't you move, old man. I'll do the same to you."

I heard Roark let out a curse, and watched him struggle to his hands and knees.

"You're a murderer," the old man hissed. "You come into my home, trying to make us feel guilty when you *kill* people for a living. You call yourselves Knights? I call you Scipio's assassins!"

Gerome's face contorted with fury, but as he took a step forward, a chime rang out. It was so calm, so kind and incongruous with the moment, that it took me a moment to recognize the source. Gerome's wrist.

The man paused, then quickly reached into his crimson uniform and drew something out. I blinked, stunned. It couldn't be. Gerome was perfect. A ten. A man beyond reproach.

In his hand, he clutched a bottle of fat, red pills.

"I'll be with you in one moment," he said hoarsely, and drew one out, then swallowed it back with a grimace. He drew in a sharp breath, and in that motion, I saw the tears vanish from his eyes. The hesitation went out of him like smoke being struck by a harsh wind.

"Now," he said, moving to stand over me. I forced my burning nerves to move, crawling to a sitting position and using the motion to disguise my left hand under my body as I pulled out the tip of the lash and palmed it in my fist. If I could hit my baton with it, I could reel it over and maybe we would stand a chance. I saw Grey struggling to his own feet from the corner of my eye.

"You're going to come with m—"

Gerome's words cut off as a loud *crack* sounded. I could only stare as he half-turned, then slumped, his eyes rolling back as he crumpled to the ground.

A young girl, perhaps thirteen or fourteen, now stood in place behind him. She was small and thin, her skin the color of porcelain, so pale I could see the light coloring of her veins. Her white-blonde hair was cut into a shaggy bob, tousled wildly around her face. She had bright blue eyes that were wide with alarm and mortification. And in her hands was a massive wrench, one edge stained with red.

For a moment, all I could do was stare as the newcomer dropped the wrench and stepped over Gerome's body, an uncertain smile flickering on her lips.

"I'm so sorry about that," she said shakily, gesticulating toward Gerome's still form. "I just..." Her hand fluttered. "Oh dear, this is a terrible way of making an introduction."

I stared blankly at the young girl, my body still in agony from the brutality of Gerome's attack, and then struggled to my feet. "I think... under the circumstances, we can overlook the oddity." The look I received from the girl was one of pure gratitude. "What's your name?"

"Oh! I didn't say? No, of course I didn't say. What was I thinking?" She sighed, her fingers dancing in front of her, and then nodded. "Christian. Tian for short."

I smiled in spite of the severity of the situation. "Don't most people choose 'Chris?'"

Tian nodded, her head moving rapidly up and down, her blue eyes wide. "Oh, yes... but most of them don't like me being a Chris, so I got

Tian. It's okay, I like Tian. It's nice to be different. This whole Tower is full of Chrises, and—"

She trailed off as I bent over and placed two fingers to Gerome's neck, her body trembling. "Is he...? Did I...?"

I shook my head. Gerome's pulse was strong and true under my fingers. "He's fine," I said. "Which means he won't be out for long. Roark, give me one of those memory pills?"

"Memory pills?" Tian echoed, her eyes darting back to the two men picking themselves off the floor. I glanced over my shoulder as well, to see Grey moving and looking more alert than before. Adrenaline—the best antidote to a sedative.

"You really sure you want to be giving him those, Liana?" Roark asked as he shakily got his feet under him. "He's been following you for some time—he might already have all the information he needs."

"I don't care. We need to—"

My skull began to vibrate, and Scipio's voice slipped into my head, catching me totally off guard. I grabbed at the area as his haughty voice sounded in my ear. *Guard down and unresponsive, Cogstown C19 quarters. One detected in room. Liana, your mission is to find and capture the one.*

The buzzing cut off violently, and I looked up, eyes wide, at Roark and Grey. "Scipio—he knows Gerome's down, and has detected a one in the room." We all immediately held up our wrists—but they all read nine.

Tian shifted uncomfortably and started gnawing her lower lip. "It's me," she announced softly. "Kind of... Technically I'm an undoc. Well not really, but kind of." She shifted nervously, and looked at Roark. "I heard you were someone who had some pills to help with rankings?"

Roark's eyes narrowed. "Heard from whom?"

"Not the time, guys!" Grey shouted, and I stood up.

"Grey's right—more Knights are coming. We need to get out of here. Roark, Grey, Tian, get the pills."

"Which ones?" Roark asked, his hands already pulling bottles and boxes out.

"All of them!" I shouted. "And give Tian some Paragon. Last thing we need is for her to set off the alarms."

I heard them moving behind me while I quickly shoved everything I could think of into a bag I found in the front closet. I piled it with food, blankets, and water, my mind already spinning as I wondered where I could hide them while they waited for this all to die down. I took a moment to consider it as I force-fed Gerome the memory pill.

"I'm taking you all up to Smallsville," I said, and Grey shot me a look. "You can hide with Sarah. She'll shelter you both for a few days."

Tian looked up, craning her neck quizzically as she tucked another bottle of pills into a bag. "Why go there," she asked hesitantly, "when we can go into the Depths? I have a place there, and it's secret. Safe. Oh! You can even meet my friends. My Cali. My Quess! Doxyyy! Oh, I'm sure you'll get along and be the brightest friends in no time."

She smiled, completely in earnest, and it was all I could do to keep from taking a step back. I felt powerless to argue against such a sweet yet decidedly odd creature. She seemed so fragile, even though she had knocked Gerome out cold. I felt like questioning her too intensely would cause her to run away, without explaining to us why she was even here. But the idea that this girl had a home in the Depths was so foreign to me, it was hard not to. She had to be mistaken, or misusing the name to refer to something else. There was no way there were people living at the bottom of the Tower. It was impossible.

Yet, as my eyes passed over Roark, the old man looked unsurprised by Tian's declaration.

"Sorry, Liana, but it's too exposed between here and Smallsville," Roark said, his gaze apologetic. He slung a bag weighted down with equipment and pills over his shoulder and nodded. "And, Scipio knows where you are, or at the very least that he sent you here. It's going to look awfully suspicious if we just miraculously escape, especially after you were supposed to kill one of us not too long ago. We're going with Tian. And you're coming too."

Tian let out a little crow of victory, and I watched as something familiar slid into her hand. She had her own set of lashes. "This is going to be so much fun!" she shouted, and with a flick of her wrist she was airborne, lashing down the hall and out the door. "C'mon!" she shouted eagerly.

We followed Tian as she lashed down the hall ahead of us, her lashes and body spinning to and fro in a way that made me feel a little bit intimidated. I might have lived for lashing, but Tian had taken to it like a bird in flight or a fish in a stream, her movements so natural and graceful that they belied the gawkiness of her frame.

She led us to an elevator shaft and stood waiting as we rushed up.

"I haven't taken an elevator in so long," she said excitedly as we approached, hopping from one foot to another. "We can take it now!"

I looked at her wrist and was shocked to see that the wristband and display were missing. The microthread was impossible to cut. "Where's your—"

She reached into her shirt and pulled out the indicator, which was hanging by a braided bit of cloth around her neck. The number showed a cool, glowing blue nine, and it reflected on her face, illuminating her excited smile. "This means I can go to the Lion's Den," she exclaimed happily, clapping her hands together.

"Tell us about it later," I said. "We have to go... to what level?"

"Five," she replied, skipping up the ramp and then performing a little twirl in midair. "You're going to like it there."

Five? That was unexpected, and not at all where I had thought "the Depths" should be. In fact, it was where Greeneries 1 and 2 were located. Why were we going there? What was she planning?

I exchanged a look with Grey and discreetly handed him Gerome's baton. Tian seemed nice, but this was all happening too quickly for us to put any brakes on. Still, that didn't mean we couldn't be prepared if the other shoe started to drop.

We all got onto the elevator, and it began to descend. Beside me, Tian looked up, her face watching the shaft above in childlike wonder. "It just keeps going up and up and up," she breathed. "Does it go to the very top? I've always wanted to go to the very top."

I frowned, my brows furrowing. "You've never been to the top?"

Tian shook her head, her features melting into sadness. "My parents fell asleep one day... and they wouldn't wake up. When the bad people came for me, I ran away, and Cali found me. I've lived with her ever since."

Cali. It was the second time she'd mentioned her. "Tian, who is Cali?"

She shrugged. "Someone who takes care of me. And people like me. She keeps us safe from the Knights. She created Sanctum."

"Sanctum?" I asked sharply, and she nodded.

"Sanctum," she said simply.

Grey barked a laugh. "Sanctum isn't real," he announced. "It's a myth, made up by the Knights to try to justify the need for so many Knights—*more*, even—in spite of the fact that there's no proof of an undoc civilization living in the Depths. It would be impossible."

"That's not exactly true."

We both turned toward Roark, who stood, wearily holding the bag of medication in his hands.

"Sanctum is real," he said.

"How do you know?" I asked, my mind racing. If there were people living down there, maybe we didn't have to wait to leave. Depending on what skills they had, maybe we could start working on figuring out how to get out of here as a group, instead of trying to recruit. Maybe we could start planning to leave *now*.

"My contact told me about it," he said, giving me a guarded look. "Told me that we would be approached eventually, and that Cali was a good person."

Tian smiled. "And the walls have eyes, but so do we, because without our eyes we couldn't see," she sang off-key, trailing off into a happy little hum. The elevator came to a stop, and we quickly got off. Tian led us through the complex network of hallways in the shell, taking us around until I started noticing the signs for Greenery 1—the Menagerie, where animals were kept—on the doorways, showing we were close to the bulk-head. A few seconds later, the hall abruptly ended, and Tian bent over to pull on the grated floor. It lifted up easily, but it was still heavy, and the little girl staggered a little as she slid it to one side. She leaned into the hole, and I heard a beep, followed by the pneumatic hiss of a door open-ing. I realized she had opened a hatch, just as a blast of hot, dry air shot out past her, immediately invading my lungs and making me cough.

"Dry heat is the best heat," Tian exclaimed as she shook out her arms. "C'mon!" The little girl immediately began climbing down into the hole. A moment later, she stuck her head out, her mop of white-blonde hair standing on end. "Lots of lights in here, but don't touch. And close the door behind you."

She dropped back down and out of sight, and I sighed, hefting the bag on my shoulder around to my front to make pushing it easier.

"Are we sure we're making the right choice?" I asked as I squatted to peer down the hole. A hatch beneath the floor plates stood open, revealing a short drop of maybe three feet below. From one side, blue-and-purple light glowed brightly, filling the short drop with neon rays.

"We gave Gerome the pill," Roark said gruffly, gingerly lowering his bag into the hole. "But it only erases the last hour or so. That means that whatever he saw *before* is still going to be there. He's going to know he went to my dwelling for a reason, and while the head trauma is a good explanation for him forgetting, he's going to figure out or be reminded about Silvan Wash. And put it all together. Which means we aren't safe up there anymore."

He was right, although I hated to admit it. Then again, I wanted to see where Tian was leading us. If there were people living down there, I wanted to know about it. There was security with people who were like you—and I was hoping these people were like me.

I helped Roark down the hole and watched as he slid out of view through the tunnel that seemed to run beneath our feet. A moment later his voice carried back up to us. "Plasma relays. Definitely do *not* touch."

Grey looked at me, and I realized he'd been uncharacteristically quiet since Tian had arrived. "Are you okay?" I asked, and he nodded.

"Just thinking."

"About what?"

He shook his head. "If Tian were any less zany, I'd suspect that this was more than coincidence. It seems too neat. I mean, what are the chances of not one but two people busting in and knowing something was going on with the pills?"

I bit my lip. The thought had nagged at me as well, but there hadn't been enough time to dwell on it. "Do you think it's a trap?" If it was a trap, it didn't seem like it had been initiated by Devon. But who did that leave? No one, really. And I doubted Devon was here, since Gerome had been the one following me (no doubt upon Devon's orders).

He hesitated, and then shrugged. "It's hard to tell. It could be that they were watching us and Tian felt like she needed to intercede on our behalf, but... What if they aren't good people? What if they are *actual* dissidents?"

"You mean like, 'take down the Tower' kind of dissidents?"

He nodded. I thought about it for a long moment, and then dropped my bag into the hole. "There's only one way to find out. Just keep that baton close, okay?"

"Yeah," he grunted as he helped me into the hole.

The crawl space was narrow, the sides crammed with plasma beams, the purple-and-blue light writhing between connection points as they hummed along. I tried not to sweat from the massive heat they were generating in the small space, but of course it was impossible. The very air felt like it was slowly dehydrating my lungs, to the point that I was wheezing more than breathing.

Pushing the bag in front of me, I wriggled forward, eager to be out of the tight space and away from the heat. I heard Grey struggling along behind me, but focused on moving forward—because if I got stuck, he got stuck. And this wasn't a place for getting stuck.

Suddenly Roark's hand appeared in my face, and I grabbed it, shoving the bag forward a few more feet and then crawling through. I gasped when I hit the catwalk and it swayed violently. I'd stepped out of an oven and into a raging storm, it seemed, as water and mist tore around us. I could hear the churning of tens of thousands of gallons of water drowning out everything else, and a thick, dense mist seemed to cling to everything.

"Where are we?" I shouted at Roark as I clung to the railing.

"Outside!" he shouted back, and my eyes widened. I looked around, and realized he was right—we *were* outside. More precisely, we were underneath Greenery 1, which hung some fifty feet off the ground, jutting out of the side of the Tower like a massive wing over the river. The churning sound I heard was from the vortex of waters below as they crashed into the hydro-turbines. The hundreds of thousands of gallons churning beneath us kicked up a thick haze of white mist that was making it difficult to see anything. I watched as Tian stepped delicately around me and began moving across the catwalk into the dense mist, turning long enough to beckon to me before disappearing in it. I looked around—the catwalk we had emerged from was flush with the side of the Tower, so the only way was forward.

I went back to help Grey out of the hole, and then shouldered my bag. It was time to see what "Sanctum" had in store for us.

Tian led us across a network of catwalks that seemed to intersect and disappear in the mist formed by the massive hydro-turbines. The catwalks were slick, but our Tower-issued boots helped us maintain steady footing as we followed her slim figure.

I looked around as we walked—I had seen the underside of a lot of greeneries before, but not this one; Knights couldn't use their lashes in this humid environment. I guessed that was why the catwalks had been built here, so that maintenance could still be performed. It was hard to make much out in the mist, but I could see the shadows of structures through it—whether they were catwalks or pieces of equipment, I didn't know.

We walked for twenty minutes, according to my indicator, before Tian began to dance forward. I followed her through a particularly hazy patch, then nearly brained myself on a massive iron door that had just appeared suddenly out of the mist.

Tian beamed up at me and then rapped on the door—three times, then twice, then three times again—and waited.

I heard something clank, and the door opened a crack, revealing a tall, statuesque woman with vibrant green eyes and jet-black hair gathered in a tight ponytail on top of her head. Her face was an imperious mask that to me read, *Yes, you should be intimidated, because I will rip your throat out.*

In an instant a knife was in her hand and she was on her guard, resting a shoulder against the inner wall and keeping the doorway blocked. "Tian," she said, her voice husky. "What have you done?"

"Doxy! I found the pill-maker," Tian chirped excitedly, clapping her hands and indicating Roark with unsubtle jerks of her head. "And he has friends!"

The woman regarded us, taking us in one by one, her eyes hard and flat. I sensed the distrust in her, and couldn't blame her. I was feeling just as distrustful at the moment. Our eyes met and grappled, and I saw hers flick down and take in my uniform, seeming to see it for what it was.

Her eyes narrowed to twin green slits. "You brought a *Knight?*" she hissed, one strong hand reaching out and grabbing Tian by the wrist to haul her back inside. Tian's eyes widened in surprise, and she caught herself on the door, resisting Doxy's pull.

"She's not like them. Like *us!*" she insisted, her jerking motions against her assailant's more muscular arm feeble and weak.

"She's standing right here," I said, not wanting this to go on. "And I really don't like how you're handling Tian right now. I don't care if you've known her longer than me."

She dropped Tian's arm as if it had bitten her and looked at me, her face quizzical and cautious. "You care about what happens to her?" she asked.

"Of course she does, Maddox," Tian said, massaging the flesh of her arm where the woman—Maddox, whose nickname was apparently Doxy —had grabbed her. "She's a *good* Knight. Like in the stories Cali tells us."

Maddox pursed her lips. Then she looked at Roark. "You really the guy?"

"In the flesh—and in great need of your hospitality."

Her eyes flicked back to Grey and myself. "And the Hand and Shield?"

"Strays that I just can't bear to part with," Roark said dryly, and I looked over to see Grey rolling his eyes theatrically.

Maddox watched for another moment, and then stepped to one side, pulling the door back. "In. Now."

I was the last one to enter, allowing the others to go first while I glanced around us, taking one final look at the misty underbelly of the Tower. Zoe was still up in the Tower. Still angry and bitter, a four on her wrist. I hadn't forgotten, so I just prayed that whatever was in store here wouldn't take too long, and that they would let me get to my friend.

I stepped inside and helped Maddox close the door behind us. She slid some bars into place on the door by twisting the strange handle.

The first thing I noticed when I finally moved back a few paces to look around was the flat black material that seemed to be on every surface, including the door. I touched it and felt the roughness of it under my fingers—a graininess that was unexpected, and not unlike sandpaper.

Turning, I realized we were in a wide-open space, with another door leading deeper into the structure. Mesh lockers lined the walls, white exposure suits inside. There were a series of showerheads on the left wall, with smoky glass partitions separating them.

"What is this place?" Grey asked, his eyes looking around.

"Save your questions for Cali," Maddox grunted, stepping around all of us. "I'm going to need you to surrender your weapons," she announced, her hands on her hips. "That's non-negotiable. I'm also going to have to search your bags."

Tian clapped her hands together, an excited smile crossing her lips, and she performed a little twirl. "Oh, can I search the bags? I already know which pieces of equipment are the 'be careful' ones!"

Maddox smiled affectionately and nodded. "Sure, Tian. Remember what constitutes a weapon?"

"Anything that can make you bleed." She grinned triumphantly.

Maddox's face was deadpan. "Maybe I'd better do it, Tian. Can you ask your new friends for their stun batons?"

My hand automatically went for the handle, and before I knew what was happening, Maddox had reached out and grabbed my elbow. Instead of trying to wrench it around my back like I expected, she pushed me to one side, her foot hooking out and catching mine to send me into a head-over-heels tumble.

I managed to catch the fall in time to roll with it, then made it back to my feet and stood, baton now clear of my belt, the end crackling with activity. I whipped around and saw Maddox staring at me, a curious light in her eyes.

We stood there, staring at each other, each one waiting for the other to make the first move, until Grey cleared his throat. "Look, I'm fine with leaving my baton here. Liana, let's just follow their lead and see what happens. It's not like we have a lot of options. I'm sure that Roark and I have just made the Tower's 'most wanted' list, if they have one of those."

"They do," said a roughened feminine voice from the door, and I looked over to see a woman bearing a striking resemblance to Maddox, only with vibrant red hair, stepping through the door. Her eyes held the wrinkles of a middle-aged woman. And I knew them. Because they were eyes that had always captivated me when I was in the academy portion of Knights' school.

"You're Camilla Kerrin," I said, my eyes wide, and she smiled, her generous mouth spreading out in a beatific smile. "You're the Knight Commander who competed against Devon for the position of Champion twenty-five years ago."

"The very same," she said with a nod. Tian bounded over, and the two exchanged a warm hug. I watched as Camilla became downright nurturing with the young woman, brushing her hair out of her eyes and planting a kiss on her forehead. "I see you've met Tian, and my daughter, Maddox. I know you," she said, inclining her head toward Roark, and then looking at Grey and me. "But I don't know you two. I also don't know why Tian brought you back here. She wasn't even supposed to be out this evening."

Tian ducked her head shyly and looked at the three of us. "I know, but I heard you and Maddox talking about how much easier everything would be if you could get some of those pills, so I decided to go check it out. But then this Knight showed up—I followed him in—and he started beating up the pill-maker and his friends! So I grabbed a big wrench from the closet and brought it down on his head. He's alive—Liana checked—and then they fed him a memory-loss pill. And then we grabbed as much of their stuff as we could, and now we're here."

If Cali was surprised by the speed with which Tian recited the story, she didn't show it. I, on the other hand, wondered how she was able to pick out all the important elements, Tian spoke so fast.

"Interesting. Can you prove that he is the pill-maker?"

Tian fumbled about with the string on her neck and produced the indicator, the glowing blue nine bright in Cali's eyes. She cocked her head at it, and then gently helped Tian tuck it back under her shirt.

I realized then that they were all wearing the same kind of clothes: all black, covering them neck to toe, in a cut similar to that of the Knights' uniforms. Everything was black microthread, from the heavy pants to the thick, sturdy-looking jackets hung upon their shoulders, probably designed to take a hit from a knife, or even a baton, if the rubber inlays I noted were anything to go by.

The design of their uniforms was surprising, and I found myself wondering how they could fabricate anything down in this secret place nestled underneath the Tower. Or how they were even *living* down here. Or how they were all somehow free from the indicator that was supposed to never leave the wrist.

Cali caught me looking, and her lips quirked up in a bemused smile. "We were just sitting down to eat," she said softly. "Why don't you join us, and we'll see if we can't hash everything out. You hungry, Tian?"

"Are we having tomatoes?"

"No."

"Then yes, I'm hungry!" The young girl's fists punched into the air with excitement, and she darted around Cali and through the door behind her, heaving it open and racing down the passage. Cali watched her leave, a bemused smile on her lips.

"She's very enthusiastic," Roark commented carefully, and Cali turned, regarding him with her bright green eyes.

"Her parents died of Whispers almost a decade ago," she said evenly.

"She watched them die, and then ran when Medica finally lifted the quarantine."

The Tower had always had its fair share of plagues over the centuries, and Whispers was one that had run its course a decade ago. It was a bacterial infection that only affected the brain, colonizing it to feast on it. Its name was derived from the way people whispered things out at random—memories from the past, slowly getting destroyed as they wasted away. As I recalled, it had hit Water Treatment the worst, and they had lost nearly eight percent of their workforce.

It could also explain Tian's odd behavior. If she'd been infected, she would've suffered some mild brain damage.

"That doesn't change the fact that something's off about the girl," Roark said roughly. "If I can get my hands on a scanner, then—"

Cali's eyebrows drew together as her face flashed with distaste. "Tian isn't a danger to anyone except those who would try to hurt her or her family. Other than that, she's as sweet as a lamb, and you'll do nothing to change that. We love who she is."

She spoke with such passion that it made me consider her and Maddox in a new light. They definitely cared for the odd, yet charming, young girl who had saved our lives—which meant that my fears about them being dissidents could be entirely misplaced. Dissidents wouldn't form family units. They wouldn't care so deeply for each other, because there was always a chance they could lose that someone in the fight. Maybe these *were* people we should know. At the very least, maybe they were people who could answer some questions.

Roark stiffened but nodded, and Cali turned her gaze to where Grey was already placing his gear into a locker. As her eyes fell on me, I slid the baton out of the loop on my belt and placed it in an empty locker, along with my bag. The lashes I kept, and she didn't seem to mind. Instead, she gave me an approving smile, and then nodded toward the open door and the hall behind her.

"Welcome to Sanctum," she announced.

Maddox led the way down the cramped tunnel. The statuesque woman practically had to bend in half to avoid brushing her head on the ceiling. I followed, suddenly grateful for my comparatively short stature. She led us to a junction that branched off into five different tunnels, but, instead of picking one, she opened a circular hatch in the floor, pulling it up and over on its hinge. I peered into it from over her shoulder, and saw a ladder leading down.

The view was lost as she swung into it in a sleek, practiced move and quickly began to climb down, her hands and feet flying on the rungs. I looked over at Grey, who shrugged and then moved into the hole after her. I wondered if he shared my tentativeness.

Roark went down next, and for just a moment, it was Cali and me. The older woman stood with her arms folded casually across her chest, watching me with a curious look on her face.

"So you're Liana Castell," she drawled, eyeing me, and I faltered.

"How did you know that?"

Her lips quirked up in a sly smile and her eyes glittered with amusement. "Because the personal friend Roark and I share told me about you."

My heart started to beat faster, and I was suddenly uncertain and nervous. I still wondered if it was Alex, but had no way of knowing, seeing as I doubted Cali would tell me either. Maybe I just wanted it to be, so that I knew he would be coming with us. Either way, Alex or not, it didn't change the fact that someone was talking about me.

"What's his name, and what did he say?"

"Nice try. He said that you had a lot of potential for leadership, but have squandered honing that skill, choosing other, non-departmental skills, instead."

That was an exact quote taken from one of my departmental assessments a year ago, written by one of my former instructors. Those files were supposed to be confidential, but if her contact was an Eye, then I was sure he could hack into it, if he really wanted to. I just wished I knew who he was.

I also felt stupid. Of course Roark had contacted him about me at some point. From what little information Grey had offered up, it seemed like they had a partnership, so Roark had let him know what was going on. If this Eye was as paranoid as Grey claimed, then he must have checked me out, accessing my information, peering into my life. It was enough to make my skin crawl, if I really thought about it.

"I see," I said, all of these thoughts flashing in and out of my mind fast enough to allow me to maintain a calm and collected exterior. "You shouldn't believe everything you read. The instructor who said that was a fairly upbeat lady who didn't like saying anything negative. I was actually really dismal in her class, but she passed me anyway. Maybe she just didn't want to deal with me anymore."

"Still, I can see how much you care about your friends," she said softly, taking a step closer to me. "You're cautious, not wanting to trust this place until you're sure it's not a threat to you or them."

I nodded. "That's true. Maybe you could save me some time and just tell me."

Cali laughed, a rich, full sound that filled the room. "I admire your wit as well. It's very rare in a person so young." She settled back down, collecting her regal posture as if she were donning a royal cape, and met my gaze, her lips curling under high, arched cheekbones. "Now, whether this place is a threat to you and your friends really sort of depends on you. I will not allow my home to be threatened, you understand? If any of you proves to be a threat, I will take care of it. Efficiently."

I couldn't tell you why, but I liked her. There was something charming about the way she spoke; whether it was the warm, sweet tone of her voice or the sparkle of good humor in her eyes, it was hard to tell. I just did. Which was disconcerting enough for me to break eye contact and immediately drop myself down into the hole, climbing down the rungs of the ladder at a swift pace. The light above me was blocked momentarily as Cali followed me down, and I kept moving, my hands and feet confident. All ladders were standardized in the Tower, which meant once you were good with one, you were good with them all. As a potential Knight, I had learned how to be *very* good.

We descended twenty feet or so before emerging into a wide, circular room with a glass floor. Half of the walls were comprised of glass, through which I could see the churning waters of the hydro-turbine seated down below, at the base of the Tower. Ahead, the river flowed toward us, snaking in under the greenery, the edge of which was visible some three hundred feet ahead. Even though we were low—perhaps fifty or sixty feet above the churning waters—I could still see out past the overhang created by the greenery above, and into a thin strip of sky now turning purple.

"This is beautiful," I said, my head tilting as my eyes absorbed the sights.

My shin connected with something hard, and I looked down to realize we were standing in a dining area in the style of the Water Treatment people. Pillows and mats littered the area around a small table that stood maybe a foot or two off the floor. There were already seven places set, along with a bowl of steamed vegetables and another bowl brimming with steamed rice.

A young man stepped around Grey, carrying a tureen, and I looked over at him as he approached, suddenly wary. His dark blue eyes seemed

to smile at me as he sat the tureen down on the table. When he straightened, his hand was already held out.

"I'm Quess," he said in a surprisingly soft voice. "Well, my full name
is Quessian, but everyone has a hard time pronouncing it, so Quess is
better."

I grinned. "Medica?"

"Born and bred," he replied with an answering grin, sharing in the
joke. The Medica were known for giving their children unusual and
never-before-heard-of names. It was a way of ensuring their prodigy and
department would stand out. "But I transferred to the Eyes when I was
fifteen, and later was a Cog."

I blinked. He'd been an Eye and then a Cog? That seemed unlikely;
Eyes were notoriously loyal, probably because disloyalty was rewarded
with harsh and corporeal punishments. Not just for the offender, but for
the offender's co-workers. Their cruel tactics may not have inspired a lot
of love, but they did inspire a lot of obedience.

"How's that possible?" Grey asked, seeming to manifest between us,
and I realized we were still shaking hands. I quickly let go, and to my
surprise, Quess winked at me before giving a nod to Grey and disappearing into the kitchen. It took me a moment to realize he had left
without answering Grey's question.

Cali stepped off the ladder and into the room, softly clapping her
hands together. "All right, everyone, we have guests tonight, so I expect
your best behavior. Doxy, I am specifically addressing you when I
say that."

I looked over to see the statuesque woman rolling her eyes, begrudg-
ingly getting back up off the sitting pillows to start shedding herself of
knives and other tools of violence. By the time she was done, I couldn't
help but feel incredibly impressed—and extremely intimidated.

She caught me looking at her and swung her long hair over her shoulder, offering me a mocking smile as she sat back down on her cushions. I
licked my lips and then chose a spot across from her, wanting to keep her
within reaching distance. Grey took up a position on my left, while Roark
took up a whole side of the square table to himself. Quess set down two

more dishes: what appeared to be some sort of marinated potatoes, and some kind of bean dish.

My stomach made a pitiful sound at the sight of all that food, and I suddenly remembered that I hadn't eaten at all today. Still, that didn't stop my mouth from opening and questions from spilling out before I could remember my table manners.

"Where did you get all this food from? How are you living here undetected? Is it only the four of you? Why did you leave the Knights? How did Quess work in two different departments? What is it you want from us?"

I paused to take a deep breath, and Cali's smile grew as she gracefully crossed her legs. Tian appeared from a door just past the kitchen and plodded over to Cali, curling up right beside her, and Cali immediately made room for the young girl.

"She has more questions than you do," she said in a stage whisper into Tian's ear, and the young girl grinned at me, showing me a toothy smile.

"Not possible," she crooned, and Cali laughed.

"Our food is grown here," Quess said. "Luckily, Maddox here got some time in as a Hand before her rank dropped to one. We have enough to take care of ourselves, although if your medication works the way that you say it does..." He turned a quizzical eye to Roark, who was already beginning to shovel food onto his plate.

Roark paused when he realized everyone was staring, his eyes going wide. "What? Were we not starting?"

"No," Cali replied amiably. "Please, dig in, and I'll do my best to explain. We are four, yes, but there are other smaller, family-like groups like ours scattered in hidden nooks and crannies all over this Tower. Not just in the Depths, but in the Tower proper. We aren't detected because of the paint that you saw on the inside of the upper levels. It's one of Quess's designs—he's quite the genius with inventions—and it blocks Scipio's scanners from detecting us down here. I am sort of the de facto leader, but that's more out of a desire or need to trade to get other supplies. As for this place, it used to be one of the water monitoring stations, back in the early years of the Tower, before Scipio was fully operational. Now that he is, the station is remotely operated, which means no one comes down here much."

She paused to pour herself some water from a pitcher in the middle of the table, and took a sip. "Let's see... Shortly after I lost out as Champion, I fell into a state of depression. If it weren't for Doxy, I'd never have gotten through it. Anyway, my rank crashed and burned. I'd actually had some suspicions about the system being skewed to begin with, but when my number refused to improve no matter how good I felt, I knew something was going on. I started digging, and the more I dug, the faster I fell. I probably would've let myself get caught, if it hadn't been for Maddox, because I was so stubborn about finding out the truth. She convinced me to run, and we ran. We've been hiding ever since."

I took this all in, and looked around the room. "What about Quess?"

"Oh, I can explain that," he said around a mouthful of broccoli. "You see, I was pretty much told to join the Eyes, which I wasn't complaining about. As a Medic, I was garbage." He grinned at me and added in a low voice, "Can't stand the sight of blood. Anyway, I was excited to go to the Eyes because I thought it'd be tough and challenging. I had a good head for numbers and tested well in basic programming. Well, it took about three years before I got bored."

I frowned. "You requested another transfer?"

Quess threw back his head and laughed loudly. "Oh, lord no. The head of IT would never have allowed it. Too many questions going on. But I didn't really have to. I just created fake credentials with a new identity for myself, and showed up the next day with new quarters in Cogstown."

"Yeah, but then what happened?" Grey asked from next to me, and I saw a muscle twitching in his jaw. I could see he didn't like Quess and his flirtatious mannerisms—and I had to admit, he looked very attractive when he was jealous.

I used my hair to hide my smile and turned back to Quess, who shrugged. "Got bored there, too. Problem is, there's no room for innovation or creation in the Tower outside of medicine. I couldn't rebuild or adjust or streamline the antiquated machinery around the place.

Everyone gets twitchy when you mention it, yet they run around like madmen trying to keep up with the day-to-day needs of the Tower. It's exhausting and depressing."

"So you fell," Roark said, again around a mouthful of food, and I couldn't stand it any longer—I began serving myself small portions, not wanting to take too much from the people we'd found. Maddox arched a taunting eyebrow as I scooped up a spoonful of the beans with some rice, but I ignored it and took a bite.

Simple, but divine after the day we'd had.

"Pretty much," Quess said. "And don't worry about giving us your backstory. We got it from Cali already. You guys really think there's life out there?"

"Selka saw it. She touched it with her own hands, and they killed her for wanting to spread the truth to everyone. The powers that be can't stand to let the Tower go, so they crack down and keep the people living in fear of the world around them."

"The Tower wasn't meant to last forever," Quess added in the wake of Roark's statement, his blue eyes sad. "Nothing we create ever does, but yeah... it will start to fall apart eventually, even with all the TLC it's given. But still, this is a huge leap based on the belief of one person."

"He's right," Maddox said, breaking her stony silence by dropping her utensil onto her now-clean plate. "You're betting everything—your very life—on believing that your wife saw what she said she saw."

"And her getting killed for it," Roark thundered, his fists banging on the table hard enough to make dishes clatter. "You think they would've executed her if she'd just been mad? No, she was a danger to their perfect image of the Tower, so they did away with her. Like she was nothing."

He looked away from everyone, but not before his eyes had filled with the bitter sorrow of a man who was railing against a faceless system. Against those who had stolen his life and wife from him.

"On that note," Cali announced softly, filling the awkward silence that had stretched out into the small space with a confident command, "we should all start getting ready for bed."

I immediately got to my feet. "Then I should go. I need to get back up there before anyone notices that I'm missing."

Cali looked at me and then stood in one fluid motion. "I'm sorry, but I can't let you leave right now."

"Excuse me?" I stared at her, trying not to gape at the woman telling me I couldn't leave.

Her face was made of stone as she shook her head at me. "You know you heard me correctly, dear. And I'm sure that your friends have already come to the same conclusion as well."

"Gerome knows something's going on between the three of us," Grey said quietly, craning his neck up to meet my gaze, his eyes also reticent. "He's going to be waiting for you to surface so he can question you."

"And people are still out looking for us—and subsequently you," Roark added. "No way they'll let you pass by them without wanting to know how your pursuit went. Where are you going to direct them? How are you going to avoid attention, even leaving this place?"

"And you're not guiding anyone back to our home," Maddox declared menacingly. "We've worked too hard to keep our location a secret for you to start screwing this up."

"Besides," Tian added, a shy little smile on her face, "I like you. You look like you can tell good stories."

I looked all around me, clearly outnumbered in more ways than one, and realized that now that I really thought about it, I didn't even *want* to go. I barely slept when I was at home, and they had all made excellent points. Still, I hadn't forgotten about Zoe and getting her those pills. She might not be talking to me right now, but she was in trouble, and if I didn't help her, then chances were she'd just continue to go down.

"I want your word that at some point soon, I'll be able to go," I said to Cali, lifting my head in challenge.

She inclined her head somewhat. "That seems reasonable, but under my terms, all right? Everyone here is my family."

"The reason I need to go is for mine, so I think we understand each other."

The two of us continued to stare at each other, and I couldn't help but feel that Cali was taking some sort of measurement of me, weighing pros and cons in her mind based on what she was seeing right now.

In the end, it was Tian who broke the stare-off, by standing up and offering excitedly to show us our room.

As we followed her, I could still feel Cali's eyes on me. Still, the exchange had gone better than I'd hoped, and I felt that she was going to make a good ally in the days to come.

Once we figured out what the heck we were going to do.

As Tian led the three of us through the kitchen and down the hall, my eyes darted around, trying to find anything that would reveal who we were really dealing with. The small kitchen area was rudimentary, just a cooking element sitting on a metal table next to a cutting board. Another table held a plastic bin filled with soapy water, but there was no faucet for it. Everything was neat and tidy, but that was because it had to be—there wasn't any space.

In the middle of the floor in the kitchen area was an open hatch with steps leading down. The smell of damp soil and vegetation wafted through, and as I passed, I caught a glimpse of greenery down below, just out of sight. Then we were walking down the long hall. String lights were draped around protruding pipes and along the wall, giving the area a whimsical feel. I saw childish paintings—likely Tian's work—on the wall in an array of colors. The one that made me pause was of four handprints, each a different size and color, with names printed just below. They had pressed their hands together so that their forefingers overlapped with the previous one's pinkie, linking them together. Tian's small hand was in pink, Cali's in red, Maddox's in purple, and Quess's in deep blue.

It was such a simple thing, but as soon as I saw it, I felt it—the love they had for each other. It gave me pause, made me think about my own family, my parents, and I truly realized that their home was not my home.

That was followed by a surprising understanding: it hadn't been my home since Alex had left.

I sucked in a breath, suddenly desperately missing my brother, on top of Zoe and Eric. They were my family, and if I was going to protect them and keep us all together, I was going to have to get them out of Scipio's control.

Tian turned, her smile glistening, and waved a long arm at me, as if she were trying to pull me forward by magic. I realized I had stopped for longer than I'd intended to, and Roark had pushed by. Grey had come to a stop next to me, though, and as I looked at him, I saw his eyes fixed to the same place mine had been.

He looked up at me, his eyes brimming with pain that echoed my own, and I impulsively reached out to take his hand in mine, squeezing it gently. His dark eyes dropped down to my hand, and I felt him squeeze my fingers in return.

We didn't say anything, but we didn't have to; we were two people sharing a moment of pain and taking comfort in the fact that we weren't alone. We stood there for a moment, and then I began to follow Tian again, and was glad when Grey retained his grip on my hand, unwilling to let me go.

The first opening we passed was a workroom, filled with tools and objects that took up almost every square inch of the place. In spite of the clutter, it was well organized: the tools were grouped together and arranged by size on the wall, and the long tables that lined the wall held objects in various stages of deconstruction. I recognized an elevator security box, a lash harness, several stun batons, a hydroponic UV light pod—random odds and ends that were small enough to be carried.

"This is Quess's room," Tian chirped, leaning in and looking around. "He sleeps there." Her hand stretched out to point at the hammock tucked away in a corner.

"No doors?" Grey asked.

"No need," she replied, craning her neck back so she could look up at him. "We're all family. Come along."

She moved down the hall to where Roark was waiting, his face impassive, and breezed by him, her small feet running in short steps. "This is Doxy's room," she announced with a flourish as she leapt up in the air and spun. Her hands made a fluttery movement as she landed, legs spread, and she pointed to the opening on the right.

I moved up to it, curious to see how the stoic woman decorated, and I couldn't have been more unsurprised. Her room was set up as a personal training room, complete with a matted area for sparring. She slept on a cot, which was in the corner across from the opening. The blankets on it were drawn tight in militant fashion. A crimson uniform with the Squire ranking on the collar hung just next to it, the folds crisp, as if she ironed it every day. Next to that sat a rack that clearly held her knives when she wasn't wearing them.

Tian turned and skipped down the hall a few seconds later, showing us her room, which was awash with paint on the wall and a simple mattress on the floor, a paint-stained blanket on top of it. Tiny crystals that I recognized as broken bits of the convex lenses used for relaying and distributing energy dangled from string and thin lengths of wire. Like the hall, this room was filled with string lights, running ragged around the walls and on the ceiling. She took a minute to introduce us to her home-made stuffed bear, Commander Cuddles.

Grey and I both indulged the odd girl, greeting the bear in turn, but Roark wouldn't participate, and I could tell that Tian's behavior bothered him. I sensed in him the need to fix her, help her to be more *normal*.

Yet as odd as she was, she was charming. Her crooked smile and single dimple seemed to light up the room. She moved as if she were dancing half the time, skipping from spot to spot, with an occasional lavish twirl thrown in here and there. There was no keeping her still, either; I didn't think she could stop, like one of those old-world humming-birds that Zoe had told me about.

"And this is Cali's room," she chirped as she led us to the doorway just past hers. Cali's room was not what I had expected at all. I had assumed her room would be like her daughter's, packed with weapons and training equipment. Instead, it was filled with books. I recognized most of them, the familiar uniform covers that were color-coded for each department: orange for Cogs, green for Hands, crimson for Shields, and so on. Shelf after shelf lined the walls of the small room, all packed with books. The collection alone made me whistle; these books were prized by their departments, coveted by others. And Cali was sitting on a treasure trove of them.

But there were more—maps of beige shapes contrasting against the dark blue behind them, with names written on them like "Germany" and "The United States of America." Books that had more than one color or picture on the cover, some depicting people, others landscapes, others objects. My gaze fell on one with a bright cover and a crude drawing on the front, my eyes going over the title: *Danny, the Champion of the World*, by Roald Dahl.

I'd never seen so many books in one place, even when I'd been to Zoe's father's shop before he died. I looked over at Grey and saw him staring at the books too, a hungry gleam in his eyes.

"Tian, does Cali ever let anyone borrow her books?" he asked, looking down at the slender waif standing between us. Her white-blonde bob dipped up and down.

"Yes, but she has very strict rules about it. I'm on a three-week suspension because I committed a hot cocoa infraction." She leaned close to Grey, her hand going up to block one side of her mouth. "It is a level nine offense, punishable by losing dinner and coloring time."

Grey smiled, his eyes softening. "That's a pretty severe punishment. Do you think you learned your lesson?"

The blonde bob started whipping back and forth before he had even finished the question. "This is my third offense." Her hands fluttered to her sides and she smoothed her clothes down primly. "Cali says I'm doomed if it happens again, but I just can't help it! Hot cocoa and stories by the window is the best! C'mon, I will show you where you three will be staying."

She led us the rest of the way down the hall, until the low ceiling lifted up and away and we stepped into a wide-open space. The floor dropped down into a pit, where several large pieces of equipment sat. On the left and the right were the same glass panes as I'd seen in the dining area, set up in a wide circle, making it look like a fish eye against the metal and concrete walls.

Tian skipped down the semi-steep staircase that ran into the trench. I watched her for a second and then whipped out my lash, swung it around once, and hit the side of the incline. I quickly lashed down to the bottom —it was only a twenty-foot drop, really—and took a quick glance around as the others made their way down.

Tian landed lightly on her feet a moment or two later, and in short order everyone was down. "So we don't really have much in the way of beds," she said, fluffing up her hair with her hands. "But we have some hammocks and a few extra blankets." She moved over to a crate and pushed open the lid, pulling out a wad of fabric, with long coils of rope spilling from the gaps in the material.

She tossed the first one in front of us with a thump, and Roark imme-diately bent over to pick it up, tucking it under his arm and stalking toward where all the massive machines sat. I watched him go, alarmed by the sudden shift in his attitude.

I was indecisive for a moment, but then I turned to Grey. "I'm going to check on Roark," I told him, my voice pitched low for his ears. "Keep Tian distracted—I don't want her overhearing anything and miscon-struing it later."

He nodded and then turned to Tian, who was now pulling a second wad of fabric and rope from the bin. I turned just as he said, "Hey, do you want to help me pick out a good place for my hammock? I'm guessing you know all the best and worst places in the room."

Tian gave an excited cry as I drew away from them, and I followed Roark's path around one of the bulky machines. The area behind it was empty, but I saw a narrow gap between two machines, and pushed through it.

Sure enough, Roark was inside, kneeling on the grated floor and unraveling his hammock on the far side of the room. He glanced up at me as I entered the small space, then continued to work.

"What's wrong?" I asked, skipping the pleasantries.

He grunted as he whipped a length of rope around some of the fabric, working to untangle the lines so he could hang the hammock. "It's not what you think."

"You can't possibly know what I—"

"You think I saw something that made me suspicious, right?" he said gruffly, peering up at me with sharp eyes. "I'm not stupid; I know you're entertaining doubts. It's too serendipitous, too coincidental." He stopped and sighed. Shook his head and frowned. "You kids don't know how to hope, not really. And it's the damn Tower's fault. Distrust and suspicion are ingrained in all of us. People willing to drop their own family members, kill unborn children in an attempt to cull the population. Sheep—and the shepherds are all wolves. These people aren't like that, Liana. They're like us—outsiders and dreamers. People who dare to think and question and defy the very system that would regulate us all to death, reduce us to a statistic, a number. They have every bit as much to lose as we do in this relationship. More, even, as this is their home. It has been for many years."

I listened to his speech, and didn't find myself disagreeing. Truthfully, the same thing had been playing in the back of my mind, my instincts warring with my more logical side. I wanted to believe in this place, because it meant that the group of people I could rely on was getting bigger. I just wanted it to include the rest of my extended family, too.

As I considered this, I looked up at him to see he was now threading his hammock's main line over and around a pipe, stringing one end up, and a question occurred to me. "Well, I'm glad to hear that, but it doesn't exactly answer my question. Why are you acting so weird? Are you okay?"

Roark looked up at me, a hard edge coming to his face. Then he turned away and said, "I didn't get a chance to grab a picture of Selka before we ran."

He said it evenly, but I could feel his pain and loss in spite of that. He had nothing left to connect him with his wife. "I'm sorry," I offered, but he shook his head.

"Don't be—it's not your fault. You fought like a banshee with that mentor of yours, and were quick on your feet in the aftermath. I'm glad you were there. And... I'm sorry I didn't believe you when you said you were being followed."

Huh. An apology from Roark was the last thing I'd ever expected. "Color me paranoid, but who is this man and what has he done with Roark?"

Roark smiled as he crossed over to the other side of the hammock, taking care not to step on the fabric. "Anyone ever tell you that you've got a smart mouth?"

"Not recently," I replied. "But then again, I've been a bit cautious about letting it free, so to speak. Didn't want to draw any attention to myself."

"Doesn't seem like it'll be a problem here—unless of course that Maddox girl and you get into it. Still, I don't see it being anything more than you two finding out who's top dog."

"I don't think I'm going to stay here long enough to find out." Besides, I was fairly confident Maddox could rip me in half if she wanted to. The girl was intimidating.

Roark gave me a pitying glance. "You know you can't leave for a while, right?"

I frowned. "What do you mean? Cali said we could talk about it soon."

"'Soon' is a vague concept, Liana. It doesn't mean tomorrow, and it doesn't necessarily mean the day after that, either. Cali's going to want to put it off for a while to keep you here."

"But..." I frowned. Looked at him. "You know I have to go to Zoe. She's up there, and she needs us. You said you would help."

"I have every intention of helping, my dear. But Gerome is out there, and he's going to have Knights watching the people you care about, waiting for you to surface. You can't bring them here and expect this place to remain a secret."

I hated what he was saying, but he was right. I was a guest here; these people were giving us shelter, and it was hard justifying any sort of rash action. I could play it cool for a day or two, be nice, be patient, and hope that Cali would help me figure out a way to leave here without drawing any attention to myself. And I needed Roark's help to do that.

"Zoe's a four, Roark. It won't be long until she's a three, and by then it'll be too late. Cali said the system is rigged, and she's right. And Zoe's going to pay the price of it because of what I exposed her to. Because of what we needed her to do in order to save Grey's life."

He stopped pulling the rope around the pipe, the hammock still slack on the floor, and sighed. "I'll talk to Cali about it, and I'll do what I can to bring her around."

"You'd do that for me?" That made me feel so much better—Roark and Cali seemed evenly matched in terms of their connection, so maybe his word would carry more weight. After all, he was the reason so much of this plan, this idea, was coming together. Was bringing us together.

He shrugged and turned back to the rope, pulling more of the slack out. "Absolutely. Because you're right—I still owe you and her both for saving Grey. So it's the very least I can do."

Gratitude welled up in my heart, and on impulse I crossed the small distance between us and wrapped my arms around his shoulders, pressing my front against his back in a surprise hug. He went still, and then his hand came up and patted my forearm.

"You're welcome, dear. Now go get some rest. From the looks of you, you haven't gotten any in a while, and today has been a very long day."

I nodded, and retreated into the main area, looking around for Grey. He was fiddling with his hammock, which was strung in the corner next to the wide windows. I looked up, realized that a second hammock was already strung just a few feet above his, and smiled.

I quickly walked over to him, and he looked up at me as I drew near, a soft smile growing on his face.

"Is Roark okay?" he asked.

"Yes, he just... He didn't grab a picture of Selka before we left," I informed him, and he nodded. "Where's Tian?"

"She helped me hang up your hammock and then said it was bedtime before lashing out of here. I'm guessing there's some sort of bedtime ritual involved."

"Probably. So... we're bunk mates?"

He grinned and ran a hand through his wild hair. I noticed that the skin on his arm was fully healed now, and felt relieved that Roark's medicine had worked so quickly. "Well, I remember you saying you liked a good view, so—"

The next thing I knew, he was shrugging off his shirt, revealing the bare lines of his chest. My mouth went dry, and I met his eyes, trying to keep my heart from tearing out of my ribcage. He was already smiling, and one eyebrow was arched.

"I didn't mean me," he said, stepping aside to reveal the window behind him, and I blushed beet red, embarrassment curling up in my stomach, but never finding a comfortable spot to sit.

Still, I was flattered that he had not only remembered that I liked a nice view, but presented one as well.

A smirk tugged at my lips, and I reluctantly looked away, just shy of being too bold. I directed my eyes toward the window, taking in the river snaking along below, the dark mass of water glinting silver under the faint light of the moon. Even though here, under the Tower, was dark and shadowed, I could just about make out the narrow edge of the horizon, the smooth, flat landscape pale in the light.

"It's pretty good," I said approvingly. *And not just the window.* I looked back at him to find him standing, his eyes fixed on me. He speared me with a look I was beginning to recognize in him, and took a step closer to me.

"You were amazing today," he said. "Calm and collected, and you fought like a beast."

My heart sped up. "I didn't win," I hurriedly pointed out, trying to deflect some of the breath-stealing intensity he was aiming in my direction. "If Tian hadn't shown up—"

"It wasn't just that," he said. "You were smart, resourceful. You thought quickly and helped get us out of there in one piece. You are impressive."

Only, in my eyes, none of that was right. I immediately brushed the compliments aside. "You realize it's my fault that we are even here in the first place, right?" I said, the words tumbling out of me, and Grey frowned.

"What are you talking about?"

My shoulders shifted slightly, trying to relieve some of the discomfort there. "What happened with Silvan is what prompted Gerome to confront us. He wouldn't have been there if I had just followed your lead during our meeting with Silvan."

Grey's eyebrows drew closer together, his frown deepening. He reached out with one hand, slowly, his eyes silently asking me for my permission. I nodded, and then his hand touched the side of my face, cupping my cheek. I felt lightheaded as he pulled me close.

"It's not your fault. You couldn't have known any of that would happen," he said, his other arm coming around my waist. I found myself licking my lips, my gaze locked on his mouth. "And you were brave and quick on your feet in the aftermath of everything. I could never be as level-headed as you."

His head was dropping down, closer and closer to mine.

"You haven't seen me cook," I managed.

He chuckled, and I watched as the angular planes of his face softened, his mouth drawing even closer. "I'm not interested in cooking," he replied. "But I am interested in you."

My breath finally gave out, but it didn't matter—his mouth was on mine, his lips and mouth hungry. A hunger of my own—unlike anything I'd ever felt before—erupted out of me, and I found myself kissing him back, my hands reaching for his bare shoulders and then the back of his neck, holding his head in place as he held mine. His breath hitched, the hand on my waist dropping to my hip. He moved us both backward, until I felt the hard press of the wall behind me.

Grey pinned me between himself and the wall as his kiss intensified, and I burned inside, desperately alone and afraid, and ready to lose myself to this undeniable attraction I felt for him.

"You know," a feminine voice spoke up, and Grey and I froze, suddenly aware that we weren't alone. "I was raised that girls and boys shouldn't kiss before they are married. But I never listened to them on that one. The one thing I *did* do, however, was wait to make love until I was married. I hope you two will understand if I pull the 'my house, my rules' card—or I'll have to split you up to bunk with Quess and Maddox."

I shifted over slightly and saw Cali standing a few feet away, a bemused smile on her lips. I hid my face behind Grey as I felt it turning bright red. Grey didn't turn around until he was certain I was ready— something I was eternally grateful for. When I was, he made sure to grab my hand before turning.

Cali's smile had only grown, and facing her now, I could see that she was genuinely amused by the two of us. She held up the blankets she was holding, and Grey let go of my hand long enough to take them.

"Relax," she said. "You're both adults—I can't stop you from getting involved with each other. But Tian runs around here all the time, and I'd prefer not to expose her, just as I'd assume you'd rather not be exposed. So, just try to be more circumspect in future, all right?"

I nodded, while Grey said, "All right."

Cali grinned, the corners of her eyes wrinkling, and then turned to leave. "Good night!" she called over her shoulder.

"Good night," we said together.

When she was halfway up the stairs, Grey turned to me. "Are you... I mean... How are you?"

My cheeks, still red from the embarrassment of Cali catching us and calling us out like that, started to inflame again, and it was getting painful. I let go of his hand and began massaging them with my fingertips.

"Incredibly embarrassed," I told him after a second.

"Because Cali caught us?"

I hesitated, and then shook my head. "Not exactly. I... I mean we..." I trailed off, flustered. How could I explain that I was a little afraid of how I just... reacted with him? To him? It was like someone had flipped a switch and I had lost all semblance of control. It was intimidating, and I didn't know how to process it on top of this already crazy day.

"Hey, hey." He stepped close, and placed his hands on my shoulders, instantly trying to console me. "It's okay... I think I get it. It's been a long day, and a whole lot has happened."

"Yes," I breathed, instantly relieved that he understood. "I just need some time to think and process and... come to terms with everything, I guess." I twisted around to face him. "Is that okay?"

"Of course it is," he said gently. "I'm sorry for—"

"Don't apologize," I interrupted, pressing my fingers to his lips. He gave me a confused look, and I smiled. "It would be like you were apologizing for kissing me in the first place, and I don't want you to... I don't want you to feel sorry about that."

His expression softened, and I sensed the moment threatening to return, and diverted it by taking a small step back. "I'm gonna head to bed, I think," I said, swallowing hard, and he nodded, moving away a few paces over to his hammock. I felt the need to add something, so I did: "Thanks for giving me a little time."

"My pleasure—just don't think I'm going to let it go," Grey said, sitting back into his hammock like an old pro. He met my gaze, a confident smile playing on his lips. "Because I'm not."

My heart continued its heavy drumming against my ribcage, and I quickly lashed up the few feet to my own hammock and gingerly climbed into it, needing some space between myself and that cocky, enigmatic face, lest I cave.

But Cali was right, and I wasn't ready to just... fall into bed with a guy I barely knew. *You know all that you need to know*, my mind whispered, but I shoved it aside. I wasn't that girl, and we had barely started acknowledging our attraction to each other. I needed for this to go slowly.

"Good night," Grey's voice said teasingly from below. "Here." Something flew up from below, spinning up and over and landing with a thump on top of my chest—the blanket that Cali had brought in.

"'Night," I called down quickly, needing there to be an end to everything. I held my breath and waited, hearing the fabric rustle as he lay back into his hammock a few feet below. I waited for things to go still, before finally starting to get ready for bed.

I quickly shrugged out of my uniform and spread out the woolen blanket that Grey had just tossed up, curling up under it. It took me a few minutes to figure out how to adjust my limbs and lie in the hammock, but I finally found a comfortable position. The hammock swayed back and forth, and I stared out the window for a long time, using my arms as pillows. I thought about everything that had happened today, and about what the next step might be. I thought about Zoe. I thought about my parents and Alex. I searched for ways out of this mess.

Long before the answers came, my eyelids grew too heavy to resist the draw of sleep, so I gave up trying.

29

I spent most of my first day in Sanctum in my hammock, fast asleep. It was, admittedly, not the wisest move to make, considering the situation, but it was as if everything had just suddenly caught up with me. I'd spent weeks not sleeping properly, barely eating, and just clinging onto the ledge with every fingertip dug in tight. Now that it felt like I was out of sight of the Tower, I could finally *breathe*. Sleep was the only natural recourse after that.

As a result, the first day there was a blur that consisted of two bathroom breaks, some sort of salad that contained an inordinate amount of tomatoes for some reason, and a visit from Grey (and that was to deliver said salad, as I had slept through dinner).

The second day there, I got sick. There was no rhyme or reason, save that my system was still rundown enough that a virus could sneak its way past my defenses. I must have brought it with me when we came down. I knew something was wrong when I woke up in a sweat, my joints aching with a deep shiver that seemed to radiate from my bones.

The chattering of my teeth woke Grey, and he quickly got Roark.

The two men lowered my hammock down, and Roark quickly began to check me over, while Grey wrapped me in another blanket. It didn't feel like enough.

Then Roark gave me some medicine, and it was lights out.

When I woke up again, I felt worlds better. I was stretching out my aching limbs and shifting slightly in my hammock, debating the pros and cons of going back to sleep, when a voice alerted me to the fact that I wasn't alone.

"No," Tian squeaked quietly. "She's still not awake, but I did see the hammock moving."

There was a pause, and I lifted my eyelids, taking in the bright light. I shifted, the fabric of the hammock moving around, and sat up, looking around groggily.

I found Tian standing a few feet away, perched on her toes like a bird about to take flight, Grey opposite her. It was clear my waking had attracted their attention and caused their conversation to die out.

"Morning," I said, my mouth inexplicably dry. I looked around dully and wrinkled my nose at the stale smell of sweat and general funk that seemed to be wafting from my body. It was... not spectacular. "What happened? How long have I been out?"

"You got here four days ago," Tian announced.

I looked up at Grey and was surprised to see that the bags under his eyes hadn't lessened. If anything, they'd increased. His eyes met mine, and the corner of his mouth quirked up.

"You had the flu," he added, for my edification, and I blinked dumbly at him. "Roark said it was because you were so tired that you became vulnerable to it. But he managed to keep you mildly sedated so you could get through the process quickly. You don't remember anything?"

I shook my head, and I saw something I could swear was disappointment flash across his face, but it was gone too quickly for me to identify it. So I pushed it aside, trying to focus on the facts. I'd been here for four days. I'd been gone from the Tower's radar for four days.

No one knew where I was, except for the people here.

I exhaled, suddenly anxious. Everyone was going to be so worried about me. They were going to think I was hurt, kidnapped, or even dead! Zoe was still up there as well, the four on her wrist dragging her inexorably down, through the Medica and into the Citadel. Into that glass cell. Oh, God, if she thought I was dead... it would tear her apart. She would be just like Sarah, crashing down to a three and then a two, before...

The image I had conjured long ago flashed back into my mind: Zoe in place of the woman Gerome had killed in the Tower, the bright light in her eyes extinguished, her body utterly still. No more of her spark, her light, the joy she created in me, just because she had gifted me with her friendship... I needed to know what was going on with her. I needed to let her know I was okay. It would help slow her descent... and maybe I could get her a month's supply of Paragon while I was at it.

I sat up and slipped my legs over the edge of the fabric, awkwardly sliding out of the hammock. Grey and Tian both looked alarmed as I landed barefoot on the cold floor, but I kept my legs under me, ignoring the wobble in my knees. I was still in my underclothes, and even if I didn't want to believe it had been four days since we'd arrived, the dried sweat stains and dirt on them were evidence enough.

"I need my clothes," I said, looking around for my uniform. "And my lashes."

"Why?" asked Grey at the same time as Tian said, "Quess has your lashes."

I blinked and looked at Grey. "I want to go talk to Cali about Zoe. Why does Quess have my lashes?" Asking the question without any panic in my voice was hard, but I didn't want to cause a scene. Still, I was concerned—I didn't like the idea of anyone else fiddling around with my equipment. Knights were trained to service their own equipment, so they wouldn't have to place their lives in someone else's hands. The fact that Quess was even now touching my gear...

"He's improving them," Tian said with a smile. "So you can use them outside like I can. Do you want to see?"

I frowned and pondered her statement and question. Use them outside like she could? I *could* use them outside, except for here under the Greenery, and that was just because the hydro-turbines kicked up too much water for the static charge to even form. Although, come to think of it, I couldn't use them in the greeneries either, and in a few of the rooms in Water Treatment where there were large exposed pools or the waters were running through a condensation process to eliminate toxins. Maybe he had a way of making them work in those environments?

"Yes, but I should probably get some clothes first. Where is my uniform?"

"Cali has it," she replied with a smile. "And she's also not here right now, but she should be home soon."

"Where'd she go?"

Tian shrugged her slim shoulders, looking slightly nervous, and I realized that I was making her uncomfortable. "I'm sorry, Tian," I breathed, moving over to her and kneeling. "I didn't mean to ask so many questions. I'm just feeling... a little out of place with all of my things missing."

"Oh." Tian bounced back and forth from foot to foot. "I'm sorry!"

"There's nothing to be sorry about—I know everyone's just trying to help."

Tian beamed at me, a dimple forming in her right cheek, and she reached over and patted my head. "You're a kind girl—not just tough like Doxy. I like you."

I managed a smile—it wasn't too hard, because Tian just seemed to naturally exude happiness—but it was hard to hold on to the moment with my worry for Zoe looming over me.

Grey cleared his throat softly, and I looked up past Tian's head to see him giving me a crooked smile. "Cali did leave you some fresh clothes while she's cleaning your uniform." He gestured to a pile of black fabric folded up on a chair next to my hammock.

"Thanks," I said, picking up the pile. "I'll just get dressed and—"

"You're not allowed to leave this room until you take a shower," Tian said primly, cocking her head. "We all voted, and you *have* to. Just like when it's my bath time."

"And just like Tian when it gets close to her bath time, you smell a little bit." I looked over at Grey to see his eyes sparkling with mischief, and rolled my eyes. I didn't need him letting me know that I was more than a little ripe. More importantly, he didn't need to know that. It was embarrassing.

Tian grinned at me, and nodded, her white bob bouncing up and down. "You smell *a lot* a bit."

And just like that, I was smiling again. I was getting the feeling it was impossible to feel any form of negativity around the impish girl. Maybe we needed to bottle the exuberance she was exhibiting—it beat the hell out of any pills the Medica was pushing.

"All right," I said, raising one hand in defeat. "Message received. Help a girl out by directing her to the showers?"

Tian pointed, her arm stiff and finger outstretched. "Up the stairs," she said primly. "There's soap and towels already in there. We'll wait here for you. Grey is going to teach me a game, so take your time!"

I looked over her head at Grey, and was surprised to see him smiling widely at the young girl, a deck of cards already spinning between his fingers. "Today, I'll be teaching you an important lesson about losing— specifically how to do so gracefully," he announced, and Tian tittered, one hand coming up to cover the crooked smile on her face.

The two of them wandered to a nearby table that had seemingly manifested out of nowhere. They must've moved it in for me, because it was covered with a few pill bottles and the remains of two meals. That meant people had been keeping me company for at least two days. I absorbed that as Grey looked up from where he was now pushing in Tian's seat, his eyes finding mine and a small smile tugging at his lips.

I stared, my heart pounding, as I suddenly connected the dots. I'd been here for four days. I'd been sick for at least two of those four days. And *he'd* been sitting with me. Vague memories tugged at me, flashes of his brown eyes brimming with concern, a strong hand wiping the sweat off my forehead with a cold cloth, the sound of his voice... No words, just the sound, strong and steady and soothing.

He broke the connection to sit down across from Tian, and I turned tail and ran, desperately needing a shower and a moment to collect myself before deciding what to do next, what I was going to do with or about Grey, and how I was going to convince Cali to at least let me check on Zoe.

The shower definitely helped me to center myself. The water was hot, and as I cleaned off four days' worth of sweat and grime, I began to feel more like a human and less like a zombie. I took some time to dry off in the small locker room, then donned the black clothes. These weren't microthread, and had a heavy, slightly cumbersome feel. The pants were a bit snug in the rear, the shirt a bit long in the arms, but overall they were a good fit. Still, I couldn't help but feel I was carrying around too much on my skin.

I stepped out of the shower and walked back down the stairs. Grey and Tian were still sitting at the table, and I could hear Grey's loud laugh over Tian's shrieking one, followed by a slamming sound as they both slapped their hands on the table. I smiled as the laughter cut short and was quickly replaced by suspicious eyes as the two glared at each other. After a long moment, they withdrew their hands and looked at the cards they had just thrown down.

Grey stood up just as Tian grabbed her face and began to moan in a dramatic fashion. "The winner and still champion!" he crowed victoriously, fists pumping in the air.

Tian's head rolled forward and planted cheek-first onto the table. "Noooooooooooooooo!" she groaned, her hands sweeping back and forth and dislodging the cards there. She didn't do it hard enough to knock any of them to the floor, but I still couldn't help but laugh, especially when she spotted me and sat straight up, with a card stuck to her cheek.

I doubled over, laughing, too entertained by their cuteness, and Grey began laughing as well. Tian looked around, blinking.

"What?" she asked, completely oblivious to the card on her face. Then she reached up, touched it, and ripped it away from her cheek with a theatrical eye roll.

"You two are *soooooooooo* immature," she said, her nose lifting up in the air as she flicked the card at Grey. She pushed off the chair and stood up, smoothing out her short skirt, and my laughter faded back into bemusement at her antics. "Ready to go see Quess?" she asked once our laughter had died out.

"Yes, please." I was beyond ready. My lashes were my life, and even though I had definitely needed the shower, making sure my equipment was okay was a very close second (since I had to wait anyway).

Tian smiled and began skipping her way to the stairs leading back to the hall and the kitchen. I made to follow her, and Grey fell in next to me, his hands shoved in his pockets.

"So, you and Tian seem to be getting along well. How have the last few days been with everyone?"

"Good," Grey replied. "I mean, when you got sick, we all took turns sitting with you."

"Grey sat with you the most," Tian called over her shoulder.

Grey's cheeks flushed, and he ducked his head, rubbing the back of his neck with one hand. "I... well... I thought you might be uncomfortable if it wasn't someone you really knew yet sitting over you when you woke up."

I was taken aback by his statement, but inordinately pleased. "Thank you," I said. He looked up at me, and I added, "That was very thoughtful of you."

"Don't mention it." The warm feeling I was holding in my heart was nice, and I wanted so much to build on it, to keep it going... but then I thought of Zoe, and just felt downright selfish. Here I was, checking my lashes and flirting with a guy I liked, and meanwhile she was worried sick wondering what had happened to me.

I looked away, suddenly heartsick, and Grey reached out to put an arm around my shoulders, pulling me over to him.

"It's going to be okay, Liana. Cali and everyone—except for Maddox, Maddox is scary—" I looked at him, and he gave a little shrug. "She's been teaching me to fight, and she's not exactly... patient?"

"Gentle," Tian chimed in helpfully from ahead. "Doxy isn't gentle. But she means well. She even taught me a few things."

And to demonstrate, the girl spun around and landed squarely on one stair, her legs spread apart. She punched her fists into the air in front of her, and shouted, "Pow, pow," as she did it. Grey and I stared at her, both of us sharing a smile as she sweetly lowered her arms and smoothed her skirt down again.

"If you'd been standing right there, you'd be dead right now," Tian whispered, before turning and skipping up the remaining few steps to the top.

"I'm sure I would be," I agreed, and Grey chuckled.

We continued to climb in silence, and then Grey said, "Oh, hey, have you looked at your indicator yet?"

I immediately looked down, and was surprised to see that there wasn't even a number on it—only a little hyphen in green, as if it were waiting for something. A quick look at Grey's wrist showed the same thing.

"Why is it—?"

"The paint that Quess developed is blocking any and all signals to and from Scipio. That means this doesn't work in here. It's been... kind of liberating, actually. Fair warning, though—Quess is going to ask you if you want to take yours off."

"He can do that?"

Grey nodded. "Apparently so."

I fell silent and rubbed my fingers over my own wristband. What would it feel like *not* to carry that burden anymore? To be judged based on myself and what I had to offer, rather than on what Scipio told others I had to offer?

"You okay?"

I looked over to meet Grey's warm brown gaze and nodded. "Just thinking what it would feel like for me."

He smiled and looked down, his hair falling to cover his forehead. "It's your decision," he said. "Maddox still wears hers around her wrist, as does Cali, but they do it in case they have to go out into the Tower for any reason."

"Is that why you kept yours?"

Grey hesitated, giving me a speculative look, and then nodded. "Yeah —you never know, and it's better just in case. Still, it's great that it doesn't mean anything in here."

"Yeah, I can see that." I had already decided to keep mine on, in case I had to go up there. It wasn't even a question for me right now. But a part of me desperately longed to be free from it.

I looked ahead and saw Tian disappearing into Quess's room, and moved to follow her. A flash of light momentarily caused gray spots to form in my eyes, though, and I winced and looked away, blinking a few times to clear my vision. When I looked back, Quess was lowering a welding wand onto the wide table in the middle of the room, and pulling up a pair of blackened goggles so they sat atop his head.

"Hey, Liana," he said, a white smile breaking free of the lines of grime and dirt on his face. "Nice to see you're feeling better. You gave us all a scare there."

"Thanks," I said, my worry over my lashes displaced slightly by the genuine warmth in his eyes. I fidgeted, trying to think of something to say that would qualify as small talk before I interrogated him on what he was doing to my equipment.

"She's worried about her lashes," Tian said after several long seconds had gone by, and I was immediately relieved. I had been drowning looking for a way out.

Quess's smile grew. "I figured you would be," he said jovially, disappearing behind the table as he squatted. He stood, his hands brimming with my lash harness, and I almost reached across the table to snatch it from him. I refrained, and watched as he gently placed the collection of straps and the circular lash housing on a clear area of the table. "Cali and Maddox are both equally protective over theirs as well. I made some adjustments to the spinner inside so you'll be able to control the lashes more precisely. It causes them to repel and retract more quickly, too, so be aware of that. I also changed out the static beads at the ends with ones of my own design—ones that allow you to create a friction bond instead of a static one."

I came around the table as he spoke, my hands immediately removing the metal dome of the lash housing. The entire rig was so familiar to me that it didn't take me long to find all the modifications that he had made. However, since a modified rig was such a foreign concept, I had no idea how it would work until I tested it out.

I eyed Quess as he continued to speak, explaining the friction bond and how it worked, and tried to gauge his competence. I didn't come up disappointed. He sounded so much like Zoe—even more technically-minded in some ways—as his explanations began to expound into theoretical physics. He fell silent when he realized everyone—including me—was starting to glaze over, and sighed.

"No one appreciates genius," he grumbled. "Anyway, test them out. I should just warn you, though, to be careful not to hit anyone with them unless you really mean it. If they're flung with enough force, they will shatter bones on impact."

"Thanks for the warning," I said, legitimately nervous about the state of my lashes. I'd definitely be testing them out as soon as I could. "Now, any chance I can find out what is going on with my baton?"

Quess smiled, but it was Cali who answered, surprising all of us with her presence. "Maddox is tinkering with it. I hope you don't mind."

I regarded her for a moment. "When will I get it back?"

She smiled, not unkindly. "When you need it."

I glanced around, and realized everyone was looking away uncomfortably. They could sense a confrontation coming, and didn't want to be a part of it. Everyone save me had gotten some time to get to know each other, and this was my chance to either make an utter fool of myself, or give a good impression. I licked my lips and decided that I would be direct, but try not to escalate the situation.

"Am I a prisoner here?"

Cali sucked in a deep breath, her smile fading some. "Not exactly, but I can't let you leave right now. Roark explained to me about your friend while you were sick, and I'm sorry, but leaving now would only jeopardize our safety. Until we know how hard the Knights are looking for you, we just can't risk you being seen up there. Especially after you've been missing for four days."

I pressed my lips together, trying to keep calm. I really didn't need a reminder of how much time I'd been away. I exhaled. "Look, I'm not like everyone here. No offense." I looked around at everyone, my hands raised in what I hoped they would understand was polite contrition, but continued ahead. "I have people in the Tower who are good people. People who know that there is something going on, and who are at risk of being punished for that knowledge. My last interaction with one of them wasn't good, and once she hears that I'm missing, she will fall. I know her —as furious as she is at me, if she thought something bad had happened to me..."

I trailed off and looked around the room, trying to find some sort of support and only finding Grey looking at me. I met his gaze, pleadingly, and was relieved when he looked over at Cali.

"I want to help her friend, too," he said. "I owe it to her. Without her, I wouldn't be alive to stand here right now. Besides, this might be your family down here, but up there—that's hers. Imagine what you would do in her shoes."

Cali stared at us both, her face an impassive mask. Then she turned to me and asked, "Do you think your friend could wait for a few more days?"

I felt my heartbeat pick up. "I think she could. Do you mean—"

"I can't make any promises," she said, holding her hand up to stop me. "And I won't give you a firm date. But I have a meeting scheduled with my contact in the Eyes in a nearby signal relay station, and he can give me a better assessment of the situation. Maybe we can come up with a plan to get your friend a meeting with you. Does that seem fair?"

I paused, aware that everyone was waiting to see if I would accept her proposition.

I met her keen gaze. "Only if I get to go with you."

She hesitated for a fraction of a second, and then nodded. "Very well."

Our deal struck, I breathed a little bit easier, relieved that Cali did indeed have a heart. Now all I had to do was keep busy until it was time for the meeting—then, hopefully, we could get the information we needed to get Zoe's rank up before things got too awful for her.

I prayed she could keep it together until I got to her.

30

F ive days later, I found myself praying *I* could keep it together. I was
bursting at the seams to get out of the tight confines of the monitoring station, to use my lashes, to do *something*. Not that I wasn't finding
ways to keep myself busy—there were all manner of ways to keep busy.
Chores, training, repair work, sparring—I'd run out of time before I ran
out of things to do.

And I got to know Tian, Quess, and Cali a bit better. Maddox as well,
I suppose, but the young woman was a tough nut to crack. She talked,
sure, but it was mostly dry witticisms, short statements with liberal doses
of sarcasm and a general disdain for whatever I, in particular, was saying
at any given time.

I'd hate her if she didn't remind me so much of myself. Just a... gruffer
version who was a little more unrefined than I'd like to think I was.
Besides, I could fully comprehend that it was hard for any of them to let
new people in. I learned that they'd been living this particular hideout for
two years, and hadn't interacted in person with too many people—neither
with their contacts, nor with the other undoc units Cali managed. The

policy kept them safe, so they couldn't be identified and so no one knew where they were.

Their closeness was palpable, that much was sure. It was hard to even transition from room to room without feeling like an interloper. Tian, Quess, and Cali all tried their best to make us feel welcome, but I was still adjusting to my new life here. Still learning who everyone really was—and how life was going to be from here on out.

Yet none of the work or bonding ever fully distracted me from the worry I felt for Zoe, Eric, and Alex. I was so scared at how worried I'd made them, a part of me fearing that when they found out I was okay, they'd never forgive me for abandoning them like that without so much as a word of what was happening.

No matter how many times I tried to remind myself that there hadn't been any time to do any of that, it still didn't ease the anxiety I was feeling. Which would probably explain why I leapt out of my hammock and onto the floor when I saw Cali descending the stairs, Roark in tow.

I moved over to intercept them, climbing the stairs. "Hey," I said when I was close enough. "Is it time?"

Cali nodded and looked at Roark. "You'll need to take Paragon before you go," he said, holding out a pill. "Just in case." I took it and swallowed it immediately and impatiently, raring to go.

"I already took mine," Cali added, glancing at Roark from the corner of her eye. "Of course, it'll be impossible to tell whether it works until we're outside."

"It works, you shrew," Roark said, and Cali chuckled, not at all offended by the rough edge of Roark's tongue.

"All right, all right—I trust in you and your work, okay? Liana, I'll meet you in the dining room in ten minutes." It wasn't a question, but I nodded anyway, immediately turning down the stairs and racing back to the sleeping area.

It didn't take me long to strip down, get my harness on, and get dressed again. I made sure to thread the lashes through my belt, opting for safety rather than speed, and fingered the new beads at the tips. I'd tested them in a limited capacity inside, but I hadn't been able to give them a real trial run.

Testing them out would keep me distracted until we got to wherever we were going, to speak to whomever Cali's contact was in the Eyes. The one who was going to help me find a way to Zoe. He had to.

I finished getting ready and hurried to meet Cali up front. She was already waiting there, Maddox standing next to her with her arms crossed, a displeased expression on her face. As soon as Maddox saw me, her eyes narrowed into slits.

"I should go with you," she snapped, her head swiveling toward her mother.

Cali's mouth pressed into a thin line that reminded me of my mom when she got angry, but, to my surprise, her voice was soft and patient. "Three have a bigger chance of attracting attention, and you know it. Liana will back me up if anything should go wrong."

Maddox's bright green eyes found mine and stared at me, hostility glistening in them. "She'd better," she said, not even bothering to disguise the threat in her voice.

I blinked as she stalked by me, turning on my heel to watch her go, and then turned back to Cali.

"I'm, uh, sorry if I caused you two to fight," I said, feeling a bit awkward. I didn't feel bad about going with Cali—I *needed* to hear whatever her contact had to say—but causing strife between mother and daughter wasn't my intention, and I did feel bad about that.

"Don't be," she replied, smoothing her clothing. "I tried to raise my daughter to have more fun, but she's got too much of her father in her. He doesn't trust easily, either."

I frowned. I'd assumed Maddox's father was dead, since he wasn't a fixture, but she'd just referred to him in the present tense. Which meant she thought he was still alive. Maybe she'd had to abandon him when she and Maddox had fled?

It was hard to tell; while I had gotten closer to Cali, she was tight-lipped about her past. I had tried asking her a few questions about her experience in the Tourney—after all, she had won a few of her own battles (not that that had affected much, as Devon had still become Champion over her). There hadn't been a real Tourney in my lifetime, and it was unlikely there would be one either. I had hoped she'd want to talk about it, but she didn't, much to my disappointment.

Cali began climbing the ladder leading back up to the entry, and I waited a few seconds before following so I could collect myself.

Outside, it was dark, the glow of the moon barely penetrating the deep shadows below. Soft lights ran along the handrails of the catwalks, helping to illuminate the path, but their light was muted and practically non-existent after a few feet. The visibility out here was downright dismal.

I looked at Cali, ready to ask her about it, when I noticed her pulling something from her coat that flopped around in her hand. She took hold of it with both hands, and a second later the one thing became two as she pulled it apart.

As she held one up to me, I realized they were goggles—much like the ones Quess had been wearing, but with red lenses. I took the pair she offered and followed her lead, fixing them over my eyes.

The haze immediately lessened, and my vision improved dramatically. The lights were brighter, clearer, burning like little white suns in the night. I tilted my head around, amazed, and then noticed something bright green from the corner of my eye. As I adjusted my gaze, I realized that it was a mark, and that there were several of them, not just in green, but also in pink, purple, and blue. I looked over at Cali in question, and saw her smile knowingly.

"Tian's a living and breathing map," she told me as she pulled her lash ends. "I swear, she never gets lost, no matter where she is. As a result, she paints directions for us, so we can find our way more easily and not get lost—the blue is for where we're siphoning our water from, pink is for heading inside, green is for the nearest greenery, and purple is for the safe routes in and out of the Tower."

I blinked, and studied the little marks. "So anyone can see these?"

"Not without the goggles. Quess designed the paint she uses to be visible only through these. It's also a way for us to leave signals for each other, in case we need a safe place to hide. So keep the goggles with you, okay?"

"Okay. So where are we going?"

Cali's answer was to whirl her lash once and launch it at the ceiling overhead as she leapt off the catwalk, trusting that her aim was true. I watched as she plummeted down another ten feet, and then the lash caught, arresting her fall and turning it into a graceful arc. I gathered my own lashes quickly and moved to follow her, praying that Quess's modifications held.

Thanks to Quess's goggles, I was able to keep pace with Cali fairly easily, although I held back some, letting her lead the way rather than attempting to catch up. The modifications Quess had made to my lashes seemed to be holding all right, although the amount of moisture in the air made me considerably twitchy at first. But after a while, I began to trust them more and more, and took the chance to really stretch out some stiff lashing muscles.

We lashed for fifteen or twenty minutes across the bottom of the Tower before Cali slowed to a stop and began retracting herself up to the structure above. As I watched, she pressed something, and suddenly a section of the ceiling drew back, revealing a dark hole above. Cali pulled herself through it, and then held out a hand for me a second later.

I drew close and grabbed it, and she heaved me up and in with a grunt. I grabbed onto the first stationary thing I saw, and helped her heft my body up farther, relaxing when I slid my hips into the room. She relaxed as well, and then stood upright and disappeared into the darkened room. Even with the goggles, I couldn't see where she had gone, or anything at all really—the room had no discernible light anywhere.

Then I heard a click, and a light blossomed, nearly blinding me with its proximity and brightness. I took off the goggles and gave my eyes a second or two to adjust, letting Cali's blurred form come into focus as she moved around. The light was being generated by a small lamp over a workstation—a workstation at which Cali was now sitting.

The rest of the room was fairly cramped and compact, rife with wires, conduits, circuit breakers, and pipes everywhere. There was maybe enough room to stand ten feet apart, but that was about it in terms of the size of the place.

She bent over and pressed something underneath the desk, and immediately the terminal turned on, the screen glowing white. Cali touched the screen, and began typing something into it.

"So this is a relay station?" I asked, looking around. "What's it relaying?"

"Orders from Scipio, ranking adjustments, location updates... As much info as they can possibly collect on the people who live here." She continued to type as she talked, and I saw screen after screen come up.

"Are you former IT or something?" I asked, impressed by how quickly she seemed to work.

"Ha, that's a funny joke. I'm no better at computers than Maddox is at making friends, bless her heart."

"But you—"

"Don't read into it. I just memorized the instructions on how to do this years ago."

Years ago? That was interesting. Especially if that meant she'd known the man in question for a long time, as *that* would mean he wasn't likely to stray at the drop of a hat. I hoped.

"So, why are we here?" I asked, trying to dig for more information on this mysterious contact. "I mean, if he's with the Eyes, doesn't that mean he can... I don't know, hide the calls or something?"

"I'm sure he can, but precaution is always the best form of safety. Using a relay station where thousands of terabytes of information are processed every day is the best way of avoiding detection."

That made sense. I waited for her to continue, but she didn't, and she hadn't really left me any tidbits for continuing the conversation. She stopped typing and leaned back in the chair, going still. The seconds ticked by, and still nothing happened.

"What now?" I asked.

"Now I wait. He's not always on time, but that's understandable, considering that he's doing it from the Core. It's dangerous, and requires excellent timing and security protocols—or so he likes to remind me when I point out that he's late."

I considered this. "How can he still be up there? It's obvious from how he's helping you and Roark that he isn't on their side. How does he avoid detection?"

"I'm not sure," she replied. "I've often wondered the same thing, and the only thing I can think of is that he managed to trick the system somehow."

I considered that too, piecing together the scraps of information that Roark had given me about him. He had contacted Roark before the old man had even finished refining the pill. Which meant he'd been helping him for some time. Cali as well. There was some trust there. It sort of dismissed the hope I carried that the contact was somehow Alex.

I exhaled, and turned back to the opening I was still half-perched in, looking down into the darkness beyond. "Can I ask you something?" I asked after a pause, and I heard the chair squeak. I glanced over to see her looking at me, her face mostly in shadows, save for the light being cast by the computer.

"I reserve the right not to answer it, but yes."

"What is the big plan here, with all of this?"

"All of this?"

"Yes," I said, and then faltered. "Not to imply that your home isn't very lovely, but, I mean... at any moment, things could go wrong for you, and there'd be no one to help you. Doesn't that scare you?"

"Every night," she admitted honestly. "I have nightmares about it. About failing to keep my family safe from this world that they, and you, were born into. It's not your fault that everything is falling apart up there, becoming a screwed-up mess, but, sad to say, you'll be the ones to fix it... or tear it down."

I frowned, her words confusing me. I'd thought we were planning to just leave the system, but she was talking about... fixing it or tearing it down? Did Cali want us to fight instead of run?

"Why do you say that?"

"No reason," she said. There was a pregnant pause, and then she spoke again. "It's just a feeling. The number of undocs has been growing exponentially for the last twenty years. When I first got out here, you could find but a handful of us. Now? I know of at least seventy people trying to survive outside the shell like this. That's a sign that something really bad is about to happen inside the Tower —nothing good."

"Right. Which brings me back to my question. What is the—"

"Shut up," Cali said abruptly, and turned back to the screen as something began flashing across it. Alarm crawled up my spine, but when she looked back at me, it evaporated under the calm control there. "It's fine; it's just him. Just try to be quiet, okay? He doesn't like surprises."

I nodded. I'd waited this long. What was a few more minutes? I watched as she hit something on the screen, and then—

"Did you secure the Medic?"

The voice—I didn't want to say "his," as it was unclear what gender the person actually was—came out of the terminal, digitally rendered to the point that it didn't even sound human anymore.

"We did," she said. "And got two strays with him. His assistant, and a Squire who's been taking the medication he created."

"Are they threats?"

Cali didn't hesitate in her response. "Not that I've seen, and my gut tells me they are trustworthy."

"I trust your assessment, but still want to get some background of my own. The Squire, is this the one Roark mentioned? Liana Castell?"

"Yes. And she needs a little help in regards to a member of her family she wants to bring down here to live with us. Apparently, she knows a bit too much, and her ranking is being adversely affected as a result."

"I see. And I suppose you want my help to try to make this happen?"

"If you can swing it. I'm not sure how bad things have been in the Tower since Tian wound up interfering."

"It has not been good," the voice replied. There was a long pause. "Give me the name of the family member in question."

"She's not biological family," I said, unable to keep quiet anymore, and the look Cali gave me should've caused me to die on the spot. "Her name is Zoe Elphesian, and she helped me save Grey Farmless's life. Her rank was a four the last time I saw her, and if what Cali tells me about Scipio is correct, then she'll continue to fall. Especially if I'm missing."

There was a silence, and then the voice returned. "I assume this is Squire Castell."

"Drop the Squire, and call me Liana. What should I call you?"

"Hey—nice try, Liana. The only name I will give you is 'Mercury.' Cali, I would be willing to discuss my assessment and findings later and in private a week from now. I trust that you'll honor that request."

"Hey, now, wait a minute," I started, my face heating as my panic grew. "My friend doesn't have a week—she might only have *days*. I need your help to get her out of there, without drawing too much attention to myself."

"Which is why we have to move slowly with these things," the voice said through the speakers. "Being fast is the same thing as being sloppy, and we can't afford to have any mess whatsoever."

"Please, Mercury. Her life is on the line. She's one rank short of mandatory treatment at the Medica, where they'll force who knows what down her throat and turn her into a little automaton who spends her life devoted to a thing that will have her killed for not being happy to devote her life to it!" Mercury had to agree—he just *had* to. I couldn't imagine that anyone who was working hard to keep so many people safe would turn his or her back on another human being in need.

"We all know the score, Liana!" Mercury reprimanded me, harsh and angry. "Lives are at stake, yes, and unfortunately, the ones down there outnumber your friend. I have spent years trying to keep them safe, and I won't jeopardize all of them for one person. So you'll either be patient while I try to help you, or I will stop helping you, have Roark dope you with as much of his memory-forgetting medication as possible, and get Cali to leave you somewhere, trussed up, for a Knight patrol to find you.

Fair warning, though: if you choose the last option, then you don't get to come back here. Clear?"

I unclenched my jaw enough to say, "Yes," and then turned away from the pad, anguished that, once again, I was going to have to wait a whole week before we had any semblance of a plan.

No, I didn't want to put any one of our new acquaintances in danger. They had been nothing but kind and welcoming the last week and a half, and I'd really grown to care about them. Especially Tian and Quess—those two had such a way about them. So happy and carefree. I couldn't bear the idea of putting anyone in danger in the process of helping Zoe. Zoe herself wouldn't even like it.

But at the same time... Zoe would've done anything for me. She already *had* done anything for me, been there when I'd most needed her, risked her ranking because of it. And if our roles were reversed, she probably would have found a way to reach me by now. The thought that I'd failed her for *days*, and might continue to fail her for more days to come, hollowed out my stomach.

I couldn't ignore the fact that I didn't know what her number was now, so I couldn't gauge exactly how imperative it was for me to get to her. On the one hand, I could see their point about needing to be cautious and waiting until the heat had died down a little bit. But on the other... I knew all too well what the Medica treatment was like. And I also knew what happened to the ones.

"Good. Cali, next time we have visitors, just announce them, won't you?"

"Sorry," Cali offered, not at all contrite. "But this is her family, Mercury—it was important for her to be here. You understand."

Mercury was silent for several seconds. "I do. I'll contact you in a week, same time."

"Over and out." Cali punctuated her goodbye by hitting a button and causing the screen to go dark. I heard her rustling around for something, then felt her hand on my shoulder. "I'm sorry it didn't go well, dear," she said, squeezing gently before removing her hand. "But he's going to look into getting her out of there. We will get her out, don't you worry."

I *was* worried, and I was sick of hearing that I was not supposed to worry. But I didn't see any other choice in front of me at the moment, so I could only ready my lashes in preparation of going home. I wasn't sure how I was going to last, not knowing what was happening back within the shell—whether my friend was all right, if her ranking was still a four or if she'd dropped to a three—it was agony. I was doing everything I could to keep it together, to be patient.

Donning my goggles, I looked down at the hole, connected my line to the side, and swung out into the air.

And then the net began to buzz violently with activity, causing me to wince slightly and falter in my next lash placement as a masculine voice was digitally synthesized into my ear.

Liana?

31

I was breathless, my eyes already darting around and searching for figures starting to race in. If he was netting me, then that meant Scipio was picking me up somehow. It meant we were in danger.

Calm down, he said soothingly, but I detected the nervous tremor in his voice. *Are you okay?*

I looked over at where Cali's legs were now beginning to poke through the underbelly of the greenery, indecisive for a heartbeat. Cali didn't know about Alex. If she found out he was contacting me, she would want me to end it immediately, as it could draw attention to Sanctum. And if I were in her shoes, I would do the same thing. But my emotions weren't allowing me to carry through, and I gave over to hypocrisy, deciding to keep talking to Alex, while hiding it from Cali. I threw my lash, moving away at a sedate pace—heading back to Sanctum, for now.

Liana?

"I'm fine," I muttered, keeping my voice pitched as low as possible so he could still hear me. I was only a little worried Cali would notice, but it was so loud outside in the cavernous space that I would need to scream for her to hear. I just hoped she interpreted my not waiting for her as a desire to be alone, and didn't decide to bridge the gap. "Why are you netting me?"

Are you joking? *Liana, we just had your funeral two days ago.* The net managed to convey his utter consternation and disdain for me at that moment, but none of that mattered.

They'd had my funeral two days ago. My parents and friends (and, up till today, my brother) all thought I was dead.

"What do they think happened?" I asked, unable to stop myself.

Your mentor was found murdered. Everyone knows you got the call from Scipio that he was down, and the net's telemetry put you first in the area, and then moving away from it at a fast speed, presumably in pursuit of the person who killed him. But when you didn't come back... and no one could find you... the Knights assumed that whoever killed Gerome had killed you too and dumped your body down a plunge or elevator shaft. What happened to you? Why didn't you come home? Are you a prisoner?

"No," I said, alarm coursing through me as his questions grew more and more invasive, and I found myself unable to process half of what he said. I glanced over my shoulder to see Cali a respectful distance behind, and tossed another lash, pressing forward.

"What do you mean, Gerome is dead?" I demanded.

They found him on the floor of dwelling C19. He had suffered a blow to the head, but it was later revealed that he died of poisoning. My heart leapt into my throat as I thought of the pill I had shoved between his lips, and I would've vomited, had Alex not added: *The toxin was injected into his body. The autopsy notes a mark on his neck and speculates that was the injection point. It's presumed Grey Farmless was the murderer, as Gerome caught him last week when he fell to the rank of one. I'm still not sure why or how he was released, but...*

He trailed off, but I barely noticed, my stomach still torn to shreds. I had left Gerome unconscious and alone on the floor of that room, and someone had killed him. I knew it hadn't been any of us—I was certain he had been alive when we left. Which meant someone else had entered after we were gone. To kill Gerome.

I just couldn't fathom why anyone would want to kill him. Sure, he had been a ten, and didn't tend to emote anything, remaining stern and stoic. And, yeah, he'd devoted himself a little too blindly to the Tower. But at the end of the day, he had been a person. A human being.

My paranoid side—never one to miss a beat—suddenly managed to put the severity of the situation into context, and realized just how dangerous communicating like this could be. It did not escape me that if I were found to be alive, I was also going to be charged with Gerome's murder. But what bothered me more was the timing of it all. It seemed so odd that everything had happened at once—and then Gerome had been killed by someone who just happened to be in the area?

It was all too surreal. Cali and I had just finished our conversation with the mysterious Eye contact, and now Alex was netting me? How had he found me, and how exposed was I?

"Alex, how did you know to net me?" I asked, following the impulse.

I... well... He swallowed hard, the sound an odd cadence of tones in my ear. *I've built a backdoor into the programming attached to your net, so that when they declared you dead and deactivated it, I could still pull it up from time to time. Just to... Just to see.*

Something inside me cracked under the pain of his words, and I felt awful. God, how terrible it must have been for him; how powerless he must have felt. He was used to taking care of me, and when he had been told I was dead, it must have devastated him.

"Alex, I'm—"

It's not your fault. I'm just glad you're alive.

I was too, but all this information was terrifying, and I kept thinking about Gerome, his murder, and what it meant for all of us. They thought Grey had done it. That meant they were looking for him. I had supposedly been in pursuit of him, and they assumed he'd killed me too. I had to be sure Alex netting me wasn't putting us all in danger.

"Alex, tell me that netting me hasn't alerted anyone to the fact that I'm alive."

You know, I am the older twin, which means I'm the smarter one, right?

"Define 'smart,'" I grumbled, but his enigmatic answer—classic Alex —was reassuring. He had taken precautions in keeping my living status protected. He wouldn't tell anyone, either. "Listen, Alex, after we are finished, can you destroy any record of this net coming up in the mainframe?"

Well, yes, but you're going to have to give me a very good reason why.

"Alex, the Knights are killing the ones. They're not even bothering to restructure anymore; they are just gassing them in cells like they're no better than rodents."

There was a long pause, followed by, *I know.*

My stomach churned. "Was this what you were talking about when you mentioned people dying?"

Yes. Although at the time I only knew that ones were dying some-how, and that was just because I'd noticed a discrepancy in the annual death rate. There was a five percent spike in accidental deaths in the Tower, starting nearly twenty years ago. Since then, the number of deaths that involve ones has nearly tripled. I only pieced together that it was the Knights a week ago, and I was grappling with how to tell you when—

"I disappeared." I closed my eyes, wishing I had figured out some way to reach out to Alex sooner, but glad he was on my side. "I'm so sorry, Alex. I feel awful for what I put you and everyone else through, but... God, this is such a long story, and I don't have a lot of time. The people I'm with are extremely cautious, and want me to lie low until the heat has passed."

Liana, that's going to take a lot longer than you think. Things... Things have changed up here.

I frowned as I lashed around an obstacle in the path. "What do you mean?"

The council voted, and it's now mandatory for anyone of rank four or lower to get Medica intervention. Threes are automatically detained there for an undetermined amount of time, and all of it is being enforced by the Knights. The council voted five to two on this, Liana. That's unprecedented.

"Who were the two against?" I asked. The information wasn't necessary, but it could come in handy if it told me where to find allies.

Mechanics Department and Water Treatment.

I absorbed the information, but moved on to my most pressing concern. "Alex, have you heard anything about Zoe and her rank? The last I saw her she'd dropped to a four. We... We had a fight, and I'm just really worried about her."

There was a long pause, and my anxiety hitched up a notch. "Alex?"

She's a two, Liana. She's being held in the Medica as a critical threat to Tower security.

For a second, I couldn't feel anything. Then it came pouring in, my greatest nightmare realized. Zoe was locked up inside the Medica, isolated, alone, and afraid—and thinking her best friend in the whole world had betrayed her and left her all alone.

And it was all my fault.

"Access her net," I said. "What's her current rank, and is it possible to tell how long it'll be before she drops to a one?"

Alex didn't offer a word of argument, so it was a little unnerving when he suddenly came back with: *She's still a two, but her levels are low. She... She doesn't have long, Lily.*

I closed my eyes, fighting against the pain and panic that threatened to consume me. "Alex, I gotta go. I need you to keep everything under your hat, and I'll try to net you soon."

Liana, what are you—

"I love you," I added, before I shut down the connection with a touch on my display.

What was happening with Zoe wasn't right, but I had no idea what to do about it. On the one hand, I wanted nothing more than to start planning a way out of here. If I could just get some of Roark's medication, I could get up to the Medica and... figure out some way to get it to her.

Yet even as I thought of it, waves of guilt washed over me. Cali had opened her home to us, even let me talk to Mercury. She was doing everything she could think of to help me, and I had no desire to put her and everyone else at risk—the thought of it alone was repulsive. But so was the idea of letting Zoe continue like this, one step away from the glass cell and poison gas.

Deeply conflicted, I continued to lash back toward Sanctum.

I didn't say much once we got back—but I wasn't really in the mood to talk. I headed straight for the bathroom. The hard edges of panic and anxiety were starting to slip in between the cracks in my armor, and I felt nausea churning deep in my gut.

It was an impossible choice, I realized—either go and rescue Zoe and risk leading someone back here, or stay here, knowing that at any moment she would drop to *one* status.

I made it to the bathroom just in time to break down, tears beginning to pour down my cheeks in hot rivers. My breathing came in ragged gasps, and I pulled at the jacket on my torso, trying to get the heavy thing off my shoulders. The stiff material fought me, so much so that it only heightened the rising tides of my panic.

Eventually, I got it off and tossed it over a bench in the locker area. My limbs felt twitchy, like they should be moving, should be doing something. I tried to shake them out, but the more I moved them, the worse it felt—like my skin was too tight and I was a stranger to my own body, to everything.

Oh, God... Zoe. I leaned against the cool tile wall and then slid down it, resting my butt on the floor. Dropping my head into my hands, I began to sob, unable to hold it back anymore. My best friend was going to die. I was going to lose her forever. All because I couldn't bring myself to risk my new friends in the process of helping her.

I jerked when a hand slid onto my shoulder, and looked up. Tian looked down at me, her eyebrows drawn together over her blue eyes. I immediately started scrubbing my cheeks with the heel of my hand, sniffling hard.

"Tian," I said, my voice coming out thick and raw. "What are you—?"

"Why are you crying?" the young girl demanded, her eyes sparkling with empathy. "What's wrong?"

I shook my head, still very much on the verge of breaking. "No—there's nothing you can do, Tian."

"Yes, there is!" Tian said, and I looked up at her blankly, unable to even imagine what she could possibly be talking about. "I can listen."

I shook my head again. There was no reason for her to know any of this, and I wasn't going to burden her with my problems. "Tian, it's really okay. I'm—"

"Worried about your friend," she finished for me. "I know—her name is Zoe, right? She has a pretty name."

I almost broke down again. I couldn't help it, and I couldn't seem to get a grip, but it hurt so much, even just talking about her. "It's because she's a pretty person. Just like you—inside and out."

"Nobody is just like me," Tian said primly, her little shoulders wriggling up and down. She sat down next to me on the floor and leaned her head onto my shoulder. "But I really want to meet her anyway."

"I want you to meet her, too," I whispered, a tear slipping free. I wiped it away, trying hard not to lose it again, and Tian shifted.

"Cali still wants you to wait?"

I nodded. "She's trying to keep you all safe, and I can understand that."

"But your friend needs help now?"

I hesitated. "Tian, it's complicated."

She gave me a crooked smile, her eyes shining brightly. "You think so? Because I don't. I think that if your friends need help, you should go help them."

"But it's dangerous. I'd be risking six other lives for the sake of one."

Tian gave me a sad little smile, suddenly looking wise beyond her years. "It's always dangerous. Even when it's Cali or Maddox—they are always worried about bringing someone back. But they're careful. You're careful. I trust you. So do the rest of us."

"This is how I break their trust, Tian," I said. "And what if someone follows me back here?"

"We'll deal with it. I'll help." Tian leaned back into me, and I lifted my arm to let the girl rest against my side, settling it in on her shoulder. "Besides, I like having new friends around—I wish Cali had let more people stay with us long ago."

I smiled and stroked Tian's hair, feeling some of the storm clouds ease. Tian's blanket approval wasn't the same as getting permission, and it wasn't even like I was getting approval from a person of authority, but... it helped make me feel better about what I had to do.

Because of course I had to help Zoe. I just had to make sure that I kept the people here as safe as possible in the process.

Hours later, after everyone had said their goodnights, and long after all the lights inside had dimmed to near darkness, I sat up in my hammock and slid out of it, the fabric rustling against my clothes. I looked over at Grey's hammock, highlighted only by the ambient light, and saw that it remained motionless, his body a still, shapeless lump.

I crept quietly past him, making my footsteps as soft as possible, and quickly grabbed my gear. I knew he'd be mad at me for going without him, but I was already risking too much on this. If I got caught, then it was on me. I couldn't risk another person I cared about on this hare-brained idea. I just hoped he would forgive me.

I had set my gear aside last night after talking to Tian, in preparation for this. Sitting with it was my crimson uniform, modified baton, and lash harness. The only thing I needed was Paragon.

And a whole lot of luck.

Alex had told me my net had been deactivated, but that only meant it wasn't actively connecting to the servers. The device was still alive in my skull, and ran the risk of getting picked up by scanners if I wasn't careful enough.

I knew this was dangerous. I knew what it would mean if I got caught.

Zoe was worth the risk.

As quietly as humanly possible, I picked up my gear and started getting dressed. I began with the lash harness, and then the uniform, pausing only to run the lash ends into place. I zipped up the front and smoothed it down, then tucked my baton into the loop.

Putting on the uniform, even after having been out of it for only a short amount of time, felt wrong, but it wasn't hard to realize why. I didn't belong to the Knights any more than I belonged to the Tower.

I belonged here. I knew what I was doing was jeopardizing their safety, but I couldn't let Zoe die. I just hoped they could find it in them to forgive me after everything was said and done. Because even though I'd known them only for a short amount of time, I didn't want to lose them so soon.

I couldn't bring the Knights down on their heads. I just couldn't. It was six lives to Zoe's one, and I knew that this wasn't the right choice, but the emotional one. But I couldn't stop it. I just had to make one hundred percent sure I didn't bring anyone back—except for maybe Zoe.

If I could do that, then, hopefully, they'd accept my apology for betraying them in the first place.

Number one on my future apology list was Roark, and I crept into his makeshift room amidst the machines and looked around. I typically didn't come into this area, out of respect for his privacy, but I needed Paragon, and I needed it now.

The pills were set up on a table next to his bed, as was all the equipment we'd been able to carry from his house. I moved over to it, treading as silently as possible, while the old man snored in his hammock. And though I was familiar with the sound, every time he made a noise, I felt close to coming out of my skin.

I was being ridiculous, and this was critical.

I finished crossing the room and began picking up pill bottles, looking for the right label.

The fourth bottle I picked up was labeled "Paragon 5," and I quickly popped open the lid, hoping that the "5" meant it was the rank it got someone to.

Roark's snores faltered for a second as the loud pop filled the air, and

I looked over at him, expecting to see his eyes open and staring at me. His eyes were closed, though, and he suddenly snorted. Then the gentle snores were back, filling the air.

I fished out a few pills—just in case—and then found the bottle marked "Paragon 9" and grabbed a few for myself, also just in case. I didn't want to take the bottles, for fear of losing them or getting caught with them—the pills at least I could swallow. I mean... I had no idea what the side effects would be, but at least they wouldn't have anything to analyze if they caught me.

I slid the pills into my pockets—Zoe's on the left and mine on the right—closed the bottle, and then took a quiet step away. Then another, and another, the sound of Roark's snores chasing me out. I couldn't imagine getting caught by him, but he did not give the impression that he was a "hug it out" kind of guy.

Though, who in this Tower was, really?

I carefully slid out of the narrow opening and headed directly for the stairs, unwilling to waste any more time. I made it to the front room easily —everyone was fast asleep in their beds, thankfully. I was on a roll tonight in the luck department.

I was starting for the ladder, and nearly screamed when a voice spoke out behind me.

"Where do you think you're—"

My hand pressed against Grey's mouth, and I pushed him back away from the entrance of the hall, deeper into the shadows of the room.

"Keep your voice down," I whispered after a moment, lowering my hand from his mouth. "You want to wake everyone?"

Grey stared at me, his eyes dark and unfathomable. "No. But then again, I'm guessing you *really* don't want me to, considering you're wearing your Knight's uniform... Where are you going?" he breathed.

I exhaled slowly, puffing out my cheeks. "Zoe's in trouble."

His eyes widened, and then narrowed. "How do you know that? I thought the contact only agreed to—"

"My brother netted me on the way back from the meeting," I whispered, interrupting him. Grey gave me a hard look, and I sighed. "He's an

Eye. But before you freak out, he's figured out what's going on, too, and wants to help. He looked up Zoe, and she's in the Medica, Grey. They are cracking down on threes, and now fours—and she's a *two*. If I don't get her out of there, they will kill her."

Grey studied me for a long moment, and then nodded. "Then there's no time to waste. I'm coming with you."

"I don't..." I hesitated, torn between wanting him to come along, and wanting to protect him. "Grey, you're wanted for Gerome's murder."

Grey stared at me, and his expression grew dark. "Gerome's *dead*? How?"

"Poisoned—an injection. But they think you killed him and... and me. They'll be looking for you."

There was a span of silence, and then Grey shrugged. "It doesn't matter. If anything, it'll be the perfect distraction if we are discovered. I'll get them to chase me."

"That..." I stopped again, giving him an incredulous look. "That's no reason for me to take you along! I'm trying to do everything in my power to keep the people here safe."

"Liana," Grey said, his hand going up to my cheek. "Stop arguing with me. I'm going—I owe it to your friend for saving my life. And there's no way I'm letting you go alone."

I stared at him, trying to find the will to fight him on this, but found myself ultimately unable to. I really was on a selfish streak tonight, it seemed—throwing the people here into danger for my friend, potentially getting Grey caught trying to help me. But at the same time... I felt just so grateful that I wouldn't have to do this alone.

"Then it'll be a fun party," announced a hushed voice, and I started, turning away from Grey to see Tian, a smile on her face. "Because I'm going too!"

Grey and I looked at each other and then back at her. "No, you're not," I retorted, just as Grey said, "Absolutely not."

Tian's eyes grew wide and large, immediately filling up with tears. "I can't... go?"

Crap. A crying Tian was the last thing we needed right now. I immediately dropped down onto a knee, putting myself at equal height with Tian. "Sweetie, don't cry. Just hear me out. You know we're already going to be in trouble for doing this. Could you imagine how mad Cali would be if we took you?"

The little girl's eyes widened in alarm, and she looked around. "Oh, my gosh, you are so right!" she said suddenly, her voice a rushed little whisper. "She'd *murder* you."

"Yes. And... I'd just feel better if you were here, okay?"

Tian hesitated, and then nodded. "Okay, but you have to take Grey with you, then. So you're not alone."

I smiled and nodded my head. "All right. I promise. Now go to bed, okay?"

"Okay." She turned to go, stopped, and then whirled around to throw her arms around my neck, hugging me tightly. "Please be careful, Liana."

"I will," I vowed, holding her tightly to me. I let her go, and watched as she made her way back down the hall, my heart heavy. I had to keep them safe. I just had to.

"You're stuck with me now," Grey said from behind me. "Tian's orders."

"I swear, that little girl's charms will be my undoing," I muttered, standing up. "Now, let's get out of here before I attract any more help in this supposedly stealthy operation."

32

We took the plunge, and I quickly learned that Grey was afraid of heights.

"It's not heights," he insisted, his arms and legs holding tightly to me. "It's the *plunge*. How you bloody Knights even attempt to navigate these things is insane!"

He winced as my arms suddenly snapped out to the left, hitting a nearby beam and using the gears in the harness to jerk us to the right to avoid a bent girder blocking the way. My other hand was already spinning, and I released the lash and felt the tug when it connected. I jerked us up, the new gears working as smoothly as if they were greased and twice as fast as they had before. The air tore at my hair as we flew ahead, the light in Grey's hand illuminating our path while the painted symbols on the wall guided my route.

I took a sudden left, and he exhaled slowly, his fingers digging into my skin as I lashed us through a tight makeshift tunnel of pipes. "Can't you just move a little slower?"

"Yes," I said with a smirk, launching us through the opening on the other side and lashing the first thing I could see above us. I was sweating from the exertion and my heart was pounding in my chest with the excitement of finally doing something to help my friend. "You okay?"

I felt Grey's weight shift slightly and compensated for it by throwing another lash and changing direction to rebalance. "I'm hanging in there. And by *in there*, I mean *on to you*. I assume this just shatters all conceptions of my masculinity, right?"

"You riding on my back and whining about the plunge?" I teased, my eyes flicking around at the marks, ready for a new danger. "Absolutely."

There was another sharp left, and I took it hard and fast, much to Grey's discomfort, the press of time heavy on my shoulders as I thought about Zoe in the Medica. At least I was finally doing something to help her. I just had to reach her in time—I couldn't get to her if she dropped and the Knights came to collect her.

"So, do you have a plan for how you're going to get in there?"

I shook my head, lashes flying. "Not so much of a plan... It's more of an outline."

"Which consists of?"

"Go to Zoe. Get her out. Go back to Sanctum."

He went silent for a minute, and all I could hear was the *tink tink tink* of my lashes as I continued to move us upward. Then: "That's literally just a *concept*."

I let his words hang between us, unable to argue with someone who was right, and focused on step one: getting to Zoe. I just continued to lash, unwilling to be swayed by something as inconsequential as the lack of a plan. This was going to happen. I didn't know how, yet, but I was going to seize every opportunity I was presented, and lie without compunction.

The exit came upon us so quickly that I almost missed it, which made my landing inside a little wobbly. I stumbled forward, Grey's weight on my back offsetting me slightly, and he quickly dropped to the ground and relieved some of the pressure. Taking a moment to collect myself, I looked down the corridor in both directions, checking to see if there was anyone around.

Thankfully, the early hour meant the halls were still fairly empty, and I quickly stepped out, put my hand on Grey's arm, and began pushing him forward.

"What are you doing?" he sputtered, his eyes widening, and I leaned close to him.

"I think I can get us inside the Medica under the premise that you're my prisoner and I'm having you checked out before I take you to the Citadel for questioning. It'll at least get us inside."

I looked at my wrist, the nine glowing brightly. I had taken the plunge to avoid the scanners, but if he or I walked through one, it would pick up on our identities and we'd be toast. Luckily, the scanners were only used when entering or leaving a department, or, in the case of the Medica, when I was checking in. If he got scanned, no doubt he'd be flagged immediately, what with Gerome's murder having taken place only nine days ago. If I was scanned, well... there wasn't really much difference in what would happen to either of us in that case.

And I still wasn't sure how I was going to avoid it yet. Although I did have the smallest kernel of an idea.

"Oh." He continued moving forward, his face thoughtful. "You might be good at this improvisational stuff."

"Shut up, prisoner," I said loudly as I saw a woman step into the corridor, a large hammer balanced on her shoulder. She waited for us to pass, her eyes curious, but I merely turned my indicator out, nodded politely, and kept my eyes straight ahead.

Once she was outside of hearing distance, I leaned close. "Good job. You okay with this?"

"It's not exactly an unfamiliar role," he replied dryly, giving me a pointed look, and I flushed, the nature of our meeting flashing through my mind.

"Hey, I'm sorry if I was a little overzealous with you," I said. "I just thought if I could finally catch a one, maybe Scipio would, you know... show a dissident like me a little bit of mercy."

He chuckled as he ducked under a bit of piping that jutted out of the wall. "I've been guilty of the same thing in the past. But you know what?

I've had some of the best times just turning my back on the system. If I died tomorrow, at least I led a life that it felt like I was living, you know?"

"Even if you're on the run and are hunted for being different?"

"Especially then," he said softly, his voice ringing with conviction. "Which is why it's important to do it. You can't make things change by sitting around and doing what everyone else does. If I die doing it, at least I'll die doing something I believe in."

His words made me look at him, and suddenly it was if I was seeing him all over again, a little piece of the puzzle falling into place to bring the picture into focus. He was, in his heart, an optimist, and he didn't try to hide it. And I admired him for it. I was too sarcastic to be an optimist, but anywhere I could find a bit of hope, it was beautiful to me.

We fell into silence as we walked, but there was so much more that I suddenly wanted to say to him. Too much more, and I wasn't even sure where to begin. From the kissing stunt he'd pulled, twice, to the way he had given me his pills and sacrificed his own safety. And then there was that third kiss and the conversation he had started almost two weeks ago, when we had first arrived in Sanctum.

He'd treated me so well, been so good to me, that it was hard not to feel my attraction for him grow, no matter how many ways I tried to tell myself it was a bad idea. We literally had to rely on each other to survive, and that could get complicated quickly, especially in such a small group of people.

And yet, my mind would inexorably lead me back to the brief images I had of him caring for me when I was sick. The way he offered me a piece of his apple, even though we weren't exactly friends. His sense of humor and loyalty.

Scipio help me, I really liked him.

And this was so not the time for that particular revelation, so I pushed it aside to focus on the task at hand.

"Name and designation?" the clerk asked, looking up at me with wide, cheerful eyes.

"Holly Castell, 25K-437. Please don't scan me—this one," I jerked his arm slightly, like I was annoyed, "seems to have damaged a portion of my net. I about peed myself when I tried to get on the elevator, the shock was that bad. I need to be checked out before I take him to the Citadel." Using my mother's name came on impulse, and I was relieved that some part of me had an idea of what to do. The lie about the scan was based on a kernel of truth; it had happened to my father once. Somehow, though, I didn't think he'd admitted that part to the Medics when he had gone in, and I derived some small, perverse pleasure in the way the clerk's cheeks flushed at that part, her eyes flicking to my indicator and back again. It put her off her game, which was good for us. Feeling flustered might cause her to overlook a detail or two here or there. Besides, if she pulled up a picture of my mother... well, with the exception of the eyes, we looked almost exactly the same. I doubted she would notice that now.

And since I was the one undergoing treatment, Grey wouldn't be scanned, but would be allowed in with me, as prisoners weren't allowed out of sight of a Knight. I'd never dreamed I'd be so thankful for protocol.

"I'm really a nice guy once you get to know me," Grey said, a smile forming on his face as he looked down at the young woman on the other side of the counter. "This is all just a huge misunderstanding. You'll see."

I narrowed my eyes at him, instantly annoyed that he was trying to flirt, and super anxious that he was going to blow our cover with this charming criminal spiel.

And then the clerk smiled in return, and I instantly hated both of them. Him for the flirting, and her for buying into it.

Scipio save me, but I was letting my self-revelation detract from the matter at hand.

"Excuse me, Medic?" She looked up at me, and I forced a polite smile onto my face. "It's really close to the end of my shift, so I was wondering if we could speed this process up?"

She nodded once and turned back to her screen, her fingers flying. "All right, Knight Commander Castell, please follow the green lights to the treatment room, and the doctor will be with you shortly."

"My thanks," I said, already tugging Grey away and following the lights. We passed through the wide white doors into the treatment center. Unlike on the third level, the halls here were busy, even in the morning, and I watched as Medics moved in and out of the doorways.

I nervously followed the green lights, wondering how I could get us out of here and to the elevator to take us up. With my mother's designation, I could override the elevator and its scanners, but I couldn't override the request to see a doctor. And the Medics would know if we didn't go to the room, as our passage was monitored by a computer system of cameras and pressure sensors.

Therefore, I went to the room. Without any better options, my hands were a little bit tied, and I wasn't certain I was ready to risk getting caught or giving away my intentions just yet.

The room the lights led us to was small, with a soft brown chair in the middle and an empty desk to one side. A portion of the wall was displaying instructions for Grey, and all at once, it came to me.

I dropped Grey's arm and moved over to the display. "Jasper?" I said, my voice rising a note. "Are you there?"

"Liana, what are you doing?"

Grey was looking at me like I'd sprouted two heads, but I ignored him. "Hey, Jasper? It's me, Liana. I'm really sorry to bother you, but I need your help. Again."

Grey looked around, his eyes squinting in confusion, and then turned back to me. "Liana, who is Jasper?"

"I'm Jasper," the voice said gruffly, and the walls began to glow warmly. "Hello again, Liana. I'm so glad to see you well. I was quite worried about you. Now, can you tell me why you revealed me to the boy I helped you get out of here, or should I just start singing childish love songs at you?"

"You're in a sassy mood," I observed. "I'm sorry I didn't ask Grey to leave, but you know that the instant he goes outside, and gets on surveillance, a nearby Medic will be alerted to drag him back in here, so cut me a break. Besides, Grey's a good guy—give him a chance. He's actually kind of... fun."

"Oh, fun... how I do long for it," Jasper sighed, and I smiled, because it felt like the whole room was sighing as he exhaled. "I miss being young."

I blinked, surprised by the whimsical nature of his voice. "You were young?"

"In a manner of speaking. Now, tell me, what do you want?" Jasper's gruff statement might have seemed abrupt, but I still couldn't keep from smiling at how he could go from reminiscent old man to grumpy old man in a matter of seconds.

"We need your help," I said. "One of my friends, Zoe Elphesian, is being held up on the third floor."

"And?" There was no hostility in the computer's voice, only curiosity.

"And, I want to get her out of here without attracting any attention." This was insane, I knew it. I had no idea whether I could really trust Jasper with this. What he had done for Grey and me had been small, possibly small enough for his programming to let go. But this? This could get us caught, right here, right now. And I was going for it full throttle.

"I see." There was a pause, followed by: "You are aware that literally everything you said is a criminal offense, right?"

I hesitated. "I am."

There was another pause. "And you still asked me?"

"Look, Jasper, I'll level with you. Zoe is my best friend, and I am trying to spare her from getting murdered just because she doesn't fit into Scipio's perfect model, but that's because the system is rigged against her. It's rigged against me, and Grey, and I just want to keep her from getting killed because she's different."

"Basically, we're desperate," Grey added, and I looked over at him to see him eyeing the walls nervously. He might have been helping, but he was definitely uncertain about what was going on. I was just glad he wasn't interrupting me with questions.

Jasper was quiet for a long time. So long that I began to grow nervous and started looking at the door, wondering if it was time to make a run for it—or if it was already too late.

"Your heartbeat is increasing again, and your adrenaline levels are starting to rise," Jasper cut in a second later. "I'm also noting that there is no evidence that you have taken the medication Dr. Bordeaux gave you."

"You notice that?"

"My sensors are very sophisticated," he replied without missing a beat. "But that's not the point. Your ranking is a nine, but you haven't been taking your medicine. Can you explain that?"

"Not in the time we have," I said, suddenly recalling that a Medic was on his or her way here soon.

"Try."

"Why should I?" I asked, and to my surprise, he laughed.

"You're contacting *me*, Liana. I think that means you're the one who needs help, not me. Either tell me or don't, but don't be surprised, if you choose the latter, that I opt not to help you."

I hesitated, and then gave in. Jasper had helped us before, and I was betting he would help us again. The computer had more programmed empathy than most people in the Tower—I was counting on it.

"A friend of ours made a medication that helps our rankings," Grey said, straightening some and crossing his arms. "But it doesn't change anything about who you are inside."

"Which means you found a way to cheat the system. Interesting. Do you have any with you?"

"What? Why?"

"I wish to analyze it. Maybe it will reveal something that can help refine the pills they are using now on the lower-ranked citizens. All data, no matter how small or inconsequential, is important for discovery."

"I'm sure it is, but... if we give you the pill, you could use it to expose us and what we're doing to circumvent the Tower. I'd... I'd need to know that you wouldn't share it with anyone."

The walls dimmed slightly for a second. "All right. I will analyze it and store it in a private server I created for myself. No one knows that I have it, so it will be safe there, even if they dismantle it. I can't promise that I won't lead the Medics toward any relevant information that I discover there, but I will destroy the pill. Will that make you more comfortable?"

I looked at Grey, and he immediately shook his head no. Biting my lip, I gave him an apologetic glance before reaching into my pocket and pulling a pill out—I grabbed from my stash, unwilling to risk one of Zoe's just to give him the weaker dose. I held it out, and something small popped out of the wall in front of me, revealing a slot. I pushed the pill through it, praying I was doing the right thing.

I knew Grey wasn't going to understand, but there was something about Jasper that made me want to trust him.

"Don't worry, I'm not going to tell the Knights," Jasper said, his voice resplendent with irritation. "Believe me, I've noticed all sorts of problems in this system since being activated, and the doctors I am supposed to be assisting don't seem to care about the suicide rate, or their own inability to keep some individuals' numbers consistently high for extended periods of time." He stopped suddenly, and I looked around, wondering if he'd maybe gone offline. "I guess I'm just saying that I was designed to save lives, not aid in murder. I'll help you."

"Really?" I asked, feeling surprised. "That would be... I mean... Thank you."

"You're welcome. I've created a path for you to your friend's room, and given you special permission to enter. You need to get in and get out, and don't stop for anything, because I can only hold back the alarms for so long. You understand?"

"I do," I replied, barely able to suppress the thrill of success I was feeling. We'd gotten in... and gotten something rather incredible.

33

"Do you really think this computer is on the level?" Grey asked me as we followed the green indicator lights on the floor. I looked around. The hall here was empty, but the curve of the walls made it impossible to see more than twenty feet ahead.

"He's different," I said, my voice whisper-soft. "It was one of the first things I noticed about him."

"He reminds me of Scipio," he replied, and I looked over at him.

"He doesn't sound anything like Scipio," I informed him, thinking of the clipped, aristocratic voice that was generated in my ear whenever Scipio handed out orders. "I mean, he acts like Scipio, in a way, but his voice is completely different. And as far as I can tell, he really does care about people. Didn't you hear the disgust in his voice when he talked about the suicide rate?"

"He's a computer. I mean, Scipio is too, but he's far more advanced, far more complex. Jasper was probably just designed to sound human. For all we know, those responses are based off parameters to get your enemy to trust you, and these lights could be leading us directly to a Knight's station!"

I bit my lip to keep from giving him a sarcastic reply, partially because I didn't want to risk starting a fight between us, but also because he was right. My interactions with Jasper made it seem like there was something more to him, but Scipio was the only AI in the Tower. There were other computer systems that were interactive, and some seemed personable, but at their core, their responses were based on an algorithm. There were no parameters for creativity on the part of the computer.

Still, I felt strongly that Jasper was different. I didn't know how, and I couldn't explain it, but I believed he was more than a series of programmed responses.

The green lights veered off into a side hall, and I followed them as they directed us toward a door leading to the staircase. Grey walked beside me, his hands in his pockets, but his eyes darting around, his shoulders hunched over.

"Relax," I told him, trying not to give away my own nervousness. I checked my wrist by habit, and the nine was still there. "You look like a criminal."

He rolled his eyes, but wiggled his shoulders slightly to work some of the tension out, and I pushed open the door into the stairwell. The green lights followed the steps up, and so did we, around and around and up.

"He led us up the stairs," I announced after a moment, and Grey looked over at me, surprise and confusion flickering over his face. "Jasper. He's making us take the stairs. Because he knows if we get scanned in the elevators, the Tower will be on alert."

"He would've known that if he led you to the elevators, you would suspect a trap."

"A machine that can think? So he is an AI after all?"

Grey shot me an annoyed look, and I smiled, pleased that I had found a partial flaw in his argument. Truthfully, though, his doubts about Jasper were making me nervous, and with each step I took up, I became more torn between the need to rescue my friend, and the need to turn tail and run. Because Grey was right—I was putting my trust into a computer that I had barely interacted with.

Even as it was happening, it all felt too easy. Like he had been too easily convinced. Which meant that he might not be on our side, and might very well be leading us into a trap. It took every ounce of my willpower to keep myself moving forward, and even then, it wasn't my trust in Jasper that propelled me, but hope.

We climbed up four stories, and as soon as we drew near a door at the top of the landing, it clicked open, allowing us entry. The lights in this hall were significantly dimmer than the ones on the other levels, and I immediately sensed that this was the right area. It was too gloomy, too depressed, too devoid of color to be anything but where they held twos. And now threes.

The green lights, dimmer now, led us down the hall to our right, and I followed them as they curved around. Another left and right, and the lights dead-ended at a section of wall where a doorway stood.

Slowing, I looked down the hall behind us, and then back up ahead. I couldn't hear anything coming from either direction, but the stupid design of this place made it difficult to tell whether we were alone. Grey didn't seem to notice, and drew nearer to the closed door.

He came to a stop in front of it, facing the doorway.

"I really hope Jasper remembers about the door," I heard him say as I turned and cast another glance down the hall behind us. "Because if not, I— Oh. Hello."

A click sounded, and I turned just in time to see Grey's expression change from surprised to fearful in front of the opening door, and then the next thing I knew, he was down on the ground with Zoe's small frame straddling him, her fists flying.

"You killed my best friend!" she screamed, lashing out, and I winced at the loud noise as it went reverberating down the walls. Grey got his arms up over his face to protect his head, but Zoe didn't seem to care as she let loose, her fists smacking loudly against his forearms. I started to move toward her when, to my surprise, Eric stepped out of the room and plucked her gently off of Grey.

Grey groaned as her weight was removed from him, his arms lowering. And then Eric's heavy foot came down on his chest, pinning him in place.

"Zoe seems to think you killed Liana," he said slowly, calmly. "Did you?"

"He didn't," I said, seizing the opportunity. "So get your fat foot off of him."

Eric's and Zoe's heads snapped toward me as I spoke, and froze as their eyes widened in surprise. Eric was the first to move, taking a step back, removing his foot from Grey's chest. For several heartbeats, no one said or did anything.

Then Zoe moved. She pulled free of Eric's hands, the mix of emotions on her face making it nigh unreadable, and then began to cross over to me, her gait steady and sure. She came toward me so fast that I couldn't help but flinch away, afraid of receiving the same treatment Grey had just gotten.

Then her arms were around me, and she was holding me tightly. I almost broke down crying right there. I was so happy to see her, had been so afraid of her rejecting me after I'd treated her so horribly, and was so mortified that my supposed death had affected her so much, that where we were escaped me for a moment.

"I'm so sorry," I said, wrapping my arms around her. "I'm so, so sorry, Zo. I didn't mean to—"

"Shut up, Liana," Zoe sniffled, her shoulders shaking slightly. "All of that stuff can wait. I'm just so happy you're not dead."

God, as messed up as it sounded, those words meant the world to me. Even after our fight, there was hope. She was going to forgive me for what I had done in leaving her alone like that.

Just as soon as we got out of here.

My eyes snapped open, the moment shattered into a thousand pieces. "Zoe, we can't stay here. You can't stay here. You need to come with us." I withdrew a pill from my pocket. "This will mask your rank enough to get you out of here, but it won't last long. You need to come with me if you want to live."

As I spoke, Zoe stepped away, her brows drawing together in a thoughtful expression. "You came to break me out?"

"Yes," I said hurriedly, looking around. Well, I had now. Originally the plan had been to get her the pill, but now all I could think of was getting her to come back with me. "And we have to go now."

"Indicators are back on," Grey announced, and I looked over Zoe's head to see him nodding toward the lights on the ground. "We have to go, Liana. The longer we stay here, the sooner they'll catch us."

Zoe exhaled and looked at Eric. "Looks like you picked a good day to visit," she said dryly.

"Shut up and take the pill, Zoe," Eric said, and I blinked at the harshness in his voice. He met my gaze, his eyes heavy, and I had a sneaking suspicion that Zoe had told Eric what was happening to the ones.

"Do you know?" I asked him.

He hesitated for a fraction of a second, and then nodded. "She told me right before she went into the Medica."

From the look on his face, he had been having a rough time. I empathized, but there wasn't any time to hash it out.

The decision came impulsively, but I didn't care. "Eric, you're coming with us as well."

Eric blinked, a slow smile coming to his lips. "You mean I wasn't invited before? You wound me."

"Not as much as I am going to wound you if you try to keep from going with us," Zoe said, and I felt her fingers grab the pill out of my hand. She took it quickly, dry swallowing it, and then nodded. "We'll catch up later, but you're right—we need to go."

As she spoke, she turned and began moving toward Grey. I kept pace, and unsurprisingly, Eric fell in behind us.

"You know I was always going to come with you," he whispered to Zoe. I was sure he meant it to be private, but his voice was too deep for it not to carry, and I couldn't help but admire the sweetness of it.

I looked over to see Zoe's reaction, and to my surprise, saw her thread her fingers through his for a moment, before letting them go. I looked away and pressed forward, suddenly feeling awkward. Their behavior was different, as if something had changed between them, and I had no idea what that was. But I would be asking as soon as we were all safe.

Jasper's lights led us down the twisting halls, which were seemingly devoid of any personnel. It seemed clear from his delivery of Zoe that he intended to get us out of here just as safely—but I wasn't take any chances. I was on the lookout for trouble the entire time.

Sure enough, as we rounded a corner, I saw the wide-open arch that was the exit from Medica come into view, and I could've burst out into a cheer—had Devon Alexander, Champion of the Knights, not rounded the corner.

His dual-colored eyes met mine, stared for a second, and—to my absolute horror—widened in recognition.

Then he began to advance.

34

"**R**un!" I cried, my hand automatically shooting to my baton. Devon was some distance away, but as soon as everyone around me started to turn, he broke into a run, charging right toward us.

Whirling, I launched into a sprint, following my friends as they headed back down the hall. Grey led the way, followed by Zoe and Eric, with me at the rear, and we flew down the halls, turning this way and that, the halls rushing by and changing faster than I could possibly keep track of.

I looked over my shoulder to see flashes of the Champion as he followed in pursuit, and just as I realized he would've called this in, a chime sounded, followed by Jasper's voice.

"Intruders on level four, near the junction of Corridors B and E," he announced into the hall, and I looked over to see that we were actually in Corridor C. He was still helping us.

"Grey!" I shouted over the message as it repeated. "Are the indicator lights on up there?"

"Wha— Hey, yeah, they are! Follow me!"

He hooked a left and pushed open a door, running into the stairwell without missing a beat. Instead of down, we climbed up, and were almost out the door on the next level when I heard the door slam open behind us, Devon still in hot pursuit. I hesitated for a second, trying to decide whether I should take the time to shut the door quietly, then heard his footsteps coming up the stairwell.

I turned and ran, hurrying to catch up with my friends. Grey led us down the curved hall and then took an immediate left, and now I could see the green lights leading us directly down the hall, in a straight shot, toward the opening that led out of the Medica.

"Go left!" I shouted, just as the Champion bellowed, "Halt! Don't let them escape!"

My breathing was coming in sharp pants, but I ignored it as I craned my neck to peer down the hall. A Knight was waiting, his baton at the ready. It took me a second to recognize him, because I was still unfamiliar with the changes to his face, but as Grey raced toward him, I saw that it was Theo who drew back the baton.

Instinctually, I cast my lash onto the ceiling and activated the gyros inside at full tilt, snapping off my feet and through the air at what felt like terminal velocity. I disconnected the line as I flew over everyone's heads, and tucked my body like I was diving into a pool, burning off excess speed as I curled my back and rolled forward onto the floor in a controlled tumble.

I rolled into a standing position and brought my baton out in a fluid motion, then stepped into Theo's attack, my baton arm blocking his oncoming blow while I slammed the baton into his side. There was a sharp pop, and he flew back a few feet, landing on his backside.

My heart skipped a beat, thinking that Maddox's modifications had killed him, but he sat up abruptly, his blond hair practically standing on end. His gaze was confused as he stared at me; then his eyes rolled back into his head and he slumped over.

I was already running when he started to fall, leaping over his still form. A quick check told me he was still breathing, and then a glance over my shoulder told me I had lost precious seconds. Devon was now close enough that I could see the hard gleam in his eyes. I poured on the speed, then switched to the lashes, trying to create some distance between us.

Ahead of me, Zoe, Eric, and Grey had reached the doorway, and were already rounding the corner, heading left. I had no idea whether Devon had seen them or not, but I made a decision, and peeled off to the right, my lashes flying. Another look over my shoulder showed him right behind me, his own lashes working.

My heart picked up speed as I threw and connected with the very edge of the platform ringing the outside. I swung into it, letting momentum draw me back up and over the ledge, where I disconnected quickly and began to run again, my finger tapping my indicator to start a net.

"Contact Alex Castell!" I said, and I felt my net buzz. Almost immediately, Alex's voice filled the line.

Liana?

I heard Devon's heavy footsteps landing behind me, and threw my lashes again, hooking onto the ceiling above and winching myself up off the ground.

"I went to rescue Zoe and had to split off from the group to draw away the Knights. Contact Zoe and tell her to keep going with Grey. I'll meet them back at Sanctum."

Liana, are you in danger?

I tossed the next line, and then the next, weaving around pillars and staircases, climbing ever upward.

"Yes," I said through clenched teeth, as I landed hard on a ledge and stumbled a few steps. Stupid—every second counted, and I could not afford mistakes. I began to run again. "I love you, but I gotta go. Get my message to Zoe."

I disconnected the line before he could respond, my lashes starting to fly again as I launched myself into the air.

Devon was relentless, I realized, as I disconnected my lines and angled my fall through the staircase and to the level below. I spotted a bridge and made for it, needing to get out of here and to a plunge. I had no idea where Grey, Zoe, and Eric were, but as long as Devon was after me, that meant they had a chance of escaping. I trusted Grey to get Zoe to Sanctum.

I just prayed I could get there as well.

I was nearly to the bridge when something yanked sharply on my foot. I was in the middle of transitioning lines, and Devon's lash was cast with perfect precision, tearing me from the air and forcing me down. There was no time to cast a new lash before I hit the ground.

The air escaped from my lungs as I slammed down, rolling a few feet before coming to a stop. I gasped, pain erupting from my back, and then sat up, the strong doses of adrenaline coursing through me helping to eradicate some of the confusion of the fall.

I scrambled to my feet, looking up in time to see Devon's lash darting for me, and I managed to shift to one side, avoiding getting hit, but also nearly tumbling over in the process. I righted myself in time to avoid another lash directed at me, and Devon retracted them, the sounds of the cables whistling as they slid back in.

Looking around, I saw the edge of the platform just a few feet away.

"Don't do it, Squire Castell," Devon said, his voice sharp. "Just come here, and we can make all of this go away. All you have to do is tell me where they are."

I met his gaze, heart pounding in fear. "'They'?"

Devon's mouth practically disappeared as his lips thinned in disapproval. "The undocs you've been hiding out with. I know that you didn't kill your mentor—that you didn't have any part in it. I can help you, keep you safe, but you have to tell me where they are."

He knew about Cali and the others. How much more did he know? How much more *could* he know? Had he killed Gerome? Or did he not know who had either?

I had to lose him. I had to get back to the others and warn them that the Champion knew they existed. Glancing again at the edge, only a few precious steps away, I considered it. I had no idea what was over the side, or if my lashes would even work after he had hit me with his, but if I didn't get out of the Medica, his backup was going to arrive, and there was no way I could take on the entirety of the Knights.

"Don't," he said. "Think of everything you've worked so hard for. You'll throw it all away."

"Good," I said defiantly.

Then I turned, and leapt.

I heard him shout, and then the air was rushing past my ears as I angled my body into a streamlined form, trying to get as far away from the Medica and Devon as possible. My eyes were already searching for lash points, and I saw one approaching fast—a footbridge that connected to the Core.

I freed my lashes and threw for it, praying Devon's lashes hadn't destroyed mine. But the first lash *tinked* off the side and then fell free. I tossed the second one on impulse, my horror growing. I watched it soar, praying I hadn't just killed myself.

The lash hit, and I immediately felt the tug as it caught me. I swung into it, relieved that it was holding my weight, and looked up, half expecting to see Devon in hot pursuit. The air above was clear, but I didn't trust it—I was still too close to Devon and the Medica for comfort. I had to get out of here, quickly, or else they'd get me.

I quickly cast another lash, crossing under the bridge to the Core and heading up, ignoring the shouts of the Eyes walking in their exposed halls below who spotted me climbing the walls of their precious Scipio. I continued to climb, angling for a massive bridge that stretched over the shell, and crossing underneath, my eyes searching for any Knights.

As soon as my feet were firmly on the ground on the other side of the bridge, I began to walk, heading to the nearest doorway leading into the shell and disappearing within, following the signs for the closest plunge shaft, and keeping an eye out for any pursuit.

Even though there wasn't any sign that I was being followed, I took the longest, most convoluted way possible back to Sanctum, first going down one plunge, then back through another, going up and down stairs and through halls, randomly changing directions.

The entire time, I searched, paranoid that at any moment Devon was going to show up and finish what he had started—and worried about the status of my friends.

But as it grew closer to dawn, I knew that I had to get out of the main Tower area and back home. No matter where I went, there would always be a chance of being seen. The only safe place was Sanctum.

I waited as long as possible, and then right before the lights came on, I threw myself down the plunge and began making my way home.

35

I dropped off the ladder and turned, my gaze sliding over Tian, Roark, Quess, Maddox, and Cali before landing on Zoe, Grey, and Eric. I let out a slow breath, relieved beyond words to see them there, and ignored Cali's angry stare to immediately move over to the small group, reaching for them.

Zoe's arms went around me, Eric's close behind, and the three of us stood there for a moment, just holding each other. The reunion was bittersweet for me; I had missed both of them so much, had agonized over their safety, and now that I knew Devon was looking for us, I couldn't help but feel like I had just dropped them both directly into the fire.

"Liana, you owe us an explanation," Cali said, and I nodded, reluctantly letting go of my friends to turn and face her. Zoe refused to let go of my hand, and I didn't force the issue as I stood, meeting Cali's angry glare.

My gaze shifted to the four individuals sitting on the stuffed pillows behind her, and took in the openly hostile look on Maddox's face, the impassive mask on Roark's, the hurt on Quess's, and the crooked smile on

Tian's. I crooked my own lips up toward her, and she nodded, looking expectant.

"I'm sorry," I told them, the apology almost ripping itself out of me. "I'm sorry I acted without telling you, and I'm sorry I betrayed your hospitality and trust, but I am not sorry for going to get Zoe. She's my best friend, and she had fallen to the rank of two, soon to be a one."

Cali's mouth tightened. "Mercury never mentioned that," she said, her tone flat. "So how did you know?"

"Her brother," Grey announced, coming up to stand beside me. "He's an Eye."

Maddox gasped and shot straight up to her feet, and Cali took a step back, her hand dropping to the baton on her side.

"No, wait. Please." Zoe stepped forward, letting go of my hand and raising hers. "Please. I've known Liana and her twin Alex for years. He contacted me during our escape from the Medica, letting me know that Liana was drawing off the Knights. He made me promise not to go after her, but I could tell it was killing him inside to do so. He loves his sister more than anything in this world. I promise you that."

I shifted, taken aback by Zoe's revelation. I couldn't believe my brother had gone so far as to make Zoe promise not to come back for me. It *must* have killed him to send that message, but he'd known how much it meant to me that Zoe escaped unscathed. Belatedly, I realized that I hadn't contacted him to let him know I was all right, and now that we were in Sanctum, I couldn't.

"He didn't want to believe I was dead," I added. "He built a backdoor into the programming attached to my net, so he was still keeping track of it even though it was officially deactivated. When I went out with you earlier, he saw my signal come back online, and reached out. I asked about Zoe, and he looked her up. After our discussion with your contact, I wasn't sure if you'd back me up, and I couldn't risk you saying no, so I took things into my own hands. Believe me when I say I didn't want to do it like this. And I'm sorry."

"I went with her," Grey added strongly. "So whatever you're going to do to her, you have to do to me."

"And they're my responsibility," Roark announced, pushing himself off of the floor and standing up. "So I should share in their punishment as well."

"Oh! Me too, me too!" Tian exclaimed, jumping up and bouncing up and down on her toes. "Because I knew she was going, and I didn't tell anyone. Oh, and also, I told her that she should go. Because you and Maddox do it all the time, and she was just really sad about her friend."

I couldn't keep the gratitude off my face, seeing all three of them come to my defense. They supported my decision to go after Zoe, and were backing me. Cali's decision was simple now—boot out all of us (and risk a massive tantrum from Tian), or keep us so she could make sure the Paragon stayed in production. Roark was the only one who knew the formula, although I was certain Jasper was analyzing it even now.

Cali looked around the room at all of us, her eyes flat and hard. "That's all well and good, but I'm not even ready to begin to address that aspect of this yet. Liana, you said you threw off the Knights that were in pursuit. How did you lose them?"

"Lashes, and a lot of luck. I stayed out for as long as I could, but as soon as the morning lights came on, I came right back here."

She nodded, her eyes flashing with approval. "Smart. Were you injured?"

"Not really, although I have never seen anyone use their lash to bring someone down to the ground like that before."

Cali cocked her head and smiled. "You got lassoed?"

"Lassoed?" I repeated, confused.

She nodded. "Basically, you use your lash and harness to entangle and reel in the criminal. It requires precise lash work, and an excellent sense of timing, especially when your opponent also has lashes. Some of the best lassoers in the Citadel could knock another lash bead out of the air."

I blew out a stream of air, extremely impressed by what she was saying. I was good, but I wasn't sure I was that good. "I guess that explains why the Champion knew how," I said. "I imagine it was one of the challenges in the Tourney."

"What do you mean, the Champion?" Cali asked sharply, her green eyes flashing in alarm. "Devon was there?"

"He was," Grey said, his words dragging in confusion at her reaction. "I mean, what the Champion was doing at the Medica at three in the morning is anyone's guess, but he was there. And he remembered us."

His words may as well have been air for all the attention Cali gave him. She was already moving directly toward me, and before I had a chance to be alarmed, she grabbed my arm in a firm grip and was pushing me down the hallway.

"Quess!" she shouted, just as the tall man brushed by her, heading down the hall toward his room.

"I'm on it!" he replied, and I looked around, alarmed by the sudden flurry of movement from the Sanctum members.

"What's going on?" I demanded, just as Grey asked, "What's wrong?"

Cali didn't answer as she propelled me forward into Quess's lab. Quess was pulling something off a shelf—a long black plastic box with some sort of rod or wand connected to it by a black cable.

He jumped off the table he had been standing on and came over to me, the wand in his hand.

"What's going on?" I asked again, as he began to pass the wand over my body, keeping it about an inch away from touching me.

"You got into a lash fight with Devon and he *hit* you," Cali said.

"Yes, I told you that, but what does that have to do with—"

A loud screeching noise erupted from the box as Quess waved it over my leg, where Devon had used his lash against me. Cali cursed and let go of me, stalking away to run a hand through her hair. I watched her, straightening up, alarmed by the nervous energy radiating off of her. After a moment, she turned.

"We have to go. Quess, get Tian and the bug-out bags. I want us packed to go in ten. Liana, leave your uniform behind."

"Wait!" I cried, and she turned. I sucked in a deep breath, feeling like I was drowning in the panic that was beginning to grip me. "Why do we have to leave?"

Cali licked her lips and sighed, waving Quess through. "Devon has special lash ends, which he can open to release a radioactive isotope. It leaves a distinct trail. He didn't follow you because he didn't have to."

I leaned heavily against the table, my knees suddenly weak. *Damn it.* I had done this. I had led him here.

"My trail..." I started weakly. "I went all over the place—that has to buy us some time."

"The equipment he has is specialized," she said bitterly. "And he'll start around these levels. He's come close to catching several cells near this greenery, so he knows we're somewhere close. The man is relentless."

"This is all my fault," I whispered, defeat starting to creep into my heart. "Your home..."

Hands grabbed my shoulders, pulling me upright, and I looked up to see Maddox standing over me, her green eyes hard. "Get it together," she said evenly. "This is just a place; the home is the people in it. We don't have any time to waste, and if you want your trip to the Medica to mean anything, you'll change your clothes, grab your gear, and get ready to go."

She let go of me abruptly, then reached over to grab a metal box on the table. It rattled as she picked it up, and I watched as she marched right out with it. In the hall, Zoe raced by, carrying a box, followed by Eric, who carried a heavy sack on his shoulder.

Maddox was right. I straightened and met Cali's gaze. "Ten minutes," I said.

"Eight, now. Hurry up."

I ran to the bathroom and changed quickly. Grey was in our room when I returned there, already throwing all of his gear, and mine, into some bags. I threw the crimson uniform to the side and took over my bag, placing my meager possessions inside. A blanket, cup, toothbrush, and soap, plus the clothes I was wearing, my lashes, and my baton were all I had left. But I didn't dwell on it, just closed the bag up and raced over to help Roark pack his gear and the medication, Grey by my side. We collected everything—we couldn't leave any of it behind. Paragon was the best and only defense we had at the moment. If the Medics got their hands on it, if they knew what it could do, then we would be lost.

With it, they could figure out where the flaw in the nets was, and make the medicine useless. That was why giving it to Jasper had been such a risk.

Grey and I worked quickly and quietly. I sensed we were both feeling pretty guilty about the whole thing, although I didn't know why he was feeling that way—it wasn't his fault. I was the one who had led them here.

As soon as the bags were filled, I hefted one up, and then stopped, looking at Grey. "This is awful."

He nodded, his eyes dark and heavy. "I know. But it'll be okay, Liana. They figured out he has a way of tracking you, and they figured it out quickly. We'll be out before he gets here—okay?"

I nodded, grateful to him for giving me the words I needed to hear. Only time would tell if they held true, but for now, it was enough to keep me going, heading up the stairs and toward the main living area.

Cali was already there, on one knee, speaking very softly to Tian, one hand on the girl's shoulder. Tian's white bob dipped up and down as she listened carefully to whatever Cali was saying, fighting back tears. She clutched her bag between her hands, shifting nervously from side to side.

A stab of guilt seared through me as I entered the room, knowing that I had put that fear in her, and I resolved to do something about it—as soon as we were all out of here and safe. It didn't matter that she had told me to go; she never could've imagined this. I dropped my bag on the floor and looked up, raking my hair out of my eyes.

Roark pushed past me, dropping the bags and moving over to grab a few notebooks on the table. I slid my bag off, turning to drop it into the pile that was collecting by the hall entrance, before turning toward Cali, intent on asking her where we were going.

A crimson-clad figure dropped from the hole in the ceiling the ladder ran through, and immediately slammed his baton into Roark's back as he moved away from the ladder. Roark screamed as his body went ramrod stiff, the notebooks in his hands clattering to the floor. Devon held the baton there for a second, then two, not breaking the connection, and Tian began screaming, a high, shrill note that resonated in my ears.

I gaped, shock rippling through me. I couldn't wrap my head around the fact that he had found us so fast.

Devon continued to hold the baton to Roark's chest, and I felt bile start to rise as I realized he was trying to kill the old man with the baton. I surged forward, my hand already snatching my own baton out of my belt, but Cali was there first, her arm sweeping up and hooking his arm, breaking the connection with Roark.

Roark toppled over, limp, but Cali ignored it as she slammed an open palm into Devon's chest, shoving him back a few feet, and then caught him in the jaw with a spinning back kick. Devon rocked back, stunned, and Cali took the opportunity to grab Roark by the collar of his faded jacket, pulling him several feet away from Devon before dropping him, to meet Devon's renewed attack.

Grey immediately raced up to grab Roark, hauling him back the rest of the way, while Tian cowered behind Maddox's leg. Maddox stared, her eyes wide as she watched her mother and Devon spar, and the stare made me realize we were all just standing around like idiots, instead of making our escape.

"Is there another way out?" I hissed, grabbing Maddox's sleeve and yanking her attention toward me. She met my gaze and then nodded, once. "Grab the gear closest and get to it," I ordered. "Don't wait for me or your mom—just go. Get everyone out of here."

Grey looked up from Roark's still form, his eyes wide and horrified. "He's gone," he whispered, and I looked down to see that the old man's eyes were wide and... empty. His expression slack. I felt a wall of pain unexpectedly slam into me, and looked away.

"Get out of here," I managed to grind out to the group of horrified people in front of me. "Mourn Roark later—but run for him now. Go!"

Eric grabbed Zoe, and they all flew apart at my command, snatching up bags—except Grey, who remained.

"You're not hanging back alone," he said, curling his hands into fists.

I shot a look at Cali, watching her block a blow and land a solid one to Devon's chest. "Grey," I breathed, "you need to lead them out—Maddox is worried about her mom, and so are Tian and Quess. They're going to hesitate."

"Eric can—" he began to protest, but I cut him off.

"They don't even know Eric. Please, *just do this.*"

Grey's face hardened, and for a second, I thought he was going to keep arguing, but then he nodded—once. "I'll be back as soon as I get them out. Wait for me."

With that he turned, and I was already spinning in time to see Devon land a blow with the baton to Cali's chest. The woman fell to her knees, her limbs locking up as the electricity rocketed through her body.

He yanked the baton back suddenly, and ran a hand through his short hair, panting.

"Dammit, Cali," he said after a moment, standing over the groaning woman. I looked around the room, and then began to creep toward the far side, trying to get behind Devon. "I should've known it was you."

Cali groaned and coughed, sliding over onto her side, her body curled up in the fetal position. "Hello, Devon," she wheezed. "Been a while."

"Twenty years, Cali. It's been twenty years since I came home and found you gone."

My eyes widened and I froze, shocked.

Devon and Cali had shared a home? Did that mean... I looked over at Cali, and saw the fear on her face as she stared up at the man who must have been her husband. "You abandoned me," he growled.

Cali gazed around the room, her eyes slightly unfocused. She locked eyes with me and then looked away, not drawing Devon's attention to me. Her hand, however, lifted slightly—a flat palm, telling me to stop. I hesitated, uncertain whether it was an order I should really follow. I glanced back at the hallway and saw Grey stepping back in. I met his gaze, and watched as he moved into the kitchen, heading for a knife on a cutting board.

"You agreed to start killing people. You voted with Scipio for it. I wasn't about to let that go." I turned back to see Cali struggling to sit up more.

Devon was quiet for a long moment, his hand on his baton. "I can't stop what's about to happen, Cali. The Knights are less than a minute away."

Grey moved onto the glass, his stance low. I moved a few steps deeper in, intending for us to flank Devon.

"Scipio is diseased, Devon, and you know it. You were part of it."

"This dream of the outside world is a fantasy, and *you* know it."

Cali laughed, a bitter sound, and shook her head. "At least I dream, Devon. And that is something that no Knight, AI, or Tower can ever take away from me."

I met Grey's gaze, and gave one single nod. Then I began to creep forward, through the pillows on the floor and toward Devon, Grey mirroring me on the other side.

"Everyone in here is going to die. I can't stop it."

Cali smiled. "You're right, but only partially," she said, and I noticed her fingers moving, and realized she was signing to me in Callivax. *L-a-s-h-e-s*, she said, and alarm coursed through me. I turned and hurriedly signaled to Grey, waving a hand to get his attention. He looked at me, and I began to sign Cali's message, translated for Grey: *G-r-a-b s-o-m-e-t-h-i-n-g*.

"And how's that?" Devon asked.

"You and I are going to die, at least."

Grey gave me a confused look, and then movement from Cali dragged my attention back to her as she lifted her right hand up—the one that had been hidden to me behind her body. I got a flash of the small black item in her palm before she slammed it down on the glass floor. There was a high-pitched tone, and then all of the glass shattered, the floor vanishing from beneath all four of us.

I didn't even get the chance to check whether Grey had grabbed something in time before I started falling, shards of glass sparkling all around me as I succumbed to the laws of gravity. My body worked from muscle memory, so used to the sensation of falling, and threw the line. It hit and connected on the ceiling above, arresting my fall some fifteen feet below where the floor had been.

Immediately I spun around, searching for Grey. To my relief, I spotted him hanging from a thick pipe on the ceiling, his arms and legs wrapped around it. He must've grabbed it as the glass broke.

With Grey momentarily handled, I spun around and searched for Cali, finding her tangled in her own lashes, forty feet beneath me, frantically trying to break free from the lines around her body. I grabbed my other bead, intent on making my way over to her, when I sensed something stirring in the shadows above us. It was Devon's dark form, clinging to a ladder, having apparently used it to stall his fall. He was moving to where Cali's bead was connected—to the metal framing the glass had been seated in. Cali looked up from where she was dangling, and I could practically see the realization in her eyes as to what was about to happen as he drew closer.

He thrust out his boot and pressed it against the bead that held her in place, disconnecting it.

"No!" I screamed, my lash already spinning out, trying to catch her with it, but it was too late and she was too far. She fell, and I was helpless to do anything at all.

Anything, except for run.

And I had to. Cali was gone, and the others needed me. There was no time to grieve.

I lashed up to where Grey was clinging to the ceiling pipe, already in a panic. Devon wasn't far away, though at least the humid atmosphere down here meant his lashes wouldn't work. Grey climbed onto my back as I watched Devon, his back still to me, staring down at where Cali had dropped into the deadly churn of the waters below. It was all I could do to not lash over there and kick him in, but the knowledge that more Knights were coming was too heavy to ignore. There wasn't anything I could do.

I threw my lash from the ceiling, connecting it to the concrete floor that made up the kitchen and swinging down between the frames of metal where the glass floor had been seated. Grey's fingers dug in tight as I used faster speeds to propel us across, under the pod that formed Sanctum, dangling under the arm of the greenery, then back up the other side, fighting back the urge to cry.

I caught sight of Quess hanging by his lashes over the pod, Eric on his back, familiar red goggles over his eyes. "Hey!" he shouted when he spotted us, and I shook my head, pressing a finger to my lips.

Eric's hands flashed in Callivax, signing for me to follow them, and I nodded, keeping pace as they lashed away. Quess wasn't a terrible lasher, but with Eric's heavy frame on top of his own, he was struggling a bit to keep their balance and momentum going. Still, he managed.

We lashed for what felt like forever, moving farther and farther away from the Tower's walls and into the open air beneath the greenery's arm. The farther we got from the hydro-turbines, the quieter and clearer the atmosphere became. Catwalks cut this way and that, and Quess took a route that allowed us to avoid swinging over or under them, just in case anyone was around to notice.

It all seemed to blur together after a while, and I just focused on keeping up with his shadowy figure. A deep weariness had settled into my bones, making me feel numb and robotic. Eventually, we stopped and crawled into a hatch where the rest of our group was inside, waiting. I looked at all of their faces, and then looked away.

"Cali's gone," I announced hoarsely, bracing myself.

Tian started crying first, softly in the beginning and then faster and harder. Maddox immediately pulled the girl into her arms and held her, rocking her back and forth. The larger girl was struggling not to cry, but her eyes were filled with anguish and horror. She looked so lost, and in that moment, so very small and vulnerable. My heart ached for her. For them both.

Quess was less overt—his expression stony, his jaw tight. I could tell he was hurting too, because he shuffled up to Maddox and Tian, clearly needing to be close to them. I wanted to cry with them, wanted to ask Maddox about her mother's marriage to Devon, ask how it had been kept so low-profile that I hadn't known about it, ask whether Devon was her father, but it wasn't the time. We still had to find a safe place, and this small room on the other side of an external hatch was not it.

"Maddox?" I said gently, and she jerked her head up to look at me, her eyes haunted. I stopped, suddenly uncertain as to what I should say, what I even *could* say. She'd just lost her mother.

"We have to keep moving," Grey added, and I shot him a grateful look before glancing around the room to see where we were exactly—another relay hub, but one of the vents had been pried from the wall.

"Do we need to go through the vent? Is that where we're going?" I asked.

"I want to go to Sanctum," Tian sniffled, and Zoe reached over and took the young girl's hand, holding it firm. Zoe met my eyes, and I could see that the guilt was weighing on her too. But it wasn't her fault. It was mine. I had led Devon back to them. I had thought I was smart and clever, but I wasn't. I hadn't been from the start.

"The safe room's through... through these ventilation ducts," Maddox choked out. "Mom... She made sure... There's supplies..." She broke then, and began to cry, long, slow sobs that seemed to twist out of her against her will. Her hands immediately went over her face, like a shield to try to push everything back inside, but it was impossible—the dam had been broken.

"It's a tight fit," Quess managed, his arms around Maddox and Tian both. "It'll be difficult to get some of the bags around the corner."

"We'll figure it out," I said. "Let's just get somewhere fast."

Quess gave me an angry look, his eyes jerking down to Maddox and Tian, both of them crying hard. I understood—I really did.

Kneeling, I placed one hand on Tian's knee and one on Maddox's, and began slowly calling their names in a calm and even voice. It seemed to work, because after a few tries, they had pushed back the fog of grief some, and were looking at me.

"I know you need to cry right now, and I understand that, but we have to keep moving, okay? Once we're inside the safe place, we can mourn... but Cali would've wanted us to keep moving."

Maddox stared at me stonily, and I hated myself for saying it, even though it needed to be said.

"Come on, Tian," the statuesque girl said hoarsely, her voice raw and bearing the weight of crippling exhaustion and shock. "Liana's right. We have to go."

The little girl nodded, her blue eyes vacant, and then sat up shakily, as if she were a ninety-year-old woman. "'Kay," she whispered, heaving herself onto her feet and swaying slightly, teetering on the precipice of breaking down.

"It'll be okay," I told her, the lie like ash in my mouth. She sniffled as she moved toward the vent, taking a light that Grey handed to her. We all got one, myself included.

The vents were tight, but manageable, and I brought up the rear, which meant replacing the grate from the inside of the vent. It took me a minute or so to get it done, and by the time I looked up, Grey's legs were disappearing around the corner some twenty feet ahead.

I exhaled and began pulling myself forward, using my palms and arms. My arms were exhausted after all the lashing I'd done, and were now starting to shake from the exertion, but I kept moving forward, not wanting to lose anyone. I clenched the light that Quess had handed me between my teeth to illuminate my way, and hurried to catch up.

I made up the distance quickly, and then slowed to a crawl. Moving the bigger bags took time. Maddox was using her lashes to help, but it was stop and go, as she had to move, then retract the lashes slowly, dragging the oblong bags forward. On corners, Eric had to go up and help shift them around before we could start all over again.

Every time we stopped, I remembered the look on Devon's face as he disconnected Cali's lash bead, and immediately was ill, wracked with guilt, terror, and horror. It took everything I had not to vomit at the fact that he had just done it—like it was nothing, like she wasn't a mother or a person who took care of the people who needed it most.

Each time I had that thought, it grew harder and harder not to break down right there in the ventilation shaft. The only thing that kept me going was the fact that I owed it to the people here to keep it together. So I did.

I couldn't say how far we had gone or how long we'd been crawling, when I suddenly tuned in to a noise.

There were lots of noises in the ducts, generated by all of us, but this one caught my attention.

"...—ere..."

It was so soft that it would be so easy to excuse it away as a figment from on overtired and emotionally overwrought mind.

"...—low..."

I closed my eyes and exhaled, trying to stay perfectly still, and listened intently.

"...—am..."

It was a voice. Coming from a vent opening just behind me. I looked back over my shoulder, the light still clenched between my teeth, and searched, half expecting to see Devon right there, grinning like a madman with the promise of death in his eyes. But the vent was empty.

The sound came again and again, and after a minute of wrestling with myself, I slid backward. The convoy was moving so slowly, I was certain I could catch up to them quickly, after I'd figured out what the strange noise was.

I slid into the vent and followed it, the voice growing louder. There was a junction ahead, and I paused, waiting. When the noise came again, I took the vent shooting left, and followed it until it dead-ended at a grate. I slid my fingers through and pushed the grate off, lowering it to the ground, and then stepped into the room beyond.

The room was decidedly out of place for the bottom of the Tower. Soft fabric covered the floor—a bright blue color—with two sofas set up, facing each other. A low table sat between them, while a heavy wooden desk took up the other side, a single chair behind it. A thick layer of dust coated everything in the room, which, given the atmosphere regulators and how aggressively they filtered the air, meant no one had been in this room for an extremely long time.

The voice had stopped as soon as I'd entered the room, and I looked around, trying to search for the source. Suddenly I felt uncertain, wondering if I *had* imagined the voice.

"Hello?" I said softly, stepping farther into the room and shining my light around. "Is anyone here?"

"—'m here," the voice replied, and I jumped straight into the air, my hand going to my chest. I moved the light around, searching for the person I had overlooked, but finding nothing.

"Hello?" I repeated, my heart pounding faster and faster. "Who's there?"

"...here!" This time the voice was cut off with a burst of electronic interference, causing there to be a strange, tonal sound at the beginning of it. "—an you... me?"

"I'm sorry," I said, bending over to check under the desk. "But I can't understand you."

There was pause. "—ow about now?"

"That's better," I said, smoothing my hand over my pants. "Are you an undoc?"

"—m not sure. —at is it?"

"How can you not be sure?" I asked, alarmed. "And where are you hiding?"

"—m with you... in the room," the voice replied calmly, and I looked around again, searching.

"I'm really not seeing you here. Are you sure you're in here?"

"—m on... desk." I looked at the desk, but the only thing on it was a computer, a coffee mug, a few file folders, and an inch of dust.

"Okay, let me try this one instead. What's your name?"

The answer brought me up short.

"My name is Scipio. Pleased to meet you."

"Of course it is," I muttered, unable to feel surprised at anything right now. I wondered how much worse one day could possibly get—and how much time we had before the Knights found us and killed us all.

READY FOR THE NEXT PART OF LIANA'S STORY?

Dear Reader,

Thank you for taking a chance on *The Girl Who Dared to Think*.

I hope it entertained you!

Book 2 of the series, ***The Girl Who Dared to Stand***, releases **September 18th, 2017**.

Visit: www.bellaforrest.net for details.

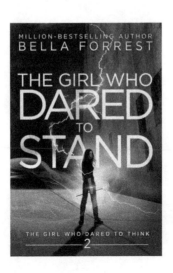

I can't wait to see you there.

Love,

Bella x

P.S. If you're new to my books or haven't yet read my **Gender Game** series, I suggest you check it out. It is where the Tower's story began and is set in the same world as *The Girl Who Dared* series—the two storylines complement each other.

P.P.S. Sign up to my VIP email list and I'll send you a personal heads up when my next book releases: **www.morebellaforrest.com**

(Your email will be kept 100% private and you can unsubscribe at any time.)

P.P.P.S. I'd also love to hear from you — come say hi on **Twitter** (@ashadeofvampire) or **Facebook** (facebook.com/BellaForrestAuthor). I do my best to respond :)

THE GIRL WHO DARED TO THINK

The Girl Who Dared to Think (Book 1)

The Girl Who Dared to Stand (Book 2)

THE GENDER GAME (Completed series)

The Gender Game (Book 1)

The Gender Secret (Book 2)

The Gender Lie (Book 3)

The Gender War (Book 4)

The Gender Fall (Book 5)

The Gender Plan (Book 6)

The Gender End (Book 7)

THE SECRET OF SPELLSHADOW MANOR

The Secret of Spellshadow Manor (Book 1)

The Breaker (Book 2)

The Chain (Book 3)

The Keep (Book 4)

The Test (Book 5)

A SHADE OF VAMPIRE SERIES

Series 1: Derek & Sofia's story

A Shade of Vampire (Book 1)

A Shade of Blood (Book 2)

A Castle of Sand (Book 3)

A Shadow of Light (Book 4)

A Blaze of Sun (Book 5)

A Gate of Night (Book 6)

A Break of Day (Book 7)

Series 2: Rose & Caleb's story

A Shade of Novak (Book 8)

A Bond of Blood (Book 9)

A Spell of Time (Book 10)

A Chase of Prey (Book 11)

A Shade of Doubt (Book 12)

A Turn of Tides (Book 13)

A Dawn of Strength (Book 14)

A Fall of Secrets (Book 15)

An End of Night (Book 16)

Series 3: The Shade continues with a new hero...

A Wind of Change (Book 17)

A Trail of Echoes (Book 18)

A Soldier of Shadows (Book 19)

A Hero of Realms (Book 20)

A Vial of Life (Book 21)

A Fork of Paths (Book 22)

A Flight of Souls (Book 23)

A Bridge of Stars (Book 24)

Series 4: A Clan of Novaks

A Clan of Novaks (Book 25)

A World of New (Book 26)

A Web of Lies (Book 27)

A Touch of Truth (Book 28)

A Shade of Kiev 1

A Shade of Kiev 2

A Shade of Kiev 3

BEAUTIFUL MONSTER DUOLOGY

Beautiful Monster 1

Beautiful Monster 2

DETECTIVE ERIN BOND (Adult thriller/mystery)

Lights, Camera, GONE

Write, Edit, KILL

For an updated list of Bella's books, please visit her website:
www.bellaforrest.net

Join Bella's VIP email list and she'll personally send you an email reminder as
soon as her next book is out: www.morebellaforrest.com